DREAMWAKER SAGA ③

lucid FATE

Lee Gabel

Frankenscript

Frankenscript Press
Box 717, #105 - 1497 Admirals Road
Victoria, BC, Canada   V9A 2P8

Lucid Fate (Dreamwaker Saga #3)

Cover illustration and design by Lee Gabel

Cover images supplied by DepositPhotos

Body font (ITC Galliard Pro) by International Typeface Corporation
Folios, heads and caps (Zapf Humanist 601) by Bitstream Inc.

ISBN: 978-1-9991856-5-7 (ebook)
ISBN: 978-1-9991856-8-8 (paperback)

Want to join Lee's Reader Group or find out more about Lee and the books he writes? Please go to:
LeeGabel.com/links

DREAMWAKER SAGA 3

lucíd FATE

Titles by Lee Gabel

Dreamwaker Saga
Lucid Bodies
Lucid Revenge
Lucid Fate

Detest-A-Pest Series
Vermin 2.0
Arachnid 2.0
Molerat 2.0

Standalone
David's Summer
Snipped
Tied

For the dreamers.
You can do anything.

Playlist

DON'T GIVE UP Peter Gabriel	MANEATER Hall & Oates
THE KILLING MOON Echo & The Bunnymen	YOU SHOOK ME ALL NIGHT LONG AC/DC
ROAD TO NOWHERE Talking Heads	A VIEW TO A KILL Duran Duran
PSYCHO KILLER Talking Heads	GONNA FLY NOW Bill Conti
STAND BY ME Ben E. King	PRIVATE EYES Hall & Oates
ALIVE AND KICKING Simple Minds	RUNNIN' WITH THE DEVIL Van Halen
BAD MOON RISING Creedence Clearwater Revival	DREAM POLICE Cheap Trick

BARRACUDA
Heart

MANIAC
Michael Sembello

I WILL SURVIVE
Gloria Gaynor

HEROES
David Bowie

STUCK ON YOU
Lionel Richie

I WANT TO KNOW WHAT LOVE IS
Foreigner

SEPTEMBER
Earth, Wind & Fire

INSTANT KARMA
John Lennon

RENEGADE
Styx

Don't Give Up

"Don't touch anything," Anson said to the nurses and doctor attending to Jezebel. He zeroed in on the doctor's name tag as they navigated the gurney past him. It read, "Maguire."

"Everything in this room is part of an ongoing investigation," he continued, "including whatever you find in her gut."

Dr. Maguire daggered her eyes at Anson. "You and I both know this scene is compromised. Get out of our way. We have a life to save."

Anson speared the trigger guard of Jezebel's pistol with his pen, lifted it off the floor, and followed Dr. Maguire and the nurses out so they could see it. Globs of congealed blood dripped off the grip. "She brought a *gun* into this hospital with intent to kill. She's a psychopath and you should let her bleed out. *You hear me?*"

Anson felt a warm hand on his shoulder. He turned to find Jake and Madeline, a comforting smile on her face. "Easy, Anson. They're only doing their jobs. Everyone deserves care." Her eyes followed the gurney as it rolled down the corridor. "Even her."

"Not if I was in charge." Anson returned to Wynter's room and transferred the pen and the hanging pistol to Cash. "Hold this. And don't touch the gun. I got to grab evidence bags from the Suburban."

Anson headed for the elevators at a brisk pace. He noticed blood on his right hand, Jezebel's blood, and wiped it on his pants in disgust as he approached the patient transport elevator.

JEZEBEL STARED AT the fluorescent lights in the ceiling, floating past her eyes like the broken white lines dividing the lanes on the interstate.

Where's the 'Cuda?

The pain in her abdomen radiated throughout her body with every breath and every beat of her heart, chasing away any coherent thought. Sweat beaded on her face and soaked through her shirt and hair.

A team consisting of two nurses and Dr. Maguire rolled Jezebel into the patient transport elevator. One nurse held a wad of gauze on her wound with a gloved hand, while Dr. Maguire tested Jezebel's iris response with her penlight. The second nurse rolled a cardiac unit alongside the gurney.

Dr. Maguire peeled the bloodied gauze away, careful not to disturb the clotting, and examined the wound's entry. The back end of the inch-wide glass shard sat just above the surface of Jezebel's abdomen and cast the elevator lights into reddened refracted patterns on Jezebel's skin. Other than the blood, the glass looked like ice, refreshing and cool. "The glass is stemming the flow of blood. I'm sure surgery would rather avoid a laparotomy, but there may be no other choice. She's running out of time."

The second nurse punched the button for emergency surgery. The doors closed quickly, then reversed as Anson jammed his foot in the door. He used his hand to keep the doors from closing.

"The world would be better off without her in it." Anson pointed at Jezebel as he glared at the doctor.

Jezebel half-grinned back at him. "Deputy Dolt," she hissed from the back of her throat.

"Let go of the door, Sheriff," Dr. Maguire said. "You're delaying emergency medical treatment. Besides, you're way out of *your* jurisdiction. I could have *you* arrested."

Anson gritted his teeth with the knowledge that the doctor was right, and begrudgingly let go of the door. "The world would be better off—" The door slid closed once again and cut him short.

The elevator lurched upwards.

"Dizzy," Jezebel croaked out. "Hurts."

Dr. Maguire glanced at the clipboard lying on top of Jezebel's legs. "Jezebel... Caine?"

The nurse applied new gauze to Jezebel's wound. "That's what that good ol' sheriff back there said."

"Immortal," Jezebel whispered.

Dr. Maguire cocked her ear and leaned toward Jezebel. "What was that?"

Jezebel extended her neck and tried to project her voice, unsuccessfully. "I'm immortal."

Dr. Maguire faced the two nurses. "Says she's... immortal."

"Is she high on drugs?" one of the nurses asked.

Maguire shook her head. "Her eyes were clear, pupils responsive."

The elevator doors opened to the surgical floor and the nurses wheeled Jezebel out.

"If she's not fixed soon," Dr. Maguire said, "she's going to find out the hard way that immortality is a fantasy. God help her if her renal artery is lacerated."

The nurses guided Jezebel into an operating room and Maguire briefed the two attending surgeons, anesthesiologist, and scrub nurse, careful not to break the sterile field.

The inner doors to the operating room closed and the doctor and two nurses stepped out.

"She's in good hands now," Dr. Maguire said.

Moments later, inside the operating theater, Jezebel's thoughts of immortality turned black. Not even Ransom would be able to break through the anesthesia.

WITH EVERY WAKING MOMENT, Wynter remembered more about what had put her in the hospital and what had happened *while* she was in a coma. Her brain, her memory, her ability to summon, and how it all worked was still a huge enigma. Medical science had advanced by leaps and bounds over her short lifetime, but doctors and scientists had barely mapped the human brain's inner workings with any great detail. Who knew what those doctors and scientists would subject her to if they discovered the power she and her friends held.

Two years ago, she had researched and written a report on comas and near death experiences for her 9th Grade Biology class. She had discovered that there was no common type of experience. Everyone's recollection was different. Some patients reported remembering nothing, floating in a vast sea of blackness, and others recalled dreams so vivid they rivaled their waking perceptions.

Wynter's experience added a new dimension of complexity. She could talk to her friends within her dreams, exist among them as a dreamwaker, and remember *all* of it. This kind of power could only be experienced firsthand to be believed. She had it and so did her father Nolan. The best part: it was a power she could share, as long as Ransom was with her.

But it was a power she was never meant to lose. Once Jezebel got her grubby hooks into Ransom, Wynter's world and her sanity began to slowly unravel. Reconnection was always in the back of her mind and as time pressed on, more of her usual thoughts were pushed aside. Her great grandmother had taken her own life because of it. Wynter needed that control back in order to survive. After the hospital discharged her, her only goal would be to recapture that control. With the help of her best friends Quinn, Cash, and Jake, Wynter believed in her heart they would be able to help make her world right again. She had no choice.

However, Madeline would never approve of Wynter's intentions, especially after her coma at the hands of Jezebel. So she decided not to tell her. Deceiving her mother would be difficult; Wynter had always confided in Madeline and trusted her implicitly. But some secrets and plans were never meant for adults. This realization set her mind at ease.

Visiting hours had ended and Quinn, Cash, Jake, and Madeline had left for the night. Her nurse wrangled dinner from somewhere, a barely palatable meal of reheated chicken, broccoli, and potatoes, with a square of lime Jell-O for dessert. The meal certainly hadn't come from the cafeteria. Despite the sub-par food, Wynter ate every bite.

Her full stomach lulled her to an intentional sleep for the first time in a week.

WYNTER OPENED HER EYES to what she thought were stars spinning above her head. As her eyes focused in the surrounding darkness, she realized that they weren't stars at all, but reflections from a hanging disco ball.

Wynter eased herself up onto her elbows. She wore a white babydoll T-shirt that exposed her midriff, denim shorts, and her favorite rainbow knee-highs that extended down her calves, culminating in a pair of white rollerskates with hot pink rubber wheels.

"The Starlite," she whispered to herself, smiling. But it wasn't the Starlite, not exactly. The familiar disco ball spun above her and she ran her fingers across the smooth wooden floor, but there were no sideboards she could see. Apart from the glow of the disco ball above and its reflected points of light, the rink faded into dark shadows.

Wynter sat up and worked herself into a kneeling position. Her arms and legs felt sluggish and it took all her effort to keep her balance.

"*Whinerrr.*"

Wynter's blood ran cold. "Jezebel!" She spun around in an attempt to find the source of Jezebel's voice. "Where are you?"

"Wouldn't you like to know, *Whinerrr.*" Jezebel's laugh echoed around Wynter's head.

"Show yourself, you fucking *coward!*" Wynter cocked her head and heard a low rumble beyond the shadow's terminator. "What the…"

The rumbling melted into the sound of rollerskate wheels on wood. Jezebel's figure breached the edge of darkness and rolled toward Wynter. She wore all black, aiding her obfuscation: black T-shirt, shorts, socks, and rollerskates. But her face grinned back at Wynter just as it always had, like a beacon from hell. A knife sat tucked alongside her waist.

Wynter felt a cold shock travel up her spine and raise the hairs on the back of her neck. The odor of blood hung heavy in the air, but she could see no evidence of it.

"Here's what's going to happen." Jezebel's words slurred together like she was drunk or stoned. "You're going to bring me out of your dream so I can cut your throat for real."

Jezebel slid the knife out from *within* her right side, not her waistband like Wynter had first thought. Thick ruby-red blood dripped off the blade's razor edge that looked more like glass than metal. She licked some blood from the knife's tip.

Wynter began skating backward. "If you think I'm going to make you a dreamwaker, you're crazy."

"Dreamwaker, huh?" Jezebel propelled herself forward on black rubber wheels. "Is that what you call it? Cute."

"What about your precious Ransom?" Wynter scowled as she increased her speed. "You kill me and he's gone forever."

"Fuck him." Jezebel snapped her fingers and "One Way Or Another" by Blondie broadcast from the inky shadows. She narrowed her eyes and pumped her legs, laughing maniacally.

Wynter's legs still felt wobbly. Had she fallen, that would have meant game over, but her strength returned surprisingly quickly. She spun on one leg and bolted in the opposite direction, away from Jezebel. But despite her speed and the cool wind on her face, she felt like she was getting nowhere. The rink's floor moved past her feet but the glow of the disco ball above her remained stationary, as if it was attached to her body by an unseen support.

Wynter glanced over her shoulder to see Jezebel gaining on her with every stride. She could not let Jezebel touch her.

"Going to get you, *Whinerrr.*" Jezebel laughed. "Going to get you *get you.*"

Wynter could feel the heat of Jezebel's hatred as she grew closer and closer. A few more seconds, a few more strides and she would be able to reach out and grab Wynter's collar.

"This stops NOW." Wynter braked, squatted, and swung her left leg out in a wide arc. Jezebel's knees struck Wynter's backside first, then her legs and feet slid out from under her. She landed on the floor hard, knocking the knife from her hands, but Jezebel was on her feet in seconds.

Wynter raced after the knife as it slid across the waxed wooden surface. Without stopping, she crouched again and grabbed the knife as she rolled past it. Spinning to face Jezebel's frenzied approach, Wynter held the knife to her left arm.

"Stay in your own head, you *bitch!*" She ran the crystal blade's edge across her forearm. The skin split open without blood, smoking and charred as if the knife had been red hot. Pain filled her body like she had swallowed a molten ingot and—

Wynter sat up, panting. Her cardiac monitor beeped frenetically, signalling her blood pressure and pulse were at dangerous levels.

A nurse burst through the door. She checked the numbers on the cardiac monitor, steadily falling as Wynter calmed herself.

"You gave me quite a scare," the nurse said as she inserted a tympanic thermometer in Wynter's ear until it beeped its reading. She jotted notes on Wynter's chart.

"Sorry. I had a nightmare."

The nurse poured water into a paper cup and handed it to Wynter. "Must've been a bad one, huh?"

"Yeah," Wynter said softly. She ran her right hand over her left forearm, the skin smooth and unbroken. "But I won."

"You killed the monster?"

Wynter nodded, a hint of a smile on her face. "I did."

The nurse glanced at her watch. "There's still a few hours until breakfast. Try and get some more sleep."

"I think I'd like to stay awake for a bit," Wynter said. "Got anything to read?"

"Let me take a look." The nurse hustled out of the room, returning less than a minute later with two publications in her hand. "*Popular Science* or *Mad Magazine?*"

Wynter balked at the two options, then said, "I'll take the *Mad Magazine,* thanks. I think my brain could use a break."

"I'll leave them both, just in case you change your mind." The nurse set the magazines on Wynter's lap and left the room.

Wynter picked up the *Mad Magazine*. The cover depicted Hulk Hogan holding Alfred E. Neuman in a strangle hold around his muscled body. She glanced at the cover of *Popular Science*. It featured "Buick's performance car for the 1990s."

She set *Popular Science* down. "Mad. Most definitely." Wynter flipped through the pages, giggling at the stupid jokes. It was just what she needed. As her body relaxed, her eyes grew heavy again. She fought against her body's weariness, but sleep would always be a relentless and endlessly patient opponent who would accept nothing but victory.

With the *Mad Magazine* open to a satire of TV's *Moonlighting*, Wynter's body rewarded her with a dreamless sleep.

AFTER BREAKFAST, DR. CORNELL performed a neurological exam to assess Wynter's recovery. She passed most of the tests with flying colors, with the exception of standing and moving her limbs.

Wynter clutched the side of the bed for stability but even her arms weren't strong enough for the task. The doctor reached out to steady her.

"Are my legs supposed to feel like Jell-O?"

"Even after seven days, your muscles weaken," Dr. Cornell said. "And your brain must relearn how to move. But don't worry. You're doing well. Just to be sure, I'll arrange for a walker to be brought to your room."

She raised a brow at Wynter's empty breakfast tray and smiled. "Looks like you'll need no help regaining your strength." She jotted notes on Wynter's chart. "I'm going to schedule a CT scan of your brain to make sure no wires are crossed in that head of yours."

"Does a CT scan hurt?"

"Nope." Dr. Cornell hung Wynter's chart down at the end of the bed. "You'll be in and out in less than fifteen minutes. It's an amazing machine." She helped Wynter back into her bed. "You should get in the habit of going to the bathroom on your own, if you're able. Just buzz a nurse if you need help."

"Thanks, Doctor Cornell."

As the doctor stepped out of the room, Madeline entered, followed by Quinn, Cash, and Jake. Cash had a white bandage on his left ear, and bright yellow fiberglass strips wrapped the top third of Jake's cast.

"Oh, hon. How do you feel?" Madeline scurried to the side of Wynter's bed. She reached out and touched Wynter's forehead, then stroked her cheek lightly.

"I feel fine, Mom. Seriously." Wynter sighed. She glanced at Quinn, winked, then clutched her stomach with stiff fingers. "On second thought..."

"What is it?" Madeline froze, ready to jump into action. "Are you in pain? Should I get the nurse?"

Wynter's feigned concern melted into a smile. "No, Mom. I'm kidding. But I am *fucking* hungry!"

Madeline gasped and tapped Wynter's shoulder lightly. "Language! And don't do that to me, Wynnie. I've been through enough this past week. I don't need your jokes and sarcasm."

"Sorry, Mom." Wynter made her best puppy dog eyes. "I bet Dad would've laughed."

"Yeah." Madeline chuckled to herself. "He probably would've."

"I think I can help with the hunger." Cash handed a white plastic bag to Wynter.

"Is it...?" Wynter peeked into the bag. "Yes! Thank you, thank you."

Cash chuckled and nodded.

Quinn shared a glance with him and gave him a playful shove. "Such a romantic."

"Well, what is it?" Madeline knew she was standing on the outside of an inside joke.

"It's..." Wynter reached in and pulled out the contents of the bag. "A Hostess Blueberry Pie and a Coke." She found Cash's eyes with hers and sent him a look of warmth and gratitude. "You know me so well. Thanks."

Cash rocked on his heels as his neck and cheeks flushed red.

Jake chuckled. "Is it hot in here, or is it just me?"

Cash elbowed him in response.

Wynter unwrapped the fruit pie and took a bite. "So good. Way better than the oatmeal and melon chunks they gave me for breakfast. Like, gag me." She cracked her Coke and took a sip. "Did you guys go back home last night?"

"Nah," Jake said. "We crashed your mom's motel room."

Wynter stopped eating and scanned the faces of her friends. "Oh. I'm so sorry. You guys must be bagged."

"I don't see how," Madeline said. "Everyone got a great sleep last night."

"Come on, Mom. You snore."

Madeline recoiled, mildly insulted. "No, I don't."

"You do so."

"I absolutely *do not.*"

Wynter took a bite of her pie and turned to Quinn, Cash, and Jake. "Did my mom snore last night? Did you guys sleep at all?"

Quinn, Cash, and Jake shared knowing glances. Jake cleared his throat. "I refuse to answer on the grounds that it may incriminate me."

"Hmph." Madeline alternated her gaze between Wynter and her friends. "Well. I think I'll go find Nolan." She stepped toward the door.

"Mom, don't be mad," Wynter called after her. "I love your snoring." She grinned and sipped from her Coke.

Madeline pulled the door open and looked back at her daughter, a sparkle in her eye and a small lopsided smile on her face. "I know, honey." She stepped out into the corridor and released her hold on the door. Cash caught it before it closed and crossed the corridor to the waiting alcove. He grabbed two chairs and carried them back to Wynter's room.

"Excuse me, young man." A nurse spotted him part-way across the corridor and gave him a questioning look.

"It's temporary," Cash said. "I'll put them back when we're done. I promise."

Hands on her hips, the nurse considered Cash's words with narrowed suspicious eyes. "Okay." She turned to walk away, then stopped and faced Cash again. "What's your name?"

"Cash Hawkins, ma'am."

"I'm going to hold you to that promise, Cash Hawkins," she said.

Cash nodded. As he carried the chairs back into the room, Wynter and Quinn were mid-conversation. "Sorry guys, got busted for stealing chairs, but it's all good."

"Dude, you're such a rebel," Jake sat in the chair Cash had slid behind him. "My leg is eternally grateful."

Cash dragged his chair to the opposite side of the bed, next to the cardiac monitor. He gave Wynter's right hand a brief and gentle squeeze and took a seat. Both Quinn and Jake noticed the gesture.

"If I had to guess," Wynter said to Quinn, "I'd say my mom knows that my dad made me a dreamwaker. They're pretty good about talking things through." She peeled more wrapping from her pie and bit into the remaining pastry.

"If your mom knows that, what else does she know?" Quinn paused as if waiting for a mind-blowing answer. She glanced at Jake and Cash before continuing. "Do you remember why your dad's in the hospital?"

"He's here?" Wynter sat up, concern clear on her face. She set her pie and Coke on the rolling side table by her bed. Cash and Jake exchanged looks.

"He's one floor up in recovery," Quinn said. "Remember why?"

"No, I..." Wynter's eyes darkened and thickened with tears. "He was burned. Our trailer... Jezebel torched it?" She looked at Quinn. "All our stuff?"

Quinn nodded. "I'm so sorry, Bug."

Wynter covered her face with her hands, but instead of tears she let loose a muffled scream.

"The doctor said you might forget things," Quinn said. "We hate reminding you, but we need you to remember as much as possible."

"Is my dad okay?" Wynter spoke through her hands as if that might protect her from the truth.

"His legs were burned and..." Quinn looked to Cash for support.

"He had a heart attack on the way to the hospital," Cash said. "I rode with him in the ambulance. But he's going to be okay. His doctor said so."

Wynter dropped her hands from her face. Instead of tears, her eyes contained fiery rage. "My gear? My books?"

"It's all gone," Cash said.

"Fuck." Wynter leaned back against her pillow and stared at the ceiling. "I hadn't returned Vinny's favorite telephoto lens yet. He's going to fire me, then kill me."

"Vinny's not going to do shit," Jake said. "We'll make sure of it. None of this is your fault."

Wynter gripped her bedcovers with white knuckles as she scanned her friends' faces. Her eyes were clear but still steeped with anger. "We have to kill her."

"No, Wynter," Cash said. "That's a bad idea."

"Why?" Wynter faced him, her red hair flipping over her pillow. "She almost killed me *and* my dad. And Quinn, Jake, even you."

Cash stood and paced beside his chair. "If we kill her and get caught, then we could go to prison. You want to risk that?"

"So we don't get caught." Wynter crossed her arms in defiance.

"Easier said than done," Jake piped up. "This ain't the movies."

"Got any better ideas, shithead?"

"Easy, Bug," Quinn said.

"No, actually I do." Jake raised his voice and propped himself up on his crutches. "Let Anson handle it. Not bringing in the police back when Jezebel sideswiped us was a fucking mistake."

"You know why we didn't get Anson involved," Quinn said to Jake. "Ransom was in Jezebel's head. We had to get him back first."

"Ransom this, Ransom that." Jake scowled. "Look where chasing his ass got us. Fucking move on already."

"I can't move on, Jake. Okay?" Wynter pointed at Jake's leg. "You need that cast to heal, right? Ransom is like that for me. I'll never be the same if I don't get him back."

Jake watched a single teardrop roll down Wynter's face. "Look, I'm sorry. I'm just frustrated."

"We all are," Cash said.

"So what happened to Ransom?" Jake faced Quinn. "You drove him here. Didn't he kiss her?"

"I'm sorry." Quinn sighed deeply and fanned her face with her hands. "This is all my fault."

Wynter reached over to Quinn and took her hand. "It's *Jezebel's* fault."

"Just tell us what happened," Cash said.

"The plan worked." Quinn grabbed a tissue and wiped her nose and eyes. "They kissed and everything was cool. I went to get a couple of coffees and when I got back, Jezebel and Roxy were there. I had to fight to get past Roxy. A gun went off and when I got into the room, Ransom drifted. Jezebel did something because she said he was back in her head again."

Quinn sobbed into her tissue. "If I hadn't left for those fucking coffees, none of this would've happened."

Jake hobbled next to Quinn and placed his hand lightly on her shoulder. "This isn't on you, Quinn. Jezebel pulled the trigger."

"And technically Ransom didn't die," Cash said. "He just got reset. It could have been much worse if you *hadn't* gone for those coffees."

Jake pulled his chair closer to Quinn's and placed his arm

around her shoulder. "The silver lining: Ransom stabbed the bitch. Jezebel's going to need time to heal. That's something she can't control and it gives us an advantage."

"It's only an advantage if we can figure out a plan in time that's foolproof," Quinn said. "So, what are we going to do?"

"I still like the idea of bringing out a creature, like a sabretooth tiger—no wait—one of those hellhounds like in *The Omen*." Jake turned to Quinn. "Remember those things? What kind of dogs were they?"

"Rottweiler," Quinn said. "But Jake—"

"Right. Rottweiler. Scary as shit." A mischievous grin spread across Jake's face. "Those dogs were mean. We could just sick it on Jezebel and she'd be ripped apart. Jesus, remember that hallway scene?"

"I do," Quinn said. "But we can only summon people. Right, Wynter?"

Wynter nodded at Quinn. "Yeah."

Jake shifted uncomfortably in his chair. "That's a stupid rule if you ask me."

"Let's say that you could summon a hellhound," Cash said. "How do you get it to do what you want it to do? Just say 'Attack Jezebel'?"

"Totally!" Jake gave the impression that he had everything all figured out. "Any hellhound I bring out of my dreams is going to understand English."

"It just doesn't work like that, Jake," Wynter said.

"Okay. No animals. What about a ninja assassin? Or the actual terminator from *The Terminator*?" Jake's eyes glossed over in awe. "Can you imagine? Schwarzenegger blowing Jezebel away?"

"Sorry, Jake," Wynter said. "The person we summon has to have some kind of special meaning for us."

"Schwarzenegger *does* has a special meaning for me." Jake said. "He's my all-time favorite movie action hero."

"A special *personal* meaning, Jake." Wynter smirked at him.

"Has anyone tried it?"

Quinn shrugged and Cash and Wynter shook their heads.

"Shouldn't we at least try? If anyone could do it, it'd be you, Wynter," Jake said. "You're the master summoner."

"I can't do any summoning if Ransom isn't back in my head." Wynter popped the remaining piece of blueberry pie into her mouth.

"That reminds me." Jake pulled himself up onto his crutches to stretch his legs. "You've all summoned someone right?"

All three nodded.

Jake turned to Cash. "Who did you summon?"

"I've summoned Ransom and my twin sister Sierra."

Jake's brows crunched, confused. "You have a sister?"

"Had a sister," Cash said. "Long story short, she died when we were six."

"Shit, dude. I'm sorry. I had no idea."

"No reason you should. I don't talk about her much."

Jake turned to Wynter. "You summoned Ransom, and..." He looked at Quinn. "Who did you summon?"

Quinn did her best to conceal the panic in her eyes. "I... I summoned Ransom, too."

Jake did a double take. "Wait. What?"

"That's how the power to summon is transferred, remember?" Quinn said. "The last person to kiss Ransom gets him in their head. But they also get the power to summon other special people."

"You kissed Ransom?" Jake looked at Quinn, confused and a little bit hurt.

Quinn shrugged it off. "It was just a kiss, nothing special. Just to get the power." She glanced at Wynter with saddened eyes. "But no one will be as powerful as Bug, the master summoner."

"Well, my dad is probably more powerful than me," Wynter said.

"Hmm. Okay. Here's where I get confused." Jake paced on

his crutches at the foot of Wynter's bed. "If we can only summon people who are special to us, where did Ransom come from? I mean he doesn't look like anyone we know."

"Really, Jake?" Quinn motioned at Cash. Jake followed her gaze, a subtle smile on his face.

"Yeah, right, guys." Cash blushed.

"He's totally made up," Wynter said. "From all the things I like in a guy. And before you ask, I guess I can do that because I'm the *master summoner*." She smiled and held her hands up like she was addressing a congregation. "I like the sound of that."

"Could your dad create some kind of super assassin then?" Jake stopped to adjust his baseball hat, his eyes cool and serious. "Totally made up?"

Wynter shrugged. "I don't know. I've never had a reason to ask."

"We should ask," Quinn said. "Most definitely."

Cash looked at his friends, his doubt showing through. "Is that our plan then? Ask Nolan if he's a grand master summoner?"

"That and getting me out of here." Wynter stretched, then drank from her Coke. "I'm no good to you guys in a hospital bed."

"Seems a little flaky," Cash said. "The plan, that is."

"We need to know what Nolan can do first. If he can summon a *super assassin*..." Quinn smiled and winked at Jake. "Then we got something to work with. Otherwise—"

"Otherwise we're fucked." Cash stood and ran his fingers through his hair.

"Not necessarily," Jake said. "If we get Ransom back and get a whole bunch of people to kiss him, then teach them how to summon, we could build an army."

Cash shrugged. "That might work. *If* we can get Ransom back. But who would we ask? How long would training take? It's got to be fast because you know Jezebel's going to recover fast. The enemy always does."

"Daytona and Hunter would do it," Wynter said. "They owe me big time."

Quinn perked up. "Maybe my boss at FreshWhip? And Anson and Mercy?"

"How about our parents while we're at it?" Cash balked. "I don't know, guys. This is getting complicated."

"A complicated plan is better than no plan," Jake said.

"Keeping things simple has power." Cash nodded at Jake. "Your super assassin idea has my vote."

"I'll talk to my dad," Wynter said. "What are you guys going to do?"

Cash grimaced. "I got to work. I'm surprised that Finn hasn't fired my ass yet."

"Finn's a teddy bear in disguise," Quinn said.

"Are you sure we're talking about the same guy?" Cash and Quinn laughed.

"Maybe I should practice summoning someone on my own?" Quinn glanced at Wynter, who responded with a thumbs up.

"I've got to dub that video I took of Jezebel shooting up the Starlite," Jake said. "Anson's going to love that."

Cash faced Wynter. "Call when you find out about your dad's superpowers?"

Wynter smiled at him and nodded. "Yeah." She reached for Cash's hand and gave it a soft squeeze. "And thanks." Her eyes flicked to the Coke can and Hostess wrapper, then back to Cash. "For everything."

"Happy to do it." Cash headed for the door, pulling it open for Quinn and Jake. "Bus or taxi?"

"Oh, shit." Quinn looked in her wallet and shook her head. "I can't afford a taxi. Can you?"

"Bus it is." Cash glanced back at Wynter as Quinn and Jake shuffled out into the corridor. She waved at him and he waved back. "Call us as soon as you find out, okay."

"For sure." Wynter watched Cash ease into the corridor as the door finished its gentle arc. She finished off the can of Coke, smiled, and rested her head on her pillow. The gentle but incessant pulse of the cardiac monitor had been her constant companion for a week without her knowing it. But after almost a day awake, she looked forward to moving on. Making a plan with her friends, even one that was as simple as asking her dad to summon a super assassin, gave her hope that Ransom would soon be back where he belonged. Back in her head.

But there was a seed of an idea in the back of Wynter's mind, an idea she couldn't yet grasp through the receding fog of her coma. Perhaps in time it would hold another answer.

ANSON SHIFTED IN his chair uncomfortably and glanced at the clock across the corridor. Its face read quarter past one in the morning. He briefly contemplated trying to gain access to the operating room as an observer, but after his run-in with Dr. Maguire and the nurses assigned to Jezebel, he thought better of it. He had already burned that bridge.

Instead, he had moved to the fifth floor recovery room and settled into the waiting alcove. After what felt like endless hours, he stood, stretched, and strolled to the nurses station. A young nurse blinked up at him. She noticed his attire and focused on his badge.

"Can I help you with something, Sheriff?"

Anson placed his hat on the counter and cleared his throat. "Yes. Could you tell me when Jezebel Caine will be out of surgery?"

"I'm afraid that's determined by the severity of her injuries—"

Anson leaned on the desk with both arms. "How severe are they?"

The nurse spotted Anson's passive intimidation a mile away. "I'm sorry. I can only share details with Miss Caine's family."

Anson scanned the corridor left and right. "Are they here?"

"If you'd like to wait, there's a seating area just over there." The nurse pointed back where Anson had just come from.

"I know. Thanks. I've been sitting there for four and a half hours already." Anson gave her his best smile. "Sure you can't give me any info? Anything at all?"

The nurse smiled sweetly at him and for a second Anson thought he had gotten through to her. "Sheriff, you know how this works. If you want information, you'll need a warrant."

Anson nodded. "Thanks." He knocked his knuckles on the countertop and headed back to the waiting room. "Wait." He sidled up to the counter again.

The nurse showed signs of agitation as she tilted her head in a silent question.

"Nolan LaCroix. Could you tell me what room he's in?" Anson watched the nurse's expression turn to one of curiosity mixed with doubt. "Funny story. See, Nolan is the father of Wynter LaCroix, who just came out of her coma one floor down. I'm Wynter's godfather. And Jezebel Caine put them both here." He paused. "Not really a funny story I guess."

The nurse blinked at him.

"Just Nolan's room. That's all I'm looking for," Anson said. "I'm not even going to talk to him. I just want to peek in—"

"Room 523." The nurse pointed down the corridor. "Remember, I can see you. I don't want to call security on the Sheriff of Newhaven."

Anson thanked the nurse and hustled down the corridor to room 523. He looked back at the nursing station and gave a thumbs up.

He poked his head into Nolan's room. The lights had been dimmed and his cardiac monitor beeped softly by the bed. Nolan's chest rose and fell in peaceful sleep.

Anson pulled his head out of the room and walked back to the waiting area, giving the nurse another thumbs up. He took a seat close to the corridor where he could keep an eye on the nurses station and found an old issue of *Popular Science*. He flipped it open and pretended to read about flying diamond wing design.

Twenty minutes later, the nurse stepped away from her desk, perhaps on her break or needing the bathroom. Anson checked the corridor was empty and wasted no time returning to Nolan's room, this time going inside.

He helped the door close and turned to see that Nolan was awake.

"Morning, Anson," he said in a raspy voice. "You wanted to talk to me?"

"Uh, right. Just want to check in. See how you're doing."

"Doing fine," Nolan said. "Doctor says my legs are healing well, but it might take another few weeks. Hopefully most of that will be at home instead of here."

"Have you heard—"

"That Wynter woke up? Yeah. Maddie told me."

"And Jezebel's here, too."

Nolan nodded. "I know. She's going to make a complete recovery."

"How..." Anson gave him a questioning look. "How do you know that? I couldn't get any information from the nurse."

Nolan shrugged. "Not sure. Just a feeling I guess."

"Look, Nolan..." Anson chose his words carefully. "I got a question for you, and it might sound a little strange."

"Shoot."

"Do you know how Wynter was at the Starlight last night and here, at the same time?"

Nolan regarded Anson with cool blue eyes that also conveyed warmth. "If I were to say 'no,' would you believe me?"

"Nope."

"Then, no. I have no idea how Wynter could be in two places at once."

Anson sighed. "Alright. Glad to hear you're okay." He glanced back at the door. "I'll check back later." He eased the door open and peeked out. "Shit," he whispered.

Nolan furrowed his brows and whispered, "What's wrong?"

"The nurse is back. Last thing I need is to be thrown out by security."

"That's Julia," Nolan said with a smile. "She's an eyeful but she takes no shit from anyone."

"I noticed." Anson thought for a moment, then grinned. "Can you buzz her?"

"I thought you wanted to avoid her?"

"I'll stand behind the door when it opens," Anson said. "You talk to her, and I'll slip out of the room. Easy peasy."

"Got it." Nolan found the call button by his bed and pressed it.

Anson heard the pat of soft-soled shoes approaching the room. He took his spot by the door's hinge and waited.

"This is exciting, eh Anson?"

Anson shushed him just as the door swung open.

"Nolan?" Julia stood at the door blocking Anson's getaway. "What can I get you?"

Nolan spoke in a whisper, then waved her over. Julia let go of the door and approached his bedside. Anson curved his body around the leading edge of the door and stepped into the corridor before spinning around and poking his head into the room again.

"Everything okay in here?"

Julia eyed Anson suspiciously. "You weren't in the waiting area a moment ago. I fully expected you to be in here."

"Bathroom." Anson smiled at Nolan. "How you doing, buddy?"

Nolan gave Anson a thumbs up.

"He's just thirsty." Julia shooed Anson. "Out. Visiting hours aren't for another five hours."

"Thanks, Julia."

Upon hearing Anson address her by name, Julia softened a little.

"I'm just going to be out here... waiting." Anson crossed the corridor and took a seat in the waiting area.

A minute later Julia left Nolan's room and headed back to the nurses station. She gave Anson a suspicious glance as she passed by.

Anson pushed three chairs together, stretched out on them, and set his hat over his face.

Jezebel had derailed his earlier plans with Mercy. The girl was like a force five hurricane, leaving nothing but injury and destruction in her wake.

Anson had realized far too late that he had forgotten to call and update Mercy about what was going on. He hoped that she would forgive him yet again for letting his work take priority over his personal life, but he knew also her forgiveness would only last so long. He was skating on thin ice as it was. He tried to dream of Mercy to ease some of his guilt, but try as he might, Anson's dreams slipped back into work mode with Jezebel front and center. He was asleep in minutes even though his makeshift bed was as comfortable as a slab of concrete.

Anson felt someone rocking his shoulder. His eyes cracked open to see Jezebel crouching over him, almost nose to nose.

With one fast and fluid movement of her right hand, Jezebel produced a Bowie knife with a blade as long as her forearm. She placed the tip of the blade under his Adam's apple. "Bye bye, Deputy Dolt." She pushed the blade through his windpipe, blocking his airflow and his attempt to scream.

Anson gasped and forced himself up off the chairs. Julia took a step back, her eyes locked on him wildly. "Sheriff Jacobs! You surprised me."

Anson tried to speak but could not. He rubbed his throat and his hand came away thickly covered with his own hot blood.

"I wasn't finished." Julia yanked the Bowie knife out of Anson's neck and threw it on the floor. She extracted a scalpel from her pocket and swung its blade swiftly against his gaping wound, slicing through his remaining neck muscles and tendons like they were gelatin.

Anson threw his legs off the chairs. His hat tumbled off his chest to the floor as he stared at the seams between the tile.

Where's the blood?

Cool air flowed into his lungs with every breath. He grabbed his neck. There was no slash, no blood, just a sheen of cold sweat covering his skin and his heart jackhammering in his chest.

Anson felt a hand on his shoulder. He looked up and saw Julia looking down on him with concern. He stood and scrambled backward. His hand went instinctively for his gun as he eyed her hands. No scalpel.

Julia must have seen the fear in his eyes because she took a step back as well. "I'm sorry Sheriff Jacobs." She crouched, picked up his hat, and handed it to him. "I didn't mean to startle you."

Anson's hand moved from the butt of his gun to the proffered hat. He ran his hand through his hair before taking the hat and placing it on his head. "Thanks." He glanced at her. "Sorry. Bad dream."

"It looked like it." Julia glanced over her shoulder at the clock across the corridor. It read five after seven. "My shift's over but I wanted to let you know your patient of interest is now in recovery room 513. She's still sedated, so questioning her won't be possible, but you can poke your head in and take a look... if that helps."

Anson ran a hand over his throat once more, his recent dream still vivid in his mind. "I'm sure a good slap would wake her up."

Julia narrowed her eyes at him, unimpressed.

"I'm joking, Julia," Anson said.

"I hope so." She gave him a sideways glance. "How do you know my first name, Sheriff Jacobs?"

"Didn't you tell me—"

"I most certainly did not."

"I, uh, must have overheard you talking with someone in the hallway."

Julia stared at Anson disapprovingly and he stared back, hoping the interrogation was over.

Anson broke the uncomfortable moment of silence. "I'll see myself to room 513. Thanks for your help." He stepped past her and hurried down the corridor, feeling her eyes on him all the way. Anson paused at the door to Jezebel's room. He looked back and saw that Julia hadn't moved from her spot at the waiting area. He tipped his hat, pushed the door open, and stepped inside.

One wall reflected the morning sunshine that beamed through the window and bathed the room in a warm glow. Considering it was Jezebel in the hospital bed, connected to a cardiac monitor, a pulse oximeter, and various IV lines to keep her alive, the warmth felt wrong. Cold and dark would have been more fitting.

Jezebel's arms and legs were bound to the bed with padded leather restraints. "At least they got that right," Anson said to himself. He imagined handcuffs instead, secured uncomfortably tight. The thought sent a shiver down his back.

He couldn't help wondering how she ended up the way she was. Jezebel's mother Frankie, a narcissist through and through, would never win mother of the year but her daughter took the sociopathic cake. Anson made a mental note to find out more about sociopaths. If he understood what made Jezebel tick, perhaps he could gain an advantage and stop her once and for all.

Anson stood beside the bed and watched Jezebel breath, her chest rising and falling, gently, steadily. He glanced toward the door to the room. The corridor outside was quiet. Not many people visited their loved ones this early in the morning it seemed.

He stepped closer to the bed but made sure there was still ample distance between them. Even though she was restrained, the image of her Bowie knife at his throat still remained crystal clear in his mind. Anson suspected that part of his recent dream would never fade.

It would be so easy. The restraints are a bonus.

Anson imagined holding his hand over Jezebel's nose and mouth. Popular film and TV had perpetuated the idea that suffocation was quick and painless. From his police training, Anson knew that it would take an average of seven minutes to end a life by suffocation. Nurses and doctors would respond to her monitoring equipment sooner than that. And death by suffocation was far from painless. Instead, victims experienced a demise that was both violent and terrifying. That aspect suited Jezebel perfectly.

But it would never happen, even if there was a hundred percent chance of getting away with it. In all Anson's years as a sheriff, and as a highway patrol officer before that, he had never taken a life, either intentionally or by accident, nor had he fired his gun at anyone. That was one perk of living in a small town. Gun violence was extremely rare. Then came Jezebel to screw up the odds.

The only scenarios in which he could imagine drawing his weapon were ones of self defense or to protect a civilian. If Jezebel had Wynter at gunpoint, would he have the nerve to pull the trigger? Anson hoped so, but he also hoped it would never come to that. Irrefutable evidence was his weapon of choice.

"Your luck is running out, Jezebel Caine," Anson said in a hushed voice. He turned and headed out of the room.

Jezebel's eyelids cracked open. She turned her head on her pillow and squinted toward the door to her room. "Is it, Deputy Dolt?" She smirked and watched the door slowly swing closed.

DR. MAGUIRE AND two nurses stood by Jezebel's bed.

"I'm sorry, Miss Caine," Maguire said. "It's going to take at least a week to heal properly."

Jezebel shook her head, working herself into a frenzy. "That's bullshit. I got to get out of here now!"

"Look, you might *think* you're immortal, but the human body has limits. You can't speed up the healing process."

"I *am* immortal!" Jezebel thrashed against her bed, tugging at the securely fastened restraints on her wrists and ankles. She glared at Dr. Maguire standing at the foot of her bed. "Roxy's going to pay for this. She's fucked up too many times." She pointed at one of the two nurses standing at the side of her bed. "Get her on the phone. She'll get me out of here."

Dr. Maguire's patience was wearing thin. "Miss Caine, we need you to calm down. You've just had—"

"Calm? I'll show you calm!" Jezebel gritted her teeth and yelled at the top of her lungs, then flexed her arms like she was trying to arm curl a barbell that was too heavy. "Don't tell me what to fucking do!"

Dr. Maguire tried again. "You've just had major surgery and if you—"

"Let me out of here, *NOW!* Wait!" Jezebel spotted Wynter and her red hair duck out of the partially opened door. "That's her, for fuck's sake! She did this! *She did this to me!* What are you waiting for? Get her!"

The second nurse looked at Dr. Maguire, unsure what to do.

"Go." Dr. Maguire hooked her thumb toward the door. "What's *she* going to do? Run after her?"

The second nurse hurried out the door after Wynter.

"That's the first thing you've done right, you bitch." Jezebel spat a thick gob of spit into Dr. Maguire's face.

Without hesitation, the doctor moved to within an inch of Jezebel's face, the spittle dripping off her cheek. "Listen here, *bitch*."

"Fuck y—"

The doctor placed her hand over Jezebel's mouth and pushed her back against her pillow, cutting off Jezebel's words instantly. "You've just had major surgery. If you keep acting stupid, you're going to tear your sutures, which will lead to more surgery and more recovery time."

Dr. Maguire glanced at the remaining nurse and made a quick nod. The nurse stepped away and busied herself at a side table. Jezebel jerked her head toward the nurse, but the doctor forced it back.

"No. Don't look at her. Look at me. And listen. You need to shut up and cooperate." Dr. Maguire matched Jezebel's furious gaze with her own. "I can have you admitted to the psych ward so fast it'll make your head spin. You think it's hard to get out of here? Wait until you're in there." The doctor stared at her. "We clear?"

Jezebel nodded, then felt a cool tingle in her arm. She glanced left to see the second nurse inject the contents of a hypodermic needle into her IV line.

"Just a mild sedative, Miss Caine," Dr. Maguire said. "To help you calm down. Are we good?"

Jezebel nodded. Dr. Maguire removed her hand and Jezebel made an uncoordinated attempt to bite it. The doctor grabbed a tissue and wiped the spittle away from her face.

The first nurse returned to the room as the second nurse and Dr. Maguire were leaving.

"I acted unprofessionally back there," Dr. Maguire said. "I would appreciate it if you kept it under your hats."

The second nurse nodded. "Under the circumstances, I think

you were totally professional. Not sure I would have kept my cool."

Dr. Maguire turned to the first nurse. "Did you find out anything with that other patient?"

"No," the first nurse said. "Just a lookie-loo."

Dr. Maguire pulled open the door, waited for the two nurses to exit, and followed them out. "I got to say, the more I get to know Miss Caine, the more I'm beginning to side with that sheriff from Newhaven."

"Jacobs," the first nurse said. "It was right there on his uniform. I've made a habit of remembering the hunky cops."

As the nurses and Dr. Maguire headed down the hallway discussing the finer aspects of the Halston police force, Jezebel sunk into a dreamless sleep. But her last conscious thoughts were of Wynter and revenge.

A NURSE ARRIVED late-morning to take Wynter for her CT scan. Wynter had been willing to use the walker that an orderly had delivered earlier in the morning, but the nurse insisted on transporting her in a wheelchair.

"It's important that you're relaxed for the scan," the nurse had said as she disconnected Wynter's monitoring equipment. "Plus, it's standard protocol."

The CT scan itself was a non-event. Wynter laid back on a motorized table and set her head in a form-fitting pillow to reduce movement. The CT technician lined up Wynter's head to the center of a donut-shaped machine he called "the gantry."

"Hold your breath for me, please, Wynter," the technician's voice buzzed from an intercom within the gantry.

Wynter drew a breath and held it. Machinery within the scanner began to spin and click as the table moved laterally through the center of the machine. She wondered if the scan would affect her ability to summon. Or maybe it would give her superpowers.

The technician repeated the process two times, the table moving slower the second time. After a brief pause, the technician's voice sounded from the intercom. "We're all done."

"That *was* fast," Wynter said to herself. Dr. Cornell had said the scan would take fifteen minutes, but it actually took less than half that. A different nurse transported Wynter back to her room, a round trip of about half an hour, and just in time for lunch.

Wynter found herself ravenous. She wolfed down a dry burger, cold fries, and postage-sized piece of carrot cake, washing it down with lukewarm tea. In any other situation she would have tossed the entire meal, but she found she did not care. Her body wanted food.

She buzzed the nurse on call. "Can you please unhook me from all the machines? I'd like to visit my dad."

The nurse gave her a confused look. Before she could ask the obvious question, Wynter added, "Oh, sorry. He's a patient here too. Upstairs."

The nurse removed the blood pressure cuff from Wynter's arm and the pulse oximeter from her fingertip, coiled the leads, and hung them on the cardiac monitor stand.

"I guess I could've done that," Wynter said. "Looks easy enough."

"It's better if we do it." The nurse jotted a few notes onto Wynter's chart. "Makes it official. You're going to use the walker, right?"

Wynter glanced at the aluminum frame with handles and rubber feet and sighed. "My legs were pretty wobbly this morning, so yeah."

"Good. If you've never used a walker before, they're real easy." The nurse gave a quick demonstration. "Push the walker forward a bit, then take a step, using the handles for balance. Then repeat. You try."

Wynter repeated the sequence a few times and moved several feet towards her door. "This is going to take forever."

"It's not fast," the nurse chuckled. "But I'm sure your dad's worth the effort."

Wynter smiled. "He is." She shuffled along the floor toward the door. "They don't call me Speedy Gonzales for nothing."

The nurse laughed. "Don't be too long, an hour at the most, and rest when you need to. Let us know when you're back."

Wynter set out down the corridor. Slide, step, step. Slide, step, step. In actuality, she moved faster than she thought she would, arriving at the elevators in ten minutes. She paused to catch her breath, then tapped the up call button.

The elevator doors slid open. She managed to shuffle inside and tap the button for the fifth floor before the doors closed.

Wynter took a moment to rest as the elevator ascended. Her mind wandered. Would she use a walker like this when she grew old? Would her dad's burns force him to use one now? And if so, how long would he need it? Her worries grew darker as she approached the fifth floor.

Annoyed with herself, Wynter pushed her thoughts aside and focused on seeing her dad but the yelling that filtered through the elevator doors stole her attention.

"Dad?" Her voice echoed within the confines of the elevator before the doors opened to a profanity-laced tirade.

Wynter knew in an instant that it wasn't Nolan yelling and she breathed a sigh of relief. She began to slide-step-step toward the nurses' station at the end of the corridor. With every step, she could feel her legs regain a small portion of their original strength. But when every step took a few seconds, even a corridor like this one appeared daunting.

Wynter passed the source of the commotion, room 513. A familiar voice screeched from behind the door, "You're fucking dead! *All of you!*"

Wynter felt the pit of her stomach drop.

Jezebel.

There was no window to this room from the corridor and she realized that she was in no danger. Wynter shuffled to the door and pushed it open enough to see the medical staff attending to the patient.

Was it really Jezebel? Wynter had to know for sure. She pushed through the door a bit more. Jezebel had her arms and legs restrained to the bed. She raised her chest and extended her neck as far as it would go.

"Don't tell me what to fucking do!" Jezebel pulled at the leather restraints. "Let me out of here, *NOW!*" She turned her head and caught a glimpse of Wynter at the doorway.

"Wait. That's her, for fuck's sake!" The tendons in Jezebel's neck stood out in angry ropes. "She did this! *She did this to me!* What are you waiting for? Get her!"

Reveling in Jezebel's fury, Wynter had moved away from the doorway too slowly. Her cover blown, she returned to her previous mission: slide-step-stepping to the nurses' station.

Wynter had moved several feet down the corridor before a nurse stepped out of Jezebel's room and approached her. The nurse stopped in front of the walker and placed her hand lightly on the top cross beam.

"Excuse me, miss," the nurse began. "Do you know the girl back there, in room 513?"

"I, um..." Wynter panicked. She couldn't tell the truth. A simple lie would be best. "No. I just peeked in there to see who was yelling. Sorry. I know it's, like, none of my business."

"She's a handful alright." The nurse looked her over. "Do you need help with something?"

"I'm just visiting my dad."

"What's his name?"

"Nolan LaCroix."

The nurse smiled. "Ah yes, Nolan. He's a wonderful man. All

the nurses love him. Unlike..." She motioned back at Jezebel's room. "He's in room 523. Second to the last room on your left."

"Thanks." Wynter resumed her two-step boogie down the corridor, keeping her eyes forward. Her legs felt stronger even after such a short time, but she was glad to have the walker for support. Thanks to the nurse, and ironically to Jezebel, she wouldn't need to walk all the way to the nurses' station.

Wynter arrived at room 523, took a deep breath, and used the walker and her body to push through the door. "Hey Dad. Long time no see."

Saturday's edition of the *Newhaven Register* obscured Nolan's face. At the sound of Wynter's voice, he flipped a corner of the paper down. His eyes lit up and a wide smile filled his face as he dropped the paper on his lap.

"Wynter! This is an unexpected surprise." He spoke a little louder than a whisper.

"Is this a bad time? I can come back—"

"Are you nuts?" Nolan laughed hoarsely. "Get your butt over here right now and give me a hug."

"Give me a few minutes." Wynter slid her walker toward the side of the bed, one step at a time. "My legs aren't operating at a hundred percent yet."

"That makes two of us." Nolan shifted his body toward Wynter, held out his arms, and pulled her into a tight embrace, nearly toppling the walker in front of her. "God, Wynter. I was so worried about you." He released her and studied her face. "Are you okay?"

Wynter sat in the chair next to the bed. "I'm fine, Dad. Well, except for the legs, but I'm getting my strength back pretty quick. I might be out of here by tomorrow."

"It's going to take me a while longer, but I heal fast." Nolan thumped his chest twice with his fist.

"I hope so." Wynter flipped up a corner of the newspaper. "The Register, huh?"

Nolan chuckled softly. "I've made a few friends in here."

"The nurses on this floor love you, apparently."

"Don't tell your mom." Nolan winked at her and flashed a wide, warm grin.

Wynter took his left hand in both of hers like she was praying to a rosary. "It's so good to see you. I mean, like when you made me a dreamwaker, that was good, but seeing you for real? That's totally awesome."

"I agree," Nolan whispered. "Most excellent."

Wynter smirked at him.

"What? Did I get that wrong?"

"No," Wynter said. "It just sounds weird when you say it."

"I guess I need practice." Nolan refolded the newspaper and set it aside. "Anson was here last night. Asking about you. Second time he's done that."

Wynter shifted in her chair. "Did you tell him that you summoned me yesterday?"

"No, but I think he knows, or at least suspects something."

"You know Anson," Wynter said. "He won't believe something unless he, like, sees it with his own eyes. Sometimes even that's not enough."

"He's stubborn," Nolan said. "Just like someone else I know." He smiled at her.

Wynter fell quiet for a moment. "Dad, we're going to get Jezebel, once and for all."

Nolan's eyes widened. "No. Bad idea. That girl is too dangerous."

"We have to. *I* have to. She's got a part of me I need back. And she's hurt too many people close to me."

Nolan pursed his lips and sighed. "I'm guessing I won't be able to convince you otherwise."

Wynter faced him, her eyes set and determined, and shook her head.

"Is there anything I can do to help you and your friends be safe?"

"There might be," Wynter said. "You summoned me, made me a dreamwaker. How did you do that? I thought I was the only one."

A cup of water sat on the rolling table next to Nolan's bed. He took a sip. "I did for a while, too. But I could summon people when I was your age. But not whenever I wanted, like you can."

"But you chose to summon me yesterday."

"Yes, but I guess the passage of time and everything else that's happened allowed me to do it." Nolan looked at her and whispered, "I don't think I could do it again. At least not for a while."

Wynter deflated.

"What's wrong?"

"I've got this power to summon whenever I want to," Wynter said. "We were hoping that since you're my dad, you'd like have that power too, maybe even superpowers, so that you could summon a super assassin or something."

Nolan reclined against his pillow and crossed his arms. "You'd want me to bring out someone to kill Jezebel?"

Wynter nodded. "Pretty much."

"Hmm." Nolan thought for a moment. "Even though it wouldn't be me doing the killing, it just wouldn't feel right. In the end I'd be responsible."

"But your assassin wouldn't leave a trace. Once Jezebel was gone, they could drift away."

"Yes, and leave us with the memory of what we'd done," Nolan said. "We're not psychopaths like Jezebel. If we kill, that memory could haunt us for the rest of our lives. It could end up destroying us." He placed a hand on Wynter's shoulder. "You should let Anson take care of Jezebel."

"But Dad, he won't listen without evidence."

"Keep trying. You're stubborn too, remember?"

"We *have* been trying." Wynter laid her head against her arms on the bed and looked up at her father. "And Jezebel keeps winning."

"I know you'll figure it out," Nolan said. "And I'll help in any way I can, except for summoning super assassins."

"You know, you never answered my question."

Nolan looked at her, confused.

"*Can* you summon a super assassin?"

Nolan smiled wistfully. "No. Your great grandmother had the true power of summoning, then it skipped a couple of generations. You're it now, kid."

"Great," Wynter said. "So it's not possible for someone else to have the true power? Like some of my friends can summon, and unfortunately so can Jezebel."

"Your great grandchild may be blessed with the power."

"Or cursed."

"Possibly," Nolan said. "But the power isn't transferable in its entirety. Your friends can only summon people they have a strong connection with. While you were able to summon Ransom, a person completely unique." He tapped his temple. "Created with your own imagination... although he does look a lot like—"

"Dad..." Wynter's cheeks flushed despite her attempt to prevent it. "Is it *that* obvious?"

"If *I've* noticed the similarity between Cash and Ransom, then surely others have too."

"I guess." Wynter clasped her hands in her lap. Thoughts of Cash and Ransom competed for attention in her mind. If she had to choose, could she? The fact remained that she needed Ransom back to become whole again. "Dad? Where are we going to live now?"

"Mom's got a motel room in Halston."

"But that's temporary. I don't want to live in a motel. Or in Halston."

"Don't worry. We'll rebuild." Nolan spoke calmly, just above a whisper and it reassured her. "That's what insurance is for."

Wynter bit her lower lip, then said, "Maybe I'll stay at Cash's place."

Nolan regarded her with surprise. "You? And Cash? Under the same roof? What do you think your mom would say about that?"

"*Absolutely not!*" Wynter said in her best Madeline impression. "But I think I could change her mind."

"You think so?" Nolan laughed. "You're welcome to try."

"What do *you* think of the idea?"

Nolan opened his mouth to speak then, paused to reconsider his words. "I'm not crazy about the idea, but I trust you and Cash to do the right thing."

"Thanks, Dad."

Nolan yawned and stretched. Wynter took that as a cue and stood up. Her legs felt slightly steadier under her than they had before.

"Looks like we're both tired." She leaned in and gave Nolan a hug, her red hair spilling around his face. "I'm going to go back to my room. I had a CT scan of my head and I don't want to miss the results."

"A CT scan? Nothing bad I hope."

"The doctor said it was, like, the last check before I get out of here," Wynter said.

"Okay. You better scoot, then." Nolan pecked her on the cheek. "I think I'm due for a dressing change. You *most definitely* don't want to be here for that." He took another sip of water.

Wynter slid her walker toward the door, turned and waved. "Bye Dad. Say hi to Mom for me. And if staying with Cash comes up..."

Nolan nodded. "I'll put in a good word."

Wynter pulled the door open and shuffled through into the corridor. She briefly contemplated exploring the fifth floor to avoid Jezebel's room, but after hearing no profanity echoing off the walls, she reconsidered. What could Jezebel do anyway? Restraints kept her tied to her bed. The direct path was the best.

Wynter slide-step-stepped back toward the elevators. She gave Jezebel's door a wide berth and arrived at the elevators faster than she expected.

Once in the elevator, she thought about her dad. The visit had felt bittersweet. Seeing him had been the best part. But Wynter did not look forward to having to tell Quinn and Jake that their plan for Nolan summoning a super assassin was a bust.

Stepping into the elevator to go down, Wynter lifted the walker for a few steps.

Getting stronger, most definitely.

But it would take more than strength to get Ransom back out of Jezebel's head. Wynter needed a back-up plan to share with Quinn and Jake. As she stepped from the elevator to her fourth floor home away from home, she began to brainstorm.

THE
KILLING
MOON

JEZEBEL OPENED HER EYES to a familiar fabric pattern above her. The stitching reminded her of the repeating diamond shapes on a storm drain cover. The gray fabric had discolored at the seams where dirt had collected over the years, unavoidable considering that the Barracuda was just as old as she was.

She reached up and ran her fingertips over the plush surface, at once reminded of velour, the cardinal sin of clothing fabric. Her fingers left a visible mark depending on the direction she moved them. A little farther away she spotted two partial hand marks from a memorable night of sex with a high school senior last summer. She had briefly tried to scrub the prints away, but they had become permanent after drying. Maybe it was the sweat or the lube. Instead, she left the stains as they were, wearing them like a badge of honor.

Jezebel sat up and oriented herself. The back seat of the Barracuda seemed bigger and more comfortable than she remembered it being. She climbed over the center console, slid into the bucket seat, and gripped the steering wheel.

Jezebel seemed to melt. "I've missed you, baby."

Through the front windshield, the headlights revealed a vast expanse of highway that faded into darkness. There was no traffic and no identifying landmarks or signs.

"Where the fuck am I?"

The passenger door opened and Ransom hopped in. "Where do you want to be?"

"Not sitting next to your sorry ass." A switchblade materialized in Jezebel's hand and she engaged the blade. She thrust the knife's point at Ransom.

"Should've thought of a gun instead."

Jezebel reconsidered her attack when she saw the pistol in Ransom's hand. He pulled the slide and rocked the hammer back.

"Shoot me then, you prick," Jezebel hissed. "It's just a dream anyway."

Ransom shook his head slowly. "No. I want out of your head."

"Too bad." Jezebel jammed the knife blade into the ignition and cranked it. The engine turned over with a growl and settled into a low rumble. She slammed her foot on the gas and the Barracuda responded like a whipped horse. "Not going to happen, fuckhead."

The dashed median on the asphalt shooting by underneath the vehicle was the only sign that the car was moving.

"Where do you think you're going?"

"I'm just driving," Jezebel said. "Feels good. Now shut the fuck up."

Ransom turned on the radio and laughed. "Road To Nowhere" by Talking Heads echoed through the car's interior. "Classic," he said.

"Shut it off."

"And if I won't?"

Jezebel glanced at the pistol in Ransom's hand and remained silent. An idea had been percolating in the back of her mind and in order to test it, the dream had to continue.

"You can't just keep driving forever," Ransom said.

"Really? Watch me."

The road flew past like they were in a game of Atari Night Driver. Jezebel concentrated on the road ahead. This was her dream, and with the exception of Ransom, she could control it.

A speck appeared on the road ahead. Jezebel smiled wildly. It was working. She floored the gas pedal, the speedometer pushing past a hundred miles per hour.

The speck changed and stretched as it got closer to the car, slowly taking shape.

Ransom squinted ahead. "What is that?"

"You'll see." Jezebel gripped the steering wheel with white knuckles, watching the object get closer, transforming into the image in her mind.

Two hundred feet away, Jezebel jammed her foot on the brake. The Barracuda shuddered under the strain as it shot past a white blob that looked more human with every second that passed. She yanked left on the steering wheel and sent the car into a slide, turning it one-hundred eighty degrees.

Ahead, in the headlights, stood a figure. Jezebel rolled the car closer and smiled with satisfaction.

Ransom stared straight ahead, eyes wide. "What the hell. That's... that's *you!*"

"No shit, Sherlock." Jezebel jumped out of the car and ran to the front bumper. In front of her stood an identical version of herself, head to toe. Same hair style, same outfit and shoes.

"Show-off," the Jezebel clone said.

"It ain't bragging if you can pull it off." Jezebel grabbed the shirt of her clone and yanked her toward her, kissing her hard.

The clone pushed her back. "What's your fucking problem?"

"Just testing you out. Making sure you got it."

"Of course I got it." The clone pushed her back again. "I'm you."

"And you're going to need a name. I'll call you Jezebel Too." Jezebel looked her over again. "You need a hoodie."

"You mean this?" Jezebel Too reached over her shoulders and

pulled a black hood out of thin air. The rest of her shirt took the form of a matching hoodie.

"That'll work."

Ransom hung his head out the passenger window. "Nice work, Jazz. You can finally go fuck yourself."

Jezebel ignored the barb. "You're going to be my dreamwaker now. You ready?"

Jezebel Too returned a familiar grin. "Abso-fucking-lutely."

Jezebel whispered something in her ear, then turned to Ransom. "Hope you like the darkness, fuck face." She grabbed Jezebel Too by her hoodie, threw her onto the hood of the Barracuda, and vanished.

JEZEBEL WOKE IN her hospital bed surrounded by the shadows of early morning. Jezebel Too careened over the side of her bed and hit the floor with a thump, banging her head on the tile. Her leg struck a metal garbage can and sent it and its contents flying. The receptacle hit the wall and rolled on its side, creating a loud clatter.

"Fuck! Hide!" Jezebel whispered loudly.

Jezebel Too rubbed her head, still dazed from her impact. "What?"

"Hide! These bitches can hear a pin drop."

The sound of hurried footsteps echoed down the corridor toward Jezebel's room.

"What are you fucking waiting for! Quick! Or we're both in deep shit."

Jezebel Too stood uneasily on her feet and looked around the room. "Hide where?"

"Fuck if I know..." Jezebel's eyes darted left and right, looking for a good spot, any spot. As the footsteps drew closer, she settled on the window and pointed. "Behind the curtains! Go!"

Jezebel Too ran to the corner of the room and stepped behind the thick woven curtains. She tried her best to settle the movement of the fabric.

"Stop moving!" Jezebel said in a forced whisper. "And shut up."

As the curtains settled in front of Jezebel Too, the shadow of feet paused just outside the door to her room.

The nurse pushed the door open, washing the room in light. Jezebel cast a casual glance at the curtains beside the window and realized a glaring error in her plan. The curtains were too short. Jezebel Too's legs and shoes were in full view. She refocused her eyes at the end of the bed.

The nurse scanned the room. "Do you need help with something, Miss Caine?" She picked up Jezebel's chart and noted the cardiac monitor's data.

"Do I look like I need help?" Jezebel scowled and shook her head.

"I heard a noise." The nurse resumed her examination, her eyes settling on the toppled garbage can and its refuse near the bed. She glanced at Jezebel's restraints, then stepped closer to the bed, righting the can.

The nurse gave Jezebel a distrustful look and rechecked the restraints one by one. "How'd that garbage can get knocked over?" She squatted to her knees and began collecting the spilled garbage and returning it to the can.

Jezebel raised her arms against the restraints. "How the hell do I know? Maybe this dump has rats."

"It doesn't get knocked over on its own," the nurse said as she worked.

"What was your first clue, genius?" She flexed her legs and tugged at her restraints again. "I can't wipe my own fucking ass. How could I knock *that* over?" Jezebel spotted motion in the corner where Jezebel Too had hidden, but now Jezebel Too was in full view, moving silently across the room.

The nurse moved the garbage can back into place and stood. She could find no explanation that placed the blame on Jezebel. "While I'm here, do you need anything? The bedpan?"

"I, uh…"

Jezebel Too had crept past the nurse, then stopped and turned. Slow careful steps brought her within striking distance. She was practically breathing down the nurse's neck.

Jezebel tried to hide her anger and angst at having her plans not followed to the letter. Her only choice was to roll with Jezebel Too's poor judgment. "There was one thing…"

The nurse placed one hand on her hip, preparing for a flippant answer. "Yes?"

Jezebel Too attacked the nurse from behind and put her into a sleeper hold. The nurse's fingers scrabbled for purchase, but Jezebel Too's grip was fast and tight. The nurse's legs thrashed chaotically, and her eyes bugged out as she struggled.

Thirteen seconds later the nurse slumped into unconsciousness but Jezebel Too continued her grip.

"What are you, stupid?" Jezebel strained to keep from yelling. "Why'd you do that?"

"For fun and excitement. What else?"

"Let her go you dumb bitch," Jezebel said. "We don't want to kill her."

"Why not?" Jezebel Too stared back at Jezebel and increased the pressure on the nurse's carotid arteries. "She was annoying."

"What are you, crazy?"

"Crazy. Like you." Jezebel Too smiled at Jezebel and for the first time, Jezebel felt her own psychopathic energy thrown back at her.

"You have a job to do," Jezebel said. "Let her go and *do it*."

Jezebel Too released the nurse and let her collapse to the floor. She flipped her hoodie over her head and bolted from the room.

From her restrained spot on the hospital bed, Jezebel could

only see the nurse's unmoving legs, white hosiery, and her white Oxford shoes.

"Come on, come on...," Jezebel whispered. "Wake up."

She counted in her head. By the time she reached ten, Jezebel began to panic. It was an unfamiliar feeling, one that she was not prepared for. How would she explain a dead nurse in her room? Her internal count reached fifteen, then twenty. What was she going to do?

"Wake the fuck up," Jezebel hissed under her breath.

Then the nurse's foot moved, then her leg. A hand reached up to the rail on the bed and the nurse pulled herself up.

"What happened?" the nurse asked, rubbing her neck.

"Weirdest fucking thing," Jezebel said. "You just dropped to the floor, and less than a minute later, you woke up."

"No." The nurse scanned the room with wild eyes. "Someone choked me from behind."

Jezebel shrugged and tried her best sweet and innocent look, hoping it would pass. "I didn't see anyone. I swear."

The nurse squinted at her with distrust. "I know what I remember." She turned and walked out of the room.

"Wait," Jezebel said. "You asked me if I needed anything. Remember?"

The nurse stopped and turned. "What can I help you with, Miss Caine?"

"Can you set up the television? I can't sleep." Jezebel smiled as sweetly as she could manage. "Please?"

The nurse sighed. "You're going to have to use headphones." She rolled the TV/VCR combo unit out from the corner of the room, plugged in the headphones, and set them on Jezebel's head. She turned on the TV and placed the remote control in Jezebel's right hand. "If I hear a peep, the TV's gone."

The nurse stood waiting. It took Jezebel a moment to clue in. "Thanks?"

"I should hope so." The nurse turned and headed for the door, smoothing down her skirt as she went. "Don't drop the remote," she said as she slipped into the corridor.

Jezebel watched her door swing close, returning the room to the pre-dawn darkness she had awakened to, but now illuminated with a flickering television glow.

She flipped through the TV's channels, most of them static or test patterns, until she found the only channel with a picture. Jezebel groaned when she realized it was a rerun of *The Waltons*. Anything would have been better. Her favorite show was *Miami Vice,* but it never aired in the wee hours. She wanted to close her eyes and dream of a threesome with Don Johnson and Philip Michael Thomas, but had to stop herself. She couldn't sleep. Her dreamwaker needed time to do her job.

Accepting this temporary fate, she sighed and settled into the episode. Soon she discovered a smile had formed on her lips. Despite a few bumps, everything was rolling along just the way she wanted them to. Ransom was still trapped in her head and Jezebel Too had taken on a mission that she couldn't do herself.

Even with restraints, Jezebel was in control. She was the boss and she planned on keeping it that way. After *The Waltons* finished, an episode of *Little House on the Prairie* began. She cycled through the channels again and ended back where she started.

Jezebel strained to focus on the TV show. It had been just over an hour since Jezebel Too had left, barely enough time to complete her mission. She fought to stay awake, but the pull of sleep was stronger. Mixed with the boring antics of the Ingalls family on the TV in front of her, the outcome was inescapable.

Her eyes slipped closed. Jezebel ended up dreaming of Don Johnson and Philip Michael Thomas after all.

JEZEBEL TOO STEPPED out of the hospital and into the cool night air. She pulled her hoodie tighter around her head and strolled to the parking lot. At quarter past four in the morning the lot was full of vacant spaces. Spotting the Barracuda was easy.

She reached under the rear bumper and located a small metal box on the left side of the gas tank, held in place by strong magnets. Jezebel Too pried the box off and slid the top open. Inside was the Barracuda's spare key.

She grinned. "There you are." Jezebel Too replaced the empty box, unlocked the door, and slid into the driver's seat. She placed both hands on the wheel and pictured the road flying past underneath the car. "Time to make it real."

She turned the key and the muscle car rumbled to life around her. The smell of oil, gasoline, and exhaust mixed with the early morning air was intoxicating. She drove the car out of her parking space and headed toward the lot's exit.

Jezebel Too merged onto Interstate 94 heading west. The highway opened up in front of her, no traffic ahead or behind, just like in the dream. But she had to remind herself that this was real as she roared past a speed limit sign.

"Fuck fifty-five," Jezebel Too stamped on the gas and the Barracuda lurched forward.

Three-quarters of an hour later, she exited onto Main Street and followed it through the center of Newhaven. Lit signs and shuttered businesses greeted her as she cruised the familiar streets for the first time. She turned left onto Mortimer Avenue, rolled past Jake's house, and pulled into Roxy's driveway.

She really wanted to lay into the Barracuda's horn but that would have drawn too much attention. Plus, it wasn't part of the plan.

Jezebel Too killed the car's engine, stepped out, and looked up at Roxy's house. Compared to what Jezebel had lived in all her life, it was a palace. "Fucking richy bitch."

She followed the walkway around the side of the house to the back door. "Breaking and entering is so much easier..." She lifted a small adobe pot to the left of the stoop and a brass key sat there, shimmering in the moonlight. "When you know where the key is." She unlocked the door, shoved the key in her pocket, and stepped inside.

HINTS OF SUNRISE mixed with the street lights seeped through Roxy's bedroom window on the second floor of the house. Even in the low light, it was clear that Roxy had everything a teenaged girl could ever ask for.

Next to her bed sat a white, ornate dresser with brass handles. A lamp with an orange and white striped shade sat on the top of the dresser with various necklaces and pendants hanging off it. A pink pushbutton phone and a digital clock radio nestled beside the lamp. The clock read eight minutes after five.

Opposite her bed stood a floor-to-ceiling bookcase filled with books, mainly mixed genre paperbacks written by every author one could imagine. Her desk sat close enough to the bookcase to look like they were one connected piece of furniture.

Roxy's stuffed animal shrine filled the small vertical space between her desk and her closet, with some of her more important stuffies laying claim to the back corner of her desk's work surface. Her mother never wasted an opportunity to tell her that she was too old for stuffed animals. Roxy ignored her.

The rest of her wall space was filled with a varied selection of rock and roll posters, including a-ha, Duran Duran, Kiss, Depeche Mode, Van Halen, The Sex Pistols, and Ozzie Osbourne. A particular favorite was a black and white portrait of James Dean in the rain. The coveted spot on the ceiling above her bed featured a poster of a shirtless and sweaty David Lee Roth.

Between the foot of her bed and the wall sat a small color TV with a cable box on top.

She's got everything, alright.

Jezebel Too stood at the foot of Roxy's bed, watching her sleep. She wanted to get rid of her and take over her life. But that wasn't *part of the plan*. Nothing she wanted to do was ever part of the plan. She felt anger rise to the front of her mind.

"Getting rid of you might not be part of the plan," she whispered to herself, "but having fun sure is."

Jezebel Too grabbed two fistfuls of covers at the foot of the bed and yanked them back, exposing Roxy in a Hello Kitty T-shirt and panties to the cool air of the room.

She leaped onto the bed, straddled Roxy, and grabbed her shirt collar. "Wake up. Time to die." Jezebel Too hissed.

"What?" Roxy squirmed to get away, then stopped, groggy and confused. "Jazz?" She rubbed her eyes. "What the fuck? What are you doing? Get off me."

Jezebel Too considered her request, then moved her hands up. She wrapped them around Roxy's neck in a tight choke hold, a move far more painful than the sleeper hold she had used on the nurse back in Halston. Roxy's face turned deep red as she fought for air. She reached to her left, found the cord to the bedside lamp, and pulled, knocking it to the floor.

With nowhere to go and her strength leaving her, Roxy settled her panicked and tear-laden eyes on Jezebel Too's.

Jezebel Too leaned in until she was nose to nose with Roxy. "You fuck up again, and I'll kill you." She released Roxy's neck and rocked back until she was sitting on Roxy's pelvis.

Roxy fell back onto her pillow, panting, sweat soaking into her T-shirt and sticking it to her body. It took a moment for her breathing to return to a semi-normal state. "I didn't fuck up. That was the plan. If things went to shit, I was supposed to split. *You* told me that."

"Shut up."

"And you're the one who…" Roxy listened for sounds of her parents waking. She continued, whispering, "You're the one who pulled the *fucking* trigger. Now, let me up."

What Roxy said had been true. Jezebel had told her those things. Jezebel Too raised her hips and let Roxy shift herself into a reclined position at the head of her bed.

Roxy rubbed her throat. Red and purple hand marks had already begun to surface on her neck. "Why did you choke me?"

Jezebel Too stared at Roxy past the point of comfort. "I'm getting used to being real."

"What?" Roxy squinted at Jezebel Too as if to make sure that her eyes weren't deceiving her. "What are you talking about? You're real. Most definitely real… How did you get out of the hospital so fast?"

"I didn't. I'm a dreamwaker, idiot," Jezebel Too said. "Jezebel pulled me out of her dream. She calls me Jezebel Too. My job was to fuck you up. So here I am."

Roxy eyed her dubiously.

"Don't believe me? Turn on the light."

Roxy reached over the edge of the bed and rescued the lamp. Setting it back on top of her dresser, she turned it on. Warm, orange light flooded the room.

"Ransom stabbed me, remember? Right about… here." Jezebel Too moved her left hand to the right side of her abdomen and pointed. "It was deep. Remember the blood? Before you ran like a chickenshit?"

"Was just doing what you told me to do," Roxy said.

"Shut up." Jezebel Too grabbed the bottom hem of her hoodie and raised it up high enough to expose the bottom swells of her breasts, far higher than she needed to. "Jezebel got out of surgery about three hours ago. Do you see stitches? Or a scar?"

Roxy's eyes widened. There was no scar.

"Go ahead. Touch my skin if you want."

"That's okay," Roxy said. "I can see what you're talking about."

"Can you?" Jezebel Too pulled her hoodie over her head and tossed it aside. "Jezebel made me in her image, but perfect in every way." She ran her hands up her abdomen, between and over her breasts, and down to her hips.

Roxy found it hard not to stare. There were no freckles or moles or imperfections of any kind. Jezebel Too's skin was perfect. *Too* perfect.

Jezebel Too let her eyes roam across Roxy's moistened T-shirt, following the hills and valleys of fabric over her breasts, lingering on her panties, before meeting Roxy's eyes again. There was undeniable heat between them, but Roxy wanted none of it.

Jezebel Too gripped the bottom of Roxy's T-shirt and ripped it up the middle, separating Hello Kitty into two pieces and exposing Roxy's bare chest.

"What the hell, Jazz!"

Roxy covered her breasts and scooted backward awkwardly on her elbows to examine the damage to her T-shirt. Jezebel Too countered and grabbed her hips, pulling her back, almost taking off her panties in the process. She placed her full weight on Roxy's hips.

"What are you doing?" Roxy hooked her hands onto the top of her headboard and struggled to break free. "Let me go!"

Jezebel Too grabbed Roxy's wrists and pressed them into her pillow next to her head. She leaned over her, close enough to feel the heat of Roxy's body on her nipples, and kissed her hard. "I want you to make me cum," she hissed into Roxy's ear. "Right now. I know you want to."

Roxy ceased her struggle and matched Jezebel Too's gaze. "After you nearly choked me to death? Fuck you." She bucked her way out from under Jezebel Too, pushed herself off the bed, and scrambled in a frenzied backward crab-walk across the floor to the bookcase. It was a bad move and left her trapped.

Jezebel Too ran around the bed. "Come on, Rox. Let's have

some FUN!" She kneeled, grabbed Roxy's ankles, and pulled her back toward her.

Roxy managed to wrap a hand around a baton balanced next to her desk and swung it around, connecting with the side of Jezebel Too's head.

Jezebel Too let go of Roxy's ankles and slumped to one side, stunned. She refocused on Roxy, her eyes narrowing. "I should've killed you when I had the chance." She lunged for Roxy, her fingers splayed like talons.

Roxy used the baton to block Jezebel Too's attack. But before she could inflict any damage, Jezebel Too vanished in a flash of bright blue energized ozone. The key to the back door plus the keys to the Barracuda rattled to the floor.

Roxy waited to make sure that Jezebel Too was really gone. She also listened in vain for parental footsteps which she knew would never come.

She crawled to her dresser, pulled out another T-shirt. She removed the tattered Hello Kitty T-shirt and tugged the fresh one over her head.

Roxy pulled herself to her feet, faced the window, and used the torn Hello Kitty shirt to wipe her tears. She could see the Barracuda parked in the driveway below, the hedges that lined the north side of her yard, and the road beyond. Dawn was breaking over Newhaven.

Across the street, she thought she sensed movement, but didn't care enough to pursue it. One thing Roxy *was* sure of: She had had enough of Jezebel's shit.

JAKE LAY STARING at his ceiling trying to distract himself, constructing images out of the random patterns in the stippled texture. His left leg had developed an itch within his cast that he couldn't reach, and it was driving him crazy. He had tried a pencil, a ruler, and even an unbent coat hanger but nothing worked.

He was crippled, hot, itchy, and aggravated. And he could look forward to another six weeks of this torture.

All because of Jezebel.

Anger seeped to the front of his mind, and he began to think of ways he could enact revenge. Jake's ideas flowed. He could poison her, cut her precious Barracuda's brake lines, give her tainted drugs, blow up her gas tank. He knew the expanding list, inspired by Hollywood blockbusters, was over the top and required toning down. Besides he couldn't intentionally kill Jezebel, even if that's what his dark desire wanted. Still, it was fun to think up ways to get rid of her.

Just as he sat to grab a pad of paper, Jake heard the low rumbling outside the house. He felt it in his chest before he heard it and recognized it instantly. He hopped to the dormer window just in time to see the black Barracuda pass his house and turn into Roxy's driveway. The engine cut out and he heard a car door open and close.

Jake had found his distraction. He grabbed his camcorder and slung it off one shoulder, grabbed his crutches, and hustled to the stairs. He had been on crutches for only ten days and he had become fast and proficient with them. But the stairs were a hurdle he had not yet conquered.

"Got to become a stair master." He chuckled quietly to his joke.

Navigating the stairs in the dark was an added danger. He sat and slid down the steps one at a time, carrying his crutches with him like he was the new kid at the playground. He paused at the front door and listened for sounds of his parents.

Nothing. The coast was clear.

Jake turned on his camcorder and pressed record, then eased the front door open. He hopped down the front walk, his bare foot gripping the concrete, and turned west, following the sidewalk until he was facing Roxy's house from the opposite side of the street. He set his crutches down and eased himself into a neighboring hedge for support.

"This is Jake Peterson reporting for Action Five News. I'm standing outside Roxy's house where suspicious activity has been reported." He aimed the camcorder at the back of the Barracuda and zoomed in. The streetlight offered just enough light to read the license plate.

"Bingo." He zoomed out, framed the car and house in the viewfinder, and waited.

Who drove the Barracuda here? And why?

Unanswered questions swirled in his head. When the recording timecode passed five minutes, he felt his impatience build. Birds had begun their early morning wake-up songs.

"Come on, come on," Jake said to himself. "Don't leave me hang—"

A light appeared in the left-most top floor window. Jake zoomed in and filled the viewfinder's frame. From his vantage point, he could see the tops of posters on the back wall of the room.

"Depeche Mode and... Ozzie Osbourne?" Jake laughed to himself. "What a combo."

A figure moved past the lower corner of the window and disappeared. Jake held the camera steady. "We've got movement folks," he whispered.

Superimposed on the viewfinder's screen, the low battery indicator began to flash. "Shit, no. Don't cut out on me now." Jake kept the window in frame and ignored the warning.

A figure ran from right to left and disappeared below the window sill. Jake glued his eye to the viewfinder. In that moment, all his aspirations of starting a video game company vanished, replaced with a life as a private investigator.

The room flashed brilliant blue for a second, then returned to normal.

"What the hell was that?" Jake braced the camcorder with

both hands in case it happened again. Instead, a figure stood up and faced the window. "Roxy?"

The figure raised something to their face (a towel?) and wiped, before reaching left to the light. They paused, then turned off the light. The room became a dark square, void of detail.

"There you have it, folks," Jake whispered. "Mysterious shit is happening in Newhaven. This is Jake Peterson, signing—"

The camcorder clicked off. All at once Jake felt exposed. Whoever was in that room could see him, but he couldn't see them. His advantage had been flipped. He waited a moment but realized it was only getting lighter as time passed.

"Fuck it." He crouched to pick up his crutches and hustled back to his house. Butt-scooting back up the stairs, he stowed his camcorder on his desk and rolled into bed.

But Jake could not sleep. His brain buzzed with what he had just seen and recorded on video. The pre-dawn surveillance mission had succeeded with another pleasing side effect: the itch inside his cast was gone.

Who had driven the Barracuda?

He sat up, dressed himself, and powered up what he liked to call his "custom designed video editing suite." In actuality, this was just two VCR machines hooked up to each other. Jake could do crude editing, but he used the machines mainly for making copies.

He plugged the camcorder's battery to charge, removed the small VHS-C cassette, and popped it into an adapter. He played the tape back several times, watching the blue flash of light in slow motion.

He began making dubs of his early morning work, one tape for himself, one for Anson. He kept the master in a safe concealed in his closet behind a false wall. Not even his parents knew of his secret stash.

Jake paused the playback and advanced the recording one

frame at a time. The blue flare in Roxy's bedroom lasted only a few frames. It reminded him of...

Wynter vanishing at the Starlite!

So much had happened over the weekend, he had forgotten about Wynter's disappearing act at the Starlite on Saturday. He ejected the master tape and inserted his dub of his covert garbage can video that he had recorded just over a day ago. Jake pressed play and fast-forwarded to the moment just after Jezebel shot Wynter.

He discovered to his horror that falling debris from the ceiling had jostled the garbage can concealing his camcorder. Most of the shot had been obscured, leaving only Jezebel visible in the top corner of the screen.

Jezebel crouched and reached forward with her pistol. A blue burst of energy that lasted no more than a split second flooded the unblocked areas of the screen, just like what he had seen through Roxy's bedroom window.

Jake sat back in his chair, conflicted. The Starlite sting operation had failed spectacularly. Yet, with his recent surveillance mission, he had uncovered a detail no one had considered. A satisfied grin spread across his face.

"Whoever drove the Barracuda was a dreamwaker." His voice sounded stark within the confines of his room.

The obvious answer was Ransom, but could there be something he was missing? Jake intended to find out.

WYNTER WOKE AT six-thirty feeling refreshed. She swung her legs off the bed and tested her muscles. They felt stronger. She grabbed the walker just in case but raised it above the floor. With quick, tentative steps, she moved across the room to the one exterior window. She winced at the brightness of the morning sun, already well beyond the horizon.

A portly food service worker knocked on the door and rolled in a cart. "Good morning. Breakfast is served." On a tray sat a bowl of oatmeal, two pieces of dry toast, a smattering of scrambled eggs and a small cup of orange juice. "I know it's not much, but it's a damn sight better than the IV 'meal' the doctors had you on, not that you'd remember that." He air-quoted the word "meal," then transferred the tray to Wynter's rolling bedside table.

"Thanks."

"You better taste it before you thank me," the service worker said, chuckling as he left.

Wynter set her walker aside and hopped onto the bed. Then it dawned on her that she had walked from the bed to the window and back under her own power. She smiled to herself and shoveled in a mouthful of oatmeal.

Cold.

Even with a plate cover, the time it took from kitchen to bedside was enough to congeal the oatmeal into a puck that needed a knife and fork rather than a spoon.

"I could teach their cooks a thing or two," Wynter said to herself quietly.

"I bet you could." Madeline stood at the door watching her.

"Mom!" Wynter pushed the rolling table out of the way, ambled over to her mom, and gave her a tight hug.

"That's what I needed." Madeline held Wynter in her arms, then ran her hands over her hair. "And without the walker, too. I'm impressed."

Wynter looked back at the walker beside her bed, surprised. "I completely forgot to use it."

"How's breakfast?"

Wynter turned her nose up. "It's something to chew."

"Maybe this will help." Madeline pulled a Burger King bag from her purse and handed it to her.

Wynter tore into it and extracted a bacon and egg Croissan'wich. "Oh God, Mom, thank you." She sat on the edge of her bed and took a bite. Her body relaxed as she chewed. "So good. And it's still warm." she said, muffled through her mouthful.

"So, I was talking to your dad yesterday." Madeline took a seat next to the bed. "He was saying that you'd like to stay with Cash when you get out of here."

"Wait." Wynter waved her hands while she swallowed her mouthful. "I know what you're going to say, that it's out of the question. It was, like, just an idea, Mom. I know you're staying in a motel here, and that it's temporary, but I don't want to stay in Halston. Cash is a good guy. He's my friend and I trust him. But if you say no, that's okay." She paused and sipped her orange juice. "Maybe I could stay with Quinn instead."

Madeline regarded her daughter thoughtfully. "Are you done?"

Wynter nodded and took another bite of her Croissan'wich.

"A year ago, I would have said you're too young, Wynnie," Madeline began. "But you're almost seventeen. You're reliable, a good worker. You do well in school, and you've done nothing but make your dad and I proud." She took Wynter's free hand in hers. "Remember, your dad and I weren't much older than you when we had you."

"It's not like I'm going to marry Cash, Mom."

"I've seen the way he looks at you... and the way you look at him."

"We're just good friends." Wynter popped the last bite of her sandwich into her mouth.

"Friendship and love go hand in hand. And trust me, I know the power of young hormones. Look at your dad and me. We got married after knowing each other for a week, and we're still together."

"If Gramma and Grampa had forbidden you from marrying Nolan, what would you have done?"

Madeline smiled. "Oh, we would have gone and done it

anyway." She raised a brow at her. "Does that mean you're going to do whatever your heart desires?"

"No, but whatever I do, I'm going to be, like, smart about it."

Madeline sighed and studied Wynter's face fondly. "I don't want to be the parent who holds her kid back and denies her experiences solely on the basis of age."

Wynter pushed her scrambled eggs around her plate with her fork. "What are you saying?"

"Is Cash's dad still working nights?"

"Yes."

"I see. That's the only part of this idea that I have a real problem with," Madeline said. "You said you trust Cash. I trust *you*."

"So, what are you saying?"

Madeline didn't answer right away.

"Mom?"

"I'm saying that it's okay with your dad and I if you stay with Cash for a while... until we get back on our feet. Just let me know where you are," Madeline said. "It has to be okay with Cash's dad too, of course."

In the back of Wynter's mind, a little voice rejoiced. If it had had a body of its own, it would have been hopping up and down. She did her best to rein in her excitement at taking one more step towards adulthood. "Thanks, Mom. I won't let you down." She leaned toward Madeline and hugged her.

There was a quick knock at the door and Dr. Cornell stepped into the room. "Oh, is this a bad time? I can come back in a few minutes."

Wynter shook her head. "No, come in." She eyed the doctor excitedly. "Is this about my CT?"

Madeline faced the doctor. "What CT?"

"Mrs. LaCroix, your daughter had a CT scan of her brain yesterday," Dr. Cornell said. "It's standard procedure after a coma as well as after a traumatic brain injury."

Madeline shivered. "I hate those words."

"I told Dad about the CT yesterday," Wynter said. "He just forgot to tell you." She looked at Dr. Cornell. "So does my pretty little head get out of here?"

Dr. Cornell chuckled and nodded at her. "The scan came back clear. So yes, you can go home, Wynter."

Wynter let go a small squeal of elation, ran to the doctor, and wrapped her arms around her neck. "Thank you so much. For everything."

"I'm glad everything turned out the way it did," Dr. Cornell said. "But if you experience any unexplained nausea, headache, blurry vision, dizziness, or see stars, you get your butt back here. Understand?"

Wynter nodded. "Got it, doc."

"Is your mom going to drive you home?"

Wynter looked at Madeline and they both smiled, a new understanding bridged between them. "No, I'm going to call a friend to pick me up."

"I'll have one of the nurses get started on your discharge papers."

Wynter ran to the door and pulled it open.

"Wynnie!" Madeline said. "Where are you going?"

"To call Quinn, of course." Wynter disappeared out the door before Madeline could respond.

She stood and held out her hand to the doctor. "Thank you, for all your expertise and hard work."

Instead of shaking her hand, Dr. Cornell pulled Madeline into a brief but firm hug. "It was my pleasure."

"It's been quite a roller coaster ride," Madeline said. "Not one I care to repeat any time soon."

Dr. Cornell nodded as she jotted some notes into Wynter's chart.

"Now I get to focus my attention on my husband upstairs."

Dr. Cornell paused as a connection clicked in her head. "*Nolan LaCroix*, right?"

"Yes, that's right." A flicker of worry flashed in Madeline's eyes.

"I should have put two and two together. Your last name is quite unique."

"Is there something I should know?"

Dr. Cornell laughed. "Not unless nurses fawning over him left, right, and center is a worry. They love him up there."

Madeline raised a brow, suspicious yet playful. "Funny. He never mentioned *that* little detail."

"Something to talk about, I guess?"

"You got that right." Madeline followed Dr. Cornell out of the room and watched her hustle down the corridor. She turned the other direction and spotted Wynter talking at a payphone, waving her free hand by her head excitedly and playing with her hair.

Madeline's love for Wynter swelled in her heart. Her baby would be okay. More than okay. She would thrive. The ugly business with Jezebel was far from over and would likely end up in court, but she reassured herself that Wynter's life-threatening roller coaster ride was over.

Regardless of her earlier misgivings about staying at Cash's place, Madeline felt confident that Wynter would do the right thing. It left her the time to focus on Nolan's recovery and finding a new home.

SWEAT BROKE OUT on Jake's neck, a combination of his exertion, the morning sun heating the neighborhood, and his nerves. He leaned on his crutches outside Quinn's house and stared at the front door's large brass knocker, briefly contemplating whether he was going to go through with his plan or not.

On one hand, he had agreed to pursue anything that led to

Ransom. On the other, this was Quinn's house at quarter to seven on a Monday morning. He could be seconds away from committing social suicide.

Jake glanced at Blue Belle parked in the driveway as if the car could give him any assurances. "Fuck it," he said for the second time this morning. "I'll do it for Wynter." He reached forward and rapped the door. When he didn't hear any immediate response, he rang the doorbell too, then regretted the decision immediately. A series of chimes that sounded larger than life echoed through the interior of the house.

Soft, padded footsteps approached the door, followed by the sound of a retracting deadbolt. The heavy oak door swung open without a sound and revealed a slender Asian woman wrapped tightly in a terry cloth housecoat sewn to resemble a kimono. Despite the early hour, not a hair looked out of place.

Jake grinned awkwardly up at her from his crutches. "Uh, hi."

She looked down at him and gave him a once-over. "Yes?"

"You must be Quinn's mom."

"Yes. I am." Mrs. Benoit waited for Jake's response. "And you are...?"

"Oh, sorry." Jake squared up his Nintendo baseball cap. "I'm Jake, ma'am. Jake Peterson. I'm one of Quinn's friends."

"It's awfully early to be calling, Jake," Mrs. Benoit said.

"I know, but it's kind of important." Jake looked at her and tried to turn up his charm.

Mrs. Benoit glanced at Jake's leg cast and determined he wasn't a threat. "Come. Wait inside. I'll call Quinn."

Jake navigated his crutches over the stoop. Mrs. Benoit closed the door behind him and padded down a marble-tiled hallway. He followed her into a well-appointed kitchen with modern brushed steel appliances. He noted a cordless phone on the wall much like the one at his house.

"I was just making some tea," Mrs. Benoit said. "Would you enjoy some?"

Jake nodded. "Uh, yes, Mrs. Benoit. Thanks."

She grabbed a second cup from the glass-fronted cupboard. "Please. Call me Lotus. I think I've heard Kirin talk of you." She poured some tea into a cup and handed it to him.

"Good things I hope?" Jake sipped the tea and winced at its bitter flavor. He imagined it was how a freshly cut lawn might taste.

Lotus laughed lightly. "Oh yes. All good." She approached a buttoned panel on the wall beside the cordless phone and pressed one of the buttons. "Kirin?" Her question floated in a sing-song voice. "You have a visitor. Jake's here."

A few seconds later, a clatter echoed from a room on the opposite side of the house, then the thumping slap of bare feet on polished tile.

"She's up. You must be important." Lotus winked at him. "That's quite the cast on your leg."

"Yeah, that's kind of why I wanted to talk to Quinn," Jake said. "Well, it's related... uh, long story."

Quinn entered the kitchen wearing black silk tap pants and a loose fitting T-shirt with *Fast Times at Ridgemont High* written across it. Her hair stuck out at odd angles.

"Jake!" She stepped quickly toward him. "What's wrong? Is everything okay?"

Quinn's bare legs and short tap pants caused Jake's brain to short circuit for a moment.

"Jake?" Quinn eyed him with concern.

He nodded. "Yeah. Yeah, everything's fine. I wanted to catch you and Cash before work." Jake glanced at the digital clock above the gas range. "Shit, Cash has probably already started work." He placed a hand on his mouth. "Sorry, Mrs. Benoit, uh, I mean Lotus."

Quinn glared at her mother. "Lotus? Seriously, Mom?"

Lotus shrugged and sipped her tea. "What? That's my name, Kirin."

"And my name is *Quinn,* Mom." She rolled her eyes, huffed in frustration, and turned to Jake. "What's so important?"

Jake rocked on his crutches nervously. "Kind of wanted to talk to both of you at the same time. But I saw the Barracuda last night... no, this morning. Two hours ago."

Quinn stared at him, her eyes wide and expectant, waiting for details. Even in her pajamas with her hair sticking up, Quinn rocked Jake's boat. He stared back at her, motioned to the front door, then took another sip of his tea, swallowing with a grimace.

"You gave him green tea, Mom? Ugh. Don't drink that." Quinn took the cup and set it on the counter. "Give me fifteen minutes." She ran back the way she came, and Jake watched her go.

Jake gave Lotus a sheepish look. "Sorry about the tea."

Lotus waved him off. "Don't worry about it. Not many like it." She studied Jake, standing strong on his crutches. "I've never broken a bone before."

Jake shook his head. "I don't recommend it."

"You like my daughter, don't you?"

Somewhere in the house the shower turned on.

"Um." Jake cleared his throat. "Uh, yes, Mrs. Benoit. I think she's great. Her knowledge of pop culture is totally amazing."

"Yes, she is amazing," Lotus said. "She's also like *bakuchiku.*"

Jake furrowed his brow.

"Bakuchiku. It means firecracker in Japanese."

Jake smiled and nodded, grasping the reference at once. "I like that, too."

"Then you two will get along fine." Lotus set her cup in the sink. "Would you like anything else? Cereal, perhaps?"

"I'm good, thanks."

Lotus tightened the drawstring of her housecoat. "I must get ready for work. Please, make yourself at home."

"I think I'm going to wait outside," Jake said. "It's nice out."

Lotus nodded and walked in the direction Quinn had gone.

Jake worked his crutches back toward the front door, pausing by the entry to a sunken living room complete with a large sectional sofa and a fireplace featured on one wall.

He opened the front door and stepped out into the morning sun, planting himself carefully on the stoop. Jake had this urge to go jogging before the day heated up but the goddamn iridescent yellow cast on his leg quashed that idea. Thankful his leg no longer itched, his thoughts drifted back to the previous night.

Ten minutes later, Quinn stepped out from the house wearing her FreshWhip uniform. She smelled like strawberries.

Quinn helped Jake to his feet. "Sorry about my mom back there. She can be mega annoying."

"I didn't find her annoying. Seriously." Jake smiled at her as he positioned his crutches under his arms. "But that tea..." He remembered the taste and shuddered. "Holy crap."

"Yeah. Both my parents drink it. It's pretty gross." She skipped down to Blue Belle. "Let's go."

They both climbed into the car. Jake had to slide the seat back to be able to fit his cast in. Quinn started the engine and backed out onto the street.

"Your house is pretty awesome."

"Thanks." Quinn turned right onto Main Street. "Maybe next time I'll show you my room." She glanced at him and smiled.

Jake felt his cheeks heat up. "Sure. Sounds cool."

"So what did you see last night?"

"This morning."

"Whatever," Quinn said. "This is more than just about the Barracuda, isn't it?"

Jake shrugged and smirked. He enjoyed drawing things out, especially if it made Quinn squirm.

"You're not going to tell me? You could walk the rest of the way, you know."

"Come on, Quinn. We'll be there in a couple of minutes. Stop busting my chops." Jake turned toward her. "And thanks for the ride. I really appreciate it."

"We'll see how much you appreciate it when you have to walk home." The sign for Finn's Gas N Go flashed a few hundred feet ahead. Quinn side-eyed Jake and a small smile curved up on the edge of her lips. "Just kidding. I couldn't do that to you."

Quinn turned into Finn's and took her usual parking spot. Cash waved at them through the front window.

"Okay, hot shot. You're up." She stepped out of the car, then leaned back in to look at Jake. "And this better be good."

Jake pulled himself out of Blue Belle and headed toward the store. Cash held the door open for them both.

"This is a surprise," Cash said. "Am I missing something?"

"Ask Jake." Quinn perused the junk food aisle. "Is Finn here?"

"Not 'til eight." Cash leaned into Jake and motioned at Quinn. "What's going on?"

Jake rested his arm on the front counter. "I couldn't sleep last night." He tapped his cast with his index finger. "Around five I heard the Barracuda pull up to Roxy's place."

Cash stepped around to the back of the counter. "Are you sure it was *the* Barracuda? I mean, last we saw that thing it was parked at the hospital."

"Come on, Cash," Jake said. "We all know the sound of that car a mile away. Yeah. It was *the* Barracuda."

"Who was driving?" Quinn asked.

Jake frowned for a moment. "It was dark. I couldn't see. But by the time I got down to the street with my camcorder, the driver was gone."

Cash's interest was piqued. "You shot video?"

Jake nodded. "I did. Was a regular Magnum P.I."

"Got to work on that mustache." Quinn winked at him.

Cash crossed his arms. "What did you see?"

"For the longest time, nothing at all," Jake said. "But then Roxy's bedroom light went on. That's when things got weird. I saw something move by the window, then, like a few seconds later a blue flash of light. Just like when Wynter drifted at the Starlight last Saturday."

"Anything else?" Cash spotted a customer roll up to the pump. "Hold that thought." He ran out and began filling the customer's tank.

Quinn moved closer to Jake. "Could you see who passed the window?"

Jake shook his head. "It was fast and it was in the corner. Plus, whoever it was, they were too far from the window to see anything."

Cash imprinted the customer's credit card, handed them their receipt, and ran back into the store. "So what else happened?"

Jake shrugged. "Roxy stood in front of the window for a bit, then turned out the light."

"I'm going to want to see that video," Cash said.

"Thought you might." Jake shifted on his crutches. "My question is who was driving?"

"It could be anyone," Quinn said.

Cash shook his head. "Not anyone. It can't be Jezebel. She might be strong, but no one is up and driving hours after having major surgery."

"Can't forget the blue flash. That makes it look like it was a dreamwaker, and that means it could be anyone Jezebel's connected with." Jake reseated his ball cap as a shiver ripped down his back. "Shit. It really *could* be anyone."

"My money's on Ransom," Quinn said.

"I don't know. I want it to be Ransom, but the last time she saw him, she shot him." Jake's eyes clouded in thought. "I think she's trying to control him, keep him in her head."

"On second thought, yeah." Quinn glanced at Jake. "She'd never trust him with her precious Barracuda."

"There's one other problem with it being Ransom," Cash said.

Jake blinked at him. "What's that?"

"As far as I know, Ransom can't drive."

"Wait. Of course," Quinn said. "Who would Jezebel trust enough to drive that car?"

Jake and Cash thought for a moment. "Roxy?" Jake said.

"Exactly." Quinn's eyes flashed with excitement and Jake fell in love with her all over again. "It makes perfect sense. Roxy as a dreamwaker drives the Barracuda home from the hospital, then drifts when she gets home."

Cash considered the idea. "It could work. But I'm still going to want to see that video."

"Sure. No prob—"

The phone next to the cash register rang. Cash picked it up. "Morning. Finn's" He paused to listen, then glanced at Quinn. "It's for you."

Quinn scrunched her brow and took the phone. "Hello?" She relaxed and covered the receiver, whispering, "It's my mom." She listened. "Okay... I will. Thanks. Bye."

"What was that about?" Cash asked.

"Wynter's getting out of the hospital today and needs a ride." Quinn looked at the two guys and smiled. "Party at Jake's on a Monday? Think your parents would go for that?"

"Yeah," Jake said. "They'd be cool as long as it wasn't too late."

Quinn faced Cash. "Want to come to the hospital?"

"For sure."

"Jake? You in?"

"I really want to say yes," Jake said. "But I don't want to sit in the back of Blue Belle with this *fargin' icehole* cast."

Quinn flashed her eyes at him. "*Johnny Dangerously?*"

Jake laughed. "You still got it."

"Was there any doubt?" Quinn turned to Cash. "I'll pick you up around six, okay? Your place."

"Sounds good," Cash said.

"Want a lift back home, Jake?"

"Sure you've got time?"

"Most definitely," Quinn said. "It's not even eight o'clock."

"Then, sure." Jake glanced at Cash, and he sent him a subtle nod and a thumbs up.

"Later, Cash."

Quinn and Jake waved goodbye. Within minutes, the teens found themselves headed north on Main Street, back the way they had come half an hour ago.

Jake dug into his jeans for his wallet. He pulled out some bills and placed it on the dash.

"What's that for?"

"Money for gas," Jake said. "It's only fair. You've been driving us around lots lately."

"I don't mind." Quinn smiled at him sweetly, then turned left onto Mortimer Avenue.

Jake took a moment to untie his tongue. "I liked your idea back there, about Roxy. It would explain a lot."

Quinn's smile evaporated. "Speak of the devil. Look."

Ahead, the Barracuda backed out of Roxy's driveway, with Roxy behind the wheel. She wore a dark hoodie.

"Stop the car," Jake said.

"What?"

"Just do it. Stop."

Quinn pulled to the curb. Before she could say anything else, Jake jumped out of the VW and made a stilted approach toward the black muscle car. She leaned out of Blue Belle's side window. "Jake! What the hell are you doing?"

Jake did not respond but instead continued his advance. Roxy shifted out of reverse and steered toward Jake in the road. He made sure she could not drive around him by staying centered with the Barracuda's front bumper.

"Jake?" Quinn popped her door open. Jake raised an arm back toward her with an open hand, indicating "stop." Understanding the signal but still confused, she closed the door and watched.

Roxy rolled the Barracuda slowly forward as Jake stepped

closer. She glowered at him through the windshield. They both stopped in a standoff, Jake five feet from the front bumper.

Jake would have never considered the move if Jezebel had been driving. Jezebel was too far gone. He banked on Roxy not being a complete psychopath, that she might have some empathy or a partially active moral compass.

He had no idea how long they stood facing each other with nothing between them except the low grumble of the car's engine. Time seemed to melt away.

Jake took a step forward. "Did you drive the 'Cuda home this morning?"

Roxy simply stared back without uttering a word.

"What happened last night? I—"

Roxy punched the gas. The Barracuda vibrated in place, spewing blue clouds of acrid smoke from behind. Then she let up on the gas, returning the engine to a rough idle.

Jake let the burnt rubber miasma roll over him, then took another step forward. Through the windshield, he spotted something that turned his theories upside-down.

"Your neck... It's all bruised." He tried his best to show concern despite his fear that Roxy would run him down at any moment.

Roxy took one hand off the steering wheel and pulled her hood over her head, shrouding the bruises in shadow. "Move," she said in a low growl.

"Who did that to you? Was it Ransom?" Jake refused to give up. "Who was it, Roxy?"

Roxy shook her head. "FUCK YOU!" She shifted into reverse. The guttural rumble of the Barracuda's engine ramped up into a scream, and the car shot backward through another drift of smoke. She turned the wheel hard left, and the Barracuda spun a hundred-eighty degrees. She fed the car just the right amount of gas to correct for the spin and tore down the road away from Jake.

He watched until the Barracuda's taillights disappeared at the opposite end of the street. Jake turned and stepped toward the sidewalk in front of his house.

"Holy shit, Jake." Quinn hopped out of the VW and ran to him. "That was fucking amazing."

Jake shrugged. "Thanks." He turned his head to look back down his street again, but Quinn intercepted him, turning him back to face her with both her hands.

She tipped up on her toes and planted a firm, warm kiss squarely on Jake's lips. He stumbled one step backward, unprepared for her advance, and used his crutches to regain his balance. There it was again, the smell of sweet strawberries.

Quinn dropped back to her soles and smiled at him.

"Whoa." Jake's wide eyes met her rich, dark ones. "What was *that* for?"

"For being badass." Then Quinn whacked him against the shoulder. "And that's for being dumb! She could've run you over."

"Well, she didn't," Jake said, pleased with himself. "The gamble paid off."

Quinn escorted Jake to his front door and he stepped inside. Pots and cutlery rattled from the kitchen.

"I think I have a new theory about what happened this morning." Jake said.

"You replacing my idea already?" Quinn pouted at him playfully.

"No, but maybe adding to it," Jake said. "Maybe Roxy was attacked."

"By who?"

"I don't know." Jake glanced at Roxy's house down the street. "We can talk about it tonight."

"Around eight?"

Jake nodded. "Sounds good."

Quinn kissed him quick on the cheek. "Later, *badass*."

Jake laughed and watched Quinn walk back to Blue Belle. She

moved with a lightness that he admired, like not many things bothered her. She started the engine, waved, and drove away.

The smell of fried bacon lured him toward the kitchen, but not even his recent kiss with Quinn could tear his mind away from his new theory.

ROXY COULD BARELY hold onto her anger as she drove the Barracuda along Main Street. She had intended the drive to calm her down, but it had done the exact opposite. At first, she had focused her rage at Jake, for asking questions she couldn't answer and for blocking her path. But he was only trying to help. She couldn't fault him for that. She even liked him and had had a secret crush on him ever since middle school. She had told no one. As she approached the downtown strip, past storefronts preparing to open their doors for business, she realized her true anger was at Jezebel.

Correction. Jezebel's dreamwaker. Jezebel *Too*.

"She almost killed me," Roxy said to the empty car. "She *would've* killed me." The gravity of her own words sunk in like shards of glass and Roxy found herself shaking, her hands gripping the steering wheel in an attempt to calm herself down. She pulled over to the curb, breathing rapidly.

Roxy turned on the radio in hopes that music would help sooth her anxiety. "Psycho Killer" by Talking Heads was playing and she turned the radio off a second later. She didn't need any reminders of Jezebel. She was already a permanent fixture in her head.

Soon her heart rate and breathing had returned to normal. Her mind began asking questions again. If the real Jezebel had been in her room last night, would she have done the same thing? Dreamwakers had free will, so it was possible that Jezebel Too was even more psychotic than Jezebel. Maybe it was like a photocopier: you always degrade the original when you make a copy.

Roxy glanced out the windshield to orient herself and realized that she had parked in front of the Newhaven Police Station. There were lights on inside. Maybe Anson was there.

She could go inside right now and confess to everything. It would be so easy. Being Jezebel's partner in crime, Roxy's story would easily pass as fact. She might avoid jail time.

But it wasn't Jezebel who nearly killed her. It had been her dreamwaker clone. She couldn't implicate someone, or some *thing,* that wasn't real. A confession would end up becoming just one more fuckup that Jezebel could hold over her head.

"Fuck that." Roxy shifted out of park and pulled away from the curb. Jezebel Too had better watch her step because next time it would be different.

Stand By Me

Wynter looked out over the city of Halston and caught her reflection in the hospital window. It felt strange to be wearing the same denim shorts and white long sleeve button-up she'd had on when she had fallen from the Main Street Overpass. But it also felt comforting. They were the last pieces of clothing she owned, and they made her feel whole again.

Luckily Madeline had dropped off a bundle of new clothes earlier in the week that included some fresh panties and a bra. It sure beat going commando for seven days straight in a hospital gown, not that Wynter remembered any of that.

She tugged at the loose waistline of her denim shorts. She had lost some weight while she had been in the hospital, an unfortunate side effect of being fed a vitamin-infused nutrient slurry for a week through a nasogastric tube. A belt was in her future.

She collected her things and stuffed them into a small wheeled suitcase. No sooner had she snapped the lid closed than Quinn knocked and pushed through the door.

"Bug!" Quinn ran to Wynter and wrapped her arms around her. "I've missed you *so much*."

"But we talked, like, yesterday."

Quinn stepped back and held Wynter by the shoulders. "I know. It's been forever."

Wynter looked past Quinn's shoulders. "Where's Cash?"

"He's downstairs. Said he had to do something." Quinn found Wynter's eyes with hers and smiled. "Probably something romantic."

"What about Jake?"

"He's getting the party ready."

"What party?"

"You'll see." Quinn winked at her. "Ready to go?"

Wynter nodded, then looked back at the room. "Wait." Hanging off one side of the head of the bed was Nolan's hope medallion. She picked it up and hung it around her neck. The hand-carved disc of wood settled in front of her heart and still carried a faint scent of birch. She raised it to her lips and kissed it lightly. A little piece of her dad had been with her during her entire hospital stay and for that she was grateful.

She rolled her suitcase next to a wheelchair and took a seat. "Will you be my pusher?"

"Maybe I should call Monty instead?"

"Don't you dare," Wynter said, glaring at her playfully. She gripped the handle of her suitcase, Quinn took hold of the wheelchair handles, and together they rolled out into the corridor.

Wynter waved back at the nurses' station before Quinn accelerated toward the elevators.

"Why do they make you use a wheelchair anyway?" Quinn used her feet to brake, sliding to a stop with inches to spare between Wynter's shoes and the wall. She punched the down button.

"To make sure patients don't injure themselves on the way out."

Quinn tilted her head and rolled her eyes. "Like *that* would ever happen."

They both laughed as the elevator doors opened and Quinn rolled Wynter inside.

"How does it feel to be free of this place?"

Wynter sighed. "Totally the best. I mean being awake wasn't bad, except for having Jell-O legs and maybe the food sometimes. I didn't remember anything about being in a coma."

"Not even talking to Cash in his dreams?"

Wynter gazed up at Quinn, her eyes wide like saucers. "I talked to him? About what?"

"Did you know he had a twin sister?"

"No... wait." Wynter paused to think. "Was her name... Sarah?"

"Close," Quinn said. "Sierra. I met her, too. Cute kid."

"What happened to her?"

The elevator doors rolled open and Quinn pushed the "Wynter train" into the foyer, her suitcase acting as caboose. "You'll have to ask Cash. I have a feeling you know already but those memories just haven't been unlocked."

Wynter scanned the foyer for Cash. "Where is he? I don't see him anywhere."

"I'm sure he's around, Bug." Panic flickered in Quinn's eyes when she couldn't find him either. She pushed Wynter past the sliding doors of the entrance, then relaxed.

Ahead, Cash leaned against one of the support pillars for the hospital's covered entry, looking cool as usual and sporting a warm smile. He held a small red gift bag in his hands.

Wynter glanced behind her. "Am I past the doors?"

"Most definitely," Quinn said.

Wynter let go of her suitcase, gripped the wheelchair's armrests, and pushed herself to her feet. After a couple of unsteady steps, her stride smoothed out and she walked, then ran to Cash and stopped.

"Hey you," she said with a grin.

"Hey yourself." Cash held up the gift bag. "I got something for y—"

Wynter threw her arms around his neck and rested her head against his chest. He had showered and smelled clean and fresh, without a hint of gasoline or oil from Finn's. She drew in a deep breath and let it go, and with it some of her worries floated away: of not making a complete recovery, whether her friends had remained the same, and what came next.

Wynter loosened her embrace and looked up at Cash and matched his gaze until her stomach began to flutter.

"What's in the bag?" Quinn asked.

"Oh, right." Wynter took the bag and pulled it open.

Cash watched her dig into the contents. "Sorry. It's not a blueberry pie or a Coke."

Wynter pulled out a small stuffed bear with a toy SLR camera hanging around its neck. Her eyes misted up and her lips trembled.

"I hope you like it," Cash said.

Wynter hugged the stuffie against her chest. "I love it. Thank you." She stepped up and kissed Cash's cheek lightly.

Quinn rolled Wynter's suitcase next to them. "We should get going. Jake's waiting for us." She gave Cash a secret thumbs up.

Cash nodded, lifted Wynter's suitcase off the ground, and headed for Blue Belle's parking space.

Wynter took her time crossing the lot. Her legs needed to adjust to walking again.

Quinn matched her stride. "How do you feel?"

"Great. So glad to get out of that place in one piece."

"If Ransom was here too, how would you feel?"

Wynter opened her mouth to answer, then the words evaporated. "I... I don't know."

"I think Cash's worried about that, too," Quinn said. "But you didn't hear it from me."

Ahead, Cash was busy loading Wynter's suitcase into the front trunk of the VW.

"Quinn?"

"Yeah, Bug?"

"Could we take a detour?" Wynter hugged the stuffed bear and regarded Quinn with serious eyes.

"Sure. Where?"

Wynter told her.

"Bug, are you sure?"

Wynter nodded.

"You got it," Quinn said. "Let's go."

All three of them climbed into Blue Belle and were soon on their way back to Newhaven.

CASH LAY STRETCHED out in the back of Blue Belle like a modern day Tom Sawyer. All he needed was a straw hat and a long blade of grass to chew on. "I'm starving."

"Me too," Quinn said, her eyes focused on the road ahead. Traffic had been light on the way back and for that she was grateful. The detour had put a small wrench in the schedule, but she'd do anything for Wynter, especially now.

"How about you, Wynter?" Cash could just make out the gentle curves of Wynter's face behind her long red hair. When she didn't respond, he pulled himself upright and propped his arms on Quinn's and Wynter's seatbacks. "You okay?"

Cash placed his hand lightly on Wynter's shoulder and she jumped, startled. She turned her head abruptly, her eyes wild. "What?"

Cash blinked, a little taken aback. "Hungry for Pizza Zip?"

"Um, I guess." Her eyes flicked to the off-ramp ahead, then focused on something distant.

"Pizza? Again?" Quinn glanced at Cash through the rear view mirror.

"Of course," Cash said. "It's Jake's go-to meal."

Quinn pouted. "Jake knows a lot about a lot of stuff, but his fast food choices need work."

Cash leaned into Quinn's ear. "I'm sure you could help him

with that." Their eyes met through the mirror, and he flashed his brows at her.

Quinn slowed the Volkswagen as she took the off-ramp. She turned left onto the Main Street Overpass.

Cash's brow scrunched in confusion. "Hey, where are you going? Jake's place is the other way."

"Bug?" Quinn glanced at Wynter. "Sure you want to do this?"

Wynter's eyes had fear behind them when she met Quinn's gaze. But she nodded.

The neon sign for Sven Dwarfs flashed and buzzed in the sky as Quinn drove past, onto the long driveway that connected with the ring road and the trailers that occupied the pads around it.

Cash could see his trailer up ahead. His dad's car still sat parked beside it, which made sense. His dad didn't leave for work for another two hours at least. He glanced at Quinn in the rear view mirror, and she shared a concerned look.

Quinn followed the ring road around to the opposite side of the field, slowed, and stopped at pad #7. She shut off Blue Belle's engine but left the headlights on. Being close to eight o'clock, the August sun had not yet fallen below the horizon, but the ambience grew dimmer by the minute. Long streaks of warm sunlight and dark shadow painted the central field.

Through the windshield of the VW, the headlights lit a yellow caution tape border set by fire investigators. The tape twisted and flittered gently in the breeze, a stark contrast to the blackened remnants and scorched ground it encircled.

Wynter opened her door and stepped out. Cash made a move to follow but Quinn held him back. "She needs some time."

Even though it had been built from wood, most of the front stoop had escaped the fire and stood intact. As Wynter walked around the perimeter, she wondered how many times she had traversed those steps and whether she ever would again.

The rancid odors of burnt wood, plastic, paint, and metal, combined with the totality of destruction, left her fighting for control of her stomach. But she soldiered onward, always staying just past the caution tape.

Most of the walls had either collapsed or were barely standing. The roof's metal support struts had sagged toward the ground, melted by the fire's extreme heat. Except for the fridge, range, and the microwave, the remnants left inside the kitchen were difficult to identify.

The phone that used to be on the kitchen wall resembled a hunk of Silly Putty stretched to its limit, its burnt edges allowing the internal wiring to stick out. Oddly, Wynter wondered if the phone still worked.

After walking around the burnt scar on pad #7, Wynter stood and faced the part of the trailer that used to be her room. Parts of the wall that separated her room from the living room still stood, but nothing else. She lifted the caution tape and approached the charred remains of her home.

"Bug! It's dangerous," Quinn called from the VW. "Don't go in."

Cash sighed. "I think she's going in."

"Should I go after her?"

"Like you said, she needs time."

Quinn turned back toward Wynter, concerned. "Be careful."

Wynter held her stuffed bear in one hand and carefully moved past the perimeter, the charred plywood floorboards creaked and crunched with each step. The blackened remains seemed warm under Wynter's feet, despite the fire having been extinguished over two days ago.

She stood in what used to be her room. The common wall she had shared with the living room was her only guidepost. There was nothing left of her bed except blackened springs and a charred frame. Pieces of her desk, books, posters, and photographs all lay on the charcoal floor. Curiously, some were not entirely burned, but all were unrecoverable.

At her feet sat a piece of a hardcover. Wynter picked it up, knowing at once which book it belonged to: *Eyes Wide Dreaming*. The green irises on a white background was the dead giveaway, even though not much of the image remained.

She walked around her bed and found her Sony Walkman, most of the red plastic shell melted, sealing a Foreigner tape cassette inside like a coffin, most likely *Agent Provocateur,* her favorite album.

A glint of silver caught her eye on the opposite side of her burnt mattress. She navigated around the incinerated remains of her room and crouched low. Wynter surveyed the spot and realized her closet must have been here, a notion she confirmed when she picked up her Pentax K1000. Made of all metal, the camera had survived the fire, but the lens was beyond repair. She picked it up and took careful steps back to the field beyond the caution tape.

She glanced at the bear Cash had given her, its own little Pentax hanging from the stuffie's neck, and dropped to her knees. She let the K1000 fall to the ground and raised the stuffie to her face, its soft fur stifling her sobs.

Quinn and Cash gave each other a knowing glance, and both stepped out of the VW. Without a word, they approached Wynter, one friend on each side, and kneeled beside her, placing their arms around her and resting their heads next to hers.

All three of them remained huddled and silent until Wynter spoke.

"That fucking bitch." She wiped her eyes with a twist of her wrist. "She took everything from me." She alternated her gaze between Quinn and Cash. *"Everything!"*

Quinn opened her mouth to say something but chose to hug Wynter tighter instead.

Cash picked up the charred Pentax. "Let's go make sure she doesn't do anything like this ever again. Okay?"

Wynter nodded.

"Plus, Jake's got food." Cash smiled at her.

The three of them walked back to the Volkswagen and climbed

inside. As Quinn drove away from the blackened patch at pad #7, Wynter found she could not tear herself away from its reflected image in her side mirror. And an anger that had been simmering since the nachos incident at the Starlite began to boil.

JAKE PACED ON his crutches in the kitchen. He was sure that Quinn had said eight o'clock. The clock on the range displayed twenty-five minutes after. Five or ten minutes late was acceptable, but not twenty-five.

The food was going to get cold. They wouldn't have stood him up, would they? What if they had been in a car accident?

Mirielle stepped into the kitchen. "They'll be here, Jake, honey. *TV's Bloopers & Practical Jokes* is on. Come watch with us."

Jake sighed, glanced at the front door, then followed his mom to the living room.

Maybe this is all a big practical joke.

Then, as if reacting to his thoughts, the doorbell rang. Jake spun around on one crutch, his feet nearly sliding out from under him. "I'll get it!"

His crutches creaked under his weight as he arrived at the front door and pulled it open. "Took you long enough!"

Cash, Wynter, and Quinn stood on the stoop all with serious faces.

Jake looked at them, confused. "What?"

"I'm mad as hell and I'm not going to take it anymore," Wynter said, the bear stuffie still clutched in one hand.

Jake raised his brow. "Um, *Network*. 1976. But—"

"Nice one, Jake." Quinn kissed his cheek as she stepped past him, Wynter following behind her.

"We know we're late," Cash said, "but we made a pitstop at Wynter's place."

"Wynter's place? But..."

Cash motioned at Wynter and shook his head subtly. He held up the blackened Pentax K1000. "You think you could fix this?"

Jake flipped the camera around in his hand. "The lens is toast." He shrugged. "All metal body? Maybe." He handed the camera back to Cash. "Why?"

"Because it's Wynter's favorite camera, that's why."

"Right," Jake said. "Of course." He maneuvered to the stairs and began his ascent. "If you're hungry, follow me... very slowly." He laughed and tried to hide his fear. This was the first time he had ascended the stairs upright.

The other three eyed him with concern as he balanced precariously on one leg, halfway up the stairs.

Jake looked back at them. "What? Aren't you hungry?" He continued up each step, balancing on his crutches and leading with his good leg. He hoped Quinn would be impressed.

Jake reached the top of the staircase and let go a subdued breath of relief. He glanced at his friends and saw that they had relaxed as well.

"Jesus, Jake," Cash said, ascending the stairs. "That took balls. Not sure I could do that."

Quinn leaned into Wynter's ear. "Totally badass," she whispered but loud enough for everyone to hear. Jake smiled to himself as he trundled toward his bedroom.

Cash scanned the room. "You've been busy, Jake. You do all this yourself?"

"Yeah. Took all day, but I had nowhere to go," Jake said. "That's how I got good on the stairs."

Wynter and Quinn followed Cash into Jake's room. A zippered insulated bag, plates, cutlery, and napkins sat on a folding table near the door, with a cooler next to that. Three extra folding chairs sat next to his VCR machines. The rest of his room remained a cluttered curiosity, one that Cash was well accustomed to.

Quinn sat on the edge of Jake's bed, ran her hands over the

duvet cover, then flopped onto her back. The bottom hem of her T-shirt pulled up just enough to reveal a small patch of smooth skin and her bellybutton. "I could just fall asleep right now."

Holy shit. Quinn Benoit is on my bed.

Jake widened his eyes at Cash and gulped. "No time to sleep. We got work to do. But first, we eat."

"What kind of pizza did you get?" Cash tugged on the zipper of the insulated bag.

"Ha. You underestimate me." Jake scooted Cash aside and unzipped the bag. One by one he removed five square containers by their wire handles, all emblazoned with a red pagoda and the words "Thank You" in an Asian type style, and placed them on the table. "All pizza and no Chinese makes Jake a dull boy."

Cash pumped his fist. "Excellent."

Wynter tickled Quinn's exposed abdomen. "Jake got Chinese food."

Quinn sat up and pulled Wynter's ear to her mouth. "I might be in love."

Wynter whispered back, "You're most definitely *something*."

Both girls stood up and peered over Jake's and Cash's shoulders. "What'd you get?" Quinn asked.

"Chicken fried rice, chow mein, sweet and sour pork, beef and broccoli, and Singapore noodles." Jake rocked back on his crutches. "Nothing too weird, except for the Singapore noodles. Golden Palace said that one was hot, so I said... what the hell."

Quinn nodded at him. "I *like* hot. And nice riff on *The Shining* back there."

Jake felt heat rise up his neck and cheeks. He took a plate, then stepped aside. "Thanks. Dig in."

Cash, Quinn, and Wynter took seats on the folding chairs and began eating. Jake filled his plate, turned to join them, and realized that holding a plate of food while using crutches was even more difficult than navigating stairs.

Cash looked up then set his plate on the floor. He took Jake's plate and spoke through a mouthful of chow mein. "You taking the captain's seat, man?"

"You know it. Thanks." Jake worked his way to the chair in front of the VCR machines.

Cash handed Jake his plate and reclaimed his own. The four friends descended on their meals as if they hadn't eaten for days. For a moment, the only sound in Jake's room was of chewing and the clinking of knives and forks on their plates.

Jake pointed with his fork. "Forgot to say, there's soda in the cooler. Sorry, Cash. No Grain Belt tonight."

Cash shrugged and set his plate down again. He opened the cooler. "We got Coke, 7up, and Orange Crush." He pointed at Wynter. "Coke, right?"

Wynter smiled and nodded.

"7up for me, dude," Jake said.

Quinn swallowed her mouthful. "Orange Crush, please."

Cash handed out the soda, took a Coke for himself, and popped the seal.

Orange Crush bubbled and fizzed over the top of the can when Quinn pulled the tab on her can. She brought her lips to the rim and quickly averted a spill.

"How's your *crush*?" Wynter smiled slyly and winked.

Quinn narrowed her eyes at her. "Just fine, thank you."

Jake opened his can, drank, then burped. "Oops. Sorry."

"I should hope so." Quinn belched, twice as loud, then began to laugh.

"That was well brought up," Cash said. "Too bad you weren't."

Jake, Wynter, and Quinn stared at him, then all four burst into hysterics.

"Wait!" Wynter said, stifling her giggles. "What about fortune cookies?"

"Oh, yeah," Jake said. "They're in the bag."

This time, Quinn leaped to her feet, skipped to the folding table, and looked into the insulated bag. She pulled out a brown paper sack and held it out. Everyone took a cookie, until there was one fortune cookie left for her.

"Okay. Everyone stop and break open your cookies," Quinn said. "Read your fortunes and add 'in bed' at the end. I'll go first." She ripped open the cellophane, cracked the cookie in half, and pulled out the slip of paper. She smiled and licked her lips. "Someone would love to cuddle up with you... in bed." She glanced at Wynter, then flicked her eyes at Jake and quickly ducked her face behind her black hair.

Jake wondered if Quinn was blushing just like he was. He turned to Cash. "Dude, what does yours say?"

Cash alternated his gaze between his fortune and the rest of the group. "Do I have to?"

"It's bad luck not to read them," Wynter said.

Cash looked across at Wynter. "Says who?"

"Just read it," Quinn said.

"Okay." Cash took a breath. "Big cats are mean, but a little pussy never hurt anyone."

"In bed," Quinn added. Cash covered his face, shook his head, and laughed.

"Bullshit." Jake beckoned with his hand. "Let me see." Cash handed the fortune to him. "Yup, that's what it says."

"Your turn, Jake." Quinn said.

Jake snapped open his cookie, tweezing the fortune out with his fingers. "Are your legs tired? You've been running through someone's mind all day long."

"...In bed," everyone said in unison.

"Well, my legs *are* tired." Jake smiled at Quinn and crunched down on the cookie.

Wynter unwrapped her cookie. Her fortune was sticking out one end so that she didn't need to break it in half. She slid the paper out and froze.

"Wynter?" Cash had been watching her reaction with concern. "Are you okay?"

"What does it say, Bug?"

Wynter looked up from her fortune and swallowed dryly. "Run."

Quinn scrunched her brows, confused. "That's it?"

Wynter turned the fortune around so everyone could see. The single word floated alone on the strip of paper.

"It doesn't even make sense if you add 'in bed' after it," Cash said.

Jake sipped his 7up. "That's creepy to the max."

"Totally." Quinn shivered then shook it off.

"Change of subject." Cash went back to the table for a second helping. "Let's start the show."

Jake set his empty plate aside. "Good idea. But... I've got a bit of bad news."

Cash exchanged looks with Quinn and Wynter. "Oh, shit. Spill it, man."

Jake placed his hand on a couple of VHS tapes sitting on top of one of the VHS machines. "Remember I hid my camcorder in a garbage can at the Starlite? Well, something hit the top of it, probably after Jezebel starting shooting up the place." He popped one tape into the top loading carriage and pushed it back into the player. "It screwed up the framing."

Cash nearly dropped his plate filled with Chinese food. "Fuck. That was the whole point. It was our backup." He slumped back into his chair and stabbed his fork into his Singapore noodles with disappointment.

"It's not a hundred percent bad," Jake said. "Let me just play it."

"Wait." Wynter sighed. "I have some bad news, too."

Cash stopped mid-chew. "What? It's about Nolan, right? Is he okay?"

Quinn held up her hand to Cash, her mama bear instincts on full display, and slid her chair a little closer to Wynter. "Let her talk."

"Remember the 'super assassin' idea we had?" Wynter waited for her friends to nod. "Well, it turns out that my dad can't do it."

Cash lowered his plate to his lap. "Jesus, should I just slit my wrists now, then?"

"God, Cash." Quinn glared at him. "Dramatic much?"

"Sorry, but we just keep hitting dead ends," Cash said. "That fucking Jezebel has a lucky charm up her ass."

Jake let out a short laugh. "I bet it's a purple horseshoe or a blue diamond. Part of a complete psycho breakfast."

"What?" Cash rolled his eyes and loaded his fork. "Not funny," he said through a mouthful of noodles.

"More like green clovers," Quinn said. "Just like those pills Monty sells."

Cash shook his head. "Enough."

Wynter continued. "Apparently, I can do it."

Quinn's eyes widened. "You can make an *assassin?*"

"I can," Wynter said. "But—"

"Of course there's a 'but.' " Cash shook his head.

"The only *butt* I see in here is you," Jake said. "Relax."

Cash puffed his chest out. "Going to make me?"

Jake gave him a sideways look, then motioned at his cast. "Obviously not, dude. Just take a couple breaths."

Cash backed down and returned to his plate of food.

Jake looked at Wynter. "What were you going to say?"

"I *can* summon an assassin," Wynter said. "I mean I could've summoned one. But since I summoned Ransom, that power has been used up."

Jake nodded slowly. "There can be only one."

"Like the *Highlander*," Quinn said quietly.

"Kind of, yeah." Wynter sipped her Coke.

"How do we get rid of Ransom for good so that you can summon an assassin?" Cash asked.

Wynter shrugged. "I don't know, but he'd have to be back in my head first."

"Back to square one." Cash set his plate on the floor. "Jake, just roll the tape."

Jake turned on the small color TV next to the VHS machines and pressed play. Snow appeared on the screen for a moment, then the image flipped and displayed the front entrance of the Starlite, framed by the blurry outline of the garbage can's opening.

"Do you want to watch all of it?" Jake looked back at the others.

"Why not?" Cash pulled his chair closer. Quinn and Wynter followed suit.

The image on the TV showed Jezebel enter the Starlite, shoot out the four surveillance video cameras, then talk to Wynter, their voices too low to understand. Only the gunshots resonated.

Something hit the garbage can lid, tipping it sideways and obscuring Wynter and most of Jezebel on the screen.

Several more gunshots rang out. Then silence.

"Watch here," Jake said. "I think this is when Wynter's dreamwaker drifted."

The off-kilter shot of the Starlite's darkened ambience flashed bright blue on the TV screen for an instant before returning to normal. Jezebel popped into the frame for a brief moment as she pointed her gun screen left, fired, and ran.

"That's most of it." Jake stopped playback and rewound the tape. "Cash grabs the camcorder and I stop recording a second later. Does anyone want to see it again?"

Cash and Quinn looked at Wynter.

"I'm good," Wynter said.

Jake ejected the first tape and inserted the second. "Now for our feature presentation." He pressed play.

The TV screen displayed hand-held images of the sidewalk in front of Jake's house.

Cash squinted at the screen. "You're on crutches, right? How are you shooting this?"

"The camcorder was hanging from my neck."

Quinn shielded her eyes. "Ugh. I'm getting motion sick."

"Jus'sec." Jake fast-forwarded the video. "There's lots of boring parts in this." When the shot revealed the back of the Barracuda, he let the tape play normal speed.

"This is Jake Peterson reporting for Action Five News," whispered Jake's staticky voice from the TV's speaker.

"Always a ham on camera." Quinn winked at him.

Jake turned down the volume as his cheeks flushed pink with embarrassment. "Sorry."

"Don't be," Quinn said. "I think it's cute."

Jake stopped playback and fast-forwarded the tape. Cash gave him a sideways look. "Trust me. There's, like, five minutes of nothing. You're not going to miss anything."

Jake restarted the video. The TV flipped up an image of Roxy's bedroom window. "Oops, just a little too far." Jake fast-reversed the playback until right before the light in Roxy's bedroom turned on and let the video play until the same quick flash of blue light bathed the second floor bedroom. A moment later, a figure stood at the window.

Cash leaned in closer and squinted at the low resolution image on the screen. "That's Roxy?"

"Pretty sure," Jake said.

The light in Roxy's bedroom window turned off and Jake pressed pause instead of stop. "I'm guessing you're going to want to watch that again."

"You'd guess right," Quinn said.

Jake cued the video at the beginning of the bedroom sequence and let it play again.

"I still think it was Roxy who drove the Barracuda home. As a dreamwaker that is." Quinn spotted confusion on Wynter's face.

"Sorry, Bug. We talked about this in the morning, before we got you."

"No problem," Wynter said. "So, you're saying that Jezebel summoned Roxy and she drove the Barracuda home?"

Quinn nodded once. "Exactamundo. Dreamwaker Roxy drives back, then drifts in Roxy's room. Makes total sense."

"But other things make sense too," Jake said. "Like if Roxy was attacked, by her dreamwaker or someone else."

Wynter narrowed her eyes in thought. "It couldn't be Ransom because he can't drive."

Cash snapped his fingers and pointed at Wynter. "That's what I said. Great minds think alike." She crinkled her nose at him.

"Then who?" Jake looked at the others. "Monty?"

"Maybe," Quinn said. "But I can't see Monty doing *anything* for Jezebel, unless it's selling her drugs."

Cash crossed his arms. "If he got behind the wheel of the 'Cuda, he wouldn't be driving it to Roxy's."

"Can you play it again, maybe slower?" Wynter said to Jake.

"Sure." Jake replayed the sequence of video several times, then advanced the video frame by frame.

Wynter remained quiet, studying the visuals on the screen. She focused on the image so intensely that everything else seemed to fall away.

Jake paused the image on the second person in the window, if it was a person at all. In total, the movement lasted only a few frames.

Wynter stared at the frozen frame of video and the person within, jittering subtly on the TV screen. Whoever it was had long hair and the jitter made it look like the hair was blowing in the breeze.

The person's head moved. Wynter was sure of it. She leaned forward. "Did you see that?"

Whoever it was launched themselves onto the window sill and crouched like a primate, creating an ominous silhouette against the light in the room. Then, as quickly as the figure appeared, it leaped off the sill and out of view.

"Guys?" Wynter's voice was barely above a whisper. "What the hell is going—"

She turned to look at Jake and saw that his eyes were no longer there, replaced by raw and torn crimson sockets with rivers of blood flowing over his cheeks. His cast lay on the floor intact, his leg sheared off at the hip.

A scream rose in Wynter's throat but before she could release it, Quinn slumped against her shoulder. She glanced right and realized that it wasn't Quinn's body, but her head. She recoiled in terror and sent Quinn's head rolling down the front of her shirt and across her lap, leaving behind a grisly trail as it hit the floor. Quinn's gaping neck oozed dark blood that contributed to an expanding pool under their chairs.

Wynter tried to push her chair backward with her feet only to discover that both her ankles and wrists had been bound to the chair with hospital-grade leather restraints. She tried to scream but nothing came out.

"*Whinerrr,*" a voice hissed beside her. She looked to her left to see Cash floating toward her, his eyes as black and lifeless as coal. His lips had pulled back and curled into a demonic Cheshire grin to expose his gleaming teeth, filed to razor sharp points.

"*Whinerrr,*" the voice came again, this time from the TV's speaker. A pale hand with scabbed nails chewed to the quick reached through the screen and grabbed at the front edge of the desk.

Tears streamed down Wynter's face as she struggled against her restraints.

A second arm pushed through the screen, veined and scratched, followed by a rat's nest of hair. Crimped hair.

Jezebel's bloodshot eyes rose past the bottom of the TV's screen and locked onto Wynter's. "Such a *whinerrr...*" Her shoulders appeared to dislocate temporarily as she crawled out of the TV's screen. She shoved the VCR machines off the table where they crashed onto the floor.

Wynter summoned all her strength and pulled against her restraints, her screams just beyond her ability to release them. "It's just a dream," she tried to convince herself.

Jezebel pulled herself out of the TV screen and squatted on the edge of the table, a soiled hospital gown tied loosely around her waist. "You're mine now, *Whinerrr.*"

"No. You're not real," Wynter's mind screamed.

"Oh, I'm real." Jezebel jumped to the floor in front of Wynter and pushed her legs apart. "And when you die here..." Her hands snaked up the front of Wynter's shirt, until they found her neck, and squeezed. "You *die* for real."

"No. No. *No! NO!*" Wynter's soundless words fought against her need for oxygen. Her brain starved and her vision clouded over like chum in water.

Despite Jezebel's grip, Wynter shook her head slowly and bared her gritted teeth. "No, you'll never be stronger than me..."

"I already am, *Whinerrr.*"

"NOOO!" Wynter threw her head back as her battle cry burst forth and pierced the enclosed space of Jake's bedroom. She drew in a fresh breath, free of Jezebel's clutches.

"Bug?" Quinn's face appeared close to hers.

Wynter blinked at her through tear-soaked lashes. "Quinn?" She kissed her and threw her arms around Quinn's neck, pulling her to the floor.

Quinn cast her arms out to stop herself from falling on top of Wynter. "Easy, Bug. You fell off your chair."

Wynter glanced around and saw Quinn, Cash, and Jake looking down on her, concern in their eyes, all of them very much alive. She let go a shuddering breath.

"Jake?" Hudson's voice and harried footsteps echoed from down the hallway outside of Jake's bedroom. "Son?" His head popped into the room. "Everything okay? We heard a scream."

Cash helped Wynter to her feet and Quinn righted her chair.

Jake wiped his forehead and straightened his baseball cap. "We're fine, Dad."

Hudson scanned the room, his eyes examining each of the teens in turn. "You sure?"

"I slipped off my chair, but I'm fine, Mr. Peterson," Wynter said. "Thank you for checking on us."

"Okay." Hudson patted the door frame. "Oh, and since it's a weekday, think about wrapping things up soon. Eleven at the latest, okay?"

"Sure, Dad. Thanks." Jake listened for his father's footsteps to fade away. "Cash, could you close the door?"

"On it." Cash crossed the room with several quick strides, eased the door closed, and returned to the group. He crouched and looked up at Wynter.

"Bug, are you okay?" Quinn flicked her attention between both of Wynter's pupils. They were big and black, like she had just smoked weed.

Wynter glanced at the TV screen and shivered. The image of the unknown person in the corner of Roxy's window held steady. "I know."

Jake, Quinn, and Cash exchanged confused looks.

"You know *what*, exactly?" Jake asked.

Wynter pointed at the TV screen. "I know who that is."

Jake glanced at the TV, then at the others. "How?"

"Forget how. Who," Cash said. "Who is it?"

Wynter faced Cash, her eyes and cheeks still damp from tears. "It's Jezebel."

"What? No way," Jake said. "That's impossible. She's in the hospital."

Wynter looked at Jake, her eyes gravely serious. "She is... but she made a dreamwaker of herself."

Jake's jaw dropped. "Holy shit. Wynter, that's it. How did we miss that?"

Cash fell out of his crouch to sit cross-legged on the floor and looked up at Wynter. "Is that even possible?"

"I've never tried it," Wynter said. "I, like, never had a reason to."

Quinn pulled her chair next to Wynter's. "Then that's what we're going to have to do next."

"I'm pretty sure I can't do it without having Ransom back." Wynter glanced at the TV screen. "And she's got him trapped."

"Correction," Quinn said. "Get Ransom back. Then make a dreamwaker of yourself. Okay?"

"I guess." Wynter yawned.

Jake stopped the VCR, rewound the tape, and ejected it. "So when are we going to get these tapes to Anson?"

"After we get Ransom back," Quinn said.

Jake sighed. "I was afraid you'd say that."

"Guys," Wynter said. "I hate to be a drag, but I need sleep."

"You can stay with me, Bug."

"Actually, I was hoping to stay..." Wynter looked at Cash with hesitant eyes. "With you, Cash."

Quinn did a double take at Wynter, then glanced at Jake. "Or you crash at Cash's. Much better idea. Right, Jake?"

"Uh, yeah, yeah." Jake nodded.

Cash opened his mouth to speak but no words came out.

"Cash? Is that okay?" Wynter asked. "My mom and dad are okay with it."

Quinn's eyes widened. "Really? Wish my parents were so easy going. I mean they don't care about much, except me bringing boys to stay for the night." She stole a quick look at Jake before hiding her eyes behind her hair.

Jake gulped dryly. "I'm sure you could stay here, Wynter. You could take my sister's room."

Quinn kicked Jake's chair and glared at him.

"Or Cash's place, of course," Jake said. "To be closer to home, er, where your trailer... uh..."

Wynter reached over and patted Jake's knee. "I know what you're trying to say. Thanks." She faced Cash, her cheeks almost dry and her eyes expectant.

Cash met her gaze and again words failed him.

Jake nudged his fork off his plate, the utensil clattering to the floor. He reached down for it, but Cash beat him to it. "Dude," he whispered. "*Say* something."

Cash handed the fork to Jake, then peered up at Wynter. From his spot on the floor, it felt like he was proposing marriage, which just added to his angst. He cleared his throat and took a breath. "Sure. You can stay at my place."

"Was that so hard?" Quinn gave him a sideways look.

Cash let the jab slide and began collecting plates.

"Leave it, dude," Jake said. "Just get Wynter home safe."

"You sure?"

Jake stood and wriggled himself on one leg and one crutch until he was next to Cash. "I'm sure." He pulled Cash closer and lowered his voice. "And don't blow it."

Cash shook his head and waved him off. He opened the bedroom door and let Wynter go through first.

"I'd see you out," Jake said. "But you know... stairs."

"That's okay, man. But let's all meet up tomorrow. Sound good?"

Jake looked at Quinn and she nodded.

"I'm going to help the cripple clean up." Quinn hooked her thumb at Jake.

"Geez, thanks," Jake said.

"I meant *badass* cripple." Quinn leaned in and kissed him on the cheek. "I say it with love."

Her voice and warm breath floated past Jake's ear and left him feeling as if he had swallowed a swarm of bees. Nervous and excited and... good.

Just don't get a hard-on.

Cash popped his head back into the room. "And Jake, thanks for shooting that video. Took balls, man."

"It was nothing." Jake waved and Cash disappeared down the hallway.

"It wasn't nothing," Quinn said, her voice low, as she collected plates, cutlery, and empty pop cans and placed them on the table. "It was *badass*."

Jake smiled and loaded the remaining Chinese food containers into the insulated bag. He turned to Quinn and found that his voice had left him. With his guts vibrating like an alarm bell, he realized what Cash must have been feeling moments ago with Wynter.

"Don't blow it," Jake had told him. What a dumb thing to say. He should have told Cash to relax and be himself. Because with his leg in a cast, he discovered being cool and showing off weren't in the cards.

"Hey, want to have some fun?"

Quinn eyed him curiously. "Sure. What'd you have in mind?"

"Come on." Jake ambled to the top of the stairs and sat down. He placed his crutches beside him. "Sit down behind me."

"What, like on the floor?"

"Yeah." Jake squared up his baseball cap. "Kind of like if we were riding a motorcycle."

Quinn lowered herself to the floor and sat with her knees pulled up to her chest.

Jake glanced backward. "That's not how you ride a motorcycle. Bring your legs down next to mine."

Quinn straddled Jake from behind and allowed her legs to rest next to his. She scooted forward and slid her arms around his waist until her chest pressed against his back. "Like this?"

Jake swallowed hard. The bees were back. "Uh, yeah. That's it." He raised his cast above the stairs and grabbed his crutches. "Ready?"

"I guess?"

"Hold on." Jake pushed off and both of them slid and bumped down the oak steps, Quinn giggling all the way down. They slid to a stop at the bottom of the stairs ten seconds later.

Jake pulled himself up on one crutch then offered his hand to Quinn. She took it with a smile. He hauled her up, surprised at how easily she rose from the floor.

Quinn handed him his second crutch. "I better not have a bruised butt."

"If you did, would you hold it against me?"

Quinn blinked at him.

"What?" The shoe dropped and Jake backpedalled. "Uh, sorry. That came out wrong."

"I know what you meant," Quinn said. "And no, I wouldn't blame you."

Jake shuffled on his crutches until they were both at the front door. He pulled it open for her. "Thanks for driving today. Thanks for everything."

"I should be, like, thanking *you* for being a such good host. The food was delish, and the tech was cool." Quinn gazed up at him, letting her eyes linger on his.

Jake looked a question at her. "What?"

"There's something about you, Jake Peterson." Quinn studied his face a moment longer, then planted a quick kiss on his lips. She bounded down the front walk to Blue Belle parked at the curb. "See you tomorrow."

Jake waved and watched her go. It was like he was replaying the morning's events except the kiss was different. Even though it was shorter, he felt the kiss carried more meaning. Time would tell.

He returned to his room and began the slow process of cleaning up. He threw the plates and cutlery into the insulated bag and transported both the cooler and bag downstairs, one at a time, using the butt-scoot method he had just shared with Quinn. But his cast made sure everything took four times as long to accomplish. His cast also ensured that Jezebel occupied a permanent spot in the back of his mind, a spot he wanted back.

THAT EVENING NURSES began removing Jezebel's restraints to allow her to exercise her legs and visit the bathroom, but only if she behaved.

"Any shenanigans out of you and I'll have you back in those restraints and sent to the psych ward," a nurse had told her earlier.

Jezebel had some choice words for her but chose to keep her mouth shut. She had a plan buzzing in her head and having her mobility back was an asset she needed to keep.

She grabbed her purse and worked her way down the corridor to the public payphone in the waiting alcove. The pain from her surgery had begun to fade but it still hurt to walk. She wouldn't be at a hundred percent for days, but she might have healed enough to get out of the hospital sooner than that. She'd still have to rely on Jezebel Too to do her dirty work.

Jezebel deposited a quarter and dialed. "Roxy," she said without waiting for a response. "I have a job for you."

Roxy began speaking excitedly on the other end, but Jezebel cut her off mid-sentence.

"Shut up and listen." Jezebel relayed what she needed done. "Visiting hours end at eight so you better move your ass." She hung up the phone and limped back to her room, favoring her right side.

Jezebel dropped her purse on a chair, beside the bag that contained her bloodstained clothes from Saturday's clusterfuck, and eased herself back into bed. Every time she twisted the wrong way, the pain reminded her of how badly Roxy had screwed the pooch. Going out of her way to make Roxy's life more difficult than it already was had become a priority.

Jezebel had returned just in time for a desiccated dinner of burger and fries and cold coffee. She wondered if the food service staff hated everyone equally or just her.

TV remote in hand, Jezebel flipped through the available channels as she choked down her meal. "Nothing but fucking news." She kept the television on the *NBC Nightly News with Tom Brokaw* as she ate just for the simulated company.

She finished the last bite of her meal and flipped the TV off at the exact moment a knock sounded at the door. It was as if the remote had caused both.

Anson stepped into the room, pushing the door wide open and flooding the small room with light from the corridor.

"Finally," Jezebel said. "I was wondering when you were going to show your ugly face."

"And a good evening to you too, Miss Caine." Anson slipped off his campaign hat. "Is this a bad time?"

"Depends on what you have in mind." Jezebel let her eyes wander over Anson's sturdy frame and made no secret about it. "I'm not eighteen yet, but I promise not to tell. Better hurry though. Never know when a nurse might walk in on us. Or maybe that's your thing." She narrowed her eyes and sent him a lascivious grin.

Anson crossed his arms. "You done?"

"Maybe."

Anson pulled out his notepad and a pen. "You seem to be recovering well from your stab wound. I don't suppose you remember how that happened, do you?"

Jezebel stared at him and shrugged. "I have the right to remain silent. Isn't that what you cops always say?"

"Your future will improve if you answer my questions," Anson said. "And right now, it's not looking very good for you."

Jezebel scanned the room. "Do you see my lawyer? Because I sure don't."

"What about earlier, at the Starlite?"

Jezebel shook her head at him with contempt. "What? They played music and people skated in circles."

Anson closed his notepad and returned it and his pen to his breast pocket. "Death and destruction always seem to follow you around."

Jezebel scoffed.

"You were there when Wynter fell off the 19th Street Bridge. I saw you," Anson said. "You were at the Starlite on Saturday, and later, here. Both incidents involved gunfire."

"You got no proof, Deputy Dolt."

Anson reached into his uniform jacket and pulled a VHS tape from an inner pocket. "Want to watch something?"

"What's that?" Jezebel glared at him, all at once consumed with rage. "Tell me."

"I have the right to remain silent," Anson said. "So I'll let the tape do the talking."

"Fuck you." Jezebel grabbed Anson's wrist and remembered the nurse's edict from earlier. She lowered her voice and spoke through clenched teeth. *"Tell me."*

"You said, and I quote, 'you got no proof.' I'm here to tell you you're wrong." Anson matched her stare. "Now let go or you're going to the psych ward."

Jezebel released Anson's wrist and crossed her arms against her chest.

Anson turned on the TV/VCR combo unit and inserted the VHS tape into the bottom. Whirrs and clicking emanated from within and the screen flipped from the news to a recording from the Starlite SuperSkate surveillance system, each of the four cameras represented in their own quadrant on screen. The date of the timecode displayed "1986-08-02."

"There's a lot here so hand me the remote, will you?" Anson beckoned with an empty palm.

Jezebel found the remote in the mess of sheets covering her lap and slapped it into Anson's waiting hand. But as she did, she spotted curious activity in one of the video feeds. Jake balanced on crutches with a camcorder before placing it in a garbage can, framing the shot, and replacing the lid.

A hidden camera! That crippled little shit.

Anson found the VCR controls on the remote and fast forwarded the tape. "You probably recognize this place, right?"

Jezebel remained silent.

"Just to be clear, it's the Starlite SuperSkate, last Saturday at around six o'clock." The images in the four quadrants on the screen zipped by at twice the speed. "Are you watching? Because this is where it gets good." Anson let the video play at normal speed.

The images on screen showed Jake, who had been standing in the foyer to help aim the cameras, hobbling toward the concession seating area.

The top left quadrant of the screen showed the foyer and the entrance beyond. Anson tapped on it. "Just to be clear, that's you."

The backlit silhouette of Jezebel entered the building and Wynter advanced to face her, standing where Jake had been.

Jezebel aimed her pistol at the admissions window and fired, fracturing the glass. She scrutinized the foyer and surrounding area before aiming at each surveillance camera and firing.

In a blast of static, one by one each quadrant on the screen went black. Fifteen seconds later only the quadrant dividing lines and timecode remained.

Anson stopped playback, ejected the tape, and turned off the TV. "Unless you have a twin, you were at the Starlite on Saturday. The video is proof. And I find that very curious."

Jezebel shrugged and diverted her eyes to the window. "How do you explain Wynter being there, Deputy Dolt?"

"Good question," Anson said. "Maybe you've got some insight on that, too."

"Doubt it." Jezebel's eyes flicked to the VHS cassette in

Anson's hand, then back to the window. She thrummed her fingers on her sheets.

"Thinking of trying to grab the tape?" Anson held the tape up and smiled at her. "Be my guest. That'd be a one way ticket to the psych ward."

Jezebel stared back at him, fuming. She balled her hands into tight white-knuckled fists.

"Didn't think so. It's a lot to risk for a copy." Anson placed the VHS cassette back in his inner pocket, deliberate and slow.

"Fuck you, Deputy Dolt."

Anson shook his head and pushed the TV trolley toward the door. "How'd you get so damaged?"

"What are you, a shrink now?"

Anson grabbed the chair next to her bed and flung it against the wall where it flipped on its side with a crash.

"What the hell are you doing?" Jezebel twisted to move her legs off the bed and felt a sharp stab of pain shoot through her right side.

Anson pulled the door open. "Should I call security?"

"No." Jezebel strained to keep her voice down. "Don't be a fucking prick."

"No? I feel the psych ward would be a good place for you."

Jezebel swallowed hard. "Please don't."

Anson let the door go and righted the chair, her bag of clothes, and her purse. "Huh. You said 'please.' Didn't think you knew that word." He rolled the TV back beside the bed.

A nurse pushed through the door, holding it open with her hand. "Everything alright here?"

Anson nodded. "Peachy keen. We're almost done."

"Good," the nurse said. "Visiting hours will be over soon and this *hellion* needs her sleep." The nurse stepped back out into the corridor and let the door close on its own.

Anson placed his hat back on. "I'm going to get you Miss Caine. It's only a matter of time."

Jezebel raised both her middle fingers at him.

"A pleasant evening to you as well." Anson tipped his hat and pulled open the door to reveal Roxy in a hoodie about to enter. He glanced back at Jezebel and scoffed. "Didn't you hear the nurse? Visiting hours are almost over."

"Not until eight." Roxy wandered in, pulled the chair next to Jezebel's bed, and sat.

"Miss Caine needs her sleep."

"I need you to fucking *leave*," Jezebel said.

Anson shook his head and left the room.

Jezebel motioned to the door. "Make sure that asshole is gone."

Roxy ran back to the door, opened it a crack, and watched until she saw the elevator doors close with Anson inside. She returned to the chair. "How are you doing?"

Jezebel rolled her eyes. "How do you *think* I'm doing? Did you get the stuff?"

Roxy dug into her purse and pulled out a small plastic bag holding at least a dozen green shamrock-shaped pills. "I cleaned Monty out."

"Good. Put them in my purse," Jezebel said. "Make sure they're hidden."

Roxy did as she was told. "When are you going to pay me back? Those shamrocks are expensive."

"When I get out of here."

"When's that going to be?"

"I don't know. Couple of days? What's with the fucking twenty questions?" Jezebel scowled at her. "It's like you're Anson all over again."

"What did he..."

Jezebel huffed at her. "They had security video at the Starlite." She stared at Roxy with an intensity that Roxy found hard to match. "And that little geek Jake had set up a hidden camera. We need *that* tape. You think you could get it?"

"I don't know," Roxy said. "I don't know if I want to do *anything* for you anymore."

Jezebel sat up, anger flashing in her eyes. "What?"

"You know," Roxy said. "You've got to know."

"What the *fuck* are you talking about?"

Roxy slumped back in her chair and crossed her arms. "Your dreamwaker tried to *kill* me."

"Bullshit," Jezebel said.

Roxy pulled back her hood and exposed purple finger-mark bruises wrapping around her neck. "That look like bullshit to you? Sure didn't *feel* like bullshit when I couldn't breathe." She looked away. "Fuck!"

The sight of Roxy's mottled neck gave Jezebel pause. Not because she cared, but because she needed Roxy on her side. She chose her words carefully.

"I'm sorry, Rox. I had no idea that happened. Really."

"Well, it did." Roxy's eyes brimmed with angry tears that refused to fall. "That shit can't happen again."

"You know I can't control what she does."

"You better do *something*." Roxy turned her eyes to the floor in an attempt to cool herself down.

"I'll talk to her, Rox," Jezebel said calmly, her voice strangely free of anger. "Hey. Look at me."

Roxy faced her.

"I promise to talk to her next time."

Roxy took a moment to consider Jezebel's words. In all the time she had known her, promises from Jezebel were rare and rarely kept. But Roxy didn't enjoy feeling angry. Against her better judgment, she agreed. The alternative would have been hell.

"So can you get the tape?"

"From Jake?"

"Yeah, that little fucker."

Roxy sighed and pulled her hood back over her head. "I'd need your help."

"Okay. I guess I can do that." Jezebel glanced back at her purse and pictured the little shamrock pills in her head. "I got options now, even if they tied me to the bed again."

Jezebel smiled at Roxy and after a moment she relented and grinned back in a rare moment of mutual forgiveness. But for Jezebel, feigning forgiveness was all part of her plan.

Alive
And
Kicking

The waning moon cast the clear night sky in a blue light as Wynter and Cash walked along Main Street, her suitcase trailing behind, both immersed in their own thoughts. Cash had grown to love that about Wynter, that they could exist together and feel comfortable in the silence, without the need to talk all the time. It felt normal.

Cash's hand had brushed past Wynter's a few times during their walk home, but he couldn't find the nerve to deliberately find her hand with his. He wondered if she had felt the same way or if she was waiting for him to make the first move. Silence was one thing, but his questions were consuming all other thought.

Ahead, the buzzing sign for Finn's Gas N Go competed with the streetlights and moonlight. For a second, Cash thought that the store was still open. As they drew closer, he realized that Finn must have left one of the overhead fluorescent lights on. He was notorious for doing that.

Wynter broke Cash out of his vortex of internal interrogation. "How old is Finn?"

"I'm not sure," Cash said. "Maybe in his sixties? He'd probably smack me if I asked."

"I'd guess he's probably close to retiring."

"I heard him say once that when he retires, he's going to sell all his stuff and move to Hawaii to be with his only daughter Bert."

Wynter raised a brow. "Bert?"

Cash chuckled. "Short for Bertha. Weird, I know. He said that she was some big-shot CEO who quit her job and moved to Hawaii to surf."

"Sounds pretty good to me." Wynter dropped her head and stole a look at Cash through strands of red hair. "What are you going to do when he retires?"

Cash shrugged. "Maybe I'd take over running the place, but I'm no mechanic."

"Do you like working there?"

"The job's okay but it's not something I'd want to do for the rest of my life." Cash smiled at her. "I'd rather help Jake build a video game empire. How about you? What's after Shooters?"

"Probably photography school, but I'm, like, not totally sure," Wynter said.

"Who is? I mean, we've got two more years of high school."

"Jake seems pretty sure."

"We're not like Jake," Cash said. "We're southies."

"True. Money's a huge factor. Photography school costs mega."

"Jake's sister goes to RISD." Cash pronounced it "ris-dee" and saw confusion on Wynter's face. "R-I-S-D. Rhode Island School of Design. I think you can study photography there."

"I'll try to remember that."

The two of them had walked past the parking lot to Stedford Plaza and headed up the incline toward the Main Street Overpass.

"Want to know a secret?"

Cash met Wynter's eyes and nearly melted. "Sure."

"Come on." She held out her hand. Cash saw his opportunity and took it without hesitation. Together they hustled along the overpass's one narrow sidewalk, the suitcase behind bouncing over the concrete, until they stood at the apex.

"I'm afraid of bridges."

"What? Really?" Cash let go of Wynter's hand and stepped to the guard rail. Below him, Monday evening traffic raced east and west on the four lane divided highway. The strip of grass separating the lanes looked like a bottomless black chasm. The memory of Wynter's fall from the 19th Street Bridge flooded his mind. He looked back to see that Wynter had frozen. "Oh, shit, Wynter. I'm sorry." He took her hand again. "Let's go."

"No. I'm okay," Wynter said. "It's a stupid fear. I got to get over it sometime."

"Maybe not right at this moment."

Wynter held steady and gripped Cash's hand tightly. "Walk with me?"

Cash nodded. "Yeah. For sure."

Wynter let go of her suitcase and advanced toward the guard rail, one step at a time, Cash mirroring her movement. She placed one hand on the railing and let go a sigh of relief. "This is where it all started."

"What do you mean?"

"Ransom."

Hearing Ransom's name caused Cash to suck in an anxiety-ridden breath, as if he had taken a sucker-punch to the gut. He calmed himself and hoped that Wynter hadn't noticed.

"I first saw him here. Just a daydream, probably." Wynter spoke like she was in a trance. "It was only later that I summoned him for real."

Cash had no words. In this instance, the silence between them felt awkward. He didn't like it.

"It seems so long ago, doesn't it?"

"I guess," Cash said. "We should go. It's getting late." He grabbed Wynter's suitcase and started toward the opposite end of the overpass, keeping himself as a buffer between Wynter and the guard rail. Ahead, the Sven Dwarfs sign flickered its steadfast neon letters, lighting a driveway both of them knew well. Somewhere along the way he had let go of Wynter's hand.

Ernie's car still sat parked next to Cash's trailer. They stepped up to the front landing.

"You sure this is okay with your parents?"

Wynter nodded and wiped her palms on her shorts. "Totally."

"Okay." Cash pushed through the doorway, holding it open for Wynter. "Hey Dad, I'm home." He set the suitcase down next to the sagging sofa.

"You're just in time. I'm about to hit the road," Ernie called out from his bedroom. He appeared wearing his janitorial uniform, surprise flashing on his face. "Oh! Wynter. You're out of the hospital."

"Yeah, got out today," Wynter said.

He strolled over to her, alternating his gaze between the two of them. "You look well."

"I got a lot of sleep."

Ernie chuckled. "I hear a good sense of humor will get you places." He grabbed his lunch kit and jacket and paused at the door. "Look, I'm really sorry about what happened to your..." He glanced self-consciously out the open door. The scorched patch of ground across the field weighed heavily on all three of them even though they couldn't see it.

"It's okay. My parents have a plan."

"How's Nolan?"

"He's going to be okay."

"Good." Ernie stepped toward the door.

"Dad? Can Wynter stay here for a while?"

Ernie sized them up. "I guess that explains the suitcase. This okay with your mom and dad, Wynter?"

"Most definitely," Wynter said. "I can give you the number to my mom's motel. And I can give you some money for groceries too."

Ernie raised his hands, palms out. "We can work out the details later." He glanced at Cash and motioned toward the front landing. "Can I have a word?"

Cash took a breath nodded. He looked at Wynter for a moment before joining Ernie outside.

"I'm not going to regret saying yes, am I?"

"No, Dad."

Ernie leaned in and lowered his voice. "You got... protection?"

Cash rolled his eyes. "Dad, it's not like that."

Ernie eyed him dubiously. "You sure about that, son?"

"Yes. She's got a boyfriend," Cash said quietly. "And I'm not that kind of guy."

"Okay." Ernie smiled at him and laid a firm hand on his shoulder. "Proud of you, son."

"Thanks." Cash remained on the front landing until the taillights on his dad's car had faded into the night. His family wasn't rich but as far as fathers go, he had hit the jackpot.

Wynter leaned against the door frame. "Everything okay?"

"Yup." He followed her back inside and closed the door. "Want a snack? Or something to drink?"

Wynter shook her head. "I think I better go to bed. I'm still feeling a hangover from what I saw at Jake's place."

"What *did* you see? Like, if you're cool with telling me, that is."

Wynter looked at him like she was expecting the question. She took a seat on one side of the tired sofa and Cash sat opposite, his arm hooked over the back.

"It was totally weird and gross," Wynter said. "You guys were all dead in the worst possible ways." Cash began to open his mouth, but she cut him off. "Don't ask how because I won't tell you. I was tied... no. There were belts around my arms and legs holding me in my chair, like the ones they use in the hospital. Jezebel crawled out of the TV and started to choke me. I thought I was going to die."

"Shit," Cash said quietly. "Sounds intense."

"Most definitely. She said that if I died in my dream, I'd die in real life."

Cash detected a subtle tremble in Wynter's hands. "That's not possible, is it?"

Wynter shook her head slowly. "It's an urban legend but the way she said it, I almost started to believe her." She shivered. "Then I was back in the land of the living."

Cash nodded. "Sleep would do us all some good." He stood and walked toward his bedroom. "You can take my bed and I'll sleep out here."

Wynter leaned over the back of the sofa. "Are you sure?"

"Hundred percent." Cash disappeared into his room, then poked his head out a second later. "You don't have PJs, do you?"

"I might," Wynter said. "I'll look in my suitcase." She unzipped the lid and dug through the clothes Madeline had found for her. Most of it was clothes, probably secondhand, but there were a few items that could pass for pajamas.

Cash returned to the living area with a long sleeve button-up shirt and a pair of sweatpants. He held them up for consideration. "How's this? And don't worry, they're clean."

Wynter jammed her clothes back into the suitcase and zipped it closed. "Looks comfy."

Cash carried her suitcase to his room and set it on the bed. "You know where everything is since your trailer is like..." He shook his head. "Shit. Sorry."

"It's okay," Wynter said. The dim light of Cash's bedside lamp hid the sparseness of his room. He had even fewer possessions than she had before the fire.

He pulled a small sleeping bag from his closet. "Let me know if you need anything." Cash closed the bedroom door and stepped around into the bathroom. *Since your trailer is like mine? Jesus.* He glared at himself as he brushed his teeth.

Cash unfurled his sleeping bag on the sofa and unzipped it.

He pulled off his T-shirt and pants and rolled them up to use as a pillow.

"How do I look?" Wynter stood just outside his bedroom, holding her arms out, one hand holding a toothbrush and a small tube of toothpaste. The cuffs of her sleeves bunched up loosely at her wrists and the sweatpants touched the floor. He wondered if she was wearing anything else underneath.

"Fits like a glove!" Cash laughed.

Wynter smiled and gave him a thumbs up before heading to the bathroom and closing the door.

Cash could hear brushing and water noises from within. He tossed open his sleeping bag and sat. Wynter sleeping in his trailer—*in his room!*—was entirely too weird and yet exhilarating at the same time. He doubted that he would be able to sleep at all.

Wynter stepped out of the bathroom. "All done."

Cash glanced back at her, hoping that she couldn't sense his excitement. "Hope you have a good sleep."

"Thanks. You too." Wynter stepped halfway through the doorway and paused. "Cash?"

"Yeah?"

Wynter shuffled across the trailer towards him. Cash stood and met her halfway. She wrapped her arms around his waist and hugged him fiercely. Slightly taken aback, he reciprocated but less intensely.

Dressed only in his boxer shorts, Cash struggled to clear his mind, but feeling Wynter's body pressed against his overrode any attempt to relax. He felt the butterflies and soon his body would begin to do things on its own. He hoped Wynter felt the same way.

"Thank you for being such a great friend," Wynter said, her breathy words tingling his ear. She gave him a brief, extra tight hug and stepped back.

"You're welcome." Cash dropped his hands and clasped them

in front of the crotch of his boxers. He hoped it looked casual and normal.

Wynter returned to the bedroom door, dipped her head, and peeked at him through her hair. "Night."

Cash nodded. "Night. And *don't* dream, okay?"

"I'll try not to."

Wynter slipped inside the room and closed the door. Cash returned to the sofa and slumped onto it. A tent had begun to form within his boxer shorts. He turned off the lights, laid down, and pulled the sleeping bag over himself.

Using a rolled up pair of jeans and a T-shirt for a pillow was not ideal but it would serve its purpose. Anything for Wynter's comfort. He closed his eyes and much needed relaxation washed over him. Sleep wasn't as elusive as he had thought it'd be.

CASH AWOKE JUST after one in the morning to the sound of sobbing. He sat bolt upright, blinking the sand out of his eyes.

He looked back at his room. In the dim light that escaped from his open bedroom door he saw Wynter's silhouette sitting on the floor, her head resting against her knees.

Cash jumped off the sofa, padded over to her in bare feet, and sank to his knees. "Wynter? What's wrong?"

She looked up at him, her cheeks damp with tears. "I can't sleep. I'm afraid to."

"That you'll dream something bad again?"

Wynter nodded. "Stay with me, Cash? Please? I don't want to be alone."

Cash wiped away a tear from Wynter's cheek with his thumb, his mind going through options. "Be back in a sec." He ran back to the sofa, grabbed the sleeping bag and his makeshift pillow, and returned, his hand outstretched to her. "Come on. Take my hand."

Wynter did. Cash helped her to her feet and they both returned to his room.

"You get into the bed first and get comfortable." Cash waited until Wynter settled herself, then spread out his sleeping bag behind her.

"You can get under the covers, too," Wynter said, looking back over her shoulder. "You don't need to use your sleeping bag."

Cash sighed and smiled at her. "Yeah, I think I do. At least for tonight."

"Okay."

Cash positioned himself in the sleeping bag to spoon Wynter and set his jean-and-T-shirt pillow under his head. "Not much room for two on this bed."

"No," Wynter said quietly.

Cash took a deep breath and let it out slowly. He could smell the sweet scent of her skin mixed with faint peppermint from her toothpaste. "Sleep well, Wynter. See you in the morning."

Wynter said nothing. She was already asleep. For Cash, sleep remained harder to recapture but at least he had the sleeping bag as a buffer should his body not cooperate again. Strangely the attraction and excitement he had felt toward Wynter earlier in the evening had changed to feelings of protectiveness. This both surprised and comforted him. An hour later, Cash joined Wynter in slumber.

ROXY GLANCED AT her bedside clock. The glowing digits yelled back at her: "12:08 AM." It was officially Tuesday. She considered watching the last half hour of *The Tonight Show starring Johnny Carson* but decided that sleep was more important. She had been using the TV as a way to escape the anxiety she felt about Jezebel showing up out of the blue. She turned off the TV with her remote.

Did she really try to kill me or was she just fooling around?

No, that was her dreamwaker. Jezebel Too. Dealing with twins, one more psychotic than the other, would take some getting used to. It was easy to get them confused.

The phone trilled on the dresser beside her bed. Roxy considered yanking the phone cord from the wall. Only one person would call her this late and talking to Jezebel was the last thing she wanted to do. But part of her enjoyed feeling needed.

Roxy rolled across her bed and lifted the handset before the third ring. "Hi, Jazz. Or is this Jazz number two?"

"What a shitty thing to say," Jezebel Too said through the handset's speaker. "Get it? Number two?" She forced a laugh. "Wait, you're not saying I'm *shit,* are you?"

"So you're the dreamwaker," Roxy said. "I'm going to call you JT for short, okay?"

"Whatever."

Roxy rested her back against the headboard. "What do you want, JT? It's late and I want to sleep."

"Sleep's for losers," Jezebel Too's voice crackled back. "Jezebel says I got to teach you how to pull people out of your dreams."

"How are you going to do that?"

"Not over the phone, dipshit," Jezebel Too said. "You're going to have to pick me up at the hospital."

"That's an hour away. Can't it wait?"

Jezebel Too paused. "You want me to ask her to wait until tomorrow?"

Roxy already knew what Jezebel's answer would be. She looked at her clock. Twelve fifteen. "Ugh. Okay. I'll be there as soon as I can." She cringed as soon as the words left her mouth.

"Sooner rather than later."

Jezebel Too hung up before Roxy could respond. She sat in

her bed until the off-hook tone bleated from the handset speaker, pulling her into action.

The drive to Halston Medical Center was a nice distraction. Despite wanting to sleep earlier, the cool night air on her face, rock and roll from KROK, and the deep rumble of the Barracuda kept Roxy awake. But as she got closer to her destination, her anxiety began to ramp up again.

Roxy had barely come to a full stop at the hospital entrance before Jezebel Too pulled open the passenger door and hopped inside.

"Let's go rob a liquor store."

"What?" Roxy stared at her, surprised yet not surprised at all. "You said you were going to help me pull out dreamwakers. Isn't that what Jezebel wants?"

"That's so boring," Jezebel Too said. "I want to fuck some shit up."

Roxy found an empty parking space and turned off the engine. "We're sticking to the plan."

Jezebel Too formed tight fists and narrowed her eyes at her. "You're so lame." She looked at the roof of the car. "What are you waiting for? Do it. Get it over with so we can do something fun."

"I thought you were supposed to help me."

"Look, it's not rocket science," Jezebel Too said. "Just go sleep, dream, and pull someone out you have a connection with."

"That's easy for you to say. You're the one that gets pulled out."

Jezebel Too shrugged. "So what? It can't be *that* hard. Just fucking do it or I'm going to bounce."

"ALRIGHT! Shut up so I can sleep."

Jezebel Too laughed. "So Roxy *does* have bite."

"Screw off." Roxy eased her seat back, closed her eyes, and tried to block everything from her mind. The parking lot was quiet at one-thirty in the morning and Halston wasn't exactly a bustling metropolis. She might have been able to sleep if not for Jezebel Too's breathing. It was so loud and... so close.

Roxy cracked open one eye and found Jezebel Too inches away from her face.

"Boo." Jezebel Too rocked back in her seat laughing.

"What the hell is your problem, JT? I thought you wanted to get this over with?"

"I got bored. So sue me."

"Then, how about you help me out and quit acting like a bitch?"

Jezebel Too's face darkened. She faced Roxy and scowled, baring teeth that looked like they had been sharpened. "The only reason you're alive right now is because Jezebel fell asleep. I would have finished the job last time. Nobody would've even missed you."

"Shut up," said Roxy.

"Your parents don't care about you. No one does." Jezebel Too sat up and leaned closer, enjoying every word. "A *waste* case. A *loser.*"

Roxy's heart jackhammered in her chest, feeding off her pent-up rage. She grabbed the steering wheel with whitened knuckles.

Jezebel Too leaned in again. "A fucking *pussy.*"

Roxy exploded, her body moving on instinct. She propelled herself at Jezebel Too and pushed her back onto her seat, knocking Jezebel Too's head against the window, stunning her.

She wasted no time with words. Instead, Roxy pulled the seatbelt out and wrapped it around Jezebel Too's neck once, twice, three times, before she could regain her composure. The woven fabric belt dug deep into Jezebel Too's neck, cutting off the blood to her head and restricting her ability to breathe.

"I am so fucking sick of your SHIT." Roxy yanked on the seatbelt, tightening it.

Jezebel Too's face shifted into shades of purple. Her lips curled back in a demonic smirk and a hiss floated from her throat.

"Who's choking now, *bitch?*" Roxy leaned backward, held the seatbelt tight, and waited. Half a minute later Jezebel Too slumped back on the passenger seat. Her eyes dulled but her horrible smile remained.

She hadn't fought back.

That wasn't like the Jezebel she knew but Roxy refused to let up. Seconds turned to minutes and Jezebel Too's eyes began to glow a familiar blue.

In a flash that lasted less than a second, a wave of blue energy spread from her eyes and down her body. Jezebel Too vanished and Roxy fell backward against the driver side door, the instantly slack seatbelt still in her grip. She had begun to despise the smell of ozone.

She scanned her surroundings for anyone who might have seen her, but the parking lot was devoid of people. Roxy returned the driver's seat to its upright position and tried to come to grips with what had just happened.

Technically she had just killed someone but Jezebel Too was a dreamwaker. Surely it was like killing someone or something in a dream. Roxy tried to convince herself that it shouldn't count, but the grooves in her hands from the edges of the seatbelt said otherwise. What she had done *was* real.

I'm a murderer.

Roxy began to shake uncontrollably. She grabbed the Barracuda's steering wheel to try and steady herself and began breathing deeply and evenly. It was one of the few useful things she had been taught by her absent mother, but it wasn't enough. She fainted and fell back into the driver's seat.

When she came to, it was just past three in the morning. She half expected Jezebel Too to leap at her from the passenger seat, but the car was empty. Roxy started the engine and began her drive back to Newhaven.

Why hadn't JT fought back? Had Jezebel told her to let herself die? Why? Questions which she had no good answers for swirled in Roxy's head during the drive back.

But she was a killer now. There was no way around that fact and the thought sent a shiver down her spine. One thing she was certain of: Jezebel had some explaining to do.

FOR ROXY, BUYING shamrock speed wasn't an odd occurrence. But when she insisted on buying all of his supply on Monday afternoon, that's when Monty sat up and took notice. She had paid a premium for it and had offered no clues as to why she needed so much. Something was going on and he was determined to find out what.

With anything that Roxy chose to do, there was a good chance that Jezebel had played a large part in her decision. The girl lacked independence. So far, he knew there was a special connection between Jezebel and Ransom, something mystical. He had seen it with his own eyes and captured it on film. But he still couldn't explain it.

He had followed Roxy to the hospital and picked a parking stall close to the Barracuda. Monty spotted Anson's police SUV parked close to the entrance.

"Great. Two movin' targets," he said to himself. Running into Anson would just slow him down. Monty held no love for playing private detective, but he believed the secrets, when revealed, would help him gain a business advantage. It was worth the effort.

The elevator Roxy had taken had stopped at the fifth floor. To reduce his chances of running into Anson, Monty took the stairs two at a time. It didn't take long to spot Roxy and Jezebel in room 513. Their conversation appeared heated.

Monty had considered confronting them both but decided to play it cool. He returned to his car and waited.

A short while later Roxy drove back home to Newhaven. Monty followed and staked out her house. Fighting sleep, the rumble of the Barracuda grabbed his attention at around midnight and gave him the shot of adrenaline he needed to stay awake. Roxy was on the move again.

He found himself back on Interstate 94 heading east. "What the hell? Halston again? Make up your damn mind." Monty wished he had onboard radar like Goose had in *Top Gun*. Then he could simply park and wait.

He ended back at the hospital, but this time Roxy never left the car. Jezebel strolled out of Halston Medical Center fit and nimble, as if she had never undergone surgery two days ago.

"What the fuck is goin' on?" Monty said to himself.

Jezebel hopped into the Barracuda and Roxy found a parking spot. Then nothing happened, except for a small blue flash a short while later. From his vantage point several parking spaces away, he couldn't be sure of anything. Even using his SLR camera with its telephoto lens didn't help to resolve any more detail. But he was sure that Roxy had left alone. Or had it appeared that way? Had Jezebel hidden somewhere inside the Barracuda? Or had he blinked a little too long while he had been watching their car and missed something? The Jezebel he had seen in room 513 hadn't appeared as agile as the Jezebel he had seen hop into the Barracuda earlier. It was a detail that defied logic and human ability.

Monty chose to let Roxy go. Following her back and forth between Newhaven and Halston would cost him a fortune in gas. He wanted answers but not if it was going to bankrupt him. Right now, those answers were behind questions within the walls of Halston Medical Center.

He committed to his plan by turning off his pager and staking out the front entrance of the hospital. Even though Halston wasn't a large city, its one and only hospital was busy, and maintaining surveillance was a full time job. He fueled himself on vending machine sandwiches and coffee.

The next morning, after no sign of Jezebel, Roxy, or Anson had presented itself, Monty headed to the fifth floor for answers.

WYNTER FOUND HERSELF standing on the front landing of Cash's trailer at midday, looking out onto the communal field of Sven Dwarfs Trail'r Park. Her hands, her arms, and her immediate surroundings had taken on shades of gray like she had stepped into an old photograph. She turned and tried the door to Cash's trailer and found it locked.

In the center of the field sat two people hunched over something in the grass. Color washed over and around them.

Wynter stepped off the landing and headed toward the two people. The grass felt cool against the soles of her bare feet, although she swore she had had shoes on moments earlier.

With every step the grass grew longer, first wicking at Wynter's heels, then her calves and knees. She was close enough to recognize Cash sitting facing her. The other person sat with their back to her, her blond silken hair flowing over her shoulders. The unknown person seemed... younger?

"Cash?" Wynter stood on the fringe of the depression in the grass and looked down on a checkers board, their game in progress.

Cash gazed up at Wynter, smiled, and returned his attention to the board.

A young hand moved a red checkers piece to the kings row. "King me."

Wynter walked behind Cash and recognized his opponent instantly.

Sierra.

Cash placed one of his captured pieces atop Sierra's piece, making it a king.

Sierra tilted her head at Wynter and beamed. She stood, the

grass coming to the waistband of her white shorts, and flicked her hair back over her shoulders. The word "ROCKY" in bold white letters glowed in the center of her black T-shirt. She held out her hand.

Wynter approached her and took Sierra's small, warm hand in hers. Cash paid no attention, but instead stared at the checker board. Tear tracks stood out on his cheeks.

"Cash?" Wynter said with concern.

Cash remained silent.

"Ready?" Sierra looked up at Wynter with eyes a vibrant blue. "Gonna fly now." She raised her hands quickly to the sky, compelling Wynter to do the same.

The two of them shot up towards the noonday sun, leaving Cash, the checker board, Sven Dwarfs, and so many thoughts and questions shrinking below them.

But one thought remained, and it fueled an idea that would change everything.

AT SEVEN O'CLOCK in the morning, Monty stepped out of the elevator onto the fifth floor of Halston Medical Center. He strolled to room 513 and propped himself in the doorway. There was a wheelchair to one side of the bed and Jezebel stood with her back to him, wearing a loosely tied hospital gown.

"I see you've been busy," he said.

Jezebel snapped her head around, the rest of her body following slowly. "Don't you fucking knock?" She collected the seams of her gown together and turned.

Monty shrugged and hooked his mirrored sunglasses off his shirt collar. "Just enjoying the view." He traced her bare legs with his eyes. "Nice underwear, *Jazz*."

"Pervert." Jezebel tucked something into her purse. "What are you doing here?"

"Just wanted to talk," he said. "I've missed you."

"Bullshit. You've missed my money."

"Nah. Roxy took care of that yesterday." Monty laughed. "I fuckin' soaked her."

"Who might you be?" A nurse stood at the doorway to the room, a dubious look on her face.

"Me?" Monty gave the nurse a warm smile. "I'm Jezebel's stepbrother. Just checkin' in on her."

"How nice," the nurse said. "Jezebel doesn't get many visitors. But you've come at a bad time. We're in the middle of a transfer."

"Can I tag along? It took over an hour to get here. I promise to stay out of the way." Monty put on a show and wrung his hands anxiously. "I could push the wheelchair."

The nurse gave him a once-over and he winked at her. "Alright." She turned to Jezebel. "Ready to go?"

Jezebel glared at Monty as she took a seat in the wheelchair and hugged her purse close to her body.

The nurse picked up Jezebel's chart. "Someone woke up on the wrong side of the bed this morning."

Monty could see Jezebel fighting against her urge to give a snide comeback. He gripped the wheelchair handles and leaned close to her ear and whispered, "What's wrong? Cat got your tongue? Nothin' a little shamrock couldn't fix."

She raised her middle finger at him in response.

The nurse led the way to the elevators, entering first. She held the doors open until Monty and Jezebel were inside.

"I heard that she was stabbed," Monty said.

"She's recovering from surgery to repair a wound to her abdomen," the nurse said. "For specifics, you're going to have to talk to her doctor."

"Must hurt when she walks, huh?"

"I'm, like, sitting *right here,*" Jezebel tightened her grip on her purse. "Jesus."

Monty smiled, taking pleasure from the aggravation in her voice.

"Jezebel's been doing better," the nurse said. "She can walk to the bathroom on her own, but longer distances are beyond her capability just yet."

"Sure, talk like I'm an invalid." Jezebel clenched her teeth.

Monty leaned close, talking through a smile. "But you can poop on your own, just like the big girls."

The trio exited the elevator onto the third floor, past the chapel to room 305. The room accommodated two beds.

"I got to *share* a room?" Jezebel turned to the nurse with a look of anger and surprise.

"Now, now," the nurse said. "Misfortune shared is misfortune halved. Which bed do you want?"

Jezebel pointed at the bed closest to the window and Monty rolled her next to it.

The nurse rehung Jezebel's chart on the end of her bed. "Let's get you under the covers." She glanced at Monty. "I didn't catch your name."

"Ty," Monty said without hesitation.

"Well, Ty, your assistance would be helpful." The nurse placed her hand on Jezebel's shoulder. "We'll—"

"Don't touch me. I can do it." Jezebel tossed her purse on the bed.

The nurse stepped back and motioned at Monty to do the same. "Alright, Jezebel. Go ahead, but we're right here in case—"

"I don't need your help." Jezebel didn't wait for the nurse to finish. She pushed up with her arms, swiveled on her feet, and sat on the edge of the bed. "See? Told you."

The nurse looked at Monty. "Your stepsister is a stubborn one. I'll leave you to help her get settled."

"Thank you..." Monty thought for a second. "What was your name?"

The nurse tapped her name tag with a finger. "Bridgette."

"Right. Thanks, Bridgette," Monty said.

Bridgette nodded. "Jezebel, your doctor will check in with you later today." She turned and left the room.

"Such a condescending bitch." Jezebel dragged her purse to her lap and held it tightly to her chest.

"She seemed nice enough." Monty glanced out the window. "Great view."

"No better than before." Jezebel eased herself back onto the bed. "Now get out."

"I've got a few questions for you first."

"Go fuck yourself."

Monty found Jezebel's surgery site and placed his right hand on it. She tried to intercept him, but he stopped her with his left hand and increased pressure on the wound. She reached over her abdomen with her left hand and grabbed his wrist. Locked in a standoff, neither of them planned on backing down.

She gritted her teeth to hide her discomfort but fighting against him only made her situation worse. She looked for the nurse call button, but it hung from a hook on the wall, too far to reach. Unable to stand the pain any longer, Jezebel relented.

"Okay. Fuck. Let me go."

"Wouldn't want your stitches to pop." Monty increased pressure.

"If you don't stop, I'll scream." Jezebel spoke between hitched breaths.

Monty slid his hands away and cracked his knuckles. The sickening sound of his joints popping sent a shiver up Jezebel's spine.

"Must hurt a lot," he said, narrowing his eyes.

Jezebel answered him with an angered glare.

"Why did you get Roxy to buy all my shamrock shakes?"

"I don't know what you're talking about."

"Really." Monty strolled around the end of the bed, walking his fingers as he went. He tilted her chart up and casually glanced at it. "You mean if I dumped that purse of yours, I wouldn't find my speed?"

Jezebel grabbed the handles of her purse and pulled it close to her body.

"What do you need speed in here for?"

"Helps me focus," Jezebel said.

"It also keeps you from sleeping." Monty studied the blank walls and took in the antiseptic smell. "I'd think you'd *want* to sleep in a place like this."

"You thought wrong."

Monty sat on the edge of her bed and rubbed the bridge of his nose. "Look. I know it hurts to walk." He looked at her abdomen. Jezebel covered it quickly with her right hand, even though she knew it would do no good if he chose to attack her again. "Care to explain to me how I saw you leave the hospital to meet Roxy six hours ago?"

Jezebel fumed at him.

"This has something to do with that guy... Ransom, doesn't it?" Monty waited for a moment before continuing. "*Jazz*... Can't you see that this would be good for all of us? We could make some serious cash."

"Time's up," Jezebel said. "In ten seconds, I'm going to scream."

"Have it your way, *Jazz*. But I'm going to figure it out eventually." Monty stood to leave, then grabbed the nurse call button off the wall and tossed it to Jezebel. "Save your pretty little voice." He put his mirrored sunglasses on and walked casually out of the room without looking back.

Monty took the stairs back to the main floor and left the hospital. With his questions remaining unanswered, he did know one thing. Whatever Jezebel was doing, she needed to be awake for it.

He returned to his Fiat, grabbing a sandwich and a coffee on the way, and resumed his stakeout.

NOLAN HAD FINISHED his oatmeal and was working on his coffee and the morning paper when a nurse he had not met yet entered his room with a wheelchair.

"Mr. LaCroix?"

Nolan looked over the top of his paper.

"I have some good news and some not so good news," the nurse said.

Nolan raised a brow and smiled. "Should I start with the good or bad..." He squinted to make out her name tag. "Bridgette? Pretty name. And you can call me Nolan."

Bridgette laughed. "They warned me you were a charmer, Mr. LaCroix. Let's start with the good. Your legs are healing well. In fact, you may be able to leave sooner than expected."

"That *is* good news. And the bad?"

Bridgette stepped around his bed noting the readings on the monitoring equipment. "We need this private room for another patient."

"That's what the go-cart's for I guess, eh?"

"You'd be correct."

"Do we need the chair? I've been going for short walks," Nolan said. "How far are we talking?"

"Third floor," Bridgette said. "And the wheelchair is hospital policy, unless you want me to arrange for a gurney."

Nolan shook his head. "No, the chair's just fine."

"Can I help you pack up your things?"

He waved her off. "No thanks. I don't have much. It won't take long."

"Would twenty minutes be enough time?"

"More than enough."

Bridgette glanced at her watch. "Fine. I'll see you at seven forty-five."

"With bells on."

Bridgette left the room and Nolan wasted no time getting to work. He hadn't worn any of the clothes Madeline had brought for him last week except the underwear. Most still had their sales tags hanging from the hems.

He gulped down the rest of his coffee and collected his meager belongings. Nurse Julia had brought him a copy of Stephen King's *Pet Sematary* on Sunday. He didn't usually read horror, preferring thrillers from Robert Ludlum and Tom Clancy, but passing endless hours in a hospital bed had convinced him to broaden his literary horizons. He was almost halfway through it and couldn't bear not knowing how it ended. Luckily there was room for the book in the duffel bag Madeline had brought him.

He sat in the wheelchair, which he found surprisingly comfortable, and unfolded the newspaper to where he'd left off. At seven forty-five on the dot, Bridgette knocked on the door frame of Nolan's room.

"Ready to go?"

Nolan folded up his paper and lifted his duffel bag onto his lap. "Ready."

Bridgette rolled Nolan out of room 523, into the elevator at the end of the corridor, and down to the third floor.

The elevator opened to the main corridor and a series of doors alongside blinded viewing windows. Bridgette pushed Nolan past a few semi-private rooms.

"The chapel is right next to the elevators, should you be so inclined," Bridgette said.

"Thanks."

She turned the wheelchair into room 305. Only a sliver of the morning sunlight slashed the walls of the room through the drawn curtains. A patient in the bed closest to the window lay facing away from him.

Nolan turned to Bridgette, concerned. "A shared room?"

"It's all we had left, and this is the last bed." Bridgette turned the wheelchair around and smiled at him. "We've had a busy couple of weeks, so consider yourself lucky."

"Oh, I do." Nolan peered down at his bandaged calves. "I thank the Great Spirit every day."

Bridgette lifted Nolan's duffel bag and placed it on a chair next to the bed. "How are you feeling? Are you in any pain? Scale of one to ten."

"Maybe a two?" he said.

Bridgette helped Nolan to his feet and guided him to the bed, assistance he appreciated since his confidence in his own legs had diminished during the trip to the third floor.

"Hey, roomie," the patient in the other bed said.

Nolan froze and his blood turned to ice-water in his veins. He knew that voice. He would never forget it.

Light it up, Roxy.

Nolan blinked, instantly transported back three days, back to his trailer that no longer existed. He stood on the stoop, his migraine pounding in his head like a jackhammer intent on breaking free. On the grass below the stoop stood two people he couldn't make out.

Migraines had always affected his vision, impairing it with static as if he was tuning into a weak channel on a television. He squinted, shaded his eyes, and forced himself to concentrate and push through the persistent throb behind his eyes.

It was Jezebel and her loyal flunky Roxy. Jezebel held a gun, and a red jerry can lay on its side next to stairs to the front landing.

"Leave now, or I call the police," he heard his voice say.

Jezebel responded, her voice echoed in his head amid the

drumming of his pulse, but he could not make out any of her words except, "Light it up, Roxy."

This is it. I'm going to die.

But Jezebel and Roxy began arguing, about what Nolan didn't care. This was his only chance to escape. If he ran down the front stoop Jezebel would surely shoot him in the back like a wild dog.

He searched for guidance from the Great Spirit and one answer bubbled up through the chaos in his mind: the only way out is in.

Nolan turned and leaped back into the trailer. An instant later a searing pain tore through his right arm and knocked him sideways over the kitchen table. He landed on the floor.

His right arm had slicked the floor red with his blood but amazingly his head had cleared. The pain in his arm combined with the adrenaline raging through his body had temporarily overpowered his migraine.

He placed his palms together under his chin. "With thanks, Great Spirit."

Flames exploded in the open doorway to the trailer and the small space began to fill with smoke. Nolan picked himself up off the floor and ran toward the master bedroom. Within seconds flames licked the windows from outside. He had to get out fast or the trailer would become his coffin.

The shower!

He entered the bathroom, ripped the shower curtain rod off the wall, and turned on the cold water. He engaged the shower head and aimed the spray at the walls first, then settled it on the frosted glass window on the back wall.

The hot smoke thickened and one by one the exterior windows on the front side of the trailer popped and smashed on the floor, sucking more smoke inside.

Nolan grabbed the shower rod with the curtain still attached and rammed it through the window like a javelin. The tempered glass shattered into a million pieces.

Wasting no time, he launched himself up and through the window just as flames worked their way around the back side of the trailer. Intense heat and fire ripped a path up the exterior walls, consuming the accelerant and everything in its path.

Nolan landed on the ground next to the back of the trailer, his legs caught in the expanding fire. The pain of his burning skin overrode all sensation and thought except one thing: survive.

Instinct took over and Nolan rolled his body across the grass until the fence separating trailer pads stopped him. Sufficiently far away, he could no longer feel heat on the rest of his body, but his calves felt like they were still burning. He forced one eye open despite the sting of smoke and saw his charred socks and pant legs, with reddened angry skin behind the blackened holes in the fabric. But no flames. He closed his eyes. He had survived.

"Long time no see." Her voice pulled him to the present.

Nolan blinked and found himself back at the hospital. He turned to see Jezebel lying on her side in the adjoining bed, staring at him with a smile that chilled him to his core.

Bridgette looked at them both with surprise. "You two know each other?"

Nolan turned to Bridgette and lowered his voice. "Are you sure there are no other rooms available? Or patients I could switch with?"

"I'm afraid not. Is there a problem?"

Nolan stood and leaned in close, too close for Bridgette's comfort. "*She* put me here."

Bridgette took a step back. "If that's true, I could try and arrange for a swap. But it'll take some time. You're going to have to stay here for the time being."

Nolan glanced back at Jezebel. She wiggled her eyebrows at him, her creepy smile melting to malice before she rolled onto her back.

"I'd appreciate anything you can do, Bridgette," Nolan said. "Thanks."

"In the meantime, maybe you can take this time to mend fences." Bridgette shifted her eyes between the two. "Forgive and forget."

"Bury the hatchet." Jezebel's words came out like a hiss.

"Whatever you want to call it," Bridgette said. "Your doctors will check in on you later in the day and I'll pop in every once in a while. You've always got the call button." She hustled out into the corridor but, unlike the private rooms, a kickdown door stop held the door open.

That suited Nolan fine. He gave a brief look at the bed next to his. "You stay the fuck away from me."

"Don't worry your pretty little Injun head," Jezebel said. "You were a happy accident. I got higher priorities now."

Nolan fought to hold back his anger and thoughts of revenge. An outburst, especially now, would go nowhere. But fate had given Jezebel too many chances. He wondered if she would ever pay the price for her actions.

WYNTER WOKE WITH an idea in her head, one so clear and profound that she wouldn't be able to forget it even if she tried. Excitement took hold and she rolled over to share it with Cash. But he wasn't in the bed.

She was alone. The side of the bed Cash had slept on was cool to her touch. On the floor by the door sat his sleeping bag, rolled up and tied. The little clock by his bed read a few minutes after six.

"Cash?" Wynter tilted her head to listen. Several birds chirped outside his window but there was a different sound mixed in, a surprisingly familiar one.

She slid off the bed, tiptoed to the door, and eased it open.

The smell of toast, bacon, and coffee flooded her nose and brought a smile to her face.

Wynter shuffled past the sofa and toward the kitchen. Cash stood at the stove preparing something she couldn't see. On the table sat placemats, plates, utensils, peanut butter, jam, and small glasses of orange juice. "Sure smells good out here."

Cash turned around and smiled at her. An apron hung loosely from his neck, and he held a spatula in one hand. "The master summoner has awoken. Did you sleep okay?"

"I did." Wynter stood beside him at the stove. On the burners in front of them sat two frying pans, one with bacon and the other with eggs. "You've been busy."

"I kept waking up, so I decided to do some cooking," Cash said. "I hope you like your eggs scrambled."

"Doesn't matter."

Cash motioned at a battered old Mr. Coffee maker on the counter. "There's coffee brewing too."

"Can I pour you some?"

"Yeah, sure."

Cash plated the bacon and eggs beside two pieces of toast while Wynter poured coffee into two mugs on the counter and carried them to the table. He presented her plate and sat beside her with his.

"Anything else we need?"

Wynter tucked a strand of hair behind her ear. "Milk? For the coffee?"

"Right," Cash said. "And sugar." He leaped from his seat and returned with a small sugar bowl and a gallon jug of milk. "Sorry, it's skim. It's all we got."

"Cash." Wynter set her hand on his. They both looked at the gesture and she pulled her hand away. She hoped it had looked casual enough. "Relax. Skim is fine."

Cash nodded. "Dig in."

They both attacked their plates, eating the first few bites in silence. Wynter worried that she had made things weird by touching Cash's hand.

"This is really good," Wynter said. "Thanks for making it."

"No problem. It's way better than Cheerios."

"Totally." Wynter crunched on a piece of bacon. "Cheerios are practically—"

"Cat food," they said in unison, then both broke out into laughter.

Wynter added milk and sugar to her coffee, stirred, and sipped. "Not bad."

"Whew. I don't make coffee very often," Cash said. "I was hoping it wouldn't suck."

Wynter took a bite of eggs, chewed, and swallowed. She set her knife and fork down. "I have something to tell you. But I don't know if I should tell you now, or when we meet up with Quinn and Jake."

Cash stopped chewing for a moment, then washed his mouthful down with a gulp of orange juice. "Seriously? I don't want to spend an entire day at work wondering what the secret is. That'll be torture."

"I just don't want to repeat myself," Wynter said.

"I'll never get tired of hearing your voice." Cash smiled at her, then cleared his throat. "Okay. If it involves Jezebel or Ransom, spill it."

Wynter placed both hands palm down on the table. "I know how to get Ransom back, without involving Jezebel... well, not directly."

Cash's jaw dropped. "What? How?"

She locked gazes with Cash. "I need to enter Jezebel's dreams, summon him, and pull him out."

"Holy shit. You can do that?"

"I have to try," Wynter said. "That dream, or vision, or whatever it was I had at Jake's place wasn't the first time. Jezebel's been popping into my dreams ever since she was stabbed. I think she's been trying to summon me and having Ransom in her head is giving her extra power."

"But why? She can't do anything to you through your dream." Cash crossed his arms against his chest. "And Jezebel's still at the hospital. It's not like she could take revenge from her hospital bed."

Wynter warmed her hands on her mug of coffee. "You know how devious she is, Cash. What if she switched me, like, with my dreamwaker, then killed me for real?"

Cash ran the scenario through his head. "I guess, technically, that's possible. If anyone can get Ransom, it's you." He looked at her with serious eyes. "But when? And does she need to be asleep for you to do it?"

Wynter shrugged. "I don't know. Probably. I can try it today from here, but I have a feeling that I'm going to need to be closer."

"How close?"

"Like hospital close."

"You can't be here during the day," Cash said. "My dad is going to be home soon, and he doesn't like distractions."

"I get it. Maybe I'll try Jake's place." She glanced back at Cash's bedroom door. "Can I leave my suitcase?"

"No problem." Cash continued eating. "I got to be at work soon. You can come with me if you want, you know, before calling Jake. That lucky bum sleeps late."

"Okay. I might head to the plaza and see Quinn on the way, too."

Now that her idea was out in the open, she felt more free, but her mind kept trying to punch holes in the logic. Wynter finished breakfast deep in thought. The idea had to work.

Bad
Moon
Rising

Wynter accompanied Cash as he headed to Finn's. Her body still felt a little stiff but with every movement she drew closer to a full recovery. Being unconscious for a week seemed like a strange dream now. Her memories during that time were still locked in a part of her brain she couldn't access. Or maybe she had no memories of that time at all. She couldn't tell.

They hurried across the Main Street Overpass. Finn's Gas N Go sign stood out in the distance.

"Thanks for letting me crash at your place," Wynter said.

"Hey, don't worry about it. You'd do the same for me."

Cash wore jeans, a white T-shirt, and a jean jacket, even though the day was supposed to be a scorcher. It was typical Cash. If Wynter could have one photograph of him, that's what she would want him to be wearing.

For once, Madeline had picked out some clothes that Wynter would have chosen for herself. In her suitcase she had found a layered ruffle skirt made from stretchy denim. Not exactly a miniskirt, the hem landed at knee level. Perfect. She pulled out a white and navy striped short-sleeved button-up that matched the blue in the denim.

Finn was already at the Gas N Go when they arrived. "Got a muffler job breathing down my neck." He filled his grubby coffee mug and disappeared back into the garage.

"It's not the center of excitement," Cash said, "but you're welcome to hang out as long as you want."

"I'll do that." Wynter scanned the back of the counter. "If you have a spare mug, I wouldn't turn down more coffee. I didn't sleep well last night."

"Tell me about it."

"What? You didn't sleep either?" Wynter crossed her arms against her chest. "Do I snore or something?"

"Uh, no." Cash found a clean mug with a Gulf Oil logo on it and filled it with coffee.

"I wouldn't be surprised if I did. You know how my mom snores."

Cash laughed. "Don't remind me. Milk and sugar, right?"

"Yup."

Cash poured a splash of milk into Wynter's coffee, added two packets of sugar, and gave the concoction a stir. He slid the cup toward her. "Try that."

Wynter sipped the coffee and gave Cash an affirmative nod. "Back to the subject." Wynter leaned on the front counter and eyed Cash playfully. "You didn't sleep well. Why? Enquiring minds want to know."

Cash leaned against the back wall and sighed. "You're not going to let this go, are you?"

Wynter shook her head as she sipped coffee.

"Honestly... I've never had a girl in my bed before. At the same time as me, that is." A mild hue of pink bloomed on Cash's neck.

"Oh." Wynter had been expecting an answer less mundane than that and she gulped coffee to give herself more time to respond. "The only boy I've had in my bed was Ransom. But he's not real so he doesn't really count."

Cash's smile faltered. "He's real to you."

"Whatever." Wynter shook her head. "Change the subject."

"What are you going to tell Quinn and Jake?"

Wynter shrugged. "Nothing special."

"Just tell it like it was, huh?"

"You got it, Pontiac."

Cash's face went ashen.

Wynter set her mug down. "Cash, what is it? What's wrong?"

He swallowed hard. "What you just said. The 'you got it, Pontiac' thing."

"What about it?"

"Why did you say that?"

Wynter shrugged. "I don't know. It just popped into my head."

"In all the time I've known you, you've never said that," Cash said. "I would've remembered it because that's what my sister would always say." His eyes blazed with remembrance as he leaned on the counter. "I summoned my sister when you were in a coma. Not sure if I told you that. You were in that dream, too. You helped me, told me what to do. And I was able to do it. I summoned Sierra. That's when she said it. 'You got it, Pontiac.'"

A single tear fell to the counter top as Cash met Wynter's gaze. His expression changed into one of revelation. "You're remembering things that happened in *my* dreams. How is that possible?"

"I don't know," Wynter said. "I guess I'm getting my strength back. At least the parts that don't involve Ransom. But I do know that's a good thing."

"Yeah." Cash nodded, then formed a small smile. "That *is* a good thing."

"What to know something else weird?"

"What?"

"I dreamed of you and your sister last night," Wynter said. "You were playing checkers in the field. She actually gave me the idea about how to get Ransom back."

Cash focused on her, his eyes clear and blue and intense. "You're amazing."

"What?"

"That was my dream," Cash said. "You were in *my* dream last night."

Wynter's eyes widened like saucers. "Oh my God. Maybe this idea *will* really work."

Cash nodded. "I think it will."

"Can I borrow your phone? I need to call Quinn."

"Yeah, sure," Cash said. "Don't be too long. Finn doesn't like it when I make personal calls." He tilted his head at her. "Friends included."

"Thanks." Wynter walked around the counter, picked up the phone, and dialed.

Cash contemplated making a coffee for himself and glanced back at the machine. Finn stood in the doorway to the garage, watching them both while cleaning a wrench with an oily rag. He approached the large man. "Sorry, Mr. O'Connor. She'll be off the phone soon."

"Bah." Finn waved him off. He set the wrench down, picked up his coffee, and drank. "I'm willing to give her a break. Poor girl's been through a lot."

Cash nodded as he watched Wynter talking animatedly into the Gas N Go phone.

"Also plain to see you love the girl." Cash opened his mouth to respond but Finn cut him off. "No point in denying it, son."

"Just keep your voice down. Please."

"No point in hiding it, either." Finn looked at Wynter, smiled, and raised his mug to her. She waved and smiled back. "Whatever problems you're having, get over them. Two people shorten the road."

"I'll tell her when I'm ready, Mr. O'Connor," Cash said.

Finn studied Cash's face for a moment. "Yeah. I believe you will, son."

Wynter hung up and ran over to them in the doorway. "Can I make one more call, Mr. O'Connor? I promise I'll be quick."

"Sure, miss. Take your time."

Wynter picked up the phone again and paused. "Cash! What's Jake's number?"

Finn chuckled. "Duty calls, eh?"

"Guess so."

"Back to that fecking muffler." Finn grabbed the wrench and shuffled back into the garage.

Cash relayed Jake's phone number to Wynter as she dialed. "Remember to let it ring."

Wynter listened to the trilling on the other end of the line. After three rings, the call connected. "Hey Jake, it's—" She placed her hand over the receiver and lowered her voice. "He's got an answering machine?"

"Must be his latest gadget."

Wynter waited for the tone. "Hey Jake, it's Wynter. Look, I need a place to crash today and was wondering if you could help me out? It's not what you're thinking, and if you were, shame on you. What if Quinn found out? You'd be in the dog house so fast, so stop it. By the way, I'm calling from Finn's. Anyway, I might be able to get Ransom back but—"

Wynter covered the receiver with her hand as they both struggled to stifle their laughter.

"You're brilliant," Cash whispered.

"Thanks." Jake's nervous chatter floated from the handset speaker as Wynter placed it against her ear. "Oh, so you *are* there. Good morning. It's about time you were up."

Cash leaned close to the receiver. "Hi, Jake."

Wynter listened. "Yeah, I just need a place to sleep for a bit. I can't stay at Cash's or Quinn's during the day, and my place is a pile of ash, so..." She paused for Jake's response. "Not now. I'll tell you all about it when I see you in maybe... twenty minutes?" Wynter handed the phone to Cash. "He wants to talk to you."

Cash took the phone. "New answering machine, huh? I'm always the last to know." Cash listened. "I can't get into it now.

Finn'll kill me. You know how he is with personal calls." He winked at Wynter as she giggled into her coffee. "Just hide your porn collection, okay?"

Anyone within three feet of the handset's speaker heard Jake's protest. "I do not have a porn collection!" he yelled.

"Yeah, yeah. Likely story," Cash said. "Kidding! Anyway, Wynter'll be there soon. Get ready. She's got a bomb to drop. Later, man." He hung up the phone and looked at Wynter. "I hope you find him. Ransom I mean."

"I do, too." She leaned over the counter and kissed him on the cheek, then bounded toward the store entrance, her ruffled jean skirt bouncing as she went. "We'll call you if we find out anything. Pretend that it's a work call so Finn doesn't chew your ass."

"He won't." Cash's eyes followed Wynter as she pushed through the door toward Main Street, heading north. He hadn't seen her in a skirt very often. It was a nice change.

Cash found himself wondering if Wynter would find Ransom today, if he'd have to again shelve all the feelings he had been having about her lately. He wished all the drama surrounding Ransom would go away forever. He was beyond tired of it all. He wanted things to go back to normal.

Little did he know how close normal really was.

LESS THAN TWENTY minutes later Wynter found herself knocking excitedly on Jake's front door. Mirielle answered in her housecoat.

"Wynter! This is a surprise," she said.

"Yeah. Hi, Mrs. Peterson." Wynter had not yet cooled down from her brisk walk from the Gas N Go and was breathing heavily.

Mirielle looked at her curiously. "It's not even eight in the morning. Is Jake expecting you?"

"Yes, I called—"

"Got it, Mom. Thanks." Jake crutch-walked down the stairs. The hair poking out from under his Nintendo ball cap looked wet and there were damp patches on his T-shirt and one-legged jeans.

"Jesus, Mary, & Joseph, Jake!" Mirielle placed her hand on her chest. "My heart does a back flip every time I see you come down those stairs like that."

"It's casual." The instant the words left his mouth, Jake's right crutch slipped to the step below and he nearly lost his balance. He grabbed the railing with his left hand and steadied himself, smirking. "See? I got it."

"You're going to give me a heart attack one of these days," Mirielle said.

"So dramatic," Jake said to Wynter as he rolled his eyes. "Want anything to eat?"

She slipped off her shoes. "Cash made me breakfast at six."

"Sure. Start bragging why don't you." Jake smiled at her, then moved into the kitchen and dug through the cereal pantry. "Don't wait up. I'll be right there."

Wynter found Jake's bedroom exactly as it had been almost twelve hours earlier, not that she was expecting it to be different. The only exception was a camcorder set up on a tripod in the dormer window, aimed across the street and one house down: Roxy's driveway.

Jake returned with a partially crushed box of Honeycomb cereal tucked under one arm.

"Jake!" Mirielle's voice floated up from the first floor.

"One sec." Jake stepped back out into the hallway. "Yeah?"

"Keep your door open, please," Mirielle said. Wynter overheard and turned away from the door to hide her smile.

"Come on, Mom." Jake shook his head in protest. "I'm not twelve."

"Exactly my point," Mirielle said from below.

"God." Jake returned to his room and made sure the door was wide open. "Sorry. My mom thinks I'm a sex fiend who can't control himself."

Wynter laughed. "Don't worry about it. My mom would do the same thing. I'm amazed that she actually let me stay at Cash's place."

Jake raised a brow as he navigated to the camcorder in the dormer window. "I assume that went okay? I mean I don't want details or anything."

"Cash was a total gentleman," Wynter said. "He makes kick-ass bacon and eggs."

Jake peered into the camcorder's viewfinder and adjusted the framing. "Did that surprise you?"

"No. I mean I didn't expect the *royal* treatment or anything, but Cash has always looked out for us."

"True." Jake set his crutches aside, sat, and stretched his leg out. "So, what's this bomb Cash said you'd drop on me?"

Wynter went over her idea a third time and with each run-through, what she had to do and how she'd do it became clearer. It was like a refinement process, and she felt glad to have told everyone independently.

"Huh," Jake said. "Consider my mind in little pieces spread all round the room. Just like in *Scanners*."

Wynter shook her head. "Sorry. I'm not good with movies like Quinn is."

"It was a lame joke, anyway. But you'd probably like the movie."

Wynter motioned at his camcorder. "You spying on Roxy again? It's almost like you've got some kind of weird crush on her."

"Roxy made a bad choice long ago and hasn't been able to escape. Kind of like Ransom in a way, you know?"

"I guess."

"Besides, I can't be watching all the time. I got shit to do."

Jake popped a couple Honeycombs into his mouth. "So how is this supposed to work?"

"You don't have to do anything," Wynter said. "I'll just lie on your bed and go to sleep. Is that okay?"

"Uh, yeah. I'm not going to need my bed any time soon."

"If it works, I'll be able to pull Ransom out." Wynter sighed. "God, I hope it works."

"Betcha Cash doesn't," Jake whispered to himself.

"What did you say?"

Jake shook his head. "Nothing."

Wynter dug into her purse and pulled out a small plastic bag. She extracted several small, dark cubes and placed them in her palm.

"What are those? Better not be drugs. My mom would shit. Probably ground me for the rest of my life." Jake leaned in closer and squinted at the little cubes. "Oh, those things. I remember them. From the Starlite, right?"

"Um, yeah. They're not drugs. Me and Quinn call them 'zees,'" Wynter said. "We made them out of sleep-inducing herbs."

"Herbs, huh? Pot's an *herb*."

"Trust me. These are legal." Wynter popped the zees into her mouth and swallowed them. "All they do is help me fall asleep faster." She pushed herself onto Jake's bed, smoothed out the ruffles of her skirt, and laid back.

"Do you need a blanket or anything? Music?"

"I don't think so. Just pretend that I'm not here." She closed her eyes.

"Okee dokee." Jake dug into the box of Honeycombs, crinkling the plastic and crunching on the sugary cereal.

Wynter felt like she was attending a movie where all the theater-goers were eating and drowning out all the important dialog. She opened her eyes and propped herself up on her elbows. "You know, maybe there is something you can do."

Jake had been looking into the viewfinder of the camcorder. "Name it."

"Stop crunching?" She smiled self-consciously.

Jake stopped his chewing, all at once aware of his noisy eating. "Oh, crap. Sorry."

"It's okay."

"How about I leave for half an hour or so," Jake said. "Would that be enough time?"

Wynter's eyes felt heavy already. "That'd be perfect."

"Ten-four, good buddy. Over and out." Jake grabbed the box of cereal and crutched out of the room, easing the door almost closed.

Wynter closed her eyes again and breathed deeply. Sleep came fast despite the copious amount of coffee she had drunk during the past few hours. As she slipped further toward REM state, she envisioned her book *Eyes Wide Dreaming* in her mind, unburned and in pristine condition. She opened it up and took control of her dream.

WYNTER BLINKED AT the ceiling above her and began to cry. Tears of remembrance and grief rolled off her cheeks and soaked into the pillow behind her head.

She knew the patterns above her like the back of her hand—the tiles that had between seventy and a hundred little holes in them, the one with a cracked corner, the water stain from the torrential summer rain they had in 1984. She had grown up with all of them.

She sat up and wiped her eyes. Wynter was back in her own bedroom at Sven Dwarfs. At the foot of her bed sat her desk and shelves of books. Her one window was open, with her favorite tattered and torn curtains playing in the summer breeze. It was all there. The posters, her photos, her closet full of clothes and photography equipment. Her mind had reconstructed her safe place right down to the last detail.

Wynter pushed herself off the bed and stepped into the connecting hallway. She peeked into her parents' room to see them both sleeping soundly. Madeline lay snuggled into Nolan's side.

She walked through the trailer to the front door, opened it, and stepped out onto the front landing. Across the field she spotted Cash, standing on the landing of his trailer. She waved at him, and he returned the greeting unenthusiastically.

A blast of hot air caught her from behind and sent her ruffled denim skirt fluttering above her knees. For a fleeting second, she felt like Marilyn Monroe in the subway scene from *The Seven Year Itch*.

She pushed her skirt back down and glanced behind her to discover the trailer was gone. A pile of charred wood and metal smoldered in its place.

"Mom! Dad!"

Deep in the recesses of Wynter's mind she knew that her parents were okay, yet seeing them in their bedroom only moments earlier clashed with the destruction in front of her.

Jezebel had been responsible for all of it. It was time to put her in her place and the first step was getting Ransom back into her head. She was certain of it.

Her anger simmered, building in intensity as she tightened her fists. "This is *my* dream, you hear me?" Wynter said through clenched teeth. "And Ransom is *mine!*"

She recalled the chapter on sleep lucidity in *Eyes Wide Dreaming*. "I am in control." She raised her fists to the sky and shot up into the blue like a superhero.

Now a few thousand feet above Newhaven, Interstate 94 cut through the Sheyenne Grasslands like the highway lines on the map that used to hang in her room. Wynter shot eastward faster than she could ever have imagined moving. Distances that took minutes to cover by car flew by in seconds. Overpasses, vehicles going about their daily business, the Red River Rest Stop, came and went at a blistering speed.

After a minute, she arrived at the small city of Halston. She could see the Shey-Inn, Zoey's Fast Fill, and her destination: Halston Medical center.

Despite having occupied a bed for a week, Wynter was not as familiar with the layout of the hospital as she had thought. Except Jezebel had been on the same floor as her dad. The fifth floor.

She found a window five floors up and hovered outside it. "This is *my* dream." Wynter sailed through the glass as if it wasn't there.

The room she had entered was unfamiliar but ahead was the corridor and her memories resurfaced. She wouldn't need a walker this time. Wynter decided she didn't need to walk at all. Instead, she floated through the room as if weightless.

She exited into the corridor several feet past the nurses' station. No one noticed this denim-skirted teenager floating by.

She paused at room 523. "Dad?" She peeked inside to find the space barren of a bed or monitoring equipment, like the room had never seen a patient. As much as she would have loved to see her dad, that wasn't the reason she was here. Her dream world had reminded her of that.

Wynter refocused and glided to the end of the corridor, to room 513. A sheet of steel had replaced the door. Again, a sudden realization dawned on her, one that replaced the reality of her waking world. "It's *my* dream. It only looks like metal."

She passed easily through the metal barrier and into Jezebel's room. A privacy curtain surrounded the bed. The sun beamed through the exterior window and made the room glow.

A shadow moved behind the curtain.

She planted her feet on the floor and made the last few steps of her approach on the cool tile. She parted the privacy curtain and to her surprise she found Ransom, instead of Jezebel, lying in a fetal position in the bed.

"Ransom," Wynter whispered. She stepped forward and her face hit what felt like glass. Instinctively her hands reached out, searching. Her fingertips slid across an invisible barrier. "Ransom?"

Wynter pulled the privacy curtain away from the entire bed, following the barrier around until it joined the wall. She let her hands drop and laughed to herself. "This is *my* dream." She walked forward and again an unknown force stopped her.

She brought her index finger to the barrier and tapped it. Tendrils of blue energy pulsed away from her fingertip in an electronic ripple.

Wynter balled her fist tightly and brought it down hard on the barrier. Blue energy shot forth from around her fist, brighter and stronger this time.

Ransom raised his head as if he had heard something.

Wynter ran around to face him. "Ransom! It's me. Follow my voice!"

He still couldn't see her, but he could hear her fist falls. Wynter punched the barrier and it responded predictably with its cerulean light show. Ransom directed his eyes to where her punch had landed.

She stared at her fist, morphing a large hammer into her waiting grip. Wynter summoned all her strength and struck the barrier. Sparks burst upon impact and left behind a small hole, its shattered and cracked edges buzzing with blue energy.

Wynter dropped the hammer and kneeled to place her mouth at the same level as the breach. "Ransom!"

Instant recognition. Ransom sat up, moved to the edge of the bed, and looked in her general direction. "Wynter?"

"You can't see me but I'm here!" She forced a finger through the crack in the invisible barrier.

Ransom zeroed in on her wriggling finger, fell to his knees, and touched it. "Wynter? Is it really you?"

She pulled her finger out and spoke into the fracture. "It's me. And I'm going to get you out." Wynter resumed her assault on the force field with her newly minted hammer. The face of the heavy iron tool knocked chunks of energy from the edges of the hole, widening it with every blow. Glowing pieces fell to the floor and vaporized like tiny firecrackers.

Ransom stuck his hand and arm out of the hole, searching blindly for Wynter. She grabbed his warm hand and held it over her heart. Tears welled in her eyes.

Her head lurched backward, and a searing pain crossed her neck. She lost the ability to talk as she fell onto her back.

"Wynter? What happened?" Ransom's voice echoed out of the energized break in the barrier.

Jezebel stood over her, dressed in surgical scrubs with a scalpel in her hand, the blade dripping with blood.

Wynter searched for Ransom's hand but could not find it. She touched her neck and found it warm and sticky with her own blood. She tried to yell for help but the air in her lungs bubbled at the gash in her neck, bypassing her vocal cords.

Jezebel crouched. "It might be *your* dream, but he's *mine*." She raised the scalpel and began to cut out Wynter's eyes.

AFTER JAKE FINISHED his breakfast downstairs, he returned to his bedroom. Wynter lay asleep on his bed. He parked his crutches against the wall and turned on the color TV next to his VHS editing decks. He connected the signal output from his camcorder to the back of one of the decks. An image of the street and Roxy's house flipped on.

He grabbed a fresh VHS tape, unwrapped the plastic wrap as

quietly as he could, and slid it into the loading carriage. He pressed record. After several clicks and whirrs, the machine settled into a low hum as it captured the camcorder's signal.

It was going to be a long day. How long Wynter would sleep was anyone's guess, but Jake imagined it could be hours.

He heard footsteps ascending the stairs, then approach his room. Mirielle knocked on the doorframe and peeked in.

Jake held his finger to his lips, silently shushing her.

She lowered her voice to a whisper. "Is Wynter feeling okay?"

"She had a bad night and needed a place to sleep," Jake said softly. "Her place burned down, remember."

"Oh. Right," Mirielle said. "I remember reading about that in the paper. Poor thing." She looked at Wynter on the bed, her chest rising and falling in a slow, relaxed rhythm. "Do the police know who did it?"

Jake had a choice. He could tell his mom everything, about Ransom and Jezebel and the power of summoning, or he could avoid the subject altogether. Part of him wanted to share. It took considerable energy to keep a part of his life secret all the time, double-checking everything he wanted to say before he said it. But his gut told him to keep everything about Wynter's situation under wraps.

"I think Sheriff Jacobs has some leads," Jake said. "But he hasn't shared anything with Wynter. I think it's a safety thing." He took pride that he hadn't lied to his mother. Holding back the entire truth was his only offense.

"Well, she's always welcome here, Jake," Mirielle whispered. "Please let her know that."

Jake nodded. "I will. Thanks, Mom."

Mirielle waved and left the room. As her footsteps descended to the first floor, Jake cursed himself for not asking her to hand him the latest issue of *Computer Gaming World*.

He turned to grab his crutches and knocked them with his

cast. He watched them fall to the floor in slow motion and waited for the inevitable clatter.

Jake closed his eyes and cringed. As the dust and noise settled, he peeked at Wynter on the bed, expecting her to be wide awake. She continued her slumber as if nothing had happened.

Jake let out a sigh of relief. He gathered his crutches and crossed his bedroom to his book case. He had sorted his magazines and books, both fiction and nonfiction, by title and date. Issue number twenty-nine of *Computer Gaming World* caught his eye and he brought it back to his editing suite.

He read the magazine almost cover to cover while Wynter slept. In the middle of the Micro Reviews, she began to stir. He set the magazine down and watched her.

Wynter's brow furrowed in concern and her eyes flipped wildly under her eyelids. Occasionally, her hands made fists. Then her entire body began to tremble, then convulse.

Jake looked to his open bedroom door and considered calling his mom for help. That would lead to more questions he couldn't, or wouldn't, be able to answer. Instead, he moved to the edge of the bed and sat. He reached out to touch Wynter's arm, then stopped, remembering reading somewhere that waking a person in a nightmare can be harmful.

"Easy, Wynter," he said softly. "It's going to be alright."

Wynter's eyes sprung open, wide with terror. She let out a single, short-lived yell and sat bolt upright. She stared at Jake, then wrapped her arms around him and began to weep.

"It's okay." Jake placed a tentative hand on her back. Her shirt was damp with sweat and warmer than he expected. "You're okay."

Despite Wynter's startling burst of consciousness, Jake found his mind wandering. Twice in less than twenty-four hours he'd had two different girls on his bed. And he still remained a virgin, not that he'd ever consider making a move on Wynter. Nice guys finished last, he convinced himself.

The smell of fear overpowered the clean scent of Wynter's skin and Jake refocused his attention, making a quick scan of his room.

With exception of Wynter, everything was in order. But Ransom was nowhere to be found. Wynter had failed and part of him was glad. He would have had a hell of a time trying to explain how Ransom had gotten into his room.

"It didn't work, did it?"

Wynter shook her head against his chest.

"What happened?"

Wynter sniffled and wiped her eyes with her wrist. Jake handed her a box of tissues. She took one and used it on her nose. "I found Ransom. I even touched him. But even though it was my dream, there were parts I couldn't control." She matched his gaze. "Jezebel got me. Again." She squared herself to the edge of the bed. "I failed. Big time."

"But you made contact. That's huge." Jake smiled at her. "I'm impressed." He placed his arm around her shoulder. "You'll get Ransom back. I know it. We'll regroup and—"

Wynter pulled his face to hers and kissed him on the cheek, but her lips touched the corner of his mouth. Jake's eyes widened as if he had seen a ghost. She pulled away and smiled. "You're a good friend, Jake. Thanks."

Jake swallowed hard and cleared his throat. "You're welcome."

Wynter wiped her eyes with the tissue. "I don't know about you, but I'm starving. Lucid dreaming is harder work than I thought." She turned to him. "I know it's your house and all, but can I make you lunch?"

"Yeah," Jake said. "That'd be nice."

They made their way downstairs and discussed next steps as Wynter prepared soup and sandwiches. Upstairs in Jake's bedroom, the TV showed an empty street, its electronic eye keeping watch like an ever-patient predator seeking an elusive prey. But some prey are easier to catch than others.

MADELINE'S ANGERED VOICE echoed down the third floor corridor and into Nolan's shared room. As he lay in his bed, Nolan listened to his wife tear a strip off the current attending nurse. He hoped it wasn't Bridgette. She had been so nice. He needed allies instead of enemies.

Placing Jezebel in his room had been an unfortunate and arbitrary decision made by someone who had not been informed of their past history. How could they have been? Each of them had arrived at the hospital at different times with injuries from different events. But Madeline could be a force of nature when she wanted to be.

"Now I know who wears the pants in the family." Jezebel set her magazine down. "You must be one pussy-whipped motherfucker. How can you live with yourself?"

Nolan ignored the taunt. Instead, he closed his eyes and breathed deeply to maintain a calm state of mind as much as possible. He had felt the edges of hate when he first discovered Jezebel would share his room. It was a feeling he tried to avoid in all situations in his life because it led nowhere positive. With Jezebel it had been particularly difficult considering the damage she had inflicted on his family.

Nolan heard Madeline's exasperated heels clack on the corridor floor before she entered the room and took a seat beside him.

"They said they can't do anything at the moment," Madeline said. "Who would put a patient in the same room with..." She glared across Nolan's bed at Jezebel. "A psycho like *her.*"

Jezebel sent back a side-glance steeped with malice.

"If it was Bridgette you were talking to—"

"It wasn't, but I'll be talking to her next. Mark my words, Nolan."

"Maddie, Bridgette told me she'd look into switching rooms," Nolan said softly. "I believe her."

"Wouldn't hurt to give her a nudge." Madeline leaned back in her chair and crossed her arms in frustration.

"Just let her do her job." Nolan looked at her with tired eyes. "Please? It makes things easier when you're not around."

Madeline glared at him. "Well. I can tell when I'm not wanted." She grabbed her purse, threw it over her shoulder, and stood abruptly.

"Maddie." Nolan reached out and caught her hand with his. "I want you here. There's no one I'd rather have by my side. But sometimes you're like a rock tossed in a lake. The ripples of your presence remain long after you're gone."

"Jesus." Jezebel snickered. "What a load of bullshit."

"You shut your damn mouth, or I'll shut it for you." Madeline made a move toward Jezebel, but Nolan held her back.

"I'd like to see you try, bitch."

Nolan met Madeline's gaze, offered a small smile and, motioned to the chair. She sat, reluctantly. He faced Jezebel. "I wonder what they do to patients with abusive tendencies? You keep talking and we're going to find out."

"You don't got the guts," Jezebel hissed.

"Try me," Nolan said. "They love me here. How about you? Who do you think they're going to believe?"

Jezebel scowled at him and returned to her magazine.

Nolan and Madeline touched foreheads and spoke in hushed voices. He hoped he had heard the last from Jezebel, at least for a while.

THE CLOCK IN hospital room 305 read eight minutes past eleven. Madeline had managed to skirt visiting hour rules and lay in

Nolan's bed, snuggled into one shoulder. Her outburst at the nurses' station earlier in the evening had made many of the nurses a little gun-shy. Avoiding another confrontation, especially going into the evening, was forefront in their minds.

The dimly lit room returned silence with the exception of ambient hospital noise and light snoring from the three occupants.

Jezebel's chest rose and fell with each deep breath and her hands twitched under the covers. Her top sheet billowed like it had been caught in a gust of wind. As the sheet floated to rest, it took the shape of a figure crouched in waiting. Jezebel lifted the leading edge of the sheet and Jezebel Too poked her head out.

"Fuck, what a rush," Jezebel Too said. "I'll never get tired of that."

"Shut up, or that'll be the last time." Jezebel shot a glance at Nolan and Madeline. They were still asleep. "Now, get off me. And be *quiet.*"

Jezebel Too slid around the side rail of the bed and placed her sneakered feet on the floor.

"Bring me my purse." Jezebel pointed with an urgent finger at the chair next to her bed.

Jezebel Too rushed around the foot of the bed and knocked Jezebel's chart to the floor where it landed with a clatter. She grabbed the chart, slid around the side of the bed, and froze. It was a poor hiding spot. The underside of the hospital bed offered no cover.

Jezebel lay back and threw the covers over her chest. She glared at Jezebel Too huddled on the floor and spoke through clenched teeth. "Shut the fuck up and *don't* move."

The two of them waited and listened. Nolan and Madeline continued their snores, and the corridor held no sounds of approaching footsteps.

When she had decided that the coast was clear, Jezebel leaned closer to the edge of the bed. "Try again with less noise, fuckwit."

Jezebel Too crept around the foot of the bed, rehanging the chart as she passed by, and lifted the purse off the chair.

"You know what to do," Jezebel whispered as she took the purse. "Don't fuck up."

Jezebel Too watched Jezebel dig out her green shamrock speed pills and place one in her mouth. "Give me one, too."

"It doesn't work on dreamwakers. But you'll feel it anyway because I control you." Jezebel waved her off. "Go. You're wasting time."

Jezebel Too scowled. She headed toward the door to the room but stopped at the foot of Nolan's bed.

"Fuck! What are you doing?" Jezebel whispered.

Jezebel Too moved to the side of Nolan's bed and leaned in until she was a few feet from their faces. She let her eyes roam over their features, reveling in their vulnerability.

Jezebel grabbed her sheets in her fists and twisted the fabric. Channeling her rage was her only alternative to screaming at Jezebel Too and she wasn't used to it. Jezebel lived for confrontation.

Jezebel Too ran her middle finger across her throat like a blade. "Can't wait to finish what *she* started," she whispered.

Jezebel pointed to the door. "Go, you idiot!"

Jezebel Too glared back at her. "If I'm an idiot, so are you."

The two girls stared at each other, both unwilling to back down. It was the subconscious movement of Nolan that broke their contest.

Jezebel Too ducked by the bed and crouch-ran to the door. She pulled up her hoodie lund peered out into the hallway. She glanced back at Nolan, then at Jezebel, made a gun symbol with her hand and shot it at her.

Nolan sucked in a breath and his eyes flicked open wide. Jezebel slumped onto her pillow and closed her eyes to slits, but open just enough to watch.

He turned his head to focus on the doorway where Jezebel Too had stood mere seconds earlier.

Madeline woke and propped herself up on her elbow. "Hon, what is it?"

He stared at the doorway to the room as if he expected someone or something to appear. Convinced that nothing was there, Nolan relaxed into his pillow and shook his head slowly. "Strange dreams."

Without warning, Nolan turned to look at Jezebel's bed where she lay feigning sleep.

Jezebel felt the heat of his stare. She watched through narrowed eyelids and waited, hoping that her ruse would be convincing enough, but she could feel the amphetamine taking hold of her body, energizing it. Even the site of her stab wound on her right side hurt less.

Jezebel fought against the urge to open her eyes wide and get out of bed. Instead, she rolled onto her right side, her back to the rest of the room. She wondered if Nolan was still watching her. She opened her eyes and let them roam the rest of the room closest to the window, searching for anything reflective that might answer her question. The low light of the room betrayed any pertinent detail.

Staying still would be a challenge. She'd give herself an hour before she'd get up and wander the corridor. To pass time, she visualized Jezebel Too following her instructions to the letter. Of course, as she had discovered with Roxy earlier, Jezebel Too had a mind of her own. And even though she could summon dreamwakers now, she really wanted to be able to see through Jezebel Too's eyes.

After an hour had passed, Jezebel sat up, completely alert. She waddled to the door. Nurses had dimmed the corridor lighting for the night. She glanced at Nolan and found he was staring at her, following her every move. Madeline lay next to him, dead to the world and to their confrontation.

"You don't fool me," he whispered.

Instead of responding, Jezebel bared her teeth and ran her middle finger across her throat, just as Jezebel Too had done while he was sleeping.

Or had he been pretending to sleep?

Jezebel didn't care. She needed to stay awake. Jezebel Too had a lot to do. She began her walkabout. By the end of the night, she'd know every square inch of the third floor.

JEZEBEL TOO STOOD in the foyer of the hospital and dug into the back pocket of her skin tight jeans. She pulled out a folded stack of twenties and counted them with nimble fingers. One hundred sixty dollars lay in her hands, more than enough to get back to Newhaven.

She stepped out of the hospital entrance and found the taxi stand. A car sat parked with its for-hire light on. Jezebel Too made a beeline for it and climbed into the back.

The cabbie gave her the once-over through the rear view mirror. "Where to?"

"Newhaven," Jezebel Too said.

The cabbie sighed and rubbed his temples. "That kinda trip is going to cost yah."

"I got it covered."

"I ain't born yesterday, honey," the cabbie said. "Prove it or move it."

Jezebel Too grinned at him and rolled over in the back seat. She pulled up the hem of her hoodie and exposed the left back pocket of her taut jeans plus a small triangle of her bare back. She slid out the stash of cash and riffled the corner of the bills. "That enough?"

The cabbie considered the display and nodded. Both of them

knew his eyes were fixated on her jeans and not the money. That was exactly what Jezebel Too wanted. She returned the cash to her pocket.

He started the car, engaged the taximeter, and pulled away from the hospital. A moment later a pair of headlights flipped up and a silver Fiat pulled out from a parking space a stone's throw from the taxi stand, following at a safe distance.

The cabbie remained silent as he navigated to the Interstate, but his eyes spoke volumes as they flicked at Jezebel Too through the rear view mirror. Once settled into westward highway travel, the questions started.

"You gonna buckle up, miss?" the cabbie asked. "Everyone's doin' it, yah know."

"I don't like seat belts." Jezebel Too ran her hands over her hips to her thighs. "Too restrictive."

"It's your funeral if we crash."

"Then don't crash," Jezebel Too said. "Besides, I'm not afraid of dying. Are you?" She laughed when the cabbie's eyes met hers in the rear view mirror.

"What's a nice girl like you doing up so late?"

"My twin sister's in the hospital. She was stabbed."

The cabbie's eyes showed zero concern. "Twin sister, huh? I bet she's a sight, too. She okay?"

"She'll pull through." Jezebel Too glanced lazily out the passenger window. "How long is this trip going to take?"

"About an hour or so. You in a hurry?"

"I might be."

The two of them drove in silence for several minutes. Jezebel Too kept tabs on the cabbie's constant leering. She stretched and puffed out her chest, wishing she had worn a tight T-shirt instead of the hoodie.

"So where are we headed, miss? Besides Newhaven?"

Jezebel Too slid her gaze to the rear view mirror but this time the cabbie was looking over his shoulder, taking her all in.

"Better keep your eyes on the road. Wouldn't want to *crash* and *die*." When the cabbie returned his attention to the road, she continued. "You know where Ollie's MovieTyme is?"

"Hell yeah," the cabbie said. "Saw *The Warriors* there before they shut it down. Damn shame. Why you wanna go there?"

"You sure ask a lot of questions."

The cabbie took the hint and flipped on the radio, turning up the volume. KROK buzzed through the speakers in the dashboard and behind the back seat.

After forty-five minutes of decent rock and roll without questions, Jezebel Too saw the off-ramp to Newhaven approaching ahead. But even with the music, the trip had bored her. Surely there wasn't anything wrong with having a little fun.

"Change of plans," she said. "You know where the Gas N Go is?"

"Finn's? Sure do. Want me to drop you there?"

"Uh, yeah."

The cabbie exited I94 and instead of turning left on Main Street, he turned right and headed north toward downtown Newhaven, Stedford Plaza, and Finn's. Hall and Oates began to sing about a "Maneater," and a wicked smile floated across Jezebel Too's lips.

This is going to be fun.

The cabbie parked in one of the customer spots in front of the store, threw the car into park, and glanced back over his shoulder.

Jezebel Too slid across the back seat and let her fingers run over the back of the cabbie's neck as she passed by. She pushed open the left passenger door and stepped into the summer night, with only the taxi's headlights and the glow of the Gas N Go sign above to light her way. She sauntered to the front of the cab.

The cabbie glanced at the taximeter. "Miss, the fare's sixty, even."

Jezebel Too pulled out the stack of bills from her pocket, leaned through the driver's side window and dropped it on the dash. She gazed at him. "Want to stretch your legs?"

The cabbie swallowed hard. "How old are you?"

"Old enough. You take tips, right?" She pulled open his door, then unbuttoned her jeans and unzipped her fly. "Interested?" It was a needless question. The cabbie's eyes and the bulge in his pants was all the answer she needed. But he still had his seat belt on.

She turned, facing away from him, her backside lit by the taxi's interior overhead light, and hitched her jeans down, past her hips to mid-thigh. The bottom hem of her hoodie covered most of her behind. Jezebel Too grinned when she heard the click of his seat belt, the jangle of his belt buckle, and the zip of his fly.

The radio broadcast AC/DC's iconic guitar intro and Brian Johnson began to belt out "You Shook Me All Night Long". The song could not have been better timed.

The cabbie swung his legs out from the footwell, set them on the pavement behind hers, and pulled himself out of the taxi. She could feel his heat and the smell of nervous sweat and stale cigarettes coming off his body in waves.

Jezebel Too turned again to face him, one of her hands cupping the crotch of his underwear. "Ready?"

The cabbie nodded.

She reached into the pocket of her hoodie and wrapped her hand around the cool hilt of a switchblade. Jezebel Too engaged the blade and brought the knife point to the cabbie's throat.

"What the fuck?" The cabbie froze, his breathing panicked.

"I'm giving you a tip, *asshole*." Jezebel Too squeezed his waning erection. "Don't fuck teenagers."

The cabbie shook his head emphatically. "I won't. I promise. I promise."

"You've got to be at least *twice* my age." Jezebel Too scowled at him. "Fucking pervert."

"Please. Let me go." The knife point had split the skin on the cabbie's neck, causing it to well with blood. "I promise. Never again."

"I believe you." Jezebel Too lowered the knife from the cabbie's neck but kept the blade against his chest. "Never again." She shoved the point of the knife into the center of the cabbie's chest until the hilt met his ribcage.

A bloom of red spread out from the knife's handle as the cabbie's knees buckled. He dropped to the pavement, staring sightlessly at the handle sticking out of his chest.

Jezebel Too pulled up her jeans, refastened them, and took a step back. The knife's hilt quivered with every beat of the cabbie's heart.

"Sicko." She wiped her hands on his jeans, turned, and ran north on Main Street. Her fun was over. It was time to get to work.

MONTY LEFT THE INTERSTATE and followed the taxi along Main Street. When he saw the vehicle park at Finn's Gas N Go, he switched off his headlights and pulled into the Stedford Plaza parking lot. He chose a spot close to the road yet far enough away to remain unseen. He grabbed his SLR and used the steering wheel to steady it.

His camera had an unexposed roll of fast film loaded and ready to go and Monty wasted no time snapping pictures of the action.

He watched Jezebel leave the car and strut to the front of the taxi. "Why are the psychos always so damn hot?" he said to himself as he clicked away.

Jezebel reached into her back pocket, leaned in through the driver's side window, then pulled open the driver's side door and turned her back to the cabbie.

"Jesus, what a *whor*—" Monty choked on the word when he

realized she was pulling her pants down. "Holy shit." His shutter finger worked in a frenzy, snapping and advancing the film.

Through the viewfinder, Monty watched the cabbie stand. Jezebel spun around to face him and a glint of something metallic flashed under his chin.

"Is that a... knife?" Monty scrunched his brows and returned his eye to the viewfinder to see Jezebel plunge the knife into the cabbie's chest. "Holy fuck."

Monty's first instinct was to run. He sat back in his seat, in shock at what he had just seen. Or were his eyes playing tricks on him? He looked again, as the cabbie slumped to the pavement, the knife sticking prominently from his chest. He captured several more photos as Jezebel ran from the scene, north on Main Street.

He stepped out of the car and ran toward Finn's. Halfway there he skidded to a stop. "Wait. What the hell am I doin'?" He took one more photo of the cabbie and ran back to his car. Arrest by police at an active crime scene fell nowhere on his to-do list.

Monty tossed the SLR onto the passenger seat and scanned Main Street, but Jezebel had vanished. He was now an official witness to a murder. As he pushed that fact to the back of his mind, another thought clicked in his head.

"I know where you are, *Jazz*." He climbed into the car and started the engine.

JEZEBEL TOO OVERTURNED the pot by the stoop of Roxy's back door. The glimmering brass key sat in the same spot as it had been the last time she took it.

"Looks like I'm still invited," Jezebel Too whispered to herself. She unlocked the door, but this time returned the key to its hiding spot.

She crept through the kitchen to the front of the house, leaving a trail of dirty footprints on the floor. With silent footsteps, she climbed the stairs and eased herself into Roxy's bedroom.

The television hissed blue static snow across its screen. Roxy lay on her side asleep with the covers half off.

Jezebel Too switched off the TV, crouched next to the bed, and let her eyes roam across Roxy's body. She remembered how exciting it had been when she had tried to choke her before. But the cabbie had been enough for tonight. She had a job to do.

Jezebel Too flicked Roxy's forehead with her index finger. "Hey shithead. Wake up."

Roxy stirred and rolled onto her back.

Jezebel Too poked Roxy's left breast. "Come on. I don't got all night."

Roxy groaned but didn't wake.

"Fuck." Jezebel Too slapped Roxy's left ear.

Roxy blinked, then recoiled from Jezebel Too, banging the back of her head on the headboard.

"Having a flashback?" Jezebel Too laughed, then her face drew serious. "How dare you fucking kill me." She punched Roxy in the shoulder. "Good job. Didn't think you had it in you. How does it feel to be a murderer?"

Roxy squinted at her in the dim light of the room. "Jeze... um, JT?"

"None other."

"What are you doing here again?"

"You got to finish your training," Jezebel Too said. "And I'm not taking no for an answer."

"What training?"

Jezebel Too smacked Roxy on the shoulder, harder this time. "Dreamwaker training, idiot."

Roxy caught the evil glint in Jezebel Too's eyes and knew that the night had headed in a bad direction.

A View
To A Kill

WYNTER AND CASH sat on the sofa engrossed in an episode of *MacGyver* while his dad busied himself with preparing lunch. Even after years of living in the trailer, Cash still found it strange when his dad made lunch at night. Now was the time to make popcorn instead of sandwiches.

Ernie had made himself a Denver sandwich and the smell was causing Cash's stomach to growl, even though he had prepared his favorite, spaghetti with Ragu sauce, for himself and Wynter three hours earlier.

"If there's any leftovers, I'll take them off your hands," Cash said.

Wynter gave his shoulder a playful tap. "What about me?"

"I'd share," Cash said.

Ernie sat at the wobbly kitchen table making short work of his sandwich and chuckled. "The odds don't look good, son." He finished his sandwich, moved his plate to the sink, and headed toward his bedroom to dress for work. "Can you fix that table at some point? One of the legs need adjustment."

"Sure, Dad." As a batch of commercials played Cash turned to Wynter. "Hey. I've been thinking."

"I thought I smelled something burning."

"Ha ha. Very funny. Seriously though. I've been thinking about your idea and what happened at Jake's," Cash wrung his hands nervously. "How can you really be sure? What if that dream you had about Ransom was all your imagination?"

"I guess it could have been my imagination," Wynter said. "I mean I'm, like, not going to go have coffee with Jezebel and talk about it."

"No shit. So how do you know? For sure?"

"It's like the dream you had, out in the field. I *was* there," Wynter said. "There were too many things in that dream for them to be separate. We didn't talk about the field and the chess board and your sister before we went to sleep. But I saw it all in my dream and so did you."

"Maybe we just had the same dream."

"The *same* dream?" Wynter cast him a dubious glance. "Don't you think that'd be a huge coincidence? Like, impossible, really? Especially if we didn't talk about it first?"

"Maybe. It could happen," Cash said. "We need to test it out once and for all."

Wynter thought for a moment and nodded. "Okay, what's your idea?"

"How about this. Make it a test for two things. I'll dream of Sierra but won't tell you what she's wearing," Cash said. "You try and make her into a dreamwaker. We compare notes after."

"Yeah, but I've been in your dreams before and we've never talked about what Sierra was wearing."

Cash sat up. "We never talked about it *after,* either."

"That's true." Wynter nibbled at her lower lip, then nodded. "Okay, let's do it. Hopefully we won't have to compare notes."

"We probably should anyway." Cash smiled. "But we should finish *MacGyver* first."

"Most definitely." Wynter sat cross-legged and placed her hands on her lap, flattening out her denim skirt.

Ernie left the master bedroom and grabbed his jacket and lunch kit. "I'm headed out. You kids going to be alright?"

"Yeah, Dad," Cash said without taking his eyes from the screen.

"MacGyver, huh?" Ernie sighed. "Night shifts are the worst. You can tell me about the episode tomorrow."

"Okay, Dad. Bye."

"Have a good shift, Mr. Hawkins." Wynter offered him a small wave.

Ernie gave her a smile and stepped out the door, closing it behind him. Moments later sounds of the Honda Civic rose up through the thin walls of the trailer, then faded away.

After *MacGyver* finished, Wynter switched off the TV. "Let's get this test going."

"But it's only ten o'clock. We could watch *The Equalizer*." Cash looked at the cupboards, his eyes lighting up. "I could make popcorn."

Wynter shook her head.

"What about *St. Elsewhere*?"

"No," Wynter said softly.

"But I'm not even sleepy."

"Hold that thought." Wynter hopped off the sofa, disappeared into Cash's room, and returned with her purse. She extracted a small plastic bag with something dark in it.

Cash eyed her uneasily, as if he was seeing a hidden side of Wynter he had never known about. "What is that?"

"Zees, remember? They'll help you… and me fall sleep quicker," Wynter said.

Cash formed a small grin. "Oh, those. Right. Quinn gave me some at the Starlite when we tried to get Jezebel."

"She did?"

"You were still in a coma then, so I guess you don't remember. They worked pretty well."

"Cool." Wynter placed three zees in Cash's hand and three in her own, then placed the bag back in her purse. "Jake thought they were drugs at first."

"Well, technically, marijuana is an herb, so—"

"Don't you start too," Wynter said. "They're perfectly fine."

Cash eyed the little cubes. He pressed one into the palm of his hand with his finger and watched the square shape bulge at the sides before returning to its regular shape. "Do we really need these?"

"Do you trust me?" Wynter locked her gaze with his.

"Yes, of course. Absolutely."

"Then believe me when I say the zees will help. Let's start this test." Wynter popped all three cubes into her mouth and swallowed. Cash did the same.

Wynter crossed the small trailer toward Cash's bedroom. She looked back at Cash still sitting on the sofa. "Are you coming?"

Cash's saliva instantly dried up. He swallowed and tried hard not to trip over his own words. "I think it would be better if I sleep out here. I mean, if this works, you're going to do it to Jezebel, right? You won't be lying in bed with *that* psycho."

Cash sensed slight disappointment on Wynter's face before she rested her head on the doorframe and smiled again. "You're right. See you in your dreams, Cash." She disappeared into the bedroom.

Cash let go a conflicted sigh. He wanted to go with Wynter and sleep beside her. He had imagined experiencing moments like that with her many times over the years he had known her. But Ransom was still in the picture and the last thing he wanted was to bare his soul only for it to be crushed again.

He laid back on the sofa and tried to convince himself that getting Ransom back into Wynter's head would help things get back to normal. But it wasn't working.

Cash's eyelids grew heavy and his mind swirled as he switched gears to focus on Sierra. It would be good to see his sister again. He wanted nothing more than the test to be successful. The results would... *might* go a long way to solving the problem. He closed his eyes and transported himself into his blackened subconscious.

A sickening punch landed in Cash's gut and sent him reeling

across the blue floor. He rolled to his hands and knees, sucking in labored breaths and trying to ignore the ache below his ribs.

"Oh my God, Cash," a voice said. "Are you okay?"

Cash raised his head to look, his vision obscured by a swath of golden hair smelling of Johnson's Baby Shampoo and hanging in front of his face. Small arms reached around his shoulders and guided his hands.

"Grab the ropes, Cashmere."

Cash smiled through his discomfort. "Sierra?"

"You got it, Pontiac."

The moment he took hold of the red vinyl ropes, red boxing gloves appeared on his hands. Cash pulled himself up and found himself in one corner of a boxing ring. A blue mat with thirteen white orbiting stars stared back at him. Sierra stood in the middle of the ring wearing red boxing gloves, white shorts, and a red T-shirt with white block letters that read, "YO, ADRIAN!" She had pulled her blond hair back into a ponytail.

Cash found his balance and staggered toward her. "Was it you who punched me?"

"Sorry about that. I was training and you got in the way." Sierra bounced on the balls of her feet, holding her gloves in front of her chest, then swung practice punches left and right.

Cash held up his gloves, palms out. "Practice on these."

"Now you're talking." Sierra threw out punches at Cash's gloves, sending them backward with every blow.

"You throw one hell of a punch."

"Thanks." Sierra wiped the sweat from her forehead with her forearm and continued her practice blows.

The bell rang behind them. Cash turned to find Wynter standing on the edge of the ring. Distracted, he caught Sierra's last punch in the jaw. Stars exploded in his eyes, and he fell to his knees. A drop of bloody saliva dripped out of his mouth and landed on the mat.

"Sorry again, Cashmere," Sierra said. "You can't deke when I'm throwing haymakers."

Wynter entered the ring, crouched, and offered Cash her hand. She wore a white tank top with shorts modeled after the American flag. "My turn at the champ." She tapped her red gloves together. "You know you just got your ass whipped by a six-year-old, right?"

"Sounds bad when you say it out loud." Cash took Wynter's hand and stood, propping himself up on his knees. He took one glove off and rubbed his jaw. "Watch it. She's got a wicked left hook."

"Thanks." Wynter shook out her arms and legs and swiveled her head to work out any kinks. "I might have a few tricks up my sleeve too." She turned to Sierra who was bounding up and down with energy that looked hard to match. "How about we practice your punches for a while."

Sierra smiled and narrowed her eyes through errant locks of hair that had slipped out of her ponytail. "Sure, but boxing is in my blood. Practicing can get boring after a while."

Wynter held her hands out and kept herself positioned in front of Sierra as the young boxer threw lefts, rights, and shifted her stance.

Cash watched the two of them move in the ring, almost like they were dancing. Grief overwhelmed him. He had lost so much since Sierra's death. What would his life have been like if she had grown up with him? What would she be like? Would his parents have stayed together? Would they have lived in a house instead of a run-down trailer in the armpit of town?

Cash leaned on the ropes and hung his head at the rows of empty arena seating. "This is bullshit," he said under his breath.

But Wynter heard him. "Hey Sierra, let's take a break and go back to your brother's place for a while. Do you remember being there?"

Sierra dropped her gloves, her shoulders slumping. "Yeah, but do I have to? I want to box."

"I know you do," Wynter said. "You'd be helping us out a lot though."

"Why?"

"Well, we're doing a test. The first time, Cash brought you back."

Cash turned around. "I took you to meet Wynter's parents."

"Yeah, I remember. It smelled weird. At first."

"I'm sure it did," Wynter said. "I want to try to bring you back this time. Everything else would be the same."

Sierra looked at her and tilted her head, confused. "Why?"

Wynter searched for the right words. "It's kind of like when Rocky decided to fight Apollo. He didn't want to at first, but he changed his mind. The fight was a test to see if Rocky could win."

"But he didn't win," Sierra said. "It was a split decision."

"He almost won. He wouldn't have gotten that far if he hadn't tried." Wynter looked Sierra in the eye. "What do you say?"

Sierra balked. "I just want to box."

Wynter scanned around the ring, at the hundreds of empty seats. "You must be getting tired of this place."

Sierra followed her gaze. "It's kind of lonely. And dark."

"What if we changed it to a real gym?"

Sierra's eyes went wide as saucers. "Like at Mighty Mick's?"

"Um... I think so?"

Cash caught the worried look on Wynter's face and managed a reassuring smile. "That's the gym in *Rocky*."

"Well, this is really your dream, Cash," Wynter said. "Could you do that? Change it into Mighty Mick's?"

"Yeah, I think so."

"Alright!" Sierra pumped her fists. "I want to try a speed bag!"

Wynter crouched to Sierra's level. "You will, but we'll try the test first. I'd like you to wrap your arms around me like I'm your best friend."

Sierra eyed Wynter cautiously. "You're Winter and winter's cold. I think I'd be friends with Summer more."

Wynter smiled. "Then think of me as Summer."

"It's okay," Cash said. "I'll be there too."

"You promise you'll make Mighty Mick's for me?"

Cash nodded and grinned at her. "You got it, Pontiac."

"Hey," Sierra said. "That's *my* line."

"I just borrowed it. Now give Summer a hug."

"Okay, Cashmere." Sierra wrapped her six-year-old arms around Wynter.

"Ready?"

"Yup."

"Here we go." Wynter swayed a moment to concentrate her thoughts, then rocked backward. She hit the mat with a thud.

Sierra lay on top of Wynter and popped her head up. "We're still here."

Wynter shared a concerned glance with Cash. "Rocky never gave up, so let's try again." She stood and embraced Sierra, then allowed herself to fall backward until the both of them landed on the mat. Wynter's head bounced off the blue canvas.

Sierra looked around. "Nope. You sure you can do this?"

"That's why we're testing it." Wynter stood, rubbed her head, and brushed herself off. She surveyed the ring. "Any ideas?"

Cash shook his head. "You're the expert."

Sierra began to run, following the circle of thirteen stars on the ring's mat, her arms stretched out from her sides.

Wynter watched her and a slow grin formed on her lips. "I know what we can do." She stopped Sierra and faced her. "I think we're gonna fly now."

Sierra gave her a smile a wile wide.

Cash looked into the empty arena and snapped his finger. The iconic brass of Bill Conti's "Gonna Fly Now" rose up around them from speakers hidden in the arena shadows. Wynter and Sierra ran the length of the ring.

"One…" At the last possible second, they turned around and let their backs sink into the ropes, propelling them forward.

The pair raced across the ring and flung themselves into the ropes on the opposite side of the ring. "Two..."

Wynter reached out and grabbed Sierra's hand, pulled her into a hug, and turned. The three stacked red ropes sprang back and shot both of them forward. Wynter spun in the air as her feet left the mat.

Sierra's ponytail had come completely undone at some point during their traversal of the ring. Her golden hair rippled behind as they sailed past Cash almost in slow motion. Wynter landed on her back and slid to the opposite edge of the ring.

Sierra opened one eye, then the other. She looked at Wynter, then up and around her. "That was fun, but nothing happened."

Wynter pulled herself up by the top rope, shook it with white knuckled fists, and screamed. "Stop that fucking music!"

Cash snapped his finger and the arena plunged into silence.

Sierra backed away. "Why is Summer so mad, Cashmere?"

Cash crouched to her level and placed his arm around her shoulder. "That test you were helping her with, well, she's been trying to make it work for a long time."

"It's my fault, isn't it?" Sierra's lips trembled as tears filled her eyes.

"No." Cash pulled her into a hug. "It's not your fault. It's just that... the world can be cruel and unfair sometimes."

"Like how you're so much older than me?" Sierra said through her sniffles.

Cash's heart ached and he closed his eyes. "Yeah. Like that." He let her go and placed his gloves on her shoulders. "But it's not your fault, okay? You believe me?"

Sierra nodded.

Cash kissed her head and glanced to where Wynter had been standing moments earlier. At the top row of the arena, he spotted a door open to bright white light. Wynter's silhouette stepped into the doorway, paused briefly to look back, then disappeared into the light, the door closing behind her.

Sierra wiped her eyes and looked around the ring. "Where did Summer go?"

Cash sighed. "She left." He turned to her. "Let's visit Mighty Mick's, okay?"

"Yeah!" Sierra threw her arms up in the air like she had just won a match.

Cash scanned the arena. "You let me know if I get anything wrong. It's been a while since I saw *Rocky*."

He closed his eyes and the mat changed under their feet, from taut canvas to hardwood flooring. The arena faded away, replaced by blue walls, with a training ring along one wall. A punching bag hung from the ceiling by a chain rope.

Sierra jumped with joy. "You made this?"

"It's my dream," Cash said. "I can do whatever I want."

"Cool! But the walls were white with pictures of boxers on them, except that one there. It was green. And there were two rings to train in. And two punching bags—no, three. And where are the speed bags?"

"Wait a sec, slow down." Cash opened his eyes to the new environment and began to change it according to Sierra's instructions. The walls faded to white, complete with full-sized pictures. The single ring morphed into two and a couple punching bags fell from the ceiling, rattling on their suspension chains. "How many speed bags?"

Sierra blanked, her face pulled back in surprise. "Um, I forget."

"How about three?"

"Okay," Sierra said. "And that wall was green, remember?"

"Right." Cash made the correction in his head and the wall responded, fading to a deep forest green. "How's that?"

Sierra stood in the center of the gym and spun around, taking it all in. "You're amazing, Cashmere!" She ran to where Cash stood. "It's *almost* perfect."

"Almost?"

"Yeah." Sierra raised her hands and shrugged. "Where are all the boxers?"

"Oh, you want boxers, too?"

"Who else am I going to fight?"

Cash scanned the environment he had created and snapped his fingers. The gym became a bustle of boxing activity, with some boxers in the training rings, and others pounding the punching bags or skipping rope.

"Better?"

Sierra nodded and ran to a punching bag. "Watch me, Cashmere!"

Cash glanced around at the world he had created and smiled. He watched Sierra hop around a black punching bag twice her size, throwing lefts and rights as fast she could. "You're pretty amazing, too, you know?"

He couldn't help but be reminded of what kind of teenager Sierra could have become had she lived. Going there once had been hard enough. A second time in one dream would be too much. He knew that it was time for him to wake up.

Cash stood behind the punching bag. "I got to go, Sierra."

"Aww. Come on. Stay and help me train."

"I can't."

Sierra stepped away from the punching bag. "It's that test, isn't it?"

"Yeah," Cash said. "In a way, it's like my own special training."

"Well, training will make you better."

"You're right."

Sierra returned to her punching bag. "I'll stay here. I'm going to become a champ."

"Okay." Cash watched her for a minute before he crossed the gym to the exit.

"Cashmere!"

Cash turned, halfway through the door. "Yeah?"

Sierra held the punching bag with her red gloves to stop it from swaying. "Are you going to visit again soon?"

Cash nodded. "You got it, Pontiac."

She smiled as he pushed through the exit, out into the same bright nothingness that had swallowed Wynter earlier.

Cash shielded his eyes, but it did nothing to stop the sting of white. He covered both eyes with his hands and felt his body jolt, with an ache centered in his chest.

Minutes or hours had passed, he had no idea which. Cash peeked out from behind his hands to see the water-stained ceiling of his trailer. His cheeks were damp from tears.

Wynter sat cross-legged on the floor beside the sofa, watching him. "I'm sorry, Cash. I don't know what went wrong."

Cash pushed himself up on his elbows and swung his legs off the sofa. "Don't worry about that now." He wiped the partially dried tears from his face and locked gaze with her. "What was Sierra wearing?"

Wynter reeled off her answer, counting each with a different finger. "Red gloves, white shorts, red T-shirt with 'YO, ADRIAN!' written on it. All capital letters." She smiled wistfully at him. "How'd I do, coach?"

"Amazing," Cash said. "Even if you didn't make Sierra a dreamwaker, we know for sure that you can enter people's dreams." He sighed. "Maybe it's for the best that she stayed in my head. Brings back too many memories."

Wynter placed her hand on his. "I'm sorry, Cash."

"Thanks. I'll be okay, though. But don't get me wrong. It was good to see her again, and for you to see her in her element. She was quite a character."

"Your memories of her are, like, totally alive still."

"I was a little surprised." Cash spoke softly. "Memories usually fade over time but not with Sierra."

"Having a photo of her by your bed probably helps."

Cash stared blankly past the sofa toward his bedroom and nodded.

"You know something?" Wynter chuckled softly. "I feel like watching *Rocky* now. I bet Jake or Quinn has it on tape."

Cash glanced at the clock on the stove. "I don't think they'd like to be woken up at four in the morning to watch *Rocky*."

"Probably not."

Cash rubbed his face in an attempt to clear his head of revisited grief. "So, why didn't it work? Any ideas?"

"I don't know exactly," Wynter said. "For all we know, it might only work with Ransom."

"Or it doesn't work at all."

"Don't be a downer, okay?"

Cash sighed and laid back on the sofa and rested his head on his raised arm. "I don't mean to be. Except it *is* a possibility."

"Let's leave it as the last possibility," Wynter said. "I think we should do another test."

"Not with Sierra, okay? Seeing her is really hard for me and making her a dreamwaker, even for a little while, would be..." Cash swallowed hard. "Can you imagine what it would do to my dad?"

"I guess in a way it's good that it didn't work."

"I guess."

"I have to try it with Quinn or Jake." Wynter rested her forearms on the sofa cushion and balanced her chin on them, her dark irises searching for his. "We could all meet up after work."

"Okay." Cash yawned, causing his whole body to shudder for a second. "I hate to be boring, but I need to sleep. I got to get up in two hours."

Wynter stood, kissing Cash's forehead lightly on the way. "I hope you have better dreams."

"Thanks, but I hope I don't dream at all." Cash rolled onto his side, his face inches from the sofa's backrest.

Wynter padded back to Cash's bedroom, pausing at the door

and looking back at the sofa. "Goodnight, Cash," she whispered across the room.

Cash responded with soft sounds of snoring. His train to dreamland had already left.

Wynter slid under the cool sheets of Cash's bed. She caught his clean scent on his pillow, probably Head and Shoulders shampoo. Her body relaxed and freed her mind to think about her episode with Sierra. Maybe there was something she could do differently next time.

She hoped there would be a next time.

Jezebel Too's eyes glinted in the moonlit shadows of Roxy's bedroom. "Who's it going to be?"

Roxy sat on her bed, her back against the headboard and her knees pulled up to her chest. She shook the cobwebs of her own fractured sleep out of her head. "What?"

"God you're slow. I said—"

"Fuck you," Roxy said, her eyelids narrowing at her. "I was asleep a minute ago. Give me a break."

Jezebel Too scanned the bedroom and picked up the baton Roxy had hit her with two nights earlier. "I'll give you a break, right down the middle of your head. Now who's your dreamwaker going to be?"

"No one. I can't do that shit."

"Stop stalling," Jezebel Too said. "I wouldn't be here if you couldn't do it."

"Sorry, can't." Roxy shook her head.

Jezebel Too gritted her teeth, her desire to choke the life out of Roxy rising in the back of her mind in angry red flashes. "You've kissed Ransom. I know because I was there."

"That was Jezebel, not you."

"Yeah, whatever." Jezebel Too pulled the rubber tip off one end of the baton. "You kissed him. That means you can make a dreamwaker. So who's it going to be?" She placed the exposed metal end of the baton under Roxy's chin and pushed.

Roxy gasped and discovered that she could not speak or swallow. She grabbed the baton's shaft and pulled it away, working against Jezebel Too's considerable strength. Once able to move her jaw, she uttered the first name that came to her head. "Jake."

Jezebel Too lowered the baton in surprise and started to laugh. "Jake? That scrawny Nintendo nerd?"

"Yeah. So?"

"Whatever," Jezebel Too said. "You like them young and hairless."

"Fuck off."

"We'll see about that, won't we." Jezebel Too grabbed Roxy's shirt by the collar and pulled her nose to nose. "Now, you're going to dream of him. And when you do, grab hold and bring him back."

"What if I can't dream of him?" Roxy said. "What if it doesn't work?"

"Then it might be your last dream."

Roxy blinked at her, confused. "What does that mean? Is that a threat?"

"I don't think you want to find out," Jezebel Too said. "Now go and dream of little Jake. Your life depends on it. I'll be right here... watching."

"Jesus, no pressure," Roxy whispered to herself. She rolled away from Jezebel Too, trying her best to ignore her, and closed her eyes.

ROXY HAD DOUBTS that she'd be able to fall asleep, especially with Jezebel Too sitting mere feet away from her. But waking from a deep sleep had its advantages. Her mind ached to return to dreamland. As soon as she closed her eyes, her body resumed where it left off. She concentrated on Jake as sleep overtook her in an attempt to make him appear in her dream. Roxy had no intention of waking without him and forcing Jezebel Too's hand. The dream was hers. Everything was under her control.

Roxy blinked and found herself in the Barracuda, the engine idling quietly in the middle of her street. A few feet from the front bumper stood Jake, balanced on a pair of crutches, his left leg in a cast. Behind him, that annoying bitch Quinn leaned out of her candy-ass Volkswagen, yelling incomprehensible noise.

Roxy pushed open the driver's side door and stepped out onto the asphalt. It was warm on the soles of her bare feet, and she could smell hints of tar rising from the road after a day in the August sun.

"Hey." Roxy stepped toward Jake, her bare legs covered just above her knees by a long football-style T-shirt with "85" on the front. She ran her sweaty hands over her hips to dry them and to remind herself if she was wearing panties underneath. She was.

"Hey." Jake's eyes flicked to the silhouette of her thighs cast on her shirt from the 'Cuda's headlights. "What are you doing out here?"

Roxy's mind raced a mile a minute. "I wanted to talk to you."

"Yeah?" Jake smiled. "Cool."

It was now or never. She closed the gap between them, took Jake's face in her hands, and kissed him. Quinn erupted and burst out of her little VW, yelling obscenities that Roxy had no interest in.

She raised her middle finger and blew on it. Quinn and her ugly little car flew backward like they had been pulled into a hurricane and vanished in a plume of glowing smoke.

Basking in the silence, Roxy smirked. "That's better."

Jake turned his head. "Wait, where did Quinn go?"

"Forget her." Roxy grabbed Jake's Nintendo baseball cap and tossed it aside.

"Hey, that's my hat," Jake said. "I want it back."

"You look better without it."

"Uh, okay." Jake returned a vacant gaze and smiled.

"I've liked you for a long time, Jake, way longer than *Quinn*." Roxy tugged at the hem of her T-shirt with nervous fists. "I never told anyone. Once I started hanging out with Jezebel, our paths never seemed to cross." She looked up at him and bit her lower lip. "Did you ever think about me?"

Jake nodded. "Yeah, sure."

Roxy tipped up on her toes and as she kissed him again, she pushed his crutches away. They vaporized before they hit the asphalt.

"Hey, I'm going to need those."

Roxy shook her head and stepped back. "I don't think so."

Jake glanced down at his left leg. His cast was gone, and his bare leg peeked through the ripped denim instead. His brows furrowed in confusion. "How did you do that?"

"Wouldn't you like to know." Roxy stepped backward, inching toward the front bumper of the Barracuda. She curled her index finger at him. "I got an idea. You coming?"

Jake glanced back again to where Quinn and her VW used to be. "What did you do to Q—"

"Who cares about her?" Roxy continued to beckon him. "It's just you and me now. Just like it should be."

Jake stared at her, entranced by her gaze. "Okay." He placed weight on his left leg and laughed. "Wicked. That cast was a pain in the ass."

The back of Roxy's calves touched the front bumper. "What can I say? I'm magical. Now, come here."

Jake quickened his pace and met her at the front of the car, the left headlight blocked by their bodies. Roxy scooted up onto the hood and parted her legs, letting the engine's heat and vibration flow through her body, awakening every nerve. She pulled Jake's body close and kissed him again. Together they rocked back onto the hood of the Barracuda.

Jezebel's Barracuda.

Fighting against their heated connection was the reason for dreaming of Jake in the first place. She had to bring him back and make him a dreamwaker. Because Jezebel said so.

Well, screw Jezebel. She could wait. Just a few moments more couldn't hurt, could it? Roxy helped Jake fumble with his belt and zipper until she heard the buckle jangle on the asphalt. She could feel his excitement through his underwear, pressing hard against her thigh.

With a trembling hand, she pulled the gusset of her panties to one side. This was it. Jezebel wasn't going to take this moment from her. "Come on, Jake," she whispered.

Jake knew what to do instinctively, despite his subdued reaction. He slid her hips down the hood and guided himself inside her. Overhead, the stars swirled in the sky and the Barracuda's engine began to rev rhythmically as if their moving bodies were working the gas pedal from outside the car.

"This could all be real, Jake," Roxy whispered into his ear. "Wouldn't that be great? You and me, together, for real?"

"This isn't real?" Jake said between hot breaths. "Sure feels real."

Roxy took Jake's face in her hands and kissed him. "Hold on to me and don't let go."

"I won't." Jake pulled Roxy's hips close and kissed her neck. She closed her eyes and felt the world spin and twist. She clutched Jake's T-shirt and pulled him against her body, unwilling to let him go.

A jolt caused both of them to open their eyes.

"Did you feel that?" Jake looked at her in surprise.

"Mmm hmm." Roxy kissed him, their bodies still moving as

one, until her eyes wandered past his head. The swirls that used to be stars moments before focused into the twisted strands of her shag carpet. She was on top of him, and the Barracuda was gone.

The light on Roxy's dresser switched on. She looked up and saw Jezebel Too sitting against the headboard of her bed.

"Finally. Was beginning to think that you'd screwed up, just like you always do."

Roxy glared at her from below. "Well, I didn't this time."

"Good job." Jezebel Too smiled lasciviously at her. "How is he? Can video game nerds fuck or what? Maybe I should try him out."

"Who're you talking to?" Jake twisted his head around but couldn't see past the edge of Roxy's bed. "Who is that?"

"Jezebel," Roxy said, resting her face on Jake's chest as the passion of the moment drained away.

"What? Jezebel's here too?"

"Shush." Roxy shifted her position on top of Jake and sat up. "He's a dreamwaker now. Happy? Now leave us alone."

Jezebel Too narrowed her eyes at her. "Sorry, no can do."

"What's a dreamwaker?" Jake said, confused.

Jezebel Too laughed. "Looks like he's missing some brain cells. That could work in our favor." She swung her legs off the side of the bed and planted a foot on either side of Jake's head. "Makes sense since he came from *your* dream."

"Go, JT," Roxy said. "Now."

"Nope." Jezebel Too shook her head and raised the broken shaft of Roxy's baton. While Roxy had been sleeping, she had snapped the end off leaving a sharp metal edge. "There's one more thing you got to do."

Roxy rolled her eyes. "Jesus... What now?"

"You're a murderer and you need practice."

Jake looked up at Roxy. "Who's a murderer?"

Roxy ignored him, knowing what Jezebel Too was going to say and afraid of it at the same time. She shook her head slowly.

"Yup," Jezebel Too said. "You fucked him. Now you got to kill him."

"No."

Jake's eyes darted around the room. "Who's killing who?"

"I had a feeling you'd pussy out." Jezebel Too slapped the sharp end of the baton into her palm where it left bloodied puncture marks. "Either *you* kill him, or I kill *you.*"

"Maybe I'll kill you first," Roxy hissed.

Jezebel Too shrugged. "I'm immortal, idiot. I'll come back and get you when you least expect it."

Roxy glanced down at Jake and swallowed hard. The reality of the situation dawned on him, and he shook his head.

"Don't do it, Roxy," he said, tears already welling in his eyes.

"God. Put the fucking pansy out of his misery already."

"SHUT UP!"

Jezebel Too leaned forward, pointing the jagged and bloodied end of the baton at Roxy. "The sooner you do it, the sooner I leave."

Roxy faced Jake and focused all her attention on him, blocking out Jezebel Too, her weapon, and her threats. "You're a dreamwaker, Jake. You're not real."

"I'm not?" Jake struggled to understand.

"No. You're from my dreams." Roxy wiped a tear from her cheek. "I'm going to send you back there so we can be alone." She placed her hands on both sides of his face and kissed him. "Do you trust me?"

Jake nodded.

"It won't hurt." Roxy had begun to roll Jake over when Jezebel Too stopped her.

"Look him in the eyes when you do it."

Roxy's face burned with anger. "I hope you rot in hell."

"Wherever I end up, you'll be right beside me," Jezebel Too said.

Jake bucked out from under Roxy but didn't get far. "I don't want to die."

Roxy scrambled on all fours toward him and straddled him again, leaning in close. "You're not going to die," she whispered. "You're just going back into my head for a while."

Jake stared up at her, uncertainty on his face.

"Don't be afraid." Roxy's trembling hand moved from his face to his neck. "Wait for me."

Jake nodded, his voice almost inaudible. "Okay."

Jezebel Too nudged Roxy with her foot. "Get on with it already. Jesus. It's not like he's real or anything."

"Back the fuck off." Roxy gritted her teeth at Jezebel Too, then returned her attention to Jake. "I'm sorry." Her words had barely left her mouth as she tightened both hands around Jake's neck and directed all her weight into her grasp.

Jake seemed to flatten into the carpet, odd clicking sounds floating from his gaping mouth. His fear turned to acceptance as his eyes glazed over.

Tears rolled off Roxy's nose and greased her hands as they twisted against Jake's neck. Time stood still as seconds morphed to minutes. No matter what Jezebel Too forced her to do, she'd never let herself get used to killing. It was ugly and difficult, and left her shattered, both mentally and physically.

Jake's eyes dulled and emitted a blue energy that expanded in waves, encompassing his body, head to toe. A second later he was gone. Roxy slumped forward, exhausted for all the wrong reasons. And she blamed Jezebel Too for it all.

"Took you long enough." Jezebel Too picked at the dried blood on the jagged end of the baton. "Maybe don't choke him next time."

Rage consumed Roxy. She leaped onto her bed and ripped the baton from Jezebel Too's hands. "That was *my* dream, you bitch! You have no right telling me what to do." She positioned the sharpened end against the center of Jezebel Too's chest.

Jezebel Too shook her head, paying no attention to the makeshift weapon in Roxy's hands. "You know you'll always be Bonnie. I'll always be Clyde. You're forever tied to me, Rox."

"Fuck you." Roxy raised the baton over her head, her muscles tensed and ready to plunge the end through Jezebel Too's chest when a rock bounced off the bedroom window, distracting them both.

"You're getting better," Jezebel Too said. "You almost killed me without even thinking about it."

"Trust me. I was definitely thinking about it." Roxy dropped the baton, went to the window, and peered down to the driveway.

"That's first degree murder," Jezebel Too said. "I'm impressed."

"Shut up."

A second stone struck the window. Jezebel Too stood beside Roxy. "Who the hell is it?" She placed her forehead to the window.

On the driveway below stood Monty. He pointed to the front door and mouthed the words, "Let me in."

"He'll break your window soon," Jezebel Too said. "What are you waiting for?"

Why was Monty here, especially now? Roxy wanted answers even though he was a loose cannon that couldn't be controlled with a baton through the heart. She padded as quietly as she could down the stairs and unlocked the front door. Jezebel Too followed her, the baton held tightly in her fist.

Roxy retracted the deadbolt and cracked open the front door. Monty stood on the front stoop grinning and gnawing a wad of gum, his mirrored sunglasses reflecting back the front entryway of Roxy's house.

Roxy glanced back up the stairs and listened for parental stirrings from the second floor. She lowered her voice to an annoyed whisper. "What the hell are you doing here?"

"I was in the neighborhood." Monty snapped his gum and let

his eyes take in Roxy's bare legs. "Thought I'd drop by." He motioned at Jezebel Too. "Can't sleep, *Jazz?*"

"Something like that," Jezebel Too said.

"Can't imagine why."

"Hey. Asshole." Roxy's voice crept up in volume. "*Why* are you here?"

"Did you try my generous sample?"

Roxy gave him a sideways look and furrowed her brow. "What sample?"

"Two weeks ago, I—"

"He means that fucking rock cocaine shit, remember?" Jezebel Too slapped Roxy's shoulder. "No, we didn't try it and no, we're not going to sell it for you. Now get the fuck out of here or we'll call the cops."

"Really, *Jazz?*" Monty slid his sunglasses down so she could feel his stare. "You're going to call the cops *on me?*"

Jezebel Too shrugged. "Just give me a phone."

Monty reseated his sunglasses shook his head in disbelief. "I know about the taxi driver, *Jazz*. I have photos."

Jezebel Too dropped the baton on the tiled entryway floor, the metal clang echoing into the recesses of the house.

"What's he talking about Jez—" Roxy faced Jezebel Too and found her face had paled in the moonlight, her earlier cockiness replaced by fear. She'd had no idea Jezebel Too could be afraid of anything. "What'd you do?"

"Nothing." Jezebel Too stepped back into the entryway.

"And it'll stay *nothing* as long as you start selling my rock." Monty spat his gum into the entryway and smiled smugly, knowing he had them both over a barrel. "Last I heard, Finn's is crawlin' with cops, most of 'em from Halston."

"Close the door, Rox."

"What'd you do, Jazz?"

Jezebel Too grabbed the baton and ran back up the stairs. Roxy moved to close the door, but Monty braced it open with one arm and pulled her hips to his with the other. He moved his hand over one of her butt cheeks and squeezed.

Roxy recoiled from his advance. The smell of sour sweat mixed with cigarettes and Drakkar Noir rose from his body in putrid waves.

"Fuckin' tease." Monty forced his words through clenched teeth. "Both of you. My place. Five o'clock, or Anson's goin' to get a mountain of photos that only have one explanation." He released her, raised his hands palms up, and backed toward the street. "Your choice."

Roxy bolted the door closed. "Jazz, what did you do?" she whispered as she ascended the stairs. She found Jezebel Too sitting in one corner of her room, her knees pulled tight against her chest.

Roxy sat and faced her. "Spill it."

And uncharacteristically, Jezebel Too did just that.

FOLLOWING HER FAILURE to make Sierra a dreamwaker the previous night, Wynter's sleep proved elusive. Instead, she went round in circles in her mind trying to figure out a reason why she couldn't pull Sierra into the real world. By the time Cash woke up and began rattling around in the kitchen, she was no closer to an answer.

After breakfast, Wynter accompanied Cash as he made his way to work. The field outside Cash's trailer dampened their shoes with morning dew.

"Still want to meet up with Quinn and Jake after work?"

Cash nodded, but with less enthusiasm than usual. "I know you want to try that test again." His eyes seemed to search the horizon for an unseen object... or person.

Wynter placed her hand on Cash's shoulder. He flinched, even though her touch had been gentle. "Sorry... are you okay?"

Cash sighed. "It's not you."

"Sierra?"

"Yeah."

"I'm sorry Cash," Wynter said. "I should've realized that seeing your sister again would be hard."

"It was, but it wasn't all bad." He turned to her and offered a brief smile of genuine happiness. "I built Mighty Mick's Gym for her after you left."

"I was going to ask."

"It was pretty good too, considering that I've only seen *Rocky* once. Plus, Sierra helped a lot."

"I'm sorry I didn't stick around to see it."

As the two of them left the field and ascended toward the Main Street Overpass, the neon sign of Finn's rose in the distance.

"Do you know about the Rainbow Bridge?"

Wynter thought for a moment. "Isn't that where a pet goes when they die?"

"Yeah, when they cross into Heaven," Cash said. "Mighty Mick's is Sierra's Rainbow Bridge. If it hadn't been for last night, I wouldn't have made the connection. So, thanks for that."

"It was your dream, Cash."

"But it was you who suggested changing the ring to a gym."

Wynter smiled and kicked a rock across Main Street as they headed for the overpass. "That's true. I guess I should definitely see the movie now, eh?" She looked up to find Cash staring into the distance, his concerned face pale in the morning light. "Cash? What is it?"

She followed his gaze to Finn's Gas N Go. Four police vehicles had parked haphazardly on the street and in front of the garage, light bars flashing red, white, and blue. One was Anson's white Suburban. Yellow crime scene tape ran from the garage doors, around the gas pumps, to the tree next to the parking spots, and back to the building.

"Finn!" Cash burst into a sprint.

Wynter followed but was no match for Cash's speed.

Anson spotted Cash's frenzied approach and intercepted him at the sidewalk in front of the garage. "Easy, Cash."

"Where's Finn?" Cash craned his neck side to side, scanning the area. "Is he okay?"

"Finn's fine," Anson said, blocking Cash's attempts to get past him. "You got to stay behind the tape."

Wynter caught up to Cash. "What's going on?" she asked between breaths.

"There's been a murder."

"What?" Cash renewed his struggle to get past Anson. "Who is it? Who died?"

"I can't tell you anything else." Anson guided Cash into the street. "If you cross the tape, I'll arrest you. Understand?"

Cash swallowed hard and nodded. "Let me talk to Finn."

"Finn went home," Anson said. "I suggest you do the same."

Wynter approached the police line and shifted her point of view. The taxi parked next to the store had its driver's side door open. A human figure shrouded with an orange tarp sat on the ground by the open door. Two lifeless legs poked out. She gasped, placed her hands over her mouth, and backed away.

"You, too, Wynter." Anson waved her over. "Go to Lucy's and eat something. Tell her to put it on my tab." He scribbled something on a business card and handed it to Wynter. "Now go, both of you."

As Cash and Wynter turned to leave, another SUV rolled up to the curb, "McLeod County Coroner" written on the side panels. Anson greeted the coroner and ushered her past the police tape.

Cash stopped and glanced back at the station. "This is the weirdest day off I've ever had."

Anson reseated his hat and pointed at him. "Go."

"Come on, Cash," Wynter said. "Anson's paying for our second breakfast." She tapped the front pocket of her shorts.

AT FIVE MINUTES TO FIVE, Roxy parked the Barracuda in front of a run-down bungalow on the southern town limits of Newhaven. Similar to Jezebel's house several streets north, regular upkeep had been ignored in favor of a lifestyle of reckless abandon. Monty's Fiat sat parked in the weed-infested driveway.

Roxy threw the car into park and killed the engine. "I can't believe you murdered someone, like for real. You're the one who fucked up royally this time."

"If you keep bringing it up, I might have to shut *you* up permanently," Jezebel Too said. "I came close before. I could do it again."

"Bullshit. You'd never kill your right hand." Roxy glanced at her and shook her head in disgust. "You don't have the balls. Not anymore."

Jezebel Too ignored her and surveyed the overgrown front yard. "Jesus. If people knew about this shithole, no one would buy from Monty."

"I doubt it," Roxy said. "Addiction's a powerful thing."

"You some kind of brainiac all of a sudden? Whatever. Let's get this over with." Jezebel Too stepped out of the car. "We need that fucking camera."

"Because you were a fucking idiot." Roxy slid her hand down the smooth lines of the Barracuda's hood, at once reminded of her recent dream of Jake and the forced aftermath. Anger simmered in the back of her mind.

The two of them walked down the crumbling driveway, cracks

spidering in all directions. Jezebel Too veered off toward the front porch.

"What the hell are you doing? He said to knock on the *back* door."

Jezebel Too ascended the steps to the front porch. "Why does it matter? He needs us. Rules don't apply."

"Monty's set in his ways," Roxy said. "I don't want to piss him off. Come on." She continued down the driveway along the side of the house to the postage stamp-sized back yard.

Jezebel Too shook her head and followed. "Jesus. You're such a tight-ass." She caught up to Roxy at the back door. "He wouldn't do anything to us. He doesn't have the balls."

Roxy side-eyed her and knocked on the door. A moment later, the locks disengaged and Monty pulled the door open enough to fit his head through. Surprisingly he wasn't wearing his mirrors.

"You came alone, right?" He eyed them both, his gaze lingering a little longer on Roxy. "You weren't followed?"

Jezebel Too laughed. "Paranoid much?"

"I can never be too careful," Monty said. "Especially with people I don't trust."

Jezebel Too dropped her jaw and widened her eyes mockingly. "What, you don't *trust* us? I'm hurt."

"We weren't followed," Roxy said.

Monty poked his head past the door frame and glanced side to side. "You sure?"

"Look, I'm not an expert at avoiding cops, but they're probably all tied up with that murder." Roxy shot a look at Jezebel Too.

"Yeah. The *murder.* You got a point." Monty stepped back into the house and swung the door wide.

Roxy and Jezebel Too entered a kitchen in a similar array of dirt and disarray as the yard. Jezebel Too began rifling through the cupboards.

"Got anything to eat? I'm starving."

Monty pushed her back toward a round kitchen table with four rickety chairs around it. "Sit."

Jezebel Too resisted for a moment, then took a chair across from where Roxy had already taken a seat.

"You got to try before you buy, right? I'll be back in a sec," Monty said. "Don't move." He walked out of the room, down a hallway, and into an adjoining room.

Jezebel Too looked under the table, then scanned the kitchen. "Did you see his camera anywhere?"

"Forget about it."

"Fuck you." Jezebel Too stood and tiptoed around the kitchen. "It's not *your* face in those pictures." She looked in a couple of cupboards, then crept down the hallway, turning left into the living room.

"Goddammit." Roxy followed as quietly as possible. The living room extended along one side of the house, ending in a large window with rotted curtains drawn. A large modern television and entertainment center sat in the corner closest to the window. A ratty and cracked leather sectional surrounded a glass coffee table covered in beer cans, several ashtrays, and a small hand mirror. All that was missing was the razor blade and a straw.

"He's such a cliché," Roxy whispered quietly to Jezebel Too.

A bookcase along one wall was filled with an assortment of trinkets and curios that didn't fit the theme of "small-time drug dealer."

"How many ceramic pigs does one person need?" Roxy whispered. "It's like someone old lived here and Monty just moved in without changing a thing."

"Got it!" Jezebel Too held up the SLR camera by its strap, complete with telephoto lens.

"Great." Roxy navigated around piles of garage sale kitsch toward the kitchen. "Let's go."

She was met with silence.

Roxy turned to see Jezebel Too on the opposite side of the

living room and headed out the second entry to the room. "What are you *doing?* Let's GO."

Jezebel Too shushed her. "Just a sec," she said as she disappeared into the central hallway.

"JT, wait!" she whispered too late. "Shit." Roxy had two choices: backtrack to the kitchen like a coward or follow Jezebel Too wherever the hell she went. She decided to follow and hustled carefully around the clutter toward the entry where Jezebel Too had disappeared moments before.

As if she knew Roxy was following her, Jezebel Too reappeared, stepping gingerly on the balls of her feet and wearing a grin a mile wide. The camera was still in her hand. "Let's book," she whispered.

Roxy studied her with concern. Jezebel Too was even more a wild card than her non-dreamwaker half. "What did you do?"

"No time." Jezebel Too pushed by Roxy. "Come on. This place stinks like ass."

"Not so fast." Monty's voice echoed from the central hallway.

The two girls froze halfway across the room. Roxy gave Jezebel Too a sideways look. "JT? What the hell did you do?"

"Yeah, what *did* you do, *Jazz.*" The muzzle of a .38 snubnose pushed past the second entry, leveled at Jezebel Too's head. "You don't listen too well, do you?" Monty appeared from the darkened hallway and scowled at them both, his eyes flicking to the camera in Jezebel Too's hand. "You see why I got trust issues? Now drop the camera on the couch and back the fuck up. Slowly."

Jezebel Too tightened her clutch on the strap to the camera. "You're not going to pull the trigger. I doubt you've even shot anyone."

"Shut up, JT," Roxy said through gritted teeth as she inched toward the rear of the living room.

Monty shot a quick glance at Roxy, then returned attention to Jezebel Too. "JT? Is that what she's callin' you now?" He pulled the hammer back with his thumb. "Well, *JT.* I don't like you. Never have."

"Feeling's mutual," Jezebel Too said. "And now you're extorting us under gunpoint to sell drugs for you. Well, fuck y—"

"I got my gun on you 'cause you been SNOOPIN' where you don't belong!" Monty's aiming arm trembled with anger.

Jezebel Too glanced at Roxy, rolled her eyes, and laughed. "You're pretty stupid if you thought I'd be a good girl and sit in the kitchen waiting for you... Wait. That's right. You *are* stupid. What kind of idiot leaves a camera with evidence on it in full view?"

"JT, let's just go." Roxy said.

"NO ONE'S GOIN' ANYWHERE." Monty alternated his aim between Jezebel Too and Roxy.

Roxy raised her hands above her head.

"What? You're afraid of this clown?" Jezebel Too backed across the living room to where Roxy stood. "He's not going to shoot us, Rox. He couldn't shoot a fly."

Monty aimed at the ceiling and fired, blasting a fist sized hole in the plaster and making the girls jump. The gunshot amplified to a deafening level in the small room. The power of his weapon was clear. "Back into the kitchen, you fuckin' bitches."

"Jesus Christ, Monty. You're crazy." The odor of cordite stung Roxy's nose. She worked at one of her ear canals with a finger as she backed out of the living and into the kitchen. "If I'm deaf, I'm going to—"

"Shut the fuck up and MOVE." Monty waved the gun at them.

"Just do it, Rox." Jezebel Too had her hands up now as well, the camera dangling by its strap from a white-knuckled fist.

Both girls found themselves standing in the kitchen, the back of their thighs against the table.

"Give me the camera," Monty said.

Jezebel Too sent Roxy a knowing glance, then squared her body towards him. "No, fuck face."

Monty cocked the gun's hammer and stepped to within a foot of Jezebel Too, aiming the muzzle at the center of her chest.

Jezebel Too stepped forward and pushed her chest against the muzzle. "Do it, then. Pull the fucking trigger."

Beads of sweat dripped from Monty's brow. He looked at Roxy and saw her fearful eyes locked on the gun.

"What are you waiting for, *tough guy*." Jezebel Too brought her free hand down and wrapped it around Monty's, pulling the gun's muzzle tighter against her sternum. "Pull the trigger. Show us how much of a *man* you are."

Monty and Jezebel Too faced off, each unwilling to budge.

"Just let us go," Roxy said. "We don't want to sell your drugs."

The tendons in Monty's jaws stood out in angry cords. He disengaged the gun's hammer, pulled it out of Jezebel Too's hand, and stepped back.

"Would you look at that, Rox?" Jezebel Too shoved her free hand in her pocket. "I told you old shit-for-brains didn't have the balls."

Monty tucked the gun into the waistband of his pants.

"Careful," Jezebel Too said. "Don't finish off the rest of your manhood."

Monty stepped back and crossed his arms, resting himself against the counter. "You think you're so smart, *Jazz*."

"Smarter than you."

"Are you letting us go?" Roxy lowered her arms part way.

Monty shrugged at her.

Jezebel Too dropped her hand and the camera swung at her side as she turned for the door.

"You'll pay that camera off, *Jazz*. Both of you will. One way or another," Monty said.

Jezebel Too ignored him and pulled open the door. "Let's go. I'm tired of dickless assholes." Roxy followed her out.

"By the way, there's no film in it."

Jezebel Too froze as she crossed the door's threshold to the outside. Looking over her shoulder, she narrowed her eyes at him. "Bullshit."

Monty crossed his arms and regarded them smugly. "I'm not as stupid as you think."

Jezebel Too stormed out of the house and back to the Barracuda. "Give me the keys."

Roxy hustled to keep up as she dug out the keys from her pocket and tossed them over the hood. "You think he's bluffing?"

Jezebel Too swung the camera around and smashed it on the driveway. The telephoto lens cracked and the film door in the back popped open, empty. No canister of film rolled out. "Fuck!"

Monty's laughter rose from the back yard as he stepped into view at the side of the house. "Who's the idiot now, *Jazz?*"

Jezebel Too hopped behind into the driver's seat, started the engine, slammed it into drive. Roxy made it into the passenger seat just in time before the Barracuda shot forward and away from the curb.

Through the open window the girls could hear Monty laughing his last words. "You'll be back, bitches!"

Jezebel Too gripped the steering wheel as the Barracuda tore down the road.

"Might want to slow down," Roxy said. "Anson's probably looking for us."

"Why?" Jezebel Too's eyed her wildly. "He's got nothing." She turned left onto Main Street and followed the road north to the I94 on-ramp.

"But the photos. What if Monty goes to Anson with them?"

"He won't," Jezebel Too said. "He thinks he has more power over me holding on to the photos. But I have something better."

Roxy scrunched her brow in thought. "What?"

"I know where his stash is."

Roxy's eyes went wide. "Wicked! Where?"

"Why should I tell you?"

"Um..." Roxy chewed at her thumbnail in a moment of

insecurity until she snapped fingers and said, "I need something to bargain with. In case Monty does something else stupid to you... or Jezebel. Or to me."

Jezebel Too considered the idea. "Not bad, Rox."

"Thank you very much." Roxy smiled, pleased with herself. "So, where's his stash?"

"There's an old vacuum cleaner in the corner of a room off the hallway," Jezebel Too said. "Looked like an Electro*sux*. I saw him dig through the stash, inside where the vacuum bag should go."

"Huh. Good hiding place. Mega weird, too." Roxy looked out the windshield at the two lanes of highway traffic headed east. "Where the hell are we going?"

"Who knows? Right now, anywhere's better than Newhaven," Jezebel Too said. "Let's go chill somewhere."

Roxy nodded and smiled. "Brill." She turned to bump fists and watched in horror as Jezebel Too drifted in a bolt of blue energized light.

Roxy glanced at the speedometer. The needle had crossed past sixty-five miles per hour and without a foot on the gas, the car began to slow... and inch into the righthand lane.

There were cars in front and behind her, all going highway speed. Roxy had no time to think. She unbuckled her seatbelt and pushed herself over the center console butt first. The shoelaces on her left foot snagged on the shifter and while she struggled to free herself, she nudged the steering wheel causing the car to swerve and change direction, drifting toward the grassy median that separated the highway.

A vehicle following behind blasted its horn, frazzling the few nerves Roxy had left. Still, she managed to steady the car with her left hand on the wheel and reached forward with her right, pulling loose the laces on her left shoe. But the laces had snagged in a knot.

"Fuck!" Alternating her eyes back and forth from the road to her left foot, she used the toe of her right shoe and forced her left shoe off her foot. It flew across the car, bounced off the passenger door and settled in the footwell.

Her left foot slid free and she tucked her leg into the foot well. She found the gas pedal and accelerated to fifty-five miles per hour. Operating the gas with her left foot in socks felt strange but it would have to do.

Her right leg remained spread and sprawled across the center console and the passenger seat. All the years she had taken gymnastics as a kid had finally paid off.

If only Jezebel could see me now.

Roxy signaled right, changed lanes, and switched on the hazard blinkers. She moved her foot to the brakes and in less than a minute, the Barracuda sat idling on the ample shoulder of the interstate.

"Holy fucking shit." She shifted into park and tried to relax, even though her body was still revving on adrenaline. Panicked sweat had soaked through her clothes. "Note to self. Never let a dreamwaker drive."

After her heart had returned to its normal rhythm, Roxy sorted out the knot in her shoe, returned it to her foot, and continued east until she found an overpass that allowed her to change direction. The last thing she wanted to do was end up in Halston.

Twenty minutes later, she found herself crawling back into bed to sleep off the chaos of the afternoon. Roxy hoped it had all been worth it. She closed her eyes and thought of Jake. This time her dream would stay a dream.

ANSON SAT RECLINED at his desk back at the station. Laid out in front of him was all the evidence he had on Jezebel: a melted jerry can, a 9mm shell casing, a blackened Zippo, and a 9mm pistol.

The items were all protected within sealed and signed plastic bags of various sizes. Even through the plastic, the jerry can leached its melted plastic and gasoline odor into his office.

Set to one side in a signed and sealed manila envelope was the switchblade the coroner had pulled from the cabbie's chest earlier in the day. Beside that were several photographs of the victim and surrounding crime scene details. He examined a close-up photograph of the switchblade. The weapon looked familiar.

Anson pulled out one of his desk drawers and took out the switchblade he had confiscated from Jezebel two weeks ago when he had arrested her for running Quinn off the road. The knife wasn't evidence and Jezebel had never asked for it back. He set the switchblade next to the photograph.

They were identical. Anson sat up and gave each weapon a closer look to make sure.

Jezebel killed the cabbie?

It didn't make any sense. He had talked with Jezebel in the hospital two days ago and she was in no condition to walk, let alone murder someone. The coincidence was compelling, but coincidence didn't prove guilt and as much as he wanted a connection, he couldn't prove that Jezebel was responsible.

Anson stood, stretched, and left his office to pour himself a coffee, closing the door behind him. The day had been rough. Murders were rare in Newhaven. In the two decades he had been a member of the police department here, he could count the number of murders on two hands, maybe one.

It was close to six o'clock and Sadie sat at her desk finishing up some paperwork. Everyone else had gone home. Anson filled his mug and stirred in a teaspoon of sugar.

"How you holding up?"

Sadie looked up at him and set her pen down. "Okay, I guess."

Anson sipped his coffee. "First murder?"

Sadie nodded. "I just don't get why someone would do that to another person."

"There's probably a thousand reasons why," Anson said, "But I couldn't begin to guess."

"Got to be pretty bent in the head."

"Damn straight." Anson returned to his office door. "You should head home. Whatever you're working on can be left 'til tomorrow."

"I'm almost done." Sadie returned her pen to paper.

"Fair enough, but not too late." He raised a brow at her.

Sadie smiled and nodded.

Anson returned to his office and stepped to the window, sipping the hot brew. It tasted bitter, like it had been sitting on the burner all afternoon. He contemplated making a fresh pot.

He heard a snap and crinkle of paper behind him. Anson turned and quickly inventoried the evidence on his desk. Everything was just as he had left it but there was a faint odor of ozone hanging in the air. He examined the evidence bags once more before realizing the envelope for the switchblade was empty.

He held the envelope up to the overhead fluorescents. The silhouette revealed only congealed blood in the shape of the knife's blade.

"What the hell?"

The impossibility of what he was seeing clashed in his mind with the physical certainty of the empty evidence envelope in his hand and what he had seen and touched moments earlier. Anson dropped the envelope, scratched his head, and scanned his office. Nothing looked out of place, but now a vital piece of evidence in a murder investigation was gone under his watch. This would look bad—very bad.

He stepped to his office door. "Sadie, you didn't see anyone go into my office, did you?"

She looked up, her face twisted in confusion. "We... were just talking. We're the only ones here."

"Yeah. Shit. I could have sworn..." Anson glanced back at his desk. The envelope for the switchblade still laid there empty.

"Maybe *you* should be going home instead of me."

"Yeah, maybe."

Sadie tilted her head as she studied him. "Anson? You feeling alright?"

"Uh..." Anson rubbed his temples, then waved her into his office.

"What is it?"

Anson took a breath. "Look, this is going to sound crazy, but tell me what you see." He pointed at the manila envelope.

Sadie stepped around his desk to get a better look and reached for the corner of the envelope.

"Don't touch it!"

Sadie pulled back her hand like she had brushed against a hot stove. "It's not going to bite. What's gotten into you?"

Anson just stared at her.

"I can't tell you what's in it without picking it up." She tweezed a corner with her thumb and index finger and held it up, feeling the weight. "Doesn't feel like there's anything in it." Sadie held it up to the light. "Nothing, except blood... in the shape of a knife."

"Shit. I was afraid you'd say that," Anson said. "Do you smell anything weird? Like ozone?"

A perplexed expression filled her face. She flipped the envelope over and sniffed it before setting it down on the desk. "All I smell is gasoline."

"Goddammit. Not five minutes ago, there was a switchblade in that envelope. The murder weapon," Anson said. "I signed and sealed that envelope this morning at Finn's, I swear to God."

"Where did it go?"

Anson shook his head slowly, his eyes falling into a vacant stare. "No clue."

"Do you have any idea how crazy that sounds?"

Anson crumpled into his chair. "Halston is going to shit bricks."

Sadie's eyes went to the other switchblade on his desk. "What's that?"

"It's not the murder weapon, if that's what you're thinking." Anson picked the switchblade up, engaged the blade, then retracted it. "I lifted this from Jezebel before bringing her in a while ago. She came in with that other kid."

"Yeah. Ransom. I remember." Sadie watched Anson set the switchblade down on the desk. "I also remember that kid disappeared into thin air. Coincidence?"

Anson opened his mouth to speak, then closed it again.

"It's the same knife as in the crime scene photos, Anson," Sadie said. "Is that a coincidence too?"

"You know I don't believe in coincidence."

"You better figure something out, something that makes sense." Sadie moved to the office door.

"I think it's time to shut this place down for the night." Anson began to collect the pieces of evidence and place them back into their evidence box. "Want to get a drink?"

"Fuck, yeah," Sadie said. "Give me five minutes to finish up."

Anson nodded. He gathered the photographs and the empty manila envelope and glanced at the evidence box at his feet. Jezebel sat at the root of all this somehow. He threw the envelope and photos into the box with the other evidence against Jezebel and locked up his office.

JAKE SAT ON an inflatable mattress in his game room and stared back at his friends on the sofa. They had pulled the sofa back to make room for the mattress between it and the TV. An empty Pizza Zip box sat on the floor nearby and the smell of pepperoni and cheese still hung heavy in the room.

"Why my dreams?" he said. "You already tried with Cash and it didn't work."

"If it doesn't work, we need to be sure," Wynter said. "Maybe I was doing something wrong. And before you ask, no, I can't make Donkey Kong a dreamwaker."

"Or Schwarzenegger," Quinn added. "You got to dream of someone else. Someone you're connected to."

Cash crossed his arms. "Face it, Jake. You're the only one left. You got to be initiated. Partly anyway."

Jake opened his palm and looked at the three gelatinous zees cubes. "You swear these aren't drugs?"

Wynter sighed. "Jake. We've been through this already. Me and Quinn made these from scratch with stuff you can buy at the health food store."

Jake looked at Quinn for reassurance.

"Would we lie to you, Jake?" Quinn sensed Wynter exchanging looks with Cash and slid off the sofa, settling into crossed-legs at the foot of the mattress. "Would *I* lie to you?" She flashed Jake a warm smile framed by her silken black hair.

Jake smiled back. "Okay. Down the hatch."

"Remember, dream about someone connected to you," Quinn said.

Wynter turned to Cash. "I guess I'm up." She popped her palmful of zees and crawled onto the mattress. "No funny business, Jake," she said, waving an index finger mockingly at him. "I mean it."

Jake shook his head and blushed. "You're funny."

"We'll be keeping an eye on you two," Quinn said.

Wynter and Jake stretched out on their backs, side by side on the mattress.

"What are we going to do to pass the time?" Cash asked Quinn. "Donkey Kong tournament?"

Cash shrugged indifference. "What about a movie?"

Wynter cracked open her eyes. "Watch *Rocky,* if Jake has it."

Jake responded with his eyes closed. "Third shelf, right side."

"I'm in the mood for some Stallone," Quinn said. "That okay with you, Cash?"

Cash sent Wynter a small smile and a wink. "Sounds good."

Quinn hopped up and found the VHS tape exactly where Jake had described it. She turned on the TV, slid the cassette into the VHS player, and pressed play.

With the remote control in hand, she took a seat next to Cash and lowered the volume as the iconic trumpet solo from "Gonna Fly Now" played over the opening credits.

"I can barely hear it now," Cash said.

"Shush... and concentrate." Quinn slouched into the leather sofa. "If we keep talking, they'll never be able to sleep."

Quinn's point made perfect sense, but since his recent dream of Sierra, he had wanted to relive the *Rocky* experience. The TV set at a respectable volume would be the only way to do that but he'd have to take a rain check tonight.

Quinn set the remote on the armrest and whispered, "You've done this before. How long will this take?"

Cash found himself remembering passages from *Eyes Wide Dreaming,* Wynter's beloved book that had been destroyed in the fire. "Dream time doesn't follow any rules. Minutes or hours for us can pass in the blink of an eye in a dream. The reverse is true too."

"So you're saying you don't know."

Cash gave her a quick sideways glance and brought his index finger to his lips, quietly shushing her back. "Concentrate, remember?"

She gave him a playful shove as both of them settled into the sofa. Cash found he didn't need dialog. He knew the story well enough to know what was going on. It was an interesting experiment to watch a movie without sound. It forced Cash to focus on the visual details, all the little things he had forgotten about when he recreated Mighty Mick's for Sierra the night before.

Fifteen minutes into the movie, Wynter and Jake were sawing logs, their snores drowning out the reduced volume on the TV.

"That didn't take long, huh?" Cash turned to see that Quinn, too, had fallen asleep. "Last man standing. Score one for Cash."

Mirielle checked in on them once during the movie, bringing in a bowl of popcorn. "Everyone else is asleep?"

Cash pictured a third person materializing out of nowhere, right between Wynter and Jake, and right in front of Mirielle. How would they explain that? "Everyone was super tired, I guess. Thanks for the popcorn."

"You're welcome, Cash," Mirielle said in a hushed voice. "Kitchen's open for about another hour before Huddy and I head to bed ourselves. Let me know if you need anything else."

"Thanks." Cash began to munch quietly.

About an hour later, just as Rocky drank five raw eggs from a glass, Wynter sucked in a panicked breath and sat bolt upright. No one else had come back with her. She pulled her knees up and buried her face.

A moment later Jake's eyes fluttered open. Cash nudged Quinn with his elbow.

"Shit, what? What?" Seeing Wynter and Jake awake again, Quinn straightened herself up. "Jake. Where's your special someone?"

He shook his head. "Didn't work. Wynter tried everything."

Wynter rested her cheek on her knees and faced the rest of them. Her cheeks were damp from tears. "Sorry. I don't know why it's not working. But thanks for taking me to the top of the CN Tower, Jake. I've never been there before."

Cash turned to Jake, looking like he had solved the world's oldest mystery. "Hold on. Was it Ella? The infamous girlfriend from Canada that no one's met?"

Jake smiled. He glanced at Quinn, her eyes questioning him. "She's not my girlfriend. We haven't talked in..." He did a quick mental calculation. "Four years."

"What'd she look like?" Quinn asked.

Wynter shrugged. "Nice enough. Blond. Smart. A little young though."

"What'd you expect?" Jake said. "My memory of her is four years old. Jeez, give me a break already."

Cash offered the half-filled bowl of popcorn as a distraction. Everyone dug in. "So why didn't it work?"

"I don't know," Wynter said between handfuls of popcorn.

"Let's go over this." Cash reclined into the sofa. "I dreamed of someone who's dead. You dreamed of someone alive, at least I assume she's alive."

"Yeah, probably," Jake said. "I think my mom would've told me if something had happened to her."

"Look. If Wynter can even do this, I think it'll only work with Ransom. He's not dead or alive. He's somewhere in between." Quinn crawled over to Wynter on the mattress and put her arm around her. "That should be the final test."

"You're probably right," Wynter said. "But getting close to Jezebel when she's sleeping might be tough."

"If we can't get to her, we're just going to have to kill her." Quinn narrowed her eyes at Cash and Jake.

Cash sent her a look of concern. "Are you serious?"

"Of course she's serious." Jake stood and began to pace. "No way. I draw the line at..." He looked at the stairs to the main floor and lowered his voice. "At killing someone. We need to get Anson involved."

"He's just going to ask a lot of questions we can't or don't want to answer," Quinn said.

Cash nodded. "Plus, he's probably focused on that murder."

Jake froze on his crutches. "What murder?"

"I thought you knew." Cash faced Wynter, a look of surprise on his face. "You didn't tell them?"

Wynter shook her head slowly. "Trying to make Sierra a

dreamwaker last night kind of burned me out. Completely slipped my mind."

"Spill, girl," Quinn said.

"Not much to say really." Wynter yawned. "Cash and I were walking to Finn's. When we got there, cops were everywhere. Police tape and everything. It was a taxi driver from Halston."

Quinn's eyes were wide as saucers. "How did he die?"

"I don't know," Wynter said. "The driver was covered with plastic. Anson made real sure we didn't get close."

Quinn scooped up a handful of popcorn. "I wonder who did it?"

"Who cares." Cash focused on the movie. "Knowing who did it isn't going to help get Ransom back."

Quinn looked up at him. "Wouldn't you want to know?"

Jake ambled over to the back of the sofa. "I know who did it. A fucking psycho, that's who."

"Wait!" Quinn held up her hands like she had just done the big reveal of a magic trick. "What if Jezebel did it?"

"I wouldn't be surprised," Cash said. "But she's still in the hospital, right?"

Wynter perked up. "She can make a dreamwaker of herself, remember?"

"True," Cash said.

"Hey, Jake." Quinn hopped to her feet, then jumped onto the leather sofa, landing on her knees. The impact made Cash bump up where he sat. "Has your video camera caught anything interesting since we were last here?"

"I don't know," Jake said. "I've got a bit of a back log to go through."

"Can we, like, fast forward through it?" Quinn pushed her glasses up her nose and blinked at him excitedly.

"Uh, I guess...?"

Jake had barely answered her when Quinn bounded over the

back of the sofa and headed for the stairs to the main floor. "Come on, Bug!" she said, then disappeared upstairs.

Jake scratched his head. "What's gotten into her?"

"It's just Quinn being Quinn." Cash stopped the VCR playback and popped the tape out. "I guess *Rocky* is going to have to wait."

"Dude! Be kind and *rewind*."

Cash placed the cassette into its protective cover. "Saving it for later. Next time, promise." Cash offered his hand to Wynter. She grabbed hold and he helped her up off the mattress.

"*Rocky,* or a locked-off shot of the street." Wynter rolled her eyes at him. "Fun times."

Cash and Wynter met Jake at the base of the stairs. "You guys go first and make sure Quinn isn't being too nosey. I'll be up in a bit."

Cash bumped Jake's fist and followed Wynter upstairs. Jake took his time navigating the steps on his crutches. Mirielle met him on the main floor.

"Sounded like a stampede of elephants just came through." She smiled and kissed his head.

"Sorry, Mom," Jake said. "We won't be too loud… or late."

"Don't worry. We'll let you know if you are." She watched him hobble up the next flight of stairs to the second level, her eyes filled with concern. "Just be careful. Watching you on those stairs gives me the willies."

"Then don't watch." Jake continued his careful ascent. Halfway up the stairs he could hear laughter floating from his room. "Don't start the party without me, guys."

He reached the second floor and glanced back. Mirielle still stood at the base of the stairs, a look of relief on her face. "See? Made it. I was kidding about the party, though."

She followed him up. "I know, son." Mirielle walked to her room, diagonally opposite from Jake's across the open staircase. "Keep it to a dull roar, huh?"

Jake nodded and she closed the door. He poked his head into his room. Quinn was busy at the controls of one of the VHS editing decks. "What are you doing?"

"I told you not to touch things, Quinn." Cash looked at Wynter and winked at her. "You made Jake angry. You won't like him when he's angry."

Quinn heaved a sigh and rolled her eyes. "Relax. I didn't stop recording on the other machine. And you labeled everything so well it's hard to screw up."

Jake stood next to Quinn. She was playing the correct tape in fast speed, covering eleven o'clock last night to seven this morning. The image vibrated on screen with lines of static moving across it. "Even in fast forward, this is going to take a while. Probably hours. Have you seen anything strange yet?"

Quinn shook her head. "Maybe this was a bad idea."

Jake shrugged and sat next to Cash on his bed. "No way around it. It has to be done, eventually."

"Go back!" Wynter pointed at the TV screen.

Quinn jerked back in her chair. "Jesus, Bug! You scared me."

"Sorry. I saw something," Wynter said. "Go back."

Jake stood and leaned in to take over the controls, but Quinn blocked him with her arm. "Hold on a second, *Gerry Todd*. I can do it."

Jake laughed. "SCTV? Classic."

Quinn reversed the playback until something moved on screen, then played it at normal speed. She looked up at Jake hovering over. "See?"

Jake smirked, backed off, and tipped his baseball cap at her.

On the TV screen, a figure ran down the sidewalk and turned into Roxy's driveway. Quinn reversed the video a few seconds, then paused it on the clearest frame of the individual.

Jake rested on his crutches. "Who does that look like to you?"

The video camera had increased the gain of the image signal due to low light, which in turn increased the graininess. Still, the streetlight beside Roxy's house brought out enough detail for identification.

Wynter slid off the bed and hunched forward to get a closer look at the TV screen. "That's Jezebel, alright."

Jezebel's face had been lit on one side while turning her head to check if she had been followed.

"But it's not Jezebel," Cash said. When the other three looked questions at him, he continued. "That's got to be her dreamwaker, right? As far as I know she's still in the hospital."

Quinn nodded. "Oh yeah. I keep forgetting about that."

Wynter returned to the edge of the bed next to Cash. "Let it play in slow motion."

Jake raised his hands and exchanged a knowing glance with Quinn. She worked the controls, setting the video playing in slow motion moments later.

On the screen, Jezebel Too ran behind a hedge and large tree in front of Roxy's house and disappeared. The tree's foliage obscured their view of the second floor bedroom window.

"That was a let down," Cash said.

"But we know that Jezebel is there." Jake pointed at the ticking time code on the VCR's display. "And we know the time, kind of."

Quinn jotted down the playback time on the VHS cassette sleeve with a black Sharpie and fast-forwarded the playback to its maximum speed. "Don't you find it interesting that Jezebel arrived at Roxy's place in the middle of the night? Yet the Barracuda's still there." She pointed at the black muscle car parked close to the hedge in Roxy's driveway.

"Like maybe she had to take a *taxi* to get here," Wynter said.

Quinn pointed at her. "Exactamundo."

"Shit," Cash said. "Jezebel's out of control."

Jake shook his head. "Since when has she *ever* been in control, dude?"

"True." Cash pointed at the TV screen. "Bogie, twelve o'clock."

"Paydirt!" Jake's eyes sparkled with excitement. "Monty and his shitbox Fiat have arrived."

Quinn queued the video and let it play. Monty parked his Fiat partway down the road. He stepped out and stood in the middle of the driveway.

Cash squinted at the screen. "What's he doing?"

Quinn rolled her eyes and shook her head. "He's doing what all guys do when they want a girl's attention. Right Bug?"

Wynter shook her head slowly and laughed. "Right, if you live on the second floor. Except he's, like, twenty-six."

The details clicked for Jake and he smiled. "He's throwing pebbles at Roxy's window instead of ringing the doorbell."

"Like the pervert he is." Quinn noted the playback time again on the sleeve.

After a minute of this, Monty stopped, then walked toward the house, the hedge obscuring his final destination.

"Probably going for a threesome," Cash said.

Quinn scrunched her nose and recoiled against her chair. "Eww, gross. Even Jezebel and Roxy's standards are higher than that."

"Ugh." Wynter shuddered. "Fast-forward."

"Wait a sec. I bet they'll send him packing. Any takers?" Quinn looked at her friends, but their eyes were glued to the screen. "Pussies." She smiled mockingly, then propped her chin on her hand and watched. A minute later Monty walked back to his car and drove into the night. "Yes! Denied!" she said laughing.

"Rewind the tape," Jake said. "We got to get this to Anson. And the other tapes, too."

Wynter looked at him. "I thought we decided not to go to the cops with this."

"That was before there was a murder." Jake reached past Quinn, stopped the tape, and rewound it. "Like a murder *for real.* I'm not counting Jezebel killing Wynter when she was a dreamwaker." He ejected the tape.

"Good point," Cash said.

"Don't you want to make copies of that?" Quinn asked. "Before you give them to Anson?"

"Not these. It'll take way too long." Jake slid the VHS cassette into its sleeve. "I've got copies of the others. And thanks for writing down the times."

"I'm not just a pretty face." Quinn gazed up at Jake and fluttered her eyelashes. "Don't you forget it."

"Most definitely," Wynter said.

Jake blushed, collected the three videotapes, and handed them to Wynter. "You've got Anson on speed dial, right?"

Cash nodded. "She does." He faced Wynter. "After nine at night on a Wednesday. I'd say call his house."

"Sure." Wynter picked up Jake's cordless phone and dialed. "Anson? It's Wynter. Are you going to be around in the next half hour?"

As Wynter sorted out details, Jake said, "You guys should go to the hospital and enter the dragon's lair."

"You should come." Cash hung his arm around Jake's neck and pulled his baseball cap down.

"Nah. This fucking cast weighs a ton. And my parents would never go for it." Jake shrugged at Quinn in an attempt to hide his disappointment. "I got to log those other tapes. Glamorous I know, but..."

Quinn stood and kissed him on the cheek. "We'll be thinking of you, Jake."

Wynter hung up the phone. "We're all set."

"How do you feel about heading to the hospital after Anson's?" Quinn asked. "Get your true love back?"

Wynter glared at Quinn, then snuck a quick peek at Cash. He averted his gaze and turned toward the door to Jake's bedroom to hide his reaction. Whether it was hurt or embarrassment, Wynter couldn't tell. She leaned close to Quinn and whispered, "Keep the Ransom talk to a minimum, okay?"

"Oh shit, Bug," Quinn said softly. "I'm sorry."

"I'm sure he's fine, but..."

Quinn nodded and whispered, "Yeah, yeah." She paused, then narrowed her eyes at her inquisitively. "Are you and Cash...?"

Wynter shook her head. "Shh."

Jake placed his hand on Cash's shoulder. "It'll blow over, dude," he said quietly.

Cash sighed. "It's getting a little lame, though, I have to admit."

"Remember, he's not real. She'll realize that sooner or later." Jake grabbed Cash's face with one hand and squished his cheeks, making his lips pucker like a fish. "Am-I-right?"

Cash broke into a smile. "Yeah. Just wish it was sooner."

"We all do, dude," Jake said.

Quinn poked her head between them, forcing Jake and Cash apart. She draped her arms over their shoulders. "Ready to go, Cash?"

He nodded.

"Lead the way." Quinn and Wynter followed Cash down the upper hallway and down the stairs.

Jake turned back into his room and sat awkwardly in front of his video editing decks. A knock on the doorframe caused him to swivel in his chair. Quinn stood in the threshold, her hands shoved in her pockets, twisting her body side to side.

"Thanks for taking one for the team, Jake." She ran on her tiptoes and leaned into him so much that his chair tipped back on its springs. As her breasts pressed against his chest, she laid a lingering kiss on his mouth. "But that one was just for you."

As quick as the kiss started, it was over, and Quinn was back at the doorway. "A lot can happen with an open door," she said with a sly grin. "Call you later."

Jake's words sat in a jumbled heap in the back of his mind. He chose to smile and wave. Then Quinn was gone.

The sound of Blue Belle's engine rose up from outside. The TV screen connected to the surveillance camera showed the headlights of Quinn's VW backing out of the driveway and into the street.

Feeling a little left out of the evening's future activities due to his broken leg, Jake focused on the job at hand: logging videotape. It was a boring task, but he found if he read next to the TV screen, he could detect changes on screen in his peripheral vision. He inserted the next surveillance tape, pressed fast-forward play, and settled into issue thirty of *Computer Gaming World*. He'd finish the magazine well before the video finished, but he wasn't above rereading past issues. That was part of the fun. If he needed a break, he could distract himself with the recent memory of Quinn's intense goodbye kiss. Just thinking about it made his cheeks feel hot.

Jake settled into work mode.

Private Eyes

QUINN PULLED UP to the curb three blocks south of Sven Dwarfs Trail'r Park. The small, unassuming house had been painted a dark blue or green, difficult to know for sure in the fading sunlight. Someone had mowed the front lawn, but not much other upkeep had been done. The front walk split into two paths: one followed the outside of the house to the back yard, and the other led to the covered front porch.

"Are you sure this is his place?" Quinn scanned the house and front yard with a slight grimace. "I would have thought Anson was a northie."

Wynter shook her head. "He might be the sheriff, but he doesn't live large."

"And that's his SUV in the carport," Cash said from the back seat.

A white Suburban with the Newhaven Police logo on the side panel sat shadowed in the covered driveway.

"I'll be right back." Wynter grabbed the VHS cassettes, hopped out of the Volkswagen, and ran down the front walk. She stepped up to the front door and knocked.

Anson pulled open the door within seconds, as if he had been standing just inside waiting. "Wynter." He looked at the video cassettes in her hand. "Those are the tapes you were talking about, huh?"

"Yeah." Wynter handed them over. "One was taken at the Starlite, and the others are from Jake's place. He lives across the street from Roxy. We wrote times on one of them. You might find them... interesting."

Instinctively Anson scanned left and right for any potential threats. He gave her a sideways look. "You said one was from the Starlite?"

"Babe?" Mercy stepped out from a room off the main hallway. She had wrapped herself in a ratty housecoat and knotted its cloth belt around her waist. Chopsticks secured her messy hair bun. "Hey, Wynter."

"Hi Mercy."

"Let me see your nails." Before Wynter could react, Mercy had lifted one of her hands and was examining her fingertips. "Haven't seen you at Bombshell for a couple weeks. You should drop by before school starts. I'll get you fixed right up."

Anson gave Mercy a smile but there was tension behind it. She recognized it at once.

"Ah. Police business," Mercy said. "I get it. Want a beer?"

"Sure, thanks."

She kissed him on his bearded cheek and shuffled toward the kitchen.

Wynter craned her neck to follow Mercy until she disappeared from view. "When are you going to marry her, Anson?"

"Yeah, Anson," Mercy's voice called back. "When are you going to marry me?"

Anson sighed. "I'm working on it."

Mercy laid a cool bottle of beer on Anson's neck. When he went to grab it, she pulled it away. "I'll hold on to this, if you don't mind. But don't be too long. I might drink it."

Anson watched Mercy walk back to the room she had came

from earlier. He faced Wynter, a sheepish grin on his face. "Seriously, I'm working on it."

"You better be," Wynter said. "She's a keeper."

Anson looked at the cassette tapes in his hand. "Backing up a bit, you said one of these is from the Starlite?"

"Um, yeah." Now it was Wynter's turn to act awkward. "It's from Jake's hidden camera—"

"Which he said had malfunctioned when I asked earlier," Anson said. "Lying to police doesn't look good on a job application."

"He, uh, he wanted to make a copy of the tape first. Just in case."

Anson glanced past Wynter at the VW parked at the curb. Quinn waved and he returned the greeting. "Is Jake out there now?"

Wynter shook her head. "He's back at home watching surveillance tapes, looking for evidence. His broken leg slows him down. A lot."

Anson set the cassettes down on a table just inside the house and crossed his arms, aware of Wynter's sympathy play. "I'll let it go this time, but be sure to let him know I've got my eye on him."

"Beer's getting warm," Mercy's voice called. "And *other* things are getting cold."

"Ten-four, Merce," Anson called back.

"You find out anything more about the mur—"

"Wynter. You know I can't discuss an open investigation."

"It was probably Jezebel."

Anson cocked his head and narrowed his eyes in curiosity. "Why would you say that?"

Wynter shrugged. "I don't know. I guess it's because she's, like, a magnet for bad."

"I see your point."

"Anyway, I had to ask," Wynter said. "I hope one of those tapes helps. Say bye to Mercy for me."

"Bye, Wynter," Mercy called from the other room.

"Good ears," Wynter said, impressed.

Anson chuckled. "She only hears what she wants to hear."

"I heard that!"

"Bye Mercy." Wynter called back. She stepped off the porch and walked briskly toward the VW.

"Thanks for the videos." Anson grabbed the door and closed it.

Wynter took her place in the passenger seat.

"About freaking time." Quinn started the Beetle's engine and pulled away from the curb. "What'd he say?"

"Nothing much," Wynter said. "I think they were fucking when I called earlier. Mercy was acting..." She glanced quickly at Cash, then back at Quinn. "I don't know. Like, thirsty."

Cash laughed. "That's one way to put it."

Quinn turned onto Main Street. "So, are we going to the hospital... again? Or are we calling a night?"

Wynter twisted in her seat and looked at them both. "I am if you guys are."

Quinn peered at Cash through the rear view mirror. "Cash? You in?"

"I don't think Finn's is going to be open tomorrow, so yeah. Let's do it."

"Yes!" Quinn pumped her fist and turned right onto the on-ramp to the interstate. "Ransom or bust!"

The little blue VW merged into traffic, heading east. The three teens inside all had different thoughts of Ransom buzzing in their heads. While Quinn and Cash wondered how they would react seeing Ransom again, Wynter felt worry eat away at her. All her attempts at bringing a dreamwaker out from *someone else's* dream had failed. Would she fail again? If she did, would it be the beginning of the end? If she couldn't save Ransom from Jezebel's head, she feared her world would become unbearable. Maybe she would suffer the same fate as her great grandmother.

ANSON PULLED BACK a curtain at the front of the house and watched the blue VW drive out of sight. He glanced at the video cassettes in his hand.

"Babe?" Mercy called out from the bedroom down the hallway. "You coming back?"

"Yeah, in a minute." Anson shuffled through the video cassettes one at a time, returning to the one with times written on the cover. He glanced back at the hallway, then at the TV in front of the sofa. The VCR sitting underneath beckoned him. "Shit."

He turned on the TV and slid the first video cassette into the VCR. The player turned on and clicked into playback mode automatically. He found the remote and fast-forwarded the playback.

Mercy, still in a loosely tied housecoat, padded into the living room and plopped herself on the sofa beside him. "It's work, isn't it?"

"Maybe. Probably." Anson focused on the screen, then put the playback into pause. He turned to her. "I'm sorry."

Mercy placed her hands on his bearded cheeks. "You're dedicated. That's one of the things I love about you. But I hate it at times, too." She kissed him.

Anson felt distraction rising within his body and in the back of his mind, but he forced himself to focus on the videotape. "I just need to see what's going on here."

Mercy held his gaze. "Then show me."

"Merce, it's an open investigation. I can't—"

"The video you're watching is connected to the murder at Finn's today. A video delivered to you by a teenager that you barred from the crime scene. A video that teenager has already seen." Mercy crossed her arms and tilted her head at him dubiously. "Come on, Anson. I'm not dumb."

"It could be dangerous," Anson said. "I don't want you to get hurt."

"It's just a video." Mercy looked at the screen. "And not a very good one." She took his hands in hers. "Let me in."

Anson smiled and kissed her forehead. "Okay. But I reserve the right to stop it at any time."

"And I reserve the right to take this housecoat off at any time." She flashed her eyebrows at him.

"Deal." Anson set the VCR into fast-forward play and watched the playback time until it matched the first time noted on the cassette sleeve.

On the screen, a person with brown spiked hair walked briskly into the driveway and disappeared behind a hedge. Anson reversed the video and let it play again.

"Who is that?" Mercy squinted at the screen. "Is that the infamous Jezebel?"

Anson looked at the empty cassette sleeve and mumbled to himself, "Eleven p.m. to seven a.m." He looked at the playback time and made a mental calculation.

"What is it?" Mercy's curiosity came out in her voice.

He fast-forwarded to the next written time and watched Monty's arrival and departure. A sly smile slid across Anson's face. He'd have to confirm the cabbie's time of death with the coroner in Halston, but the video appeared to match the timeline of the cabbie's murder. And now he had two potential suspects.

Anson turned to Mercy and nodded. "Yeah. It could be Jezebel." He glanced back at the TV. "But how?"

"I'll tell you how."

Anson stopped the playback, ejected the cassette, and returned it to its sleeve. "Okay. I'll bite." He faced Mercy to find her reclined on the sofa, her bleach-blond hair fanned out over the backrest and her housecoat laid open, wearing nothing else.

She blinked at him, her eyelashes heavy. "Yup. You took that bait like a pro."

Anson shook his head in mock frustration. "Working on a Wednesday night? What was I thinking?"

"Clearly you weren't."

Anson peeled off his T-shirt. He had barely enough time to loosen his pants and underwear before Mercy pulled him down, their bodies entwined.

"Do me, Sheriff Jacobs." She laughed at her choice of words, then kissed him hard.

Anson let his lips travel Mercy's body. Yet, despite their passion, the contents of the videotapes pulled for his attention.

It couldn't be Jezebel on that tape. She's still in the hospital. But if not Jezebel, then who?

Anson kicked off his pants and underwear and forced his work thoughts to the back of his mind. The rest of the evening was all about Mercy. He picked her up and carried her into the bedroom, lip-locked the entire way.

CASH OPENED HIS EYES to the sound of knocking. He sat up in bed to orient himself. A video camera sat atop a tripod, aimed out the dormer window. The morning sun cast a beam of warm light through the room.

Next to the tripod stood a table perpendicular to the wall with two VHS machines and their accompanying TV screens. Cash was sure of one thing: he wasn't in his own bedroom.

"Jake?" He waited for a response, but none came. Cash stood and peered out the window, taking in a regular summer morning. "Hey, man. What's going on?"

The knocking continued. He turned toward the bedroom door and spotted a closeup of Roxy's face on *both* TV screens. It looked like she was screaming and pounding on a door.

The front door?

"Jake? Where are you?" Maybe Jake had gone to the bathroom. Cash stepped into the second floor hallway, approached the bathroom door, and pressed his ear to it. "You in there, man?"

No reply. The only sound that reached his ears was the incessant knocking.

Cash leaned over the railing to the central staircase. "Hello?" His voice echoed through the house.

He descended the first step of the staircase before he realized that his feet were covered in...

Blood?

Sticky red footsteps led all the way back to Jake's bedroom. "What the fuck?" Cash contemplated going back to Jake's room to investigate, but the knocking that had momentarily stopped started up again, capturing his attention.

He continued down the stairs and approached the front door. Cash peered through the spyhole and reconfirmed Roxy's presence outside. He opened the door and Roxy threw her arms around his neck and buried her face into his chest.

"You have to stop her, Cash!"

"Whoa." Cash took Roxy by the shoulders and pushed her back, taking a couple steps backward himself. "What are you doing here—"

He felt something bump against his back. Startled, Cash spun around to find Jake strung up by his hands and legs between the staircase banisters with bright yellow nylon rope. Blood dripped from his swollen face and mouth onto a torn Nintendo T-shirt. His cast was irreparably shattered, and more blood oozed from the cast's toe hole onto the hardwood floor.

Ransom sat three steps up from Jake, gnawing on a wad of gum.

"Holy fuck, Jake!" Cash approached him but refrained from touching him for fear of hurting him further. He glared at Ransom. "What the hell did you do?"

Ransom shrugged, his smug smile never wavering. "Didn't do shit."

"Cash... Cash..." Jake's words mumbled through a slurry of gore draining from his mouth.

"What, man? What're you saying?"

"Watch out," Jake said, but it came out sounding like one raspy "chout" coated with maroon drool.

Cash scrunched his brow and tried to decipher Jake's message when he felt a sharp sting in his right side. He looked down and saw a red blossom spread out through the fabric of his T-shirt. He reached down with his right hand and touched the rapidly soaking T-shirt as if he was expecting it to all be an illusion. His hand came away painted with deep red. "What the...?"

Cash pivoted just in time to catch the flash of cold steel in Roxy's hand but not soon enough to defend himself.

Her knife tore across his throat, slicing through his skin, muscles, tendons, and veins like they were made of Jell-O. Cash placed his hands to his neck to stem the flow of his blood but it was an impossible task.

He fell to his knees, then rolled to his side, his hand pressed against his throat. Cash watched Ransom hold one of Jake's crutches like a rifle and pretend to pull the trigger.

"Boom," Ransom said, then bellowed laughter that echoed through the foyer.

Cash found Jake's eyes and locked onto them. "Jake. Hold on, man."

A single tear rolled down Jake's face, accumulating blood and taking his life with it.

"Jake? Jake!" Cash reached out as Jake's eyes clouded over. "No!"

"Cash?"

He felt a warm hand on his shoulder. Cash opened his eyes to Wynter reaching back from the passenger seat of Blue Belle. "Runnin' With The Devil" by Van Halen played through the dashboard speakers.

"Are you feeling okay?" Wynter's eyes held a look of concern and reassurance. "You yelled out."

"You called out for Jake," Quinn said.

"Shit." Cash rubbed his eyes, then moved to his forehead. "Just had one hell of a dream."

"Do you remember what it was about?" Wynter squeezed his shoulder lightly, then let go.

Cash decided to lie. "No, but it was fucked up. I know that much." He gave Wynter a weary smile. "I needed you in there with me."

"Whatever it was about, I'm sure we'd kick ass."

"You'd kick ass."

Quinn pulled off the interstate. "Time flies when you're dreaming. We're almost there."

Wynter sat back in her seat and stared at the roof of the VW. "Jesus, I never thought I'd be back here so soon."

"Yeah," Quinn said. "I'm getting sick of this parking lot and, like, everything really." She glanced at Wynter. "You got to make this work, Bug."

"Jesus, no pressure." Wynter sighed. "What if I can't?"

"I guess we'll figure something else out." Quinn turned into the hospital parking lot and found an empty spot.

"We'll beat Ransom out of her if we have to," Cash said. "Let's go."

It was past eleven o'clock when the three teenaged liberators entered the front of the hospital. Wynter was first to step from the elevator on the fifth floor. Most of the overhead lights had been turned off or dimmed to aid patients with sleep.

"Jezebel's in room 513," Wynter said. "Last time I was here, she freaked out. I'll go and see if she's asleep."

Cash touched Wynter's arm and caught her attention. "If she's asleep, we need to... well, *you* need to work fast. If she makes a dreamwaker of herself again, we're fucked."

Wynter nodded and tiptoed down the corridor. The door to Jezebel's room was open and she slowly advanced close to the wall until she could get a good view without blowing her cover.

"I hope that bitch is asleep," Quinn said.

Cash exchanged a worried look with her. "Me, too."

Wynter's shoulder's slumped. She slid her feet backward until she was out of direct line of sight from within Jezebel's room and hustled back to join Cash and Quinn.

"She's not there."

"What do you mean she's *not there?*" Quinn's eyes widened with alarm. "What, is the bed empty?"

"No. There's someone in the bed," Wynter said. "It's just not Jezebel."

"Fuck." Cash began to pace. "We should have called first."

Wynter chewed at her bottom lip as she rolled scenarios through her mind. "Wait. I can ask my dad. He might know and he's on this floor too. Way down there." She pointed. "523."

Quinn bolted down the corridor, then pivoted to walking backward with the same intensity she had started with. "What're you guys waiting for?"

Cash and Wynter smiled at each other and ran to catch up. Quinn arrived at room 523 first and walked in without hesitation. A second later, she backed out with a nurse giving her the third degree.

Wynter and Cash caught up mid-way into the nurse's interrogation. "Quinn, don't run off on us like that."

The nurse stepped toward Wynter, looking her up and down. "You know this person?"

Quinn whispered into Wynter's ear, "Your dad's not in there."

Wynter shifted her attention back and forth between the nurse and Quinn. "What?"

"Visiting hours are long over." The nurse scrutinized all three teens. "Come back tomorrow."

Cash seized the moment and casually peered into the room. An elderly woman smiled weakly at him. He nodded an awkward greeting.

"Not so fast Magnum P.I." The nurse kept her gaze on Wynter. "Stop your snooping."

Cash backed away from the door, his eyes wide with surprise. He caught Wynter's attention and mouthed, "Not there."

"I'm sorry, uh..." Wynter spotted the nurse's name tag. "Bridgette? My friends were helping me find my dad, Nolan LaCroix. He was in this room a few days ago because I talked with him. Can you help me find him?"

Bridgette softened. "Oh. Yes. Mr. LaCroix was here, but another patient with greater needs required a private room. He was transferred elsewhere."

"Where?"

Bridgette pursed her lips and narrowed her eyes at Cash, Quinn, and back to Wynter. "You're welcome to check the front desk when visiting hours open tomorrow. You can wait there if you want." She pointed to the waiting alcove on the opposite side of the corridor. "But if you try any funny business, I'll call security. Understand?"

Cash nodded. "Yes, ma'am."

All three teens exchanged looks as Bridgette hurried back to the nursing station.

"What a bitch," Quinn said with no attempt to speak quietly.

Cash tapped Quinn's shoulder. "What the hell? You *want* us to get kicked out?"

"Sorry, but she pissed me off."

"She's just doing her job," Cash said.

"Whatever." Quinn looked at Wynter, who had begun to nibble at her lower lip and pace back and forth. "What's the plan now, Bug?"

"We could work our way down, floor by floor, checking each room," Cash said. "They've got to be here somewhere."

"Your dad didn't get discharged, did he?" Quinn asked.

Wynter shook her head, then hesitated. "No. I don't think…"

"Would your mom know?" Cash pointed to the waiting alcove. "I saw a pay phone back there."

"Good idea." Wynter charged over to the small waiting area, Cash following close behind.

Quinn saw that Bridgette had been watching them from the nurses' station. She grinned and motioned an acknowledgment at the nurse, then turned toward the waiting area, the grin dissolving into a scowl. "Fucking bitch," she whispered to herself.

"Quinn? Got a quarter? I left my purse at Cash's place."

"Just a sec." Quinn jammed her hand into her satchel and rummaged around by feel. A second later she pulled out a twenty-five cent piece and handed it to Wynter.

Cash shook his head in amazement. "How the hell do you do that?"

"Us women are magical," Quinn said. "I'm surprised you don't know that by now."

Wynter picked up the handset, deposited the coin, and punched in a phone number. She placed the handset to her hear and waited.

"See?" Quinn hooked her thumb at Wynter. "There's another example. Bug's a human Rolodex."

"No shit," Cash said. "You guys are amazing."

"You know it."

The call trilled, then connected in Wynter's ear. She keyed in the room number and a second later she heard her mom's voice. It had been a few days since she had last spoken to Madeline and it eased her mind at once, anchoring her to better times. "Mom? It's me."

As Wynter talked, Quinn picked up the July issue of *People* magazine and flipped through it. "A blind date with Prince? Oh my God, most definitely." She showed Cash the cover. In the photo Prince wore a sharp yellow suit and stared into the camera with his dark bedroom eyes. "Isn't he hot?"

Cash shrugged. "He's not ugly, I'll give him that."

"He's a dream." She brought the cover up to her lips and kissed it.

Cash shook his head and laughed. "You don't know who else has touched that."

"Don't care," Quinn said.

The click of the pay phone handset returned to its cradle caught Cash's attention. "Wynter? Everything okay?"

Wynter appeared stunned. "I don't know. My dad's on the third floor. Room 305." She faced her friends. "You'll never guess who's sharing the room with him."

Cash exchanged a casual look with Quinn. "Who? Jezebel?"

"Yes, actually."

His eyes went wide like saucers. "You've got to be shitting me."

Wynter shook her head slowly. "Nope."

"Holy crap, Bug. You know how awesome that is?"

Wynter stared at Quinn, still trying to process this unwelcome turn. "What the hell are you talking about?"

"Look at it this way," Quinn said. "This gives us, like, a totally legit reason to be close to Jezebel." Her eyes gleamed with excitement.

"She tried to *kill my dad,* Quinn. I don't want to be anywhere near that fucking psycho bitch, and I'd guess my dad doesn't either. And sleeping there?" Wynter shook her head. "No way. That's mega creepy and psychotic."

"Who said anything about sleeping in the same room?" Quinn pushed her glasses up her nose and gave her a sideways look.

"I think a trip to the third floor is in our future," Cash said.

"Damn straight." Quinn left the alcove, headed for the elevators. Cash and Wynter barely had a chance to follow before she turned around and returned. She took the *People* magazine with Prince on the cover and shoved it into her satchel. "Nobody saw nothing. Now let's go!"

Wynter took a deep breath and followed Cash and Quinn to the elevators.

MUCH LIKE THE FIFTH FLOOR, Quinn, Cash, and Wynter stepped out onto a darkened third floor. The buffed floor reflected the warm task lights of the nurses' station at the opposite end of the corridor.

"Let's not bump into a nurse this time," Cash said with a smirk directed at Quinn.

"Cash, you're so funny I forgot to laugh."

Wynter shushed them as they walked down the corridor.

Quinn pointed and whispered, "305's the next one." She charged ahead on as much tiptoe as her Vans would allow.

"Quinn. Stop," Wynter said in a forced whisper. "Everyone get behind me. I don't want to blow our cover."

"Oh. Yeah." Quinn shuffled back to where Wynter and Cash stood. "Sorry."

Wynter led the way along the left wall of the corridor. She heard the gentle beep of a pulse monitor before she could see past the doorway, and it brought back the memory of her own recuperation. She counted herself lucky that her time here had been spent in a private room.

Wynter approached the door frame to room 305. During the day, three teenagers walking with their bodies flat against a wall would have raised red flags. But the limited lighting and lack of other people in the corridor gave them an advantage. For now.

She eased herself forward and peered in, heaving a sigh of relief when she saw Nolan asleep in the first bed. A few more inches forward revealed more of the room, the back wall, the head and pillow of the second bed, then a tuft of spiky hair.

Jezebel.

Wynter hoped that Jezebel was sleeping because getting close enough to make sure wasn't in the cards. This had to be a surprise attack, both in reality and in dreams.

Wynter backed up, turned to Cash and Quinn, and whispered, "She's in there. She might be awake but there's no way in hell I'm going to find out." She caught Quinn's eagerness. "Neither are you. We're just going to have to take a chance."

Quinn nodded. "Okay." She scanned the corridor up to the nurses' station. "So, like, where's the waiting area?"

"There isn't one on this floor," Cash said. "But there's a chapel near the elevators."

"Right, I forgot about that." Quinn held her hand out to Wynter. "Ready?"

"Abso-fucking-lutely." Wynter took Quinn's hand and Cash followed them back toward the elevators and left into the chapel.

There were four rows of pews inside the converted hospital room, with a central aisle ending at an altar with fresh flowers and a bible laid open in front of it. A lectern stood in one corner. Behind the altar, the only exterior window had been painted to resemble intricate stained glass. The walls left and right incorporated false windows, both painted to resemble stained glass. A cross hung on one wall and the Star of David mirrored it on the opposite wall. It was clear that the hospital wanted to appeal to multiple religions.

Like the corridor, the chapel lights glowed at half their brightness, giving the space a welcoming air of peace and tranquility. The three of them had the chapel to themselves.

"Where do you want to do this, Bug?"

Wynter stepped down the aisle until she faced the altar. A shiver ran the length of her back and she spun around, her eyes connecting with Cash's for a brief intense moment. "How about the first row? No one will see me if they walk in."

"Good plan." Quinn joined Wynter at the first row and threw her arms around her. "Let's get you comfy. Where you going to sit, Cash?"

When there was no answer, they turned to find Cash nowhere in sight.

"What the hell?"

"Probably went to the bathroom." Wynter sat on the right pew in the first row. There was some padding, but it wouldn't provide comfort for long. She swung her legs up and laid back. "Oh, this is going to be tough."

"Luckily I still have some zees." Quinn dug into her satchel and pulled out a plastic baggie with just over half a dozen little black cubes. "Want some?"

"Yeah. Three'll be okay."

Quinn handed the little gelatin cubes to Wynter. "We're going to have to make some more soon."

"Maybe after tonight we won't have to." Wynter threw the gelatin into her mouth and swallowed.

"Yeah maybe."

The sound of shoes squeaking on tile rose up from out in the corridor and grew louder with every passing second. Quinn froze. Wynter began to sit up, but Quinn held her hand up and shook her head.

"What?"

Quinn shook her head again more intently in response.

"They can't kick us out," Wynter said. "This is a house of worship. It's not like were drinking or getting wasted—"

Cash rounded the corner into the chapel entrance holding something wadded under his arm.

Quinn relaxed. "Or having sex." She smiled and motioned toward Cash. "He's so obviously into you."

"*Shut up,*" Wynter whispered through her teeth, then slapped Quinn's arm playfully.

Cash sat on the pew behind Wynter and held up a wad of blue scrubs. The girls stared back at him confused. "Fold them up. Use them like a pillow."

Quinn took the pile of clothes. "Is this really going to do anything?"

"They will, trust me." Cash rested his chin on the back of the first pew and looked at Wynter. "I slept here the first couple of days you were in a coma."

"Wait." Quinn gave Cash a sideways look. "Are these clean? They could have surgeon sweat all over them."

Wynter turned up her nose. "Gross."

"Of course they're clean." Cash looked at them both. "I've got connections."

All three of them folded the scrubs into a makeshift pillow and Wynter placed it behind her head. "It's actually not that bad."

"See? What did I tell you?" Cash looked down at Wynter, winked at her, then locked his gaze with hers, all at once serious. "Now go get Ransom so we can finish with Jezebel once and for all."

Wynter nodded and closed her eyes. Quinn exchanged a doubtful glance with Cash. He shrugged in response as she sat next to him.

With the aid of the zees Wynter had taken, dreams came quickly. She knew what she had to do, but deep down she had doubts whether she could do it. Jezebel would always be an unpredictable wildcard.

LONG GRASS SURROUNDED Wynter's body like a shield and the cloudless blue sky above her seemed so close she could touch it.

She reached up but felt nothing but the warmth of the summer sun.

Wynter sat up, her head rising above the level of the grass. The sunshine that had warmed her hands moments earlier now illuminated her face. She closed her eyes and faced the sun's brightness and drew in a deep breath, in through the nose and out through her mouth.

She caught the smell of wood smoke in the calm breeze and all at once memories of family camping trips tugged at the edges of her dream.

Wynter opened her eyes, shading them from the sun at first, then turning and surveying her surroundings. Lines of smooth stones radiated from a central point directly behind her heels and cut channels through the long grass. Each line of stones culminated at an outer ring of similar stones.

She scanned the horizon and discovered the source of the wood smoke. A tepee covered with a mosaic of sewn animal hide sat near one of the rocky spokes. Tendrils of smoke rose from the top of the conical structure.

Wynter followed the line of stone until she stood in front of the tepee's entrance. She parted the break in the hide and stepped in.

The smell of smoke and animal hide was stronger inside but not overwhelming. Instead, it was a comfort. In the center of the tepee a small fire burned within an indentation in the earth, encircled and contained by larger river stones. A metal pot hung over the flame.

Nolan sat to one side of the fire, sipping something warm from his favorite mug. He looked up at her and smiled. Opposite Nolan, Quinn slept on her side atop flattened grass, the fire warming her face and her hands tucked under her right cheek. Cash mirrored her, his back to hers, facing the outer circle of the tepee.

"Dad?" Wynter shifted her gaze between Nolan and her friends. "What are you doing here?"

Nolan stared at her with his dark, warm eyes and smiled. He set his mug down and directed his gaze to the lazy smoke rising to the tepee's open smoke flaps. A feather had found its way inside and twisted, tumbled, and floated down on hazy eddies.

Effortlessly, Nolan reached out and grabbed the feather by its quill. He made wide circles through the rising smoke before, then presented it to Wynter.

She shook her head, perplexed. "Dad? What do you want me to do with this?"

He answered her with just a smile, then raised his left arm to a second entrance at the rear of the tepee.

Wynter sensed pride and assurance in Nolan's face and navigated carefully around Quinn, Cash, and the fire. She parted the opening in the hide and stepped out. A dark grey cloud head had disrupted the blue sky, roiling on the horizon and drawing closer with each passing second.

"I am a warrior." Wynter rolled the feather's quill between her fingertips and let the vanes brush past her lips and nose. She took the quill and secured it in her hair.

Nolan's weathered hand landed on her left shoulder. He gave it a gentle squeeze and pointed at the outer ring of river rock.

Wynter gazed down and saw a visible break in the ring of stone. She looked at Nolan and he nodded once, then cast his eyes outward, across the grasslands to the brewing storm.

Wynter placed a tentative foot outside the circle of stone. Everything remained as it was, except for the storm. She looked back at Nolan. "I love you, Dad. And... I'm sorry." She wiped away a tear with a quick swipe of her wrist.

Nolan held his palms over his heart and smiled warmly, then pointed once again at the dark clouds approaching.

Wynter faced the storm and stepped beyond the circle. In an instant, day became night. The tepee disappeared behind her and in front sat Jezebel's dilapidated house. The dark storm front swirled around her as she stood in the eye of her final test.

She climbed the rotting steps to the front porch. The second to last step gave way under her weight and her right leg plunged through, splinters raking gouges into her calf. Wynter grabbed the top step and pulled herself up to the landing. Blood dripped from the swollen gashes and soaked into the top of her white socks.

To her surprise, her anxiety appeared to have no effect on her body. Her hand held steady when she grabbed hold of the doorknob. She turned the knob and pushed the door open with ease. There were no locks. Why would there be? She was in Jezebel's dream world now.

Wynter wanted to yell for Ransom at the top of her lungs, but decided to stay silent, even though staying hidden in someone else's dream was like bleeding in shark infested waters. Jezebel probably knew she was there already.

In front of her a line of closed doors stretched down an impossibly long hallway, too long for the house she had just stepped into. Wynter let go of the doorknob on the front door and took one step forward.

A *slam* behind her took her by surprise. She spun around expecting to find the front door locked, but there was no door at all, or exterior or interior walls. Just the hallway and unopened doors remained, with mottled black and grey smoke swirling around her. The change in Wynter's surroundings reminded her that moving forward was the only way through someone else's dream. She began opening doors.

The original wood of the first door showed through the paint job in ragged streaks and made Wynter think of a wild animal bent on escape. She ran her fingertips over the surface and promptly caught her index finger on a long sliver. She yanked her hand back and stuck the injured finger in her mouth to sooth the pain. The taste of her own blood swirled across her tongue like the turbulent clouds above her head.

Wynter grasped the doorknob, twisted it, and pushed open the door. Inside was a decrepit bed, a torn mattress sitting on a rusting bed frame, the air heavy with the smell of stale beer and body odor. An unshaven man she did not recognize was engaged in rough sex with a woman that looked a little like Jezebel but not quite. There was no love between them.

Frankie?

A young girl, no older than Sierra had been in Cash's dream, stood next to the bed watching the two adults.

"Get the *fuck* out of here or you're next." Without pause, the man swung out his right arm and backhanded the girl's face, causing her to tumble to the floor by the door.

Wynter crouched down to the girl's level. "Are you okay?"

The girl looked up at her with tears in her eyes but a scowl on her face. "Leave now. *Whiner.*" Even without hearing her derogatory nickname, Wynter could see Jezebel in the girl's young features.

Wynter stumbled backward into the hallway. She glanced at the bed and found the man and woman glaring at her with hatred in their eyes. She pulled the door closed.

"Jesus," Wynter said softly to herself. What the hell did she just witness? She thought for a moment. "Jezebel's memories?"

The long line of doors stretched away from her, too numerous to count. She would never be able to open them all in time.

Wynter moved on to the next door and opened it to find Frankie pacing back and forth in a run-down kitchen, screaming at a ten year old Jezebel cowering in the corner.

"You're a little *bitch!*" Frankie balled her hands into fists and shook them at Jezebel. "He left because of *you.*"

Wynter moved on to the third door, opening it to the food preparation area of a restaurant. Jezebel, maybe twelve years old, wore a food-stained apron and stood beside a cooking station that included a deep fat fryer, a griddle, and several gas burners. A different man than before had one hand against Jezebel's throat, pinning her against the door to a walk-in freezer. His other greasy hand palmed her young breasts.

Jezebel met Wynter's gaze. Her disgust morphed into a mask of evil. "*Whiner...,*" she hissed.

Wynter shivered and shook her head slowly, closing the door behind her.

The doors that followed revealed a history of abuse that soon saw Jezebel as the instigator, whether it was torturing a classmate in the school washroom, forcing a teenaged boy to have sex with her in the back seat of her Barracuda, or killing Frankie's beloved cat.

The rooms painted a bleak portrait of how Jezebel had become the psychopath she was today. Why Wynter was being shown these vignettes was anyone's guess. Maybe deep down, Jezebel wanted to be seen as normal, to be understood. Wynter's heart ached for her, just a little, despite her own memories of the past abuse Jezebel had inflicted on her and her friends.

The next door Wynter faced had no doorknob. A latch hung slack, missing its padlock. She pushed the door open and revealed the interior of a grimy shed. Against one wall stood several metal shelves that stored maintenance equipment and other tools. The door swung wider and revealed a soiled mattress, then two feet poking out of denim pant legs... a black hoodie, white T-shirt, blond curls, and blue eyes. Those piercing blue eyes.

"Ransom?"

He looked up at her and gave her a weary smile. "Hey, beautiful. I knew you'd find me eventually."

Wynter ran toward where Ransom sat and heard the door close behind her. Instead of disappearing like before, the door merged with the wall, leaving no escape. She scanned the small space. "Where's Jezebel?"

"She'll get here eventually." Ransom stood up on the center of the mattress. "She always does."

"Then we don't have much time." Wynter reached for Ransom's hand, then froze, remembering the difficulty she had before. "Is there a barrier around you?"

Ransom shook his head slowly. "No idea. Probably."

Wynter approached the mattress and extended her hand toward Ransom, and he mirrored her. Their fingers touched and a blue static discharge arced from their hands, but there was no resistance like last time. "It must be because I'm so close... I have more power," she whispered to herself. She locked her gaze with his, took a deep breath and stepped onto the mattress.

The static washed over her body like she had walked through a band of fine mist. Wynter threw her arms around Ransom's neck, kissed him hard, then hugged him tight. She stood for a moment and took in the feeling of his body against hers. It was a risky move but one she felt she had time for.

Ransom pulled back slightly and winked at her. "You've tripped the alarm now."

As if his words held magic, Wynter felt the energy barrier build up again between them, trying to push them apart. She discovered she could still overpower the forces of Jezebel's dream if she concentrated, but they needed to be touching for her to bring Ransom back.

"Take my hand and don't let go, no matter what."

"Got it." Ransom interlocked his fingers with Wynter's.

"*Whinerrr...*" Jezebel's disembodied voice floated within the small space. "You're trespassing, *Whinerrr.*"

"Shit." Wynter hurried around the shelves and examined the walls for any hint of a door. "Any secret escape hatch in here?"

Ransom shrugged. "There might have been, if this place was really Ollie's MovieTyme, but it's all a dream."

Wynter snapped her fingers. "Jesus. That's it!"

"What is?"

"This! I can do anything in a dream." Instead of searching for a way out, Wynter sorted through escape ideas in her head. "Jezebel created this place, but I still have limited power here."

She turned to the wall and concentrated. A doorknob appeared on the wall without a door. "Dammit."

"*Whinerrr...*"

Wynter shook her head. "It's got to be unconventional. Unexpected." Her eyes flicked to the corners of the room, the ceiling, floor. "Get off the mattress."

Ransom barely had a chance to comply when Wynter let go of his hand to pull the mattress aside, exposing a hatch underneath with a rope handle attached to it. She pulled it open to reveal a set of wooden stairs without a railing descending into darkness.

She hopped down onto the second step and held out her hand to Ransom. He coupled his hand with hers once again. A small energy barrier kept them from making skin-to-skin contact, like two repelling magnets, and both scrambled down the stairs. Wynter could have squeezed her hand harder and broken through the barrier, but she had funneled all her concentration into creating an escape route.

"I got you now, *Whinerrr...*" Jezebel's silhouette stood at the top of the stairs, her unblinking red eyes watching them descend. Instead of giving chase, she stepped off the first step like she was jumping into a pool.

Three steps below Wynter, Jezebel punched through the tread boards wearing a demented and hate-fueled ear-to-ear grin. Wynter froze and Ransom ran straight into her back, almost toppling her forward.

Wynter looked left and right at an abyss of nothing but inky black. "Trust me?"

"Absolutely," Ransom said.

"Okay. Hold on and roll with me." Wynter turned right and stepped off the stairs. After a brief fall of unknown distance, they both landed on hardwood with rollerskates on their feet. Lit from an unseen source from above, Wynter tugged Ransom across an endless expanse of roller rink.

She tried to picture Nolan, the tepee, and the medicine wheel from Windspeaker Park, but any thought that took her away from her escape weakened her ability to maintain her grasp of Ransom.

Out of nowhere, Wynter and Ransom skated straight into a reflection of themselves, bouncing off the edgeless mirror. She helped Ransom up and rolled in a different direction, only to run into themselves again.

Jezebel stepped out of the mirror, a switchblade in one hand. "You're in deep shit now."

Ransom clones began stepping out of the shadows behind Jezebel.

Two clones attacked Ransom from behind and pulled him away. Wynter lost her grip on him and Jezebel kept her at bay with wild swings of her knife.

Wynter shifted her thoughts and a Bowie knife materialized in her hand. "Come on, bitch. I can take you."

Jezebel shook her head and laughed. "Such an idiot." She plunged her knife deep into her own chest, pulled it down to her abdomen, and pulled it out with no visible wound. "I can't die. But *you* can."

Wynter turned to the group of identical Ransoms. They were all holding out their hands beckoning her to take it. If she grabbed the wrong hand, it would be all over.

"Come on," said one Ransom clone. "Take my hand."

"I'll keep you safe, Wynnie," said another.

Their pleas came fast and urgent.

"Come with me if you want to live."

"Don't pick them. Pick me."

"I'm the *real* one."

"I love you, Wynter."

"Love? That's rich." Jezebel stepped closer, passing her

switchblade from one hand to another. "Whatever your little plan is, it's going to fail."

The Bowie knife in Wynter's hand collapsed on itself like it had been made of soft rubber. She dropped the useless weapon and narrowed her eyes at Jezebel.

"And now you're going to die. Again." Jezebel launched herself at Wynter, swiping the switchblade from side to side.

Wynter stood her ground and concentrated. Starting with her face, she morphed herself into Frankie. "You little *bitch!* You'll *never* amount to *anything!*"

Jezebel skidded to a stop, cowering at her mother's fury. "I... Mom?"

Wynter continued, drawing on the scene she had witnessed earlier and infusing it with her own rage. "He left because of *you!* It's all your fault. I should've abandoned you in the *fucking* alley."

Jezebel had curled into a fetal position. Wynter knew she only had seconds before she'd lose her advantage. She let go of Frankie's visage and singled out one of the Ransom clones. It was now or never.

Wynter charged forward and wrapped her arms tightly around a Ransom clone. She had felt no charged barrier between them and hoped it was the right one. Cheek to cheek, with her mouth by his ear, she whispered, "What are the magic words?"

Ransom whispered back without hesitation, recalling the dialog from *The Terminator* as if they had just watched it at Quinn's cabin. "Come with me if you want to live."

Thank God for Quinn.

Wynter nodded. "Ready?"

"Yes."

Wynter concentrated with all her strength and pushed Ransom backward through the crowd of other clones, all of them reaching and pulling at her clothes. Jezebel stood up behind them, her eyes blazing with red fire, as the world spun into darkness.

Jake had worked into the wee hours of the night. Logging videotape was one thing, but four straight hours of watching a locked-off shot was quite another. He finished his *Computer Gaming World* magazine and afterward cracked out his pristine premiere issue of *Teenage Mutant Ninja Turtles* from its protective plastic sleeve. Flipping carefully through the pages, Jake concluded that the comic was going places. He could feel it.

By one-thirty in the morning he had one tape left to log, but Jake needed sleep badly. He set his alarm clock for six in the morning and crawled under the covers.

It wasn't his alarm that pulled him from sleep four hours later, but a clicking sound by his camcorder. Still dressed, he yawned, maneuvered off the bed, and padded in a bare foot and crutches to where his camcorder sat atop the tripod. He cocked his head to the side and listened.

Click.

Jake examined his camcorder as much as he could without altering its framing on the street below. Then he heard it again.

Click.

But it wasn't a click. More of a tap, coming from his window. He maneuvered around the tripod as best he could without moving it and placed his forehead on the window pane. The sun had just broken free of the horizon and cast an orange glow on the shadows of the front yard. Just as his forehead made contact, a small pebble struck the glass, bounced off, and tumbled back down the shingled roof.

Roxy stood on the lawn below looking up at him. She smiled briefly and waved, then pointed to the front door.

Jake scrunched his brows. "What the hell is *she* doing here?" He couldn't talk to the enemy, could he? What good would that do? Then he remembered a line from *The Godfather, Part Two*. "Keep your friends close, but your enemies closer," he whispered to himself. Maybe he'd find out something that Wynter, or even Anson, could use against Jezebel. He pictured himself coming to the rescue with information only he could provide. Quinn would be so impressed.

A small smile curled at the corners of his mouth. Jake cast his eyes at her below and nodded, hoping his duplicity hadn't shown through.

Making sure he didn't wake his parents, Jake took slow and careful steps along the upper hallway and down the central staircase. He had grown to appreciate how stealthy moving on crutches was, effectively cutting out half the noise of his footfalls. Navigating up and down stairs still remained his kryptonite.

Jake paused at the front door and listened for any noise from upstairs. Confident that his parents were still asleep, he unlocked the dead bolt and pulled open the door.

Roxy stood on the front stoop in bare feet, blackened with dirt, which Jake found odd. She wore a pink miniskirt and a Hello Kitty T-shirt, and her hands tapped at her thighs anxiously. The swell of her breasts and a hint of her nipples showed beneath the T-shirt, and he averted his eyes.

"Roxy?" Jake whispered as he scanned the front yard left and right, looking for an ambush.

"It's just me, I swear."

Jake swallowed hard. "What do you want?"

"Uh, can I talk to you for a second?"

"Okay. We're talking."

"Inside?" Roxy crossed her arms against her chest and rubbed her arms. "It's, like, kind of cold out."

"Uh..." Jake glanced up the stairs, his ears primed for any parental noise and part of him hoping for it. The rest of the house remained silent.

"So... can I come in?"

Jake nodded and pulled the door open. "Keep quiet. I don't want to wake my parents."

"For sure." Roxy stepped into the foyer.

"What did you want to talk to me about?"

Roxy stepped close enough for Jake to feel the heat of her body. Into his ear she whispered, "Somebody's got to stop her."

Jake realized immediately that she was talking about Jezebel. He took a step back and raised a brow at her. "And that somebody's *me?*"

Roxy gazed up the stairs. "Can we go somewhere private?"

"No one's going to hear—"

Roxy bolted up the stairs, her footfalls silent as if she weighed nothing.

"Shit." Jake pushed the front door closed and chased her up the stairs as quickly and quietly as he could, but on crutches he was no match for her speed. He had reached the third step when Roxy mounted the top of the staircase and turned down the upper hallway to his bedroom. "Shit shit shit."

It felt like it had taken an eternity to get to the top landing. Jake paused and listened for his parents, but all he heard was Roxy rummaging in his bedroom. He cursed himself for being so trusting, so stupid.

He arrived at his room and peered inside. Roxy paced on the opposite side of his bed, dark ribbons following her as she moved. The light from the rising sun did little to penetrate the shadows in his room. Jake turned on the room light and his blood went cold.

Roxy leaned against the wall beside the dormer window. She held a VHS cassette in her hand and was yarding handfuls of videotape out of the front.

"Fuck!" Jake's words came out in a strained whisper. He eased his door closed. If there was ever a time to ignore the cardinal "doors open" rule, this was it. "Put that down!"

Roxy tossed the cassette into a tangled mess of videotape on the floor and picked up the cassette's protective sleeve. " 'Roxy and Jezebel' it says on here. And a list of times?" She tossed the sleeve across the room and placed her eye to the camcorder's viewfinder. "Are you in love with me or something?" She shoved the pan-handle causing the camcorder to spin atop the tripod, tangling the wires coming out the back. "Or are you some kind of perv?"

"Don't touch the camera." Jake clenched his jaws and took a step forward. "I mean it."

"Afraid I'll break your toys?" Roxy's eyes lit up but there was nothing playful about the way she looked at him. "We should make a *sex tape*." She grabbed for the last surveillance tape.

"Put that down."

"Or what, tough guy?" Roxy looked him up and down with a scowl. "I've had a crush on you since middle school, but you fucking *ignored* me."

"What? You started hanging out with *Jezebel*." Jake tugged the brim of his baseball cap for emphasis. "She has a way of ruining everything." He motioned at his cast. "Like *this* bullshit."

"I wasn't driving."

"You could've stopped her."

Roxy narrowed her eyes and flipped open the videotape guard built into the VHS cassette. She tweezed out black tape, one loop at a time, taunting him.

Jake had reached his limit. Without figuring out his next move, he lurched forward on his crutches, closing the small distance between them.

Roxy let him get halfway across the room before she kicked out one of the tripod's legs and sent it careening away from the dormer window. The cables anchored to the VHS deck on the desk reached its limit and snapped off the back. Jake altered his approach and extended his cast. The neck of the tripod struck his plastered foot and bounced to one side, the camcorder's lens hitting the floor first.

"Fuck." Jake turned to her, his face filled with anger. "That camcorder was one of a kind."

"Oops." Roxy shrugged as she continued her willful destruction of the cassette. "Where are the other tapes?"

All Jake wanted to do was inspect the camcorder for damage, but his cast got in the way as usual. "I don't know what you're talking about."

"Don't play dumb. I saw you outside my window the other night. And then there was that hidden camera at the Starlite." Roxy spotted Jake's anger mix with surprise. "Yeah, I know about that one too." Roxy tossed the damaged cassette across the room where it hit one of the closet doors.

She followed Jake's worried gaze. "What's in there, *Jakey-poo*. Got a secret stash?" She bolted through the pile of videotape and pushed back the closet door. Roxy began digging through the magazine back issues and plasticized comics, tossing Jake's private collection out into the room without care.

Instead of pursuing her, Jake swung one of his crutches like a baseball bat, connecting hard with Roxy's right hip and knocking her off balance. He positioned the crutch's axillary support against Roxy's throat and leaned into it. "I'll break your fucking neck if you don't get out of here right now."

"Bullshit." Roxy's voice strained against the crutch. "You couldn't hurt a fly."

They stared at each other, a standoff of wills, each trying to judge the other's intent. Roxy grabbed the crutch and pushed back with strength that Jake hadn't anticipated.

He flew backward, hopping on one leg, his balance compromised, and fell backward onto his bed. Roxy was on him in seconds, straddling his waist. The hem of her miniskirt slid up to her hips, exposing Hello Kitty panties to match her T-shirt.

Her lips found his ear. "Mmm. This could get interesting," she whispered as one of her hands snaked down to the waistline of his pants and the other gripped his throat. "Are you a *virgin,*

Jake? I've already fucked you in *my* dreams, but I bet you're a virgin for real."

Jake's body responded to her aggressive advance, his teenaged hormones paying no heed to the danger. But his mind remained clear. "So what if I am? You're the last person I'd want to fuck, you *psycho.*"

Her grin was back and it chilled Jake to his core. Before Ransom had entered the scene, he had never known of Roxy behaving so recklessly. She was usually the silent sidekick to Jezebel's psychopathic assaults. This version of Roxy scared him deeply.

She sat up and peeled off her Hello Kitty T-shirt, exposing her bare breasts. "Touch me, Jake. You know you want to."

She was right. Jake wanted to touch her, even though she disgusted him, even though he wanted Quinn more than any girl he had ever met. His mind waged a war between desire and logic and desire was winning.

"Okay," he said softly. He used his arms to push himself to a sitting position on the bed. Roxy ran her fingers through his hair and pulled his face between her breasts, expecting him to kiss her.

Jake glanced to his left where mountains of torn videotape lay in a pile on the floor beside his coveted JVC GR-C1, probably damaged beyond repair. Roxy had destroyed hours of work in a few short minutes. His anger broke through her attempt at seduction like a fire burning away fog.

"NO!" He shoved Roxy with all his strength. Arms flailing, she sailed backward and struck the back of her head on one of the TVs and again on the corner of the desk on the way down. She landed in an unconscious heap on the floor.

Jake sat on the edge of his bed, catching his breath and listening. The house had been silent, but now he heard the tell-tale signs of waking parents. He slid off the bed and crouched on one leg. From his new vantage point, he could see an expanding pool of blood collecting behind Roxy's head. He placed his fingers against her neck.

No pulse.

"Oh fuck." Jake scanned the room with wild, panicked eyes. "Oh *fuck*." What he wanted was a hand mirror, but it was in the bathroom and he couldn't risk leaving Roxy alone. Not like this.

He grabbed one of the VHS cassettes Roxy had destroyed and brought the clear tape spool window to her mouth. "Please please please..."

No breath condensation appeared on the smooth clear plastic. "*Oh fuck.*"

Jake heard the familiar squeak of his parents' bedroom door opening, then footsteps in the hallway. His mind raced, fueled by adrenaline and the sudden realization that his life would now take an irreparable turn for the worse. A partially naked girl was lying on his floor, dead as a doornail. And his door was closed.

"Jake, honey?" Mirielle called from the hallway.

Jake grabbed his bedspread and dragged it off the bed and covered Roxy as best he could with a full leg cast. The rest of his room lay in disarray with no time to set it right. He picked up the crutch he had used as a weapon and settled onto it.

Jake had taken two steps toward his door when Mirielle knocked softly on his door. "Jake?"

"Yeah, Mom?"

"Are you okay? We heard noises."

Jake glanced back at the carnage. Blood had begin to seep into the bedspread covering Roxy. "I'm fine, Mom. My editing decks kind of went haywire."

"Are you sure? Can I open the door?"

She doesn't believe me.

Jake faced a crossroad. He could let her in and face the inevitable fallout of his mom's disappointment and horror upon finding Roxy's body. Or he could refuse his mom entry. Then he'd have to deal with removing a dead body from the second floor of his house, secretly, while Mirielle was still in the house. It was a monumental task for anyone. Sporting a full leg cast, the task seemed impossible. He could face manslaughter or maybe murder charges either way. Frankly, both options sucked.

Jake approached the door and placed his hand on the doorknob. Maybe if he stood close to the door and blocked her view, Mirielle wouldn't see Roxy. Maybe she wouldn't come in.

He cracked open the door wide enough for his shoulders to fit through.

"Are you feeling okay?" Mirielle placed her hand on his forehead. "You look flushed and you feel hot." She looked down and saw a comic book leaning against the baseboard, bent and half out of its protective plastic sheath.

Their eyes met and Jake prepared for his life to crumble around him. He'd never been able to lie successfully to his mom. "What's really going on?"

Jake stepped back with a sigh and pulled the door open wider, exposing more of the room and surrounding shambles. He remained between Mirielle and Roxy in the hopes that she'd stay in the hallway, but Mirielle took the open door as an invitation.

She stepped past him. "Good lord, Jake. What a mess. What happened?"

He rested his forehead on the door, closed his eyes, and chose not to answer. What could he say that wouldn't make this situation worse?

He heard Mirielle gasp. "Oh my God. This is more than your video machines going *haywire*, Jake. You've got some explaining to do."

Jake could feel the rise of burning tears behind his eyes. "I'm sorry, Mom. I didn't mean to. It was... it was an accident."

"How is this an accident?" When Jake didn't respond, Mirielle continued. "Look at me, Jake."

It was time to face what he had done, even if it wasn't intentional. Jake shifted on his crutches and looked at Mirielle.

Standing on the opposite side of the bed, she held up his issue of *Teenage Mutant Ninja Turtles* number one. There was a small rip in the corner of the cover. "This was a gift from your dad. He paid a *fortune* for it."

Jake gazed at his mother, stunned. He stumbled forward, stealing a glance at the floor for only a second. His bedspread lay on the floor just as he had left it moments earlier, but Roxy was gone and so was the pool of blood from her head wound. That could only mean...

Mirielle set the comic on top of a TV. "What happened? And I want the truth."

The truth? He struggled to stifle the nervous laughter that rose in the back of his mind. This was no time to start telling the truth. However, partial-truths would work.

"I'm stuck here doing grunt work while my friends get to do the cool stuff. All because of this stupid cast." The tears from earlier were still percolating and Jake could turn on the waterworks at any time if he wanted. "The first tape jammed and I lost everything on it. I tried the second tape and the same thing happened." He let one tear slide. "I got mega angry and started throwing things. I know it's stupid."

"It's not stupid, Jake." Concern and compassion showed on Mirielle's face. "You've been through—"

Jake heard her but continued as if he hadn't and moved toward his closet. "I was going to my back issues, you know, to find something to read, to calm myself, and my crutch must have caught the corner..." He reached for the *Teenage Mutant Ninja Turtles* comic in Mirielle's hand. "I was reading it earlier, you know, taking a break. I guess it fell on the floor. Then I freaked out and..."

The most valuable comic he owned had been made worthless through his own stupidity. He should have never taken it out in the first place. Jake's sorrow was genuine, and his tears fell without forcing them. "I'm so sorry. I'll find a way to replace it."

Mirielle wrapped her arms around him. "Shh. It'll be okay."

Relief washed over him. He may have just lost something

priceless, but at least he wasn't going to jail. His future was still unwritten. "Don't tell Dad, okay?"

"Don't you worry." Mirielle kissed his head. "Want help tidying up?"

"Maybe just my bed," Jake said. "Thanks, Mom."

Mirielle smiled and nodded as she picked his bedspread up off the floor and threw it back over his mattress. Jake caught a faint whiff of ozone as the fabric settled.

Roxy had been a dreamwaker the whole time and Jake had fallen for it, hook, line, and sinker. What had been her endgame before he accidentally killed her? Was it just the videotapes? Was Roxy actually into him or was that just part of her plan?

Mirielle finished tucking in his bedspread and headed to the door, stopping at the doorframe. "That cast will be off in a month or so, honey. Things will be back to normal before you know it."

"I hope so." Jake stepped to the dormer window. The sun now sailed past the rooftops of the houses across the street, including Roxy's. "I don't know if I can take another month of this," he whispered to himself.

Jake righted the tripod and examined the camcorder. He spotted a hairline crack in the lens. Flipping on the power, he placed the viewfinder to his eye. The crack affected the lower left corner of the image and the power zoom toggle no longer worked. Manual zoom was the only option now. Other than that, the camcorder still looked to be in working order.

He collected the magazines and comics scattered across his room and placed them in a careful pile on his desk. As he gathered the strewn videotape and transferred it to his waste basket, he came across one of the cassette sleeves noting important playback times. In actuality, the tapes held very little evidence of anything except Roxy and Jezebel leaving in the Barracuda. And even if Roxy had gotten into his safe, Anson had copies. It wasn't as bad as it looked.

As Jake tidied the room, he found himself caring less about

the tapes, his camcorder, and his magazines, and more about Roxy's death. Even if she wasn't real, his actions *had* been. The whole encounter had left a dent in his psyche that he hoped he could move past.

Dream Police

CASH HAD FLOATED on the edge of sleep but never quite got there. The pews in the chapel were damn uncomfortable. Apparently, this place of worship didn't embrace loitering. Quinn had fallen asleep next to him soon after Wynter, and now she was slumped over, resting her head on his shoulder. Yet another thing keeping him awake. He didn't want to wake her but after more than four hours of sitting, his body ached and he had to pee badly. Relieving himself where he sat wasn't an option. For all he knew, it was probably a sin, too.

He shifted under Quinn and gently moved to one side. Cash tried to hold her head steady as he made his escape, but she groaned and her eyelashes fluttered back to life.

"Shit. Sorry," Cash said. "Didn't mean to wake—"

They both heard Wynter gasp from the pew ahead of them and fall to the floor. Any residual sleepiness in Quinn evaporated in an instant. She met Cash's gaze with concern and excitement.

"Did it work?" Quinn whispered.

Cash shook his head and whispered back, "I don't know."

"Should we look?"

"Do you want to?"

"Yes... Why are we whispering?"

Cash shrugged. Together, they placed their hands on the first pew's backrest and let their eyes rise slowly over the top like a pair of peeping toms.

On the floor between the altar and the first pew lay Ransom in his blue jeans and black hoodie, with Wynter on top of him engaged in a deep kiss.

"Holy shit." Cash knew this moment was coming and he had prepared for it, but now that it was here, it was difficult to hide his hurt. No matter how hard he tried, it still felt like his heart had broken again.

Quinn saw the disappointment on Cash's face at once. "You okay?"

"Forgive me, Father..." Cash said softly before trailing off.

"What?"

"I got to piss." Cash stood and hustled out of the chapel.

Quinn watched him go, then hung her arms over the back of the pew. "Bug."

Wynter and Ransom continued to kiss. His hands moved down her backside to the waistline of her jean shorts where he hooked his thumbs into her belt loops.

Part of Quinn wanted to watch, but this wasn't the time or place. "Hey Bug." She reached over the pew and poked Wynter in the shoulder. "This is a place of worship, you nympho."

Wynter turned to her with a wide, satisfied smile on her face. Then it melted to an expression of concern and panic. She sat up. "Shit. Where's Cash? Did he see?"

Quinn nodded. "Totally." She narrowed her eyes at her and grinned. "Somebody's been practising." She cast a quick glance at Ransom.

He lay on the floor with his hands clasped behind his head. Ransom smiled at her and beckoned with his eyebrows. Quinn looked away. She had strayed once before. Never again. But it would be hard to resist that smile... and those eyes.

Quinn held out her hand to Wynter and helped her up. Wynter

did the same to Ransom. He took her hand and she pulled him to his feet.

"Long time no see," Quinn said.

Ransom brushed himself off. "Good to be back."

"You did it."

Wynter spun around to see Cash standing at the entrance to the chapel. "I know you saw me kissing Ransom and—"

Cash shook his head and waved her off. "It's okay. I know it's the only way to keep him in your head." He had given Wynter an out, even though they both knew it had been more than one kiss. "Let's book before Jezebel wakes up." He headed for the elevators at the end of the corridor.

"She's going to be pissed," Quinn said.

"Totally." Wynter grabbed Quinn's and Ransom's hands and led them out of the chapel. "She's going to wig out, big time."

Cash stood by the elevator, holding the door open. As they shuffled in, Cash exchanged a quick and wary glance with Ransom. Losing his cool would be easy but he chose to keep a lid on his feelings for Wynter's sake. And if it meant Jezebel got what she deserved, all the better.

Outside in the parking lot, the four teens piled into Blue Belle. Quinn drove to the interstate and headed west, hopefully for the last time.

IT WAS JEZEBEL'S HEAVY BREATHING that woke Nolan from a sound sleep at close to five in the morning. He cracked open his eyes to orient himself. So far, his hospital stay had been less than a week, but it still required some effort to orient himself after waking. Being in a new hospital room with a psychopath as a roommate didn't help.

Nolan's eyes led the turn of his head. Nurses had pulled the privacy curtain around Jezebel's bed earlier but not far enough to obscure it completely. Her head and spiked hair thrashed back and forth on her pillow and her labored breathing continued.

She's fucking dead.

At least that's what Nolan *thought* he heard, low and raspy, mixed with the sound of rustling fabric and the low hum of the air circulation system.

He was about to close his eyes when the sounds of anguish ceased. All at once the room was quiet again, except for... whispers? And the breathing sounds of *two people*.

Nolan's heart jackhammered within his chest. He was glad not to be hooked up to a cardiac monitor because nurses might have mistook his fear for a heart attack.

He didn't scare easily, but what Nolan saw petrified him. Another Jezebel leaned forward, nose to nose with the Jezebel lying in bed. They turned their heads in unison, four eyes blazing at him through the gap in the privacy curtain. The eyes of the second Jezebel were glowing orange.

Is that a...

He froze his body in place and shut his eyes to squinted slivers, feigning sleep to maintain his terrified vigil. His lashes reduced the amount of detail he could perceive to lights and darks, as if he was looking through layers of gauze.

The second Jezebel perched on the edge of the bed, yanked back the privacy curtain, and hopped to the floor. Her nimble feet landed without a sound. This version of Jezebel wasn't injured in the slightest.

She wore dark street clothes which made it difficult for Nolan to track her movements in the predawn light.

The Jezebel clone moved past the foot of Nolan's bed and out of range of his peripheral vision. He would have to turn his head to keep his eye on her, but that would blow his illusion.

Nolan focused his left ear on the door to the room. He had learned over the past few days that it made a slight squeak when opened and closed. He listened but the squeak never came. That could only mean...

Nolan turned his head to the left just in time to see the second Jezebel standing at the side of his bed, but not fast enough to prevent her hands from wrapping her surprisingly strong fingers around his throat.

"Your little bitch stole something from me," the clone said through clenched teeth as she pressed her weight onto his neck. "And you're going to pay for it."

Nolan tried to call out but his throat spasmed against any attempt to form words. He should have been able to stop her attack with his bare hands, but seven days in the hospital had weakened his arms and legs.

Any rational thoughts of defense shattered in his oxygen-starved brain. Nolan thrashed on his bed, kicking out his sheets. His head felt as if it would bust open like an overripe melon. In his struggle, his right hand slid inside his pillowcase. Smooth metal brushed over his fingertips and for a second his backup plan flashed to the front of his mind.

The fork.

Nolan had secured it soon after discovering his roommate would be a psychopath. The dinner staff hadn't noticed it was gone and he had hidden it inside his pillow.

He wrapped his right hand around the handle in a tight fist, and as his strength and vision faded, he swung his arm around toward the clone's head.

Nolan may have lost strength from his hospital stay, but his body proportions hadn't changed. And his arms were longer than Jezebel's doppelgänger.

The tines of the fork sunk into the side of the clone's neck with little effort. Nolan twisted his fist and pulled the fork down, opening a two-inch gash in her left carotid artery. Warm blood cascaded over his hand and down his arm.

Jezebel's twin convulsed and released the grip on his neck. She placed one hand on her gaping wound unable to stem the flow of blood around her fingers. She stumbled backward and collapsed between the wall and the bed.

Dark red soaked the side of the bed, the sheets, and mattress. Nolan still gripped the bloody fork in his hand as he turned his head to the right.

Jezebel stood by her bed, her hospital gown in a pile at her feet. She pulled on her T-shirt over her bra, careful of her incision site, grabbed her purse, and approached Nolan's bedside. Her incision must have hurt because she walked favoring her right side.

"You and your little *bitch* ruined everything."

Nolan thrust his bloodied hand toward her, still trembling from adrenaline release. "Get any closer and I'll kill you too." His words came out raspy against his bruised throat.

Jezebel snarled. "Third time's a charm... and I always get what I want." She kept her distance from Nolan's weapon.

The corner of the room filled with a burst of bright blue light, as if both of them had been caught in a paparazzi's flash. The blood on Nolan's hand and bedsheets vanished before his eyes.

"Holy shit. She was a *dreamwaker?*"

"Seriously, old man? Thought you'd have clued in when there were fucking *two of us.*" Jezebel placed her hand on the door handle. "Watch your back, 'cause we're not finished." She slipped out and pulled the door closed, making an unconvincing attempt to hide her pain.

As soon as the door swung shut, squeaking as expected, he laid back on his pillow, damp from his own sweat, and reminded himself that this almost became his deathbed. Relief washed over him.

Through the room's window, he could see the red orange glow of sunrise forming on the horizon. Nolan closed his eyes. He had had enough of this hospital and of Jezebel to last the rest of his life. Now he had the room all to himself. Within minutes he was asleep, dreaming of Madeline, Wynter, and new beginnings.

The morning sun had begun to filter through Anson's bedroom curtains. He laid in bed and stared at the ceiling, deep in thought over the mounting evidence against Jezebel, unfortunately all circumstantial.

"Work?"

Anson turned his head to find Mercy lying on her side facing him, her hands tucked under her pillow. She wore his Chicago Bears three-quarter-sleeve T-shirt jersey with Richard Dent's 95 on the back. There was no need to imagine what she wore underneath.

"Yeah, what else?"

"Oh, you could've been thinking about last night." Mercy smiled and ran her hand lightly down his jawline, letting his trimmed beard tickle her fingers.

"Merce, you're the only thing getting me through these days." Anson sighed. "This town has a cancer and I got to get rid of it."

"Jezebel Caine."

Anson nodded subtly. "Yup. Jezebel fucking Caine."

Mercy snuggled up to Anson's side and trailed her finger along his chest in small circles. "What are you going to do?"

"I want to get her for the cabbie's murder. And for the LaCroix arson and attempted murder. She'd go away for good. But there's no direct evidence." Anson recalled how the murder weapon had disappeared without a trace the previous day. He briefly considered telling Mercy about that detail but decided against it. It was better if she didn't know. She would have thought he was out of his mind anyway.

"I can get her for unlawful discharge of a firearm at the

Starlite," Anson continued. "But that'll only get her off the streets for a month. You can't cure cancer with a Band-Aid. You got to cut it out." He rubbed his face in frustration. "Looks like I'll be heading to Halston Medical Center to pay our little psychopath a visit. But first, a shower."

"Not so fast, Sheriff." Mercy ran her fingers down his chest, past his navel, and under the covers. "If it's true that I get you through the day, I better start your engine." Her head disappeared under the covers.

Anson felt her lips on him although his body needed no coaxing. He cleared his mind of all things Jezebel and focused on the woman he had loved for seven years. Mornings had been their favorite time of day to make love and they often stretched weekend wake-ups until noon. And as much as Anson wanted to stay in bed, it was a work day.

Mercy hadn't finished but Anson couldn't hold back any longer. He pulled her up to his lips and kissed her hard. Moving together, they welcomed Thursday morning.

AT JUST PAST EIGHT in the morning, Anson found himself heading east on I94. Again. The glow he felt from his morning with Mercy hadn't left him yet and he savored it as long as he could. Any interaction with Jezebel tended to spoil any good mood he was in.

An hour later Anson arrived at Halston Medical Center. Due to his underpowered police radio, he found a pay phone in the foyer to call dispatch.

"Morning, Sadie."

"It's after nine. Was beginning to worry." Sadie's voice buzzed through the handset's speaker.

"Yeah, I'm in Halston, about to arrest Jezebel Caine for unlawful use of a firearm," Anson said. "I don't expect any trouble."

"Well, good luck anyway."

"Thanks. I'll need all I can get. She's a real piece of work." Anson glanced toward the elevators. "I'll check in before I leave."

"Copy that," Sadie said.

Anson hung up the phone and took the elevator to the fifth floor. As he headed down the corridor to Jezebel's room, he passed Julia walking in the opposite direction.

She stopped and turned. "Sheriff Jacobs?"

Anson stopped to think, then spotted her name tag and snapped his fingers. "Julia."

Julia winked at him. "You forgot my name, didn't you?"

"You got me." Anson sighed. "I've had a lot on my mind lately."

Julia nodded and studied him.

Anson cleared his throat and hooked his thumb towards Jezebel's room. "I have the pleasure of arresting Newhaven's resident psycho."

Julia nodded. "Right. You mean Jezebel Caine."

"Good memory."

"Yeah, well I always remember the weird ones." Julia shook her head slowly. "She was... a challenge."

A mix of panic and unease swept through Anson's mind. "What do you mean, *was?*"

"Oh!" Julia waved him off. "She was moved to the third floor..." She leaned in and lowered her voice. "Unfortunately, she's still alive."

"Whew. You had me worried for second."

"Sorry." Julia let out a nervous laugh. "Look, I'm just finishing my shift. Do you... God I never do this, but... do you have time for a coffee?"

Anson gave her a warm smile. "Uh, thanks, but I'm on duty. Besides... I'm in a relationship."

"Ah ha," Julia said. "The *real* reason slips out. Lucky woman." She blinked at him.

He motioned to the elevators. "Walk you down? At least to the third floor?"

"Sure."

The two walked to the end of the corridor in silence. Anson couldn't tell if it was awkwardness or sudden indifference. Julia punched the call button with her knuckle and a moment later the elevator doors rolled open. Anson waited for Julia to enter first, then followed her. She selected floors three and one and silence enveloped them once again as the door closed.

"How long have you been *in a relationship?*"

Anson detected a subtle edge to her voice. "Uh, going on seven years now."

"Seven years?" Julia whistled. "*Someone's* afraid of commitment." She looked him up and down. "I'd guess it's you."

"Why do you say that?"

"Tell me, what does your girlfriend do?"

Julia would have made a good interrogator. Anson didn't appreciate the scrutiny but rolled with it. "She's an aesthetician. Nails are her specialty." He replayed some of the morning in his head and smiled.

That wasn't her specialty this morning.

Julia crossed her arms against her chest. "And you're the chief of police. Need I say more?"

"No, I think you've covered it." The elevator doors opened at the third floor. He headed down the corridor toward the nurses station. "Thanks for the chat, Julia."

"Hey, Sheriff."

Anson looked back at Julia just as the elevator doors began to close.

She didn't wait for his response. "Quit stalling or cut her loose."

"Everybody's got an opinion," Anson said to himself as he

recalled countless others who had offered similar points of view in recent years. Maybe it was time to listen to them. But not now. He had a psychopath to arrest, and he wasn't looking forward to it.

A nurse redirected Anson to room 305. He backtracked and stepped through the door, half-expecting it would be the wrong room, prolonging what had become a series of dead ends.

The room had two beds. The first had a patient with their head buried behind a newspaper. The other bed several feet away had been stripped to the mattress, with the privacy screen pulled all the way back.

Another dead end.

"Sheriff?"

Anson turned to the familiar yet raspy voice. Nolan had laid his paper on his lap and smiled back at him.

"Nolan!" He shared a firm handshake with the Native American. "I'm surprised to find you here."

"At the hospital? Or in the same room as Jezebel?" Nolan refolded his newspaper. "That *is* why you're here, right?"

"Uh, yeah. You don't waste any time getting to the point." Anson glanced at the empty bed. "But as usual, she's always a step ahead of me."

"She left last night."

"What? You actually saw her leave?"

Nolan winced as he swallowed. "I did."

"She give you any idea where she was going?"

Nolan shook his head.

Anson sighed. "I know. Long shot."

"She left me with this." Nolan touched his bruised throat gently. "Pull up a chair. I need to tell you something."

Anson knew Nolan to be a straight shooter and there was something dark behind his eyes that scared him. He pulled a chair from beside the spare bed and positioned it next to Nolan's. By habit, he extracted his notepad and pen from his breast pocket. "Whenever you're ready."

"Have you heard anyone talk of summoning before?" Nolan asked hoarsely. "Or the power of summoning? Wynter, perhaps?"

Anson jotted down the word 'summoning' and underlined it. "No. I can't say I have."

"To be gifted with the power of summoning allows one to pull a person from their dreams into reality," Nolan said. "There are different levels of the power, and it can be shared, within reason."

Anson set his pen down and leaned backward.

Nolan smiled half-heartedly. "I can already see you're having doubts. You need to keep an open mind."

"Nolan, I live in a world of black and white, of fact and evidence, guilty or not guilty."

Nolan pointed at his neck. "I'm bruised and it hurts a great deal. Would you say that's a fact?"

"Yes, of course."

"Would you say it's evidence of an attempted strangulation?"

"I'd have to talk to a doctor, but sure." Anson narrowed his eyes at him. "What are you getting at?"

"Jezebel did this to me, but she had been summoned from a dream."

Anson blinked at Nolan, his mind at war trying to process an idea that sounded crazy.

"Wynter calls them dreamwakers. It's a good name."

Anson narrowed his eyes with curiosity. "Are you sure *you* weren't dreaming?"

"You can't die in a dream, right?"

"No, I don't believe you can."

"I was very much awake," Nolan said, "and I almost died. If it hadn't been for the fork I used to kill her, I wouldn't be talking to you right now."

"Wait." Anson paused his note writing. "You *killed* Jezebel?"

"Yes." Nolan reached under his pillow and pulled out a metal fork. "With this. But she was from a dream. A *dreamwaker.*"

"From *whose* dream?"

Nolan held Anson's gaze for a second. "From Jezebel's dream."

Anson set his pen down again. "So you're saying Jezebel pulled *herself* out of her own dream?"

"Yes. Exactly." Nolan leaned forward and raised his voice slightly above a whisper. "And I saw her do it."

Anson sighed. He couldn't deny the reality of Nolan's bruises, but he had a difficult time believing those injuries had been caused by a dream. "Nolan, can you explain to me how a dream, something that doesn't exist except in our minds, can impart any physical damage?"

Nolan took a moment to collect his thoughts. "While a dream isn't real, a dreamwaker is as real as you, or me, or this fork." He tapped the tines into the center of his palm. "A dreamwaker eats, drinks, breathes, bleeds, fucks... anything we can do, they can do. Except sleep. If they sleep, they disappear, returning to their summoner. And another thing. A dreamwaker can bring their own inanimate objects with them, like clothes or jewelery."

"So... I got to ask. What happens when a dreamwaker dies?"

"Simple," said Nolan. "They disappear, including any inanimate objects they brought with them."

The switchblade.

In his mind, Anson was back in his office, staring at an empty, sealed evidence bag. "Like a weapon for example."

"Yes. If this fork had been brought out by a dreamwaker, it would disappear the moment they died."

"Or fell asleep," Anson added.

"Yes."

Anson was more a believer in dreamwakers now than when he had first entered the room. Nolan's explanation fit the unexplained mystery of the disappearing switchblade. But he still wasn't completely convinced. At his core, he still needed hard evidence.

"Just so we're clear, the dreamwaker version of Jezebel tried to choke you, and you stabbed her with a fork?"

Nolan nodded, then tapped the left side of his neck with his left index finger. "Right in the carotid. She disappeared a minute or two later."

"Including all evidence, and I imagine quite a lot of blood."

"Yes."

Anson scribbled notes. "What happened to the real Jezebel? She didn't attack you as well, did she?"

Nolan shook his head. "She got dressed and crept out of the room. Told me to watch my back."

He closed his notepad. "I have to admit, Nolan. Your story is compelling. And some details check out with my investigation. But I need to see it to believe it."

"Chances are good that you've seen it already and didn't realize it," Nolan said. "But I understand your hesitancy." He swung his legs out from under the sheets and placed his feet on the floor. "Can I ask why you wanted to see her?"

"I was here to arrest her," Anson said. "That's all I can say."

"Whatever the reason is, I'm sure she deserves it."

"This time there's plenty of direct evidence."

Nolan pushed himself off the bed and into a standing position. Anson reached toward him to help, but Nolan waved him off and grabbed a cane by the bed. "It's okay. Things are getting better every day. The pain is manageable with Tylenol."

Anson watched Nolan shuffle toward the window, placing one foot in front of the other. The occasional wince revealed that perhaps the pain was more intense than Nolan had let on.

He admired the man's tenacity. The fact that Jezebel had put Nolan here in the first place made Anson even more determined to put Jezebel away for good.

Anson joined Nolan at the window. The morning sun warmed their faces. "Beautiful."

"Yup," Nolan said. "Even from a hospital window."

"Look. Thanks for trying to teach this old dog a new trick."

Nolan offered a single nod and kept his stoic gaze facing the glorious morning outside.

"I'm going to get her. You have my word on that."

"I know you will." Nolan faced him. "I've seen it."

Anson tipped his hat. "I'll be in touch. Say hi to Madeline for me."

"Will do. Travel safe."

Anson paused at the door and took one last look at Nolan, framed by sunshine and blue sky. He headed toward the elevators with a gut feeling of where his wild goose chase would end.

JUST OVER AN HOUR LATER, Anson parked at the curb in front of Jezebel's ramshackle house. Frankie's orange Pinto sat in the weed-infested driveway, but the Barracuda was curiously missing.

Maybe this chase isn't over after all.

Anson radioed dispatch and informed them of his whereabouts and intended action.

"Feels like déjà vu," Sadie crackled back.

"Tell me about it. Frankly, it's getting a little old. Anson out."

"Ten-four."

Anson reseated the radio handset and stepped out of the Suburban. He touched the butt of his gun so maybe he wouldn't have to touch it during or afterward. The ritual grounded him and helped him focus on the task ahead. It was something he tried to do before every arrest. As he strode toward the weathered front porch, he hoped it would be enough.

Anson knocked on the door and waited. The hands on his

watch read ten to eleven. Someone should be up by now. He rapped his knuckles against the door again, this time sounds of activity rising within the house. He decided to poke the bear and knocked again.

"All right all right, hold yer fuckin' horses."

Anson groaned. Dealing with Jezebel would be unpleasant enough, but throwing Frankie into the mix made a bad situation even worse. He took a fortifying breath and prepared himself.

Frankie worked the deadbolt, pulled open the door, and rolled her eyes. "Anson Jacobs." She settled her weight onto one leg and pulled the door closer to her body. "Last time I saw yah, you were spouting off on how to raise my kid. This better be good."

"Morning, Frankie. I'd like to speak to Jezebel please."

"What's the little bitch done now?"

"Just do us both a favor and get her for me."

Frankie shrugged and poked her head part way out the door, scanning the driveway. "Don't see the 'Cuda. She's probably not home."

"Can you check?"

Frankie narrowed her eyes. "What's in it for me?"

"My undying gratitude," Anson deadpanned.

"Now *that's* some bullshit if I ever heard it. Wait here." Frankie pushed the door closed and headed to the top of the stairs at the end of the hallway.

The door hadn't latched properly. Anson gave it a nudge and listened.

"Jeze-BEL!" Frankie banged on the doorframe. "Get your ass up here!"

Anson heard a muffled voice float through the floorboards. "She's probably not here, *my ass*," Anson said to himself.

"Now, DAMMIT! I ain't got all day."

A door slammed somewhere in the house followed by thumping on the stairs. "What?"

There was the familiar voice he had grown to despise. Anson smiled and whispered, "Gotcha."

"Sheriff's here to see you," Frankie said.

"What for?"

"How the fuck should I know? Now move it!"

"Just a second," Jezebel said, followed by thumping back down the stairs.

"Yah better not cut and run." Frankie waited a moment for Jezebel's response. "You HEAR me?"

More thumps, then, "I'm not! Fucking *lay off.*" The sound of Jezebel ascending the stairs echoed through the house. She pushed Frankie backward against the wall. "I ain't got nothing to hide."

Not expecting the sudden outburst, Frankie backed off and recomposed herself.

Jezebel strode toward the front door in bare feet, confidently at first, with her hair hanging in greasy clumps. When she met Anson's unimpressed gaze, she slowed her pace, winced slightly, and placed her right hand gently on her side. Anson could see a corner of gauze bandage sticking out from underneath her Megadeth T-shirt and jean shorts. Frankie followed, keeping her distance.

Jezebel stopped just short of the door. "What?"

"Put on some shoes," Anson said.

"Don't need shoes."

"Suit yourself. Now step out onto the porch, please, Miss Caine."

"Why?" She snarled her questions at him. "What for?"

Anson slipped a piece of folded paper out from his back pocket. "I have a warrant for your arrest."

Jezebel smirked at him. "Another bullshit charge, Deputy Dolt?"

"Unlawful discharge of a weapon in a public place," Anson said. "Last Saturday at the Starlite SuperSkate. You can read it if you like."

Jezebel fidgeted with her hands and shifted her weight on her feet. Her eyes flicked to the warrant and back, but she made no attempt to reach for it.

"You're developing quite a reputation." Anson placed the warrant back in his pocket. "Don't even think of running. I can, *and will,* pursue, adding evading arrest to your list of charges."

Jezebel glanced back at the doorway that led downstairs, then at Frankie.

"She didn't hurt anyone, did she?" The chip on Frankie's shoulder was gone, apparently replaced with concern. But Anson knew it was mostly an act.

"Shut up," Jezebel hissed.

To Frankie, Anson said, "No. Everyone was fine." He motioned at Jezebel. "Step onto the porch. Face the wall with your hands up and spread your legs."

Jezebel's face flushed red with anger and grudgingly did as she was told. Anson unclipped a pair of handcuffs and tightened them around her right wrist.

"What, aren't you going to read me my rights?"

"Don't need to," Anson said. "I've got all the evidence I need." He brought her left wrist behind her back and secured the cuffs. "But feel free to open your mouth and give me more I can use."

Frankie took several steps toward Jezebel before Anson told her to stop. Softly, she said, "Jezzy, that's not how I raised you—"

"You didn't raise me *AT ALL!*" Jezebel spat at her, the gobs of saliva speckling Frankie's face. "You're not a mother. You're a *fucking whore!*"

Frankie looked like she had been slapped. She wiped her brimming eyes and the dripping saliva away with trembling hands.

"Alright. Enough." Anson grabbed Jezebel's bicep and guided her down the porch steps and through the weed infested lawn to his parked SUV.

"Everything's going to be okay," Frankie called out to them. Neither responded.

Anson opened the door to the back bench seat and escorted Jezebel inside.

"I didn't do nothing," Jezebel said, her eyes glaring at him through strands of unkempt hair. "I'll be out in no time."

Anson strode around the front of the Suburban and hopped into the drivers seat. "The video evidence I have will keep you behind bars for a month." He turned and locked his eyes on her. "I'm going to use that time to put you away for good."

"Fucking Roxy," Jezebel muttered to herself.

"What was that?"

Jezebel ignored him and glowered through the window at Frankie standing on the porch.

Anson faced forward, started the engine, and unhooked the radio handset. "Sadie, Anson here. Enroute with Jezebel Caine. ETA three minutes. Anson out." Dispatch squawked acknowledgment as he rolled away from the curb.

In the rear view mirror, he thought he spotted a grin on Jezebel's face. Subtly, he shook his head in disdain as he began the short drive to the station.

ANSON PARKED AT the station and unloaded Jezebel from the back seat. "Okay, Miss Caine. No funny business. You're in enough trouble as it is."

He expected a snide comment in return, but Jezebel remained quiet and relatively compliant as he directed her forward, his left hand grasping her right bicep, her wrists cuffed at the small of her back.

As they approached the front entrance to the station, Anson spotted Monty and another young man exchange a special handshake. He felt Jezebel hesitate and bump into him.

"Watch it. I still hurt." Jezebel's eyes hovered on the two men for a moment longer than what seemed normal to Anson, then she glanced at him. "You got any pain killers?"

"Yeah. Inside," Anson said. "Let's go."

Monty remained on the steps to the station as the young man hustled away from Anson's approach. A wide toothy smirk spread on his face. He crossed his arms against his chest and watched them approach behind his mirrored sunglasses.

"Well, well, well. Jazz is in *trou-ble*," he said in a sing-song voice.

"Keep your distance, Monty, or you're going to join her."

Monty held up his hands, palms out. "Don't want no trouble, chief." He slid his sunglasses an inch down his nose to get an unobstructed view. "But damn, joinin' *Jazz* wouldn't be *that* bad. Joined at the hip, that is."

"Fuck off, sleaze bag." Jezebel lunged at him, but Anson pulled her back.

"Ignore him." Anson led Jezebel up the steps and opened the door for her. She paused at the threshold and looked back. Monty stood propped against the railing, sporting his shit-eating grin.

"I got you, *Jazz*. You know I do." He kissed his index and middle finger, then pointed them at her like a gun and fired.

Anson watched Jezebel's jaw tighten and ball her hands into tight fists. He pulled her away and they both entered the station.

Once the exterior door closed, Jezebel glanced back at the entrance once more as Monty walked away. "What would you say if I told you I got dirt on that asshole." Her voice was barely above a whisper.

Controlled rage.

Curiosity piqued, Anson faced her. "I'm listening."

"If I tell you, will you let me go?"

Anson had no intention of letting Jezebel go. She had to know that. What was her end game? It couldn't be as simple as wanting to get rid of the local drug dealer. But maybe it was.

"I'll see what I can do," he said. "*If* your information checks out. But you're going to wait it out in juvie."

Jezebel considered his words as she scanned the station, past Sadie at her desk and the one other officer on duty. The holding cells were empty. "Where can we talk?"

Anson and Sadie exchanged glances as he led Jezebel to his office and closed the door.

Barracuda

Quinn could see the off-ramp to Main Street ahead. She glanced at Cash in the front passenger seat, then at Wynter and Ransom in the back. They sat close and appeared to be talking to each other in whispers. If they had been alone, they would have been all over each other, just like back at the chapel. But with Cash in the car too, there was a different vibe, and it wasn't entirely pleasant.

Still, with the exception of Jake, all her friends were back where they were supposed to be, and that was something worth smiling about. She sailed past the exit to Main Street.

"Hey wait." Cash twisted in his seat to watch the back of the exit sign recede behind the VW. "What are you doing? That was our exit."

Wynter hadn't noticed but looked out the rear window to confirm Cash's observation.

Quinn kept her eyes on the road. "A successful rescue mission demands a celebration."

Wynter found Quinn's gaze in the rear view mirror. "Lucy's?"

"Correctamundo," she said. "On me. What do you say, Cash?"

"I say... two thumbs up." But Cash's enthusiasm didn't quite match his words. "I already know what I want."

"Too bad Jake's not with us," Wynter said. "He's part of this rag tag fugitive fleet."

Quinn's eyes lit up. "Battlestar Galactica! Nice one, Bug."

Cash turned to Wynter. "Movie quotes now? Who *are* you?" He managed a wink and faced forward again.

"I don't know where that came from," Wynter said. "You must be rubbing off on me, Quinn." She faced Ransom. "Hungry?"

Ransom nodded, then leaned in and kissed her. Wynter kissed him back, clearly enjoying the moment, then pulled back and shook her head.

"Not here," she whispered. Ransom backed off.

Quinn caught the exchange and sent Wynter a short look of disapproval. "I'm going to get Jake some takeout."

Ten minutes later, Quinn left the interstate and rolled Blue Belle into a parking spot near Lucy's front entrance. Lucy's was always busy, but at six in the morning a parking spot always seemed to be available.

She opened her door and inhaled. "Oh my God, I'm dying for some bacon. Come on!"

The four teenagers wandered inside and had no problem securing a table. Rhonda spotted them and grabbed four coffee cups and a carafe of fresh brew.

"I never pegged you for an early riser, Quinn." Rhonda distributed the cups and poured four coffees.

"I'm not." Quinn looked at her friends, her lips curling into a small grin. "We, like, stayed up all night, so..."

"Huh. Youth is wasted on the young." Rhonda set her carafe down on the table and flipped open her order pad.

"Then wisdom is wasted on the old." Cash smiled at her from behind his blond curls.

"Touché, Mr. Hawkins." Rhonda surveyed the teens expectantly. "Ready to order?"

They were. Wynter and Quinn ordered Belgian waffles with blueberries, whipped cream, and a side of bacon. Ransom chose what he had ordered the last time: the New-Heaven Big Bite. Cash picked the Eighteen-Wheeler, which consisted of three bennies, three pancakes, sausage, bacon, hashbrowns, and toast.

Fifteen minutes later, Rhonda appeared with all four meals balanced on her hands and forearms. After distributing the food, she placed her hands on her hips. "Anything else I can get you party animals?"

The only one without their mouth full was Cash. "I think we're good. Thanks." He cut into his bennie and looked across the table. "So, Ransom, what's it like to be inside the head of a psychopath?"

Ransom swallowed his mouthful. "Most of the time it's just black. Like, pitch black, as if you've been buried alive." He carved a piece of sausage and speared it with his fork. "Her dreams aren't much better."

"What *does* Jezebel dream about?" Quinn asked.

"Most of what I saw were dreams about her past. She's had a rough life." Ransom set his fork down. "She doesn't know who her father is because her mom…" He leaned in to the table and lowered his voice. "Her mom, like, screwed a different guy every night." He sat back and popped the bite of sausage into his mouth. Between chews, he continued. "The dreams I was in… let's just say she treated me like a piece of meat, like a sex doll."

Quinn and Wynter exchanged glances across the table.

Ransom shook his head. "She's filled with rage."

"That's exactly why we can't give up," Wynter said. "Now that you're back, we have to figure out how we're going to nail Jezebel for good. I know she could get at least five years for burning my house down."

"If Jake were here, he'd want to take things to Anson," Cash said.

"Shit!" Quinn slapped the table in frustration. "Jake. I meant to order something for him."

"Just do it when you pay," Wynter said.

Quinn nodded at her. "Don't let me forget."

Cash continued. "Maybe going to the police is our only option now. I mean, like, what else can we do that we haven't done."

Quinn raised her brow at him. "Kill her?"

Cash rolled his eyes. "Not this again. Be serious."

"I am." Quinn turned to Ransom. "You could kill her. *And* get away with it 'cause you're a dreamwaker."

Ransom blinked back at her.

Quinn continued. "Would you do it?"

"You *are* serious." Cash set his fork down. "Jesus, Quinn, there's got to be a better way."

She turned on him. "Yeah? Like what, exactly?"

Cash stammered. "I... I don't know. But I'm not going to be a part of..." He lowered his voice. "Of murdering someone in cold blood."

"That's what she'd do to us." Quinn glared at Cash, then at Wynter and Ransom. "In a heartbeat. You know she would."

Wynter reached across the table and placed her hand on Quinn's. "I used to think the same way. I mean she almost killed me. Twice. But you're better than Jezebel. We're better."

Quinn sighed. "Okay. We go to Anson with everything we know. And I mean everything." With serious eyes she met Wynter's gaze, then looked at Ransom, then Cash. "Agreed?"

Cash reached out and placed his left hand on her right, giving it a gentle squeeze. "Agreed."

Wynter and Ransom mirrored the gesture of solidarity. "Agreed. Most definitely," she said.

Quinn took a gulp of coffee. "You guys have any idea what Jake's favorite meal is here?"

Without hesitation, Cash spoke up. "Bronco Buster with the works. And fries."

"You sure?"

"Hundred percent." Cash leaned in to her. "Honestly, Quinn, you could bring him a bag of dog shit and he'd be happy. He's into you big time."

Quinn's eyes flicked to Wynter's and she swallowed hard.

"Okay. Thanks." She flagged down Rhonda and ordered Jake's take out.

The four of them polished off their meals. Quinn paid and met the others at the car. She handed Jake's food to Cash to hold, and they all piled inside the little car.

"I'm going to run by Jake's to drop off his food, then drop you guys off," Quinn said.

Cash shook his head. "No. You'll take us to my place *first,* then go to Jake's."

"Yeah, and make your move already," Wynter said.

Quinn smiled. "Okay. Then we meet later, and spill to Anson."

"Right," Cash said.

Quinn started Blue Belle's engine and began the journey home to Cash's trailer, then to Jake's. She felt excitement rise in her stomach. Even though it had been less than a day since she had last seen Jake, she had missed him. She hoped he had missed her, too.

QUINN STOOD AT Jake's front door, one Bronco Buster and fries in one hand, and the other thrumming nervous fingers against her leg. The bag of food from Lucy's still felt warm against her leg and the smell made her stomach growl, even though she had just eaten.

She rang the doorbell and waited. After a minute passed, Quinn considered ringing again. She wanted to hand deliver the food to Jake. Leaving it on the front stoop wasn't part of her plan.

Quinn reached out to press the doorbell again but pulled her hand back when she heard the deadbolt retract.

Jake opened the door. On any other day, his eyes would have lit up and he would have given her a big smile. There was no joy in his face and his eyes were set within grey circles. Something was up.

"Hey, Jake. Brought you something." Quinn raised the bag and smiled at him in an attempt to lighten the mood. "Bronco Buster and fries."

"Why?"

Quinn frowned for a second, then leaned against the door frame. " 'Cause you're part of our team, even *with* that cast on."

"Thanks. Want to come in?"

"Most definitely!"

Jake shifted backward and pulled the door open wider to let her through.

Quinn stepped into the foyer in front of the stairs. "Hope you're hungry."

"I haven't eaten yet," Jake said. "I've been a little busy."

"Oh." Quinn found herself holding back, trying to use Jake's vibe as a guide. "Is this a bad time?"

A small chuckle and a hint of a smile broke through Jake's funk. "No. I just had one hell of a morning."

Quinn blinked at him, waiting for the rest of the story.

He hooked his thumb at the stairs. "You can head up. I got to tell my mom that you're here."

Quinn watched Jake walk toward the back of the house, then headed up the stairs to Jake's room. She mused about the difference between her parents' way of doing things and Jake's. Her mom wouldn't have cared to know who she invited up to her room as long as she didn't do drugs or get pregnant. Perhaps Jake's parents weren't much different, except for their naive idea that an open bedroom door would prevent teenagers from doing teenaged things. Teenagers always found a way. Quinn was no exception.

She stepped into Jake's room and her jaw dropped. Normally cluttered in a neat and organized way, the room looked like a cyclone had gone through it. Half of his magazine collection sat in jumbled piles, divided between his bed and his desk. A twisted mound of unspooled videotape overflowed the waste basket. The tripod set in the dormer window no longer had a video camera atop it.

"What the hell...?" Quinn trailed off as she surveyed the room, carefully stepping around more videotape on the floor.

"What a fucking mess, huh?"

Quinn turned around to see Jake, framed by the doorway. "What happened?"

Jake navigated around his bed and sat, laying his crutches next to him. Quinn handed him the bag from Lucy's and took a spot on the bed next to him.

Seemingly without breathing, Jake unloaded the morning's events and Quinn sat and listened. Two weeks ago, she would have accused him of making it all up, but nothing surprised her now.

"I killed her, Quinn." Jake's hands had tightened to fists on the paper bag.

Quinn leaned into his slumped shoulder. "You didn't kill her, Jake. A dreamwaker is just an extension of a dream. And dreams aren't real."

"Whatever she was, she died because of what I did. Dream or not." Jake's reddened eyes were thick with tears ready to fall.

"Haven't you ever killed something in a dream?"

Jake paused to think, then shrugged.

"I think we all have at some point," Quinn said.

Jake faced her. "Have you ever killed something, like, while you're awake?"

Quinn shook her head slowly, not taking her eyes off his.

"It's different." Jake looked down at the bag from Lucy's Burger Stop. "I'm never going to forget what I did as long as I live."

"It's going to be okay, Jake."

He shook his head and quickly wiped his tears away. "It's not. Because there's more."

Quinn tried to imagine what he had left out but came up blank.

"She was practically naked when I killed her." Jake closed his eyes. "All she had on was a miniskirt and her underwear. She wanted me and I wanted her, even though I didn't." He found Quinn's eyes with his. "Does that make sense?"

"Did you—"

"No. I'm saving that for..."

Jake didn't need to say it. Quinn knew that he meant her. It was the sweetest thing anyone had *almost* ever said to her. She closed her eyes and swallowed hard, her own secret weighing heavily on her.

"You're quite the guy, Jake Peterson. Whatever happened between you and Roxy doesn't change things between us. At least for me it doesn't." Quinn sighed, knowing the only way forward was through the truth. "But I've got a confession too."

"About Roxy?"

"No." Quinn took Jake's hands off the cinched top of the bag and held them in hers. "This happened before we got closer."

"What did?" Jake's eyes were uncertain. He wanted answers but Quinn saw that he feared them as well.

"I had sex with Ransom. Twice." There. It was out. Quinn held her breath and waited for an inevitable explosion.

Jake slid his hands away. His eyes wandered from her face to the closet in front of him, to the floor, to the bag on his lap. "Was he your first?"

"No, but I feel terrible about it," Quinn said. "I still do. I hurt Wynter and now I've hurt you."

Silence descended onto the room. Quinn desperately wanted to know what Jake was thinking, whether she had just torpedoed any possibility of a future with him. But she also knew that she had to wait for his response.

"I'm not going to ask why," Jake said. "He's a good looking

guy. But it was you who told me a few seconds ago that I didn't really kill Roxy."

"It was an accident, Jake. With me, it wasn't. I planned it." Her eyes fell to her unclasped hands with anxious worry. "That makes it so much worse."

"Except I didn't know Roxy was a dreamwaker until she drifted. Who knows what would've happened if she hadn't fallen. I might've lost my virginity to her." Jake shuddered at the thought, then looked at her. "Maybe you didn't *really* have sex with Ransom. You know? Since *technically* he's not real."

They looked at each other, both knowing that the logic of Jake's reasoning was flawed, both not caring.

Quinn relaxed and took his hand in hers. "I'll say it again. You're quite the guy. And I'll tell you a secret. You're not a virgin in *my* dreams."

Jake's heart flipped in his chest. His steamy yet frustrating dreams of Quinn rushed to the forefront of his mind, almost impairing his ability to talk. He tried his best to conceal his surprise but failed in a mostly endearing way.

"You've *dreamed* of me?"

"Uh huh," Quinn said, a playful smile on her face. "And since it's confession time... I also made a dreamwaker version of you, and..."

Jake blinked at her, looking a little stunned. "And?"

"And... like I said before, you're *not* a virgin in my dreams."

Jake gripped the top of the burger bag with two anxious fists and swallowed hard. "I've dreamed of you too, but they always ended too soon... if you know what I mean."

"Maybe we can change that later, for real." Quinn nudged the bag on his lap. "Now eat up while it's still a little bit warm."

Jake glanced back at his open bedroom door. "What if I want dessert first?"

It was a cheesy line, but Quinn didn't care. Anything that

restarted the heat between them was fine by her. "Then maybe you should—"

Jake let go of the bag. He held Quinn's face with gentle hands and kissed her. She kissed him back fiercely. They eased down onto his bed, on their sides facing each other, pushing piles of magazines out of the way as they went.

Quinn was surprised at how well Jake kissed, considering his professed lack of experience. She slipped her hand under his shirt and ran her fingertips up his back. He pushed off his baseball cap and responded in turn with more intense kisses.

She could feel his hands slide gently around her bra and the swell of one of her breasts. Quinn also sensed something happening below Jake's belt. She led with her hand, over his hips and past his cast to the crotch of his jeans. She felt hardness and heat and a desire within her she had not felt this strongly before. Sex with Ransom had been good and exciting, but her feelings for Jake raised every sensation to a higher level.

She took off her glasses and set them aside before rolling onto her back and pulling Jake on top of her. He had been unprepared for her boldness, the move made more awkward by his cast. He tried to lift it over her legs, but the cast's weight pulled him backward toward the edge of the bed and the toe of his cast hit the floor with a *thump,* crushing his toes.

Jake clenched his teeth and grimaced at the pain of the impact.

"I'm sorry I'm sorry," Quinn whispered. Jake rolled onto his back, sucking air through his teeth.

"Everything okay up there?" Mirielle's voice floated up from the main floor.

"Yeah, Mom," Jake called back. He looked at Quinn, smiled, and rolled his eyes. "Just dropped my crutch."

Quinn stifled a laugh and slid her hand down his stomach and under the button of his jeans. She imagined going down on him right then and there and blowing his mind.

Jake shook his head. "I want to, Quinn, I really, *really* do, but my mom's got, like, a sixth sense or something. She's probably going to bake something and—"

"I just put blueberry muffins in the oven, if you want some," Mirielle's voice said from below.

"Yeah, sounds good." He lowered his voice for Quinn. "See? What'd I tell you? Let's put things into pause, okay?"

She nodded. "But you better eat your burger and fries first, or I might get offended."

Jake picked the bag up from the floor and unrolled the top. He pulled out the burger and a cardboard sleeve of fries and placed them on the flattened bag. "I still detect some warmth." He unwrapped the burger and took a bite. "I taste a particle of pre-animate pickle caught between the patties." A glob of ketchup oozed out onto the corner of his mouth.

"*Star Trek II: The Wrath of Khan,*" Quinn said with a smile. "But just barely." She leaned over and licked the smeared tomato sauce from his face.

"I thought you didn't like ketchup."

"It tastes pretty good on you." She leaned back to a sitting position and bounced lightly on the bed. "Hurry up and eat. I want a blueberry muffin." The bed squeaked with each bounce.

Jake paused his eating and smiled at her. "You probably should stop bouncing. You're going to give my mom a heart attack."

Quinn clued into the sound she was making and giggled. "Oops. Sorry."

He presented the half eaten burger and fries. "Want some? It's damn good."

"No thanks. I'm holding out for muffins."

Jake continued to eat and spoke between bites. "I got to get my magazines reorganized. And get my other camcorder set up."

"I don't think we're going to need it," Quinn said.

Jake scrunched his brow, confused, and side-eyed her.

"Oh! I forgot to tell you. This afternoon we're going to give

Anson everything we know." Quinn found her glasses on the bed and returned them to her face. "I guess I got a little... *distracted*."

Jake chuckled. "Me too." He finished the last bite of burger and wiped his fingers on a napkin. "It's about time we got Anson involved."

"Cash said you'd say that."

"I'm that predictable, am I?"

"Not *that* predictable." Quinn placed her hands on his cheeks. "You're a great kisser."

"Are you surprised by that?"

"A little bit... but mostly not." She gave him a quick smooch. "Let's get some of your stuff cleaned up or your mom might get ideas. I don't want to get on her bad side."

"Okay." Jake moved to his right bedside table. "Feel like some music?" Quinn nodded and Jake turned on his clock radio. "Maniac" by Michael Sembello burst through the radio's small speakers.

"Oh!" Immediate recognition from Quinn. "From—"

"*Flashdance!*" they said in unison.

Quinn started moving her legs to the electric piano riff, trying hard to mimic the dance scene in the movie. "Am I a steel town girl?" She moved her body next to Jake and gazed up at him. "Or am I *cra-zy?*"

"You're a maniac. Most definitely." Jake bobbed his head, swayed side to side on his crutches, and moved his right leg back and forth in rhythm with the music.

Quinn used Jake's limited mobility to her advantage and danced around him. It was more fun than she had had in months. She found herself looking ahead to a time when Jake's cast was off. They'd be able to do so much more together. So much more.

The radio played and the two of them danced more than they tidied. Quinn didn't care about the noise they were making, and Jake didn't seem to mind leaving his magazines for later. They existed only for each other until the smell of fresh baked muffins lured them downstairs.

"YOU SAID YOU'D cut me loose!" Jezebel scowled at Anson through the rear view mirror. "That was the deal. You fucking *crossed* me."

"I said I'd think about leniency, if your story checked out."

Jezebel's wrists scraped against the handcuffs behind her back. She kicked the plexiglass divider in front of her and cursed under her breath.

After taking Jezebel's information about Monty and processing her misdemeanor at the station, Anson had loaded her back into the Suburban. His next stop was MacLeod County Juvenile Detention Facility in Lake Gilberg.

The facility had existed at the north end of Lake Gilberg long before the town had become a desired location for upper middle class families to settle. New residents had repeatedly beat the drums of lowered property value and increased crime as reasons for the facility to be shuttered or relocated. Despite the residents' vocal opposition, the facility remained, and the town grew up around it. In actuality, Lake Gilberg's crime rate had remained surprisingly low, a fact protesters conveniently ignored.

The detention facility served both female and male residents, separated visually and physically from each other. The Green Wing housed beds for twenty females and the Black Wing provided forty-five beds for males.

"You're lucky there was a bed available," Anson said as he took Exit 183 to Lake Gilberg. "MacJuvie is considered posh by most standards." He glanced at her through the rear view mirror. "But you've always had a lucky horseshoe around your neck, haven't you, Miss Caine."

Jezebel ignored him and watched the elm and boxelder maple trees fly past the window.

"Tell me. Why did you shoot up the Starlite?" Anson kept his eyes on the road but could sense her anger coming at him in waves from the back seat.

"Do you see a lawyer here?" Jezebel shot back.

Anson responded with a small nod. She wasn't going to talk, and his curiosity could wait. It would be better not to provoke her anyway.

Twenty minutes later, Anson turned into the parking lot of the detention facility and navigated to the secured drop-off zone for law enforcement. The gate opened and he advanced the Suburban forward. As he waited for the gate to close behind him, he shut the engine off and turned in his seat to face Jezebel.

"You ever been here before?"

Jezebel continued to stare out the window. Anson noted the same clenched jaw muscles she had displayed with Monty.

"Once inside, they're going to give you new clothes and do an intake interview," Anson said. "It'll be just a bunch of questions about you and your situation. Tell them what they want to know. They use the information to keep you safe. If you lie, they'll find out eventually and it'll make your situation worse. They'll want you to shower and change. Don't be difficult. Your time here doesn't have to be bad."

"Gee, thanks *dad.*"

Anson unbuckled his seatbelt, stepped out of the SUV, and walked to the opposite side. He pulled open the rear passenger door. "Let's go, Miss Caine."

Jezebel shifted off the seat and extended her right leg to the asphalt. Anson noticed that her bandage was hanging loose out of her shirt and pointed at it.

"You might want to fix—"

"I *got* it!" Jezebel pulled up the hem of her T-shirt, then glared up at him. "Do you *mind?*"

Anson stood back to give her space and averted his eyes. After she had reaffixed her bandage, he escorted her inside the facility.

He worked in tandem with another Corrections Officer and switched Jezebel's handcuffs with a pair supplied by the facility, locking her hands in front of her. The Corrections Officer led her toward a series of locked doors.

Jezebel stopped at the first door. "You better not fuck me over, Deputy Dolt."

The *old* Jezebel that he knew was back. Anson shrugged. "Depends if your story checks out."

The Corrections Officer pulled her past the first door and let it close with a heavy metallic clunk. The first door locked automatically, before the Corrections Officer could open the second door to the inside. Anson had toured the inner sanctum of the detention facility two years before and had no interest in going any farther.

Jezebel was right where she needed to be. Anson left the building and began his journey back to the station. He had thirty days to nail her coffin shut for good, even if her dirt on Monty worked to her advantage.

AFTER JEZEBEL HAD COMPLETED her intake interview, a Corrections Officer waited for her to shower and change into her new standard facility clothes. Her forest green T-shirt with "M C J D F" on the back in block letters matched her forest green pocketless sweatpants. She wasn't permitted a bra or shoes and the panties provided were worn and stained. At least they smelled fresher than they looked.

The Corrections Officer issued Jezebel her bedding and escorted her to a six by eight cell, one of five in pod D, dubbed "The Divas" by a handwritten paper sign on the wall.

"When do I get my phone call?"

The Corrections Officer looked at her with tired eyes. "Leave your stuff and follow me."

The officer led her to a bank of phones, most occupied. Jezebel picked up a free handset. "Hey, what time is it?"

The Corrections Officer glanced at his watch. "About quarter to one."

A small grin formed on Jezebel's lips as she dialed. The line trilled twice, then connected. "Hey. Yeah, it's done... yeah, totally. I wish I could see his face when Deputy Dolt arrests his ass... Look, I got to bounce. Got eyes on me... Yeah. Phase two... Got it." She hung up.

Jezebel returned to her cell in pod D. The other cells were vacant, their residents elsewhere in the facility. She sat on her built-in bunk and surveyed her new space. A toilet, sink, desk, and stool lined the opposite wall. It wasn't comfortable, but it was livable. That didn't matter because she wouldn't be here for long.

"Phase two," Jezebel said quietly. She stretched out on her bunk and let her eyes wander the patterns on the water-stained ceiling tiles. The passing minutes brought a small self-assured smile to her face.

JEZEBEL'S INSTRUCTIONS HAD been very specific: don't let Quinn out of her sight. Roxy had backed the Barracuda into her driveway to make surveillance easier. Focusing on the small reflected image of Jake's house in the rear view mirror had left her with a crick in her neck. Now facing the house, she could recline in the 'Cuda's cloth and vinyl bucket seats.

Roxy had no idea why Jezebel wanted her to follow Quinn but did not want to disappoint her. She slid down in the driver's seat until she was just high enough to see over the steering wheel and dashboard.

Quinn's blue Volkswagen had been parked in front of Jake's house since the morning. As Roxy watched the house, her mind replayed the dream she had had with Jake. She could have had so much fun with him in dreamwaker form. But no, Jezebel had to make her kill him. Roxy had gotten no pleasure from it.

Her eyes floated up to Jake's dormer window. *What's taking so long? What are they doing in there?* Roxy's eye narrowed. *That could've been me. But he...*

Roxy made a sudden realization. "He *killed* me?" The memory in her head was fuzzy and she didn't quite trust it, but she could see Jake's room in perfect detail even though she had never set foot there.

It was my dreamwaker.

Roxy had cloned herself almost six hours ago, yet another task Jezebel had made her do, this time to destroy Jake's videotapes. When her dreamwaker twin hadn't returned, she had assumed everything had worked.

Bits and pieces of memories surfaced: of being almost naked on his bed, of Jake's interest, his rage, and her pain. As Roxy tried to fill in the details, the more the memories faded. Something good and bad had happened and now she'd never remember the truth.

It was well past lunch time, and her growling stomach didn't help with her mood, magnifying her simmering anger and envy. A quick snack would do her good. It wouldn't take long.

Roxy took one last glance at the VW as if forming a mental image of the scene would prevent it from changing. She ran into her house to the kitchen and grabbed an apple from the refrigerator. Cool water straight from the faucet quenched her thirst but the sound of running water woke up her bladder. She took a bathroom break and grabbed a Nature Valley granola bar from the pantry as she headed for the front door.

Roxy leaped back into the Barracuda, the granola bar in her hand and the apple clamped in her jaws. She eased the car door closed and gazed across the street.

The Volkswagen was gone.

She dropped the apple to her lap. "Shit!" Her excursion had taken only a few minutes. But Jezebel would know she had screwed up again. And a car could travel a long way in a few minutes.

Roxy started the engine and turned down Mortimer Avenue in the direction that the VW had been facing. Newhaven was a small town. Where would Quinn go? Possibly anywhere.

She had a brain flash. Roxy doubled back on the next street over, Hobbs Avenue. Quinn's house, Jake's, and hers were so close you could throw stones from one to the other. Right now, she wanted to throw stones at Quinn's VW, even at Quinn herself. Roxy slowed the Barracuda, letting the engine settle into a low rolling rumble.

Quinn's house sat beside a hedge on the left side of the property, separating it from the next door neighbor. As Roxy drove closer, the iconic chrome bumper from the Beetle inched into view in the driveway. She pulled to the curb and watched, just like Jezebel had instructed.

From behind the hedge, Jezebel stepped out from Quinn's driveway and into the street, a bat gripped firmly in one hand and no happiness to see her.

I Will Survive

On most days, Ernie would cross paths briefly with Cash in the morning as his son left for Finn's. At the very least there would be evidence of breakfast still on the stove. If he was lucky, Cash would have left him some bacon or eggs or both. But he returned this Thursday morning to find the trailer empty.

Scenarios ran through his head.

Was Cash in trouble?

Had Cash left for work already?

He peeked into Cash's bedroom. His bed was still partially made, which meant he hadn't slept in it last night. It was an odd occurrence to happen on a Wednesday night, but after the murder at the Gas N Go less than twenty-four hours ago, Finn had given Cash a couple of days off.

Probably just blowing off steam.

Tired from his shift, Ernie hustled himself into bed and was asleep before eight. Even though he had reassured himself about Cash's safety in his head, his sleep was restless. He knew his son was responsible and made good choices, but he was a teenager. Sometimes even responsible teenagers made mistakes.

Ernie woke at two-thirty in the afternoon, an hour earlier than most days, and his fears were soon put to rest. He found Wynter asleep in Cash's bedroom and Cash asleep on the sofa. His son had impressed him once again.

"Son?" Ernie had barely touched Cash's shoulder when his eyes flicked open, Cash scooted backward on the sofa, almost like he was preparing to defend himself. Once he met Ernie's gaze, Cash relaxed.

Ernie took a step back. "Tough night?"

"Just long." Cash sat up and ran his hands through his hair.

Ernie nodded toward Cash's bedroom. "Wynter's still asleep. Go wake her and I'll put on a pot of coffee."

Cash yawned and rubbed his eyes. "Thanks Dad."

Ernie gave Cash's shoulder a light squeeze before heading to the kitchen counter to begin the coffee. And bacon. It was a bacon kind of afternoon.

CASH PEERED INTO his bedroom. Wynter lay on her side, snoring lightly, her red hair spilling out across his pillow. He longed to be beside her but knew it was not in the cards as long as Ransom was around. He was back in her head, back where he belonged. Good for Wynter. Bad for him. He wasn't about to rock the boat.

Maybe I should *rock the boat...*

Cash didn't see himself as the jealous type, but denying his feelings became more difficult as time marched on. And as if his thoughts were being broadcast out loud through a megaphone, Wynter's eyes blinked open.

As he watched her wake up, he realized that Wynter had woken up *alone*. It was obvious now but with the unpleasantness of jealousy clouding his thoughts, he had completely missed it. Either Wynter hadn't dreamed of Ransom, or if she did, she chose to leave him in her head. Maybe he wouldn't have to rock the boat at all. Maybe he could just be himself.

Cash took a spot next to her on the bed. He offered a small smile which faltered when his eyes floated to the ruffled bedsheets at Wynter's back. Ransom wasn't visibly in the room, but he was there just the same.

"Did you..."

"What?" Wynter sat, her face lit up with disappointment and anger. "Do you really think I'd do that, like, in *your* bed?"

Cash swallowed hard. "Did you sleep okay?" He looked at her even though his heart ached to do so.

"Oh." Wynter blinked, embarrassed, and shrugged her shoulders, making her joints pop under her T-shirt. "I thought you meant—"

"I'd never ask you about that." Cash directed his gaze to the floor. "It's none of my business."

Silence descended and wedged itself between them. Finally, Wynter sighed and said, "I'm sorry. Do over?"

"Sure."

Wynter sat up and nodded, appearing to stare at the same spot on the floor. "I slept pretty good. No dreams for once." She squinted at the bright afternoon light streaming in through the window in his bedroom. "What time is it?"

Cash motioned at his clock radio. "General Electric says it's quarter to three."

"Shit. It's late." Wynter swung her legs off the bed. "We need to call Quinn and Jake."

The aromatic results of Ernie's cooking floated into the bedroom and made Wynter's stomach growl. Cash laughed quietly. "How about some coffee and bacon?"

"Most definitely. But bathroom first." Wynter tiptoed out of the room.

Despite the misunderstanding, Cash thought their exchange went well. He returned to the kitchen and began setting out plates and cutlery.

Ernie gave him a wary glance. "Everything okay?"

Cash nodded. "Is there enough for all of us?"

"Are you kidding?" Ernie laughed. "I'm the king of big breakfasts."

"Don't get too crazy, Dad," Cash said. "I'm still working on one of Lucy's Eighteen-Wheelers."

Ernie waved him off. "You worry about your friend."

Wynter stepped into the living room. "Something smells good."

"There's going to be lots, but I'm not that hungry." Cash flopped onto the sofa.

"I should call Quinn," Wynter said. "Can I use your phone?"

"Go for it."

Wynter sat at the end of the sofa next to Cash, picked up the phone's handset from its cradle, and punched in Quinn's number. She waited while the call trilled in her ear.

"She's taking a long time to answer."

"She might be asleep, too," Cash said.

Wynter listened but alarm bells were flashing in the back of her mind. If she had plans with Quinn, especially exciting ones, they'd both be glued to the phone. After the fifth ring, Quinn answered.

"Hey, it's me. What's up?" Wynter said. "When do you want to meet?" She waited for a response. "Quinn? You there?"

Cash watched a look of puzzlement cross Wynter's face, then a short smile. She covered the receiver with her hand and whispered, "She's just tired."

Cash gave her a tentative thumbs up.

"Okay. What about four o'clock?" Wynter nodded. "You want to call Jake and we'll, like, meet you there?" The confused look was back. "You know. At the police station."

What was going on over there? Was Quinn high? Drunk? Did she take one of those homemade sleeping cubes? Cash concentrated to try to hear Quinn's side of the conversation from where he sat, but the noise of Ernie's cooking proved too distracting. All he could go on was Wynter's facial expressions, which were not in line with a conversation with Quinn. Not at all.

Wynter hung up the phone and turned to Cash. "Well, that was weird."

"Looked like it," Cash said. "What did she say?"

"It was, like, more what she *didn't* say." Wynter shook her head. "She sounded totally out of it. And get this. She wanted *me* to call Jake. I would've thought she'd be all over that."

"Maybe something happened, like after dropping us off."

"Maybe." Wynter was not convinced, and neither was Cash.

Ernie placed a plate of bacon, eggs, and toast on the table. "Grub's up. Get it while it's hot."

Wynter was first to the table. "Looks great, Mr. Hawkins. Thank you."

"My pleasure, Wynter."

"I'll be right there." Cash walked around the sofa to the phone on the end table. "Going to call Jake and let him know what's going on." He picked up the handset. "Four o'clock, right?"

Wynter nodded, her mouth already filled with a bite of bacon.

Cash dialed and Jake picked up on the second ring, which made the call to Quinn all the more curious. He filled Jake in on their plans, then joined Wynter and Ernie at the table.

Even though Lucy's Eighteen-Wheeler was still moving through his body like a lead ball, Cash found some room for breakfast and coffee.

He thought ahead to their upcoming meeting. The plan was to lay all their cards on the table, including Ransom. But would Anson believe them?

Jezebel sat cross-legged on her bed, wearing shorts and a T-shirt. Despite the summer warmth, her basement bedroom was always comfortably cool. Last year's school yearbook sat in front of her.

Newhaven High School served just over three hundred students from grades nine through twelve. Next year she'd be a senior. Grade fucking 12. And if Jezebel Too had stuck to the first phase of her plan, soon Anson would have more than enough evidence to put Monty away for a long time.

She could take over his territory. Someone had to. Leaving that opportunity up to someone else would be a huge waste. She had the advantage. Being able to pull out dreamwakers of her own to do the dirty work would make selling drugs a whole lot easier. A sly grin spread across her lips.

But first things first. Dismantling Wynter's circle of friends was her priority now. They had already created too many problems for her. She flipped open the yearbook and found the section dedicated to 11th Grade students. Color pictures of ninety-one students, spread out over four pages stared back at her. Jezebel scanned through the head shots, five rows per page, five students per row. It took just a few seconds to find Quinn Benoit near the bottom of the first page.

"There you are." She placed her finger on top of Quinn's face, obscuring it. "You're mine, *bitch*."

She brought the photo close and studied Quinn's face, her glasses, her hair, the shirt she was wearing. Jezebel turned several pages ahead and read her write-up aloud. "President of the Film Fan Club, Quinn can't wait to graduate, move to Hollywood, and make movies."

"Hollywood? Fat chance, *chink*." Jezebel sneered as she turned to the yearbook's Film Fan Club page. Quinn had her arm hooked around Wynter holding an SLR camera and several other classmates sat on desks beside them with filmmaking equipment in their hands. They were all laughing. "The only place you're going is six feet under."

Jezebel flipped back to Quinn's mug shot and gave it one more look. "Phase two, I'm coming for you...," she said in a sing-song voice, like it was straight out of *A Nightmare On Elm Street*.

She propped the yearbook up beside her pillow, open to Quinn's photo, and lay down next to it, taking one last look before closing her eyes.

JEZEBEL STOOD IN the center of the "The Nexus", a common area of Newhaven High School where four corridors branched off leading north, south, east, and west. Lockers of a different color, each representing a different grade, lined each corridor. Students had voted blue as the color for 11th Grade. She would have preferred black.

The floors had been polished to an almost mirror shine, but the absence of students made the whole place feel surreal. Jezebel envisioned running into the cast of *The Breakfast Club* at any moment.

At the far end of the corridor, one student stood at their locker rummaging through the contents. The reflected sunlight made her eyes sting and forced her to squint to see any detail. Jezebel reached up and a pair of Ray-Ban Wayfarers materialized in her right hand. She set them in front of her eyes.

"There you are." A devious smile curled up one side of her lips as she pulled open the closest locker door. In front of her was Quinn, searching for something in her locker, as if a portal had opened up between them bridging the distance. Except Quinn couldn't see her. Yet.

Quinn's hair looked exactly as it did in Jezebel's yearbook, hanging in wavy strands with bangs curled up. Her shirt was a jumbled mess, part T-shirt, part button down, and she wore bootcut jeans with white Reebok High Tops.

"That's not going to work." Jezebel blinked and Quinn's top

morphed into a T-shirt with the word "HOLLYWOOD" written across it in its iconic lettering. "Gotta keep up the illusion."

She pushed through the void between lockers, grabbed Quinn by the throat, and kept moving until she had Quinn's back against the lockers across the corridor. "Surprise, fuck face."

Quinn's eyes popped in surprise, but she didn't struggle against Jezebel's assault. "What're you doing?"

"Yeah, what *are* you doing?" The voice came from behind. *Her* voice.

Jezebel glanced back and saw Jezebel Too, arms crossed against her chest and giving her a sideways look.

"Phase one went off without a hitch." Jezebel Too gave a wily smile, leaned against the lockers, and looked Quinn over. "This *cheap copy* ain't going to cut it."

"Got a better idea?"

"Actually, yeah," Jezebel Too said. "Surprised you haven't thought of it already." She leaned in close. "Maybe I'm smarter than you."

"Fuck off. Now what's your brilliant idea?"

Jezebel Too sneered and shook her head. "You keep forgetting that this is all just a *dream*."

Jezebel faced Quinn. Then things clicked. It all made sense. *She's just a shell that* looks *like Quinn*.

"Watch me... *disappear.*" Jezebel Too wiggled her fingers like she was casting a spell, strolled toward Quinn, then merged with her, matching her stance until Jezebel Too no longer was present. Quinn might still be a shell, but she had Jezebel Too inside her head.

Jezebel Too, acting as Quinn, raised her hands in a flourish. "Presenting Quizebel."

"Okay, that might work," Jezebel said.

"Of course it'll fucking work." Jezebel Too surveyed her new body through Quinn's eyes. "But I hate looking like this bitch. Let's get this over with."

Jezebel grabbed Quizebel's T-shirt with two fists. "Ready? Time to wake up." She pulled Quizebel off the lockers and propelled her toward the floor. Beams of light broke through the floor tiles as the two of them fell through the widening cracks.

Brightness overtook them both as remnants of the school twisted and shattered around their bodies. Jezebel jerked backward like someone had grabbed her by the shoulders and pulled. The sensation of flying tipped upside-down into a feeling of freefall.

Energy, bright and hot on her face, steeped her surroundings. For a moment Jezebel could no longer see Quizebel, despite knowing that the fabric of her T-shirt was still held firmly in both her fists.

She broke the beam of heat and realized that she had been looking straight at the sun. Autumn sunshine beaming through the one small window in her room had temporarily blinded her. Jezebel looked down and saw she was straddling Quizebel. The yearbook sat closed near the edge of the bed.

"What are you waiting for?" Quizebel said. "Get the fuck off me."

Jezebel slid off Quizebel's hips and sat next to her at the head of the bed, her back resting against the wall. Quizebel pushed herself to a sitting position next to her.

"You sure you can do this?" Jezebel picked up the yearbook and flipped through the pages.

"Uh, yeah. It'll be easier than that fucking cabbie," Quizebel said. "I'm *you*, not Roxy."

Jezebel pulled out the drawer from her bedside table, retrieved a small baggie of shamrock speed pills, and placed one on her tongue.

"Like *you* need to focus." Quizebel scowled at her.

"Shut up. Let's go." Jezebel picked up a bat from the corner of her room and led Quizebel out of the house.

"We're walking? Where's the 'Cuda?"

"Roxy's got it," Jezebel said. "She's tailing the real Quinn."

"Fuck her." Quizebel primped. "I'm the real Quinn now."

Quizebel may have looked identical to Quinn, but her mannerisms didn't match. Jezebel worried that the entire plan might derail because of Quizebel's attitude.

"Well, if you can't talk and act like her, you better just keep your damn mouth shut."

Grudgingly, Quizebel took the hint. Twenty minutes later the two of them walked past Quinn's house. The driveway was empty, and it appeared that no one was home. They stepped off the sidewalk and obscured themselves in the hedge that separated the property next door.

"So your brilliant plan is to just stand in the bushes and wait?"

"Remember what I said about talking?" Jezebel said.

Quizebel crossed her arms. "I'm definitely the smart one."

"Shut the fuck up!"

As if on cue, the sound of Quinn's Volkswagen rose from down the street, then passed the hedge and turned into the driveway.

"Showtime." Jezebel whispered as she faced Quizebel. "Walk up the driveway from the sidewalk and distract her. I'll get her from behind."

Quizebel offered a scowl in response.

"Just do it, asshole," Jezebel said. "You'll be playing little miss rich bitch in no time."

Quizebel concealed herself behind the hedge until she had reached the sidewalk, then reversed direction and strode quickly toward Quinn as she opened the Beetle's door. She had crouched into the vehicle to search for something.

Quizebel saw Jezebel position herself in the hedge. "Hey."

Quinn spun her head around, startled that someone was behind her. "What the..." She forgot whatever she was looking for in an instant and took a couple of uncertain steps toward Quizebel.

"Jake has a message for you."

Jezebel stepped from the hedge and raised the bat behind her head.

"What?" Quinn's eyes searched Quizebel for clues but couldn't get past her own face staring back at her. "How is this possible? You're me. You're..." Her eyes cleared and widened in horror. "You're a dream—"

Jezebel's bat struck the back of Quinn's head with a sickening *tock*, like a softball had just been knocked out of the park. Quinn stumbled forward and fell to the ground unconscious next to the VW's left rear tire.

"She's a smart cookie," Quizebel said.

"She's a dead cookie now." Jezebel reached into the VW, pulled out Quinn's satchel, and tossed it to Quizebel. "Get the hell inside before someone sees you."

Quizebel nodded. "Fucking A."

"Yeah, well don't fuck it up."

Jezebel walked down to the curb and scanned the street both ways. "Where the hell are you, Roxy? Goddammit." She glanced back at Quinn's body crumpled next to the Volkswagen. She had to get her out of sight as quickly as possible.

Jezebel hustled back to the VW and pulled Quinn's dead weight into a sitting position. She opened the door, tilted the seat forward, and grabbed Quinn under the arms and around the chest, as if she was giving her a bear hug. The thought disgusted her.

The iconic popcorn rumble of the Barracuda drifted up the street, breaking her concentration. Jezebel dropped Quinn to the pavement and headed back to the street.

Roxy had the Barracuda parked on the opposite side of the street, idling about a half block away from Quinn's driveway.

Jezebel imagined introducing her bat to Roxy's head and smashing her face in. She smiled at the thought, diffusing some of her anger as she sprinted toward the car.

"About fucking time."

Roxy let Jezebel's wrath slide over her. "I didn't want to follow too close."

"Whatever." Jezebel pointed at Quinn's driveway with the bat. It was then that she noticed dots of blood and several strands of black hair stuck to the end. "Back into her driveway and make it fast."

Roxy drove to the end of the street and parked the Barracuda in Quinn's driveway just as instructed. Jezebel ran to meet her, stopping on the way to run the end of the bat through the lawn of the neighboring house.

"Pop the trunk and help me." Jezebel tossed the bat into the back seat of the Barracuda. "Hurry your ass."

The trunk released and Roxy ran to the rear of the car. "Holy shit."

"Don't just stand there. Grab her arms."

Roxy hesitated. "Is she dead?"

"Who gives a shit?" Jezebel said. "Help me get her in the trunk."

Jezebel grabbed Quinn's feet and Roxy took her arms. With hands slicked with sweat, they dragged Quinn's body to the back of the Barracuda. Moving one-hundred twenty pounds of dead human weight across eight feet was more difficult than Jezebel had expected.

She wrapped her arms around Quinn's ankles and Roxy grasped Quinn's armpits and after two attempts they were able to transfer her into the trunk.

Jezebel slammed the trunk closed. She looked back at the house and saw Quizebel standing in the front window.

"Let's get the fuck out of here." They both jumped into the car and Jezebel threw the engine into drive. Fighting against her urge to floor the gas, she eased the Barracuda toward Main Street.

"Where we going?"

"Where nobody'll find her." Jezebel's eyes narrowed. "Until it's too late," she added under her breath.

"What if all this…" Roxy waved her hands around and continued. "What if it doesn't work?"

Jezebel curled her lip up at her. "Then *you're* going to have to get rid of Wynter. Once and for all."

"Why do *I* have to do it?"

"If you don't, you're *next*." Jezebel set her dark eyes upon Roxy for an uncomfortably long time. "Understand?" The Barracuda began to drift into the oncoming lane.

Roxy's jaws tightened. "Fine," she said through clenched teeth. "Just keep your eyes on the damn road."

"Pussy," Jezebel whispered to herself through a sneer. She pushed Roxy's pathetic resistance to the back of her mind. Her plan had been set in motion. Now it was up to Quizebel. She punched the gas pedal and sped south.

ANSON SAT IN HIS OFFICE and faced the window, his feet propped up on his desk. He mulled over the notes he had taken while Jezebel implicated Monty. What was her angle? Was it simple self-preservation or something more? If luck was shining down on him, he could rid Newhaven of two bad seeds in one fell swoop. But Anson didn't believe in luck.

Jezebel's information against Monty had been compelling. He was a known drug dealer that had eluded arrest for the past five years. It was a worthwhile lead that needed follow-up.

Anson craned his neck to see Sadie at her desk. "Did Monty's warrant come through while I was out? I had left a call for Judge Traxler from MacLeod County District Court. She's usually pretty quick when it matters.."

Sadie spun in her seat and approached the fax machine near the back wall. She collected several sheets from the machine's collector tray. "Myles Mancini?"

"That's it." Anson hopped up and met Sadie halfway, where she handed him the pages. "Going to have to send Traxler flowers or something."

"Try a bottle of scotch instead," Sadie said. "All judges like scotch, right?"

"Hell if I know."

"Just don't make it remotely romantic. I think she just got divorced."

"Noted." Anson returned to his desk, reclined with his feet up, and scanned through the warrant.

The station phone rang. Sadie answered and listened for a moment, then called at him through the open door of his office. "MacJuvie on one."

The phone on Anson's desk rang. He set Monty's warrant down and stared at the button for line one blinking at him relentlessly. Any guesses why they'd be calling were met with more questions his brain didn't want to entertain. Maybe Jezebel was injured, or better yet, dead. A girl like her didn't play nice with anyone. Whatever the call was about, it was bound to complicate things.

"Anson?" Sadie stared at him across the common area. "You going to get that?"

"Yeah." He picked the handset up off the cradle and punched line one with a finger. The button for line one burned solidly, like the end of a cigarette. "Sheriff Jacobs."

As he listened to the voice on the other end, the color drained from his face.

Sadie noticed. "Anson?"

He answered by holding up his hand to her. Anson dropped his feet to the floor and sat up, his body all at once at attention. "You sure about this?" He listened and nodded. "Alright. If she shows up, let me know. Thanks." He returned the handset to the phone's cradle and stared at the red light for line one as it flickered for a second, then went out.

"What is it?" Sadie stood at the door to his office.

Anson stood and rubbed his beard before locking gazes with Sadie. "Jezebel is gone. She just vanished. Poof." He ran his hand through his hair and began to pace. "MacJuvie ain't maximum security, but it's certainly not easy to escape from. Especially if you don't know the layout or routine."

Sadie watched him with careful eyes.

"They found her scrubs laid out in her bunk, nice and neat. But get this..." Anson leaned against the corner of his desk and crossed his arms. "Her surgery bandage was inside her shirt. They're going to get the blood typed, but it's going to be a match. I'm sure of it."

"Sounds a lot like that kid we had in the cell a while back." Sadie thought for a second. "Ransom."

"And the switchblade," they said in unison.

"Jinx. You owe me a Coke." Sadie grinned at him, but Anson didn't see it. His recent conversation with Nolan had rushed to the forefront of his mind.

He pulled out his notepad and flipped back through the pages. *Dreamwakers disappear, including the inanimate objects they bring with them.* He had underlined that sentence. The bandage had remained behind. That could only mean...

"I got to go." Anson rushed past Sadie.

"What is it?"

He bolted toward the exit. "I'll tell you later," he called back. "But I think I—" Anson stopped cold.

Cash, Wynter, Jake, and Quinn had just stepped inside the station, blocking his path.

"Anson, we need to talk to you," Cash said.

Anson looked at the gauntlet of teenagers. "Does it have to do with Jezebel?"

Cash turned to his friends. Wynter placed her hand on his shoulder and nodded in reassurance. He faced Anson again. "It has to do with everything."

ANSON LED THE FOUR TEENAGERS into the station's conference room and closed the blinds. He sent Sadie a knowing look as he shut the door.

Cash and Wynter took chairs next to each other. Quinn settled on the chair next to Cash and Jake sat next to her. Anson took a seat opposite, pulled out his notepad from his breast pocket, and stared back at the four teens across the conference table, thrumming his fingers. Jake, Quinn, Cash, and Wynter stared back.

"So, this is about *everything,* huh?" Anson alternated his gaze between each youth in turn. "Where's your friend?" He tapped his notepad with his finger. "Ransom. That's his name, right?"

Quinn's ears perked up upon hearing his name.

"That's right," Wynter said.

He pointed at Jake with his pen. "What's with the video camera?"

Jake had set his JVC GR-7 camcorder on the table top and was busy at the controls, preparing to record.

"You want concrete proof, right?" Cash glanced at Jake at the end of the table, then looked back at Anson. "We're going to give you that."

Jake reseated his Nintendo baseball cap. "In other words, Wynter is going to summon Ransom and I'm going to record the whole thing." He pointed the camcorder at Anson and pressed the record button. "You'll have no choice but to believe us."

Anson flipped through a couple pages on his notepad. "And Ransom is the dreamwaker, correct?"

All eyes and the lens of Jake's camcorder focused on Wynter. She returned a look of concern. "Yeah... How do you know that?"

"Your dad and I had a little chat."

"Do you believe him?" Wynter focused on Anson's notepad like she was trying to decipher the contents with her mind.

Anson sat back in his chair and Jake followed the action with the camcorder lens. "I'm getting there."

"So let's get on with it." Quinn stammered upon realizing how abrupt her voice had sounded.

Jake turned the camcorder toward her and winked beneath the brim of his hat.

"Get that *thing* out of my face!" Quinn pushed the camcorder away, almost knocking it off the end of the table.

"Jesus, Quinn. Chill!" Jake glared at her as he cradled the camcorder in his arms. "What the hell's wrong with you?" he said softly.

Quinn ignored him and kept her eyes forward.

Anson shifted his eyes to Wynter. "So, are you ready?"

"Yeah, I think so," Wynter said. "I'm just going to need some zees. And don't worry. They're not drugs."

Anson furrowed his brow in confusion. "Sorry. What aren't drugs?"

"We call them zees. Quinn and I made them out of a bunch of natural herbs that help you fall asleep."

Anson gave her a dubious look.

"You know, like chamomile and lavender. Here, I'll show you." Wynter reached past Cash. "Quinn, give me the zees."

Quinn looked unsure. "I, uh…"

"They're in your bag." Wynter tugged at the strap of Quinn's satchel. "I'm sure you had a few left."

Quinn recoiled and moved her satchel out of reach. "Let me look." She pulled the bag to her lap and dug through the contents.

"It's the baggie with the little dark cubes," Cash said.

"I know what it fucking looks like."

Anson watched Cash, Wynter, and Jake exchange worrisome looks with each other. Something wasn't right and he made a note of it.

Quinn threw a baggie on the table with six little black cubes in it. Anson reached for it and turned the worn and wrinkled plastic bag around in his hands. He opened the top and sniffed. It wasn't a marijuana derivative. He thought he smelled hints of... lime Jell-O?

"These help you sleep, huh?" He slid the baggie across the table to Wynter's hand.

"Yeah. They help me get into the REM cycle in, like, half the time."

"REM cycle?" Anson gave Wynter a curious glance.

"Rapid eye movement. That's when we dream."

"And that's good?"

"I can only summon a dreamwaker during REM," Wynter said. "So, yeah."

Anson continued jotting notes.

"She can sleep in here. We'll put some chairs together." Cash was already on his feet moving his chair against the wall. "That okay, Anson?"

"Sure, sure. Go for it."

Jake stood and offered his chair to Cash, whispering, "What's up with Quinn?"

Cash shrugged and lined up Jake's chair with the others.

"And did you see her shoes?"

"What about them?" Cash glanced casually back at Quinn's feet and recognized the difference immediately. "High Tops?" he said quietly.

Jake whispered back, "She always wears—"

"Vans," Cash and Jake said softly in unison, sharing a look of concern.

Quinn stood and pushed her chair away. "I'll stay and help Wynter sleep."

"I don't think that's a good idea," Cash said, positioning himself between Wynter and Quinn. "Wynter needs to be alone."

"Who asked *you*?" Quinn hissed. "I'm talking to Wynter."

Jake rocked back on his crutches. Holding his camcorder at arm's length, he aimed the lens up at Quinn.

"Cash is right," Wynter said. "It's better if I'm alone."

"No, you're wrong." Quinn flashed wild eyes at her. "Friends help each other out."

Wynter took a step toward Quinn, but Cash grabbed her hand gently and stopped her. "You know how this works, Quinn... What's wrong with you?"

Anson observed Quinn's agitation escalate. What he saw contradicted everything he knew about the girl. He rested his hand on the butt of his gun and eased the snap off the holster. It popped with a small metallic click.

Most people wouldn't have thought twice about the small sound, but Quinn oriented to his unseen holster below the table. Panic blazed in her eyes.

"Quinn? Are you—"

Quinn crouched fast and pulled out a knife that she had hidden in her sock. She pressed a button in the hilt and a silver double-edged blade popped out and locked in place. Anson recognized the weapon in an instant.

Wynter stared at her in confusion. "What are you doing?"

"We're getting out of here, Wynter."

Anson stood up slowly, his hands out in front of him. "Put the knife down, Quinn."

"Fuck you, *Deputy Dolt*." Quinn beckoned to Wynter. "Come on. They're trying to trick you." She backed against the door and twisted the doorknob.

Cash stood in front of Wynter like a shield. "She's not going anywhere with you."

Anson advanced around the table with slow, careful steps, his hands still raised. "Easy Quinn. You don't need to do this. You're safe here."

Quinn shifted her panicked gaze around the room. "Wynter!

Don't be stupid!" Her voice was angry now. She pulled the door open. "Come on!"

Wynter stood her ground. "You're not Quinn."

Anson saw Sadie turn in her desk. She spotted Quinn's knife, stood, and drew her gun.

He shook his head almost imperceptibly, but Quinn caught the gesture. She glanced behind her and found herself staring down the barrel of Sadie's gun.

"Drop it," Sadie said firmly as she made careful steps toward Quinn, blocking her escape route through the front entrance.

Quinn moved her hand side to side to defend herself against Sadie in the main office and Cash emerging from the conference room. Her hand gripped the knife with a tight fist.

Her only escape was backward, past the two interrogation rooms and into the bathroom. It had to have a window she could force herself through. Quinn spun on her heels and bolted. Cash followed like the wind.

She pushed through the door to the woman's bathroom. There was a small frosted glass window set into the wall opposite the door but it was ten feet from the floor with no visible hand holds.

Cash exploded through the door. Quinn turned to face him, backing herself up against the wall.

"Who the fuck are you?" Cash said between breaths. " 'Cause you sure aren't Quinn."

"Wouldn't you like to know?"

Cash charged across the tiled floor. "Tell me."

"Fuck you." Quinn took the knife in her right hand, reached across her neck, and plunged the razor-sharp tip into the left side of her neck. It must have hurt because Quinn flinched when the knife sliced through her muscles, tendons, and left carotid artery. Already beginning to convulse from rapid blood loss, she used the last of her strength to guide the blade around the front of her neck and through to the right side.

Gushers of maroon flooded over her T-shirt and spattered the floor. Quinn lost all control of her head as it lolled backward like an unhinged Pez dispenser. She dropped her satchel and collapsed to the floor, her body spasming in a bright red pool of her own blood. The knife hit the tile and bounced under the sink.

Sadie came through the door next, her gun raised, and nearly knocked Cash over from behind.

"Jesus Christ," she said, her mouth suddenly dry as bone. She turned to the nearest sink and retched into it.

"We got to get out of here." Cash tugged Sadie's shirt. "Jake... Jake can't see this. Come on."

Sadie grabbed a paper towel and wiped her mouth, unable to take her eyes off the carnage at the far end of the bathroom. She holstered her gun.

"Hurry!" Cash pulled open the door just as Jake made his approach. Anson and Wynter followed close behind.

"Where is she?" Despite his crutches, Jake barreled into Cash, pushing him back against the bathroom door. "Where's Quinn?"

Cash held him back. "You don't want to go in there, man."

Sadie took Anson aside and briefed him quietly.

"Are you sure?" he whispered back.

She glanced back at Cash struggling to hold Jake back, then returned her gaze forward and nodded.

"What happened?" Anson tried to imagine the scene behind the bathroom door.

Sadie shook her head. "Not here."

Jake shoved Cash back against the bathroom door, took his right crutch, and swept Cash's feet out from under him.

Cash hit the floor, knocking the wind out of him. Still, he tried to grab Jake's right foot to stop him. Jake hopped past his grasp and disappeared into the bathroom.

Anson moved to follow, but Cash held up his hand. "Let him go."

Wynter offered her hand to help Cash to his feet. She leaned in close to his ear. "That wasn't Quinn."

Cash shared her concern. "I know." He cocked his ear toward the door, expecting to hear an anguished cry but none came.

"She's gone." Jake had propped himself between the door and the frame, a look of confused defeat on his face. "She must have escaped through the window." He held up the satchel. "But she left her bag behind."

Wynter took the satchel and dug through it. The items inside, tubes of lip gloss, cash wallet, FreshWhip name tag, a *People* magazine with Prince on the cover, it all fit Quinn perfectly.

Anson looked at Sadie and motioned to the bathroom. Once they were both inside, he closed the door and spoke in a hushed voice.

"Is this what you saw moments ago?"

Sadie's jaw dropped as she let her eyes scan the bathroom. "No. It was a bloodbath in here, Anson. There, under the window. The girl had cut her own throat, ear to ear." She pushed open the doors to the two bathroom stalls, fully expecting that they'd be empty. "How could anyone do that?"

Anson pulled out a paper towel. He crouched under the window and ran the paper over the grout between tiles. Traces of dirt showed up but no blood.

"Did you see the knife?"

Anson nodded. "It's the same one I took from Jezebel when I arrested her before." He stood and tossed the towel in the garbage. "The knife is one of her tells. She called me 'Deputy Dolt' in the conference room. That's another one."

Sadie looked at his reflection in the mirror. "So Quinn was actually... Jezebel?"

"I think so," Anson said. "The kids call them dreamwakers. Waking manifestations of dreams."

"How is that possible?"

Anson shook his head. "Don't ask me." He headed to the door. "Now we get a front row seat to see it in action." He pulled the door open for Sadie and followed her out.

Wynter, Cash, and Jake stopped their hushed talking and faced the two officers. "That was Jezebel in disguise," Wynter said.

These teens were quick. Anson headed back to the conference room. "A dreamwaker, right?"

"Yeah." Wynter and the others followed. "I think she wanted to kill me. For real."

"Why would she want to do that?"

"Jezebel always said that if she couldn't have Ransom for herself, then no one could," Wynter said. "And I'm the source of the summoning power. With me out of the way, no one can summon. And Ransom's gone."

Anson faced the rest of the group. "I've got an idea, but we're going to need Ransom for it to work. You think he'll cooperate?"

"He'll do anything for me," Wynter said.

Cash jammed his hands into his pockets and directed his gaze to the floor.

Anson cast a serious glance at Wynter. "Time for that concrete proof?"

"Most definitely." Wynter stepped into the conference room and closed the blinds on the exterior windows. She swallowed three zees, jamming the rest in her pocket, and stretched out on the chairs.

Jake set his camcorder on the table and framed Wynter in the shot. "We're ready for your close-up, Miss LaCroix."

Wynter stuck her tongue out at him.

Cash crouched next to her. "Think you'll be able to do it?"

"No sweat," Wynter said. "He's my creation, remember. And he's glad to be back in my head. I think putting Jezebel away would be at the top of his list."

Cash studied her face for a moment, then kissed her forehead. "Be careful."

"I will."

Cash escorted the rest of the group out of the conference room and closed the door.

Anson looked at the others. "Now what?"

"Now we wait." Cash glanced at Jake balanced on his crutches, Quinn's satchel in one hand. He rolled an office chair over to him. "Take a load off, man."

"Thanks." Jake collected his crutches and settled into the chair. He closed his eyes, relief clear on his face.

Anson stood next to the closed door to the conference room. If anything happened, he wanted to be first in the room. "How long does it take to find a dreamwaker?"

Cash shrugged. "Maybe an hour or two? It depends on what's going on in the dream." He exchanged a knowing glance with Jake.

"We need to find Quinn," Jake said.

Sadie narrowed her eyes. "What makes you think she's missing?"

The question struck a nerve and Jake turned on her, shaking Quinn's satchel in anger. "Where else would she be? Like, if you were a psychopath, would you leave your victims lying around?"

"Probably not," Sadie said.

"Exactly. If Jezebel made a switch, she wouldn't want Quinn talking." Jake began to wring his hands and lowered his voice. "She might be dead already."

"Whoa, whoa, man," Cash said. "Don't go there."

Jake locked gazes with Cash, his eyes brimmed with tears. "It *is* possible. I *have* to go there. Jezebel is all about hurting Wynter in the worst way possible. This fits."

"You're right, Jake." Anson crouched to his level and placed a light hand on his shoulder. "It is possible, but let's not get too carried away without evidence."

Jake let out an anxious breath and looked away.

"She was acting weird earlier, when Wynter called her," Cash said. "Before we got here. Like she didn't know what was going on. So whatever Jezebel did, it was before that."

"And her shoes," Jake said.

"What about her—"

Jake had reached his limit and cut Anson off. "She wears fucking *Vans*. That's her thing. I totally missed it."

"And she didn't call me Bug," Wynter added.

Anson stood. "That's not evidence."

"Gonna have to disagree with you, Sheriff. We know our friends…" Cash looked at Jake and gave him a small nod. "And we know when they're not themselves. She never leaves her bag lying around." He faced Anson. "And earlier today Quinn wanted *Wynter* to call Jake."

Anson exchanged a glance with Sadie. "Why is that important?"

"Because Quinn and Jake are a *thing*," Cash said.

"Well…" Jake calmed and offered a sheepish grin. "Not quite, but *enough* of a thing to *be* a thing." He looked up at Anson. "She would've wanted to call me today. Trust me."

"Oh-kay," Anson said.

Jake scrunched his brows and side-eyed him. "Sheriff, does Mercy love you?"

"Huh? What does that have to do with…" Anson realized where this was going.

"How do you know?" Jake nodded in agreement. "Because you *know* Mercy. It's not concrete evidence though, is it?"

Anson smiled and pointed at him. "Touché."

"Speaking of Mercy," Sadie said. "When you going to marry that girl?"

"Jesus Christ. Don't start." Anson picked up Sadie's desk phone. "Who's hungry? Burgers from Lucy's?"

Jake nodded. "I could go for that."

"Got to keep our strength up, right?" Anson directed his gaze at Sadie. "Right?"

"What the hell. I'm in," Sadie said.

"Me too." Cash glanced at the closed blinds on the conference room windows. "Get something for Wynter too."

"And Ransom," Jake added.

"Right," Cash said, then lowered his voice to a whisper no one else heard. "Don't forget Ransom."

HALF AN HOUR LATER, all four were digging into the best burgers in Newhaven.

"I should talk to the mayor and get Lucy's designated an essential service," Anson said between mouthfuls.

Jake held up a greasy thumbs up. "You have my vote."

A loud thump rattled the conference window. The group stopped chewing and talking and directed their attention to the glass. The blinds within the conference room hung askew and swayed gently against the window frame.

Anson exchanged looks with Cash as they both dropped their food and rushed toward the door. Anson arrived a second after Cash.

"I'm first inside, remember?" he said, guiding Cash aside. "Besides, I'm the sheriff."

Cash held his hands up and backed off. "Be my guest."

Anson placed his ear to the conference room door and knocked lightly. He could hear laughter and muffled talking. "Wynter? It's Anson. I'm coming in."

Before he could twist the doorknob, the conference door opened inward. Wynter and Ransom stood in the doorway.

"Anson," Wynter said, "I'd like to officially introduce you to Ransom."

"Right, right. Don't mean to be rude, but..." Anson glanced back at Jake. "Mr. Nintendo, you're up."

Jake crammed a handful of fries into his mouth, hopped onto his crutches, and followed Anson into the conference room. He gave Wynter a quick hug and a nod to Ransom as he went by. "Glad you guys are back."

Anson had rolled an old cart with a TV and VCR stowed on top next to the table. "Work your magic."

Jake began disconnecting wires leading into the VCR and reconnecting them to his camcorder. "What I'm doing? It's not magic. But what's on this tape might be." He rewound the tape in the camcorder and cued it using the viewfinder.

Anson plugged in the TV and turned it on. As the TV warmed up, a jittering still frame of a sleeping Wynter appeared on the screen. "Alright, people. Presenting exhibit A." He nodded at Jake. "Roll it."

Jake pressed play and stepped aside, taking a seat on one of the chairs lined up against the wall. Sadie took a spot on the edge of the conference table beside Wynter and Ransom.

Cash remained at the door. He watched Ransom move his hand toward Wynter's, but she didn't reciprocate. She gave Ransom a stern eye, then glanced back at Cash.

"You okay back there?"

Cash nodded. "Eyes forward. You're going to miss the show."

She gave him a quick smile and faced the TV. Her own sleeping image stared back at her with muffled conversation from the other room filtering through the TV's small speaker.

"Your performance is Oscar-worthy." Jake winked at her.

"Ha ha." Wynter rolled her eyes and shook her head.

The image on the TV blipped, then went haywire as if someone had placed an old running vacuum next to it. Then as quickly as the interference began, the TV image settled again and showed Ransom rolling off Wynter and onto the floor. She fell to her knees and they embraced.

"God, I've missed you," Ransom's voice said through the TV's speaker.

"Shit," Jake whispered to himself. He shot a glance at Cash, then hopped to the table, fumbling with the playback controls before placing the camcorder into pause. He looked at Anson. "That proof concrete enough for you?"

Anson tapped his finger on the table. Part of him still thought it was all made up, that dreamwakers were just figments from angsty teenager imaginations. But the other part of him, the one that sought logical explanations could not dispute what he had just witnessed. Dreamwakers were the real deal.

"I'll be damned," he said. "I thought you all were full of shit, but this…" Anson shook his head. "I'm sorry. I take it all back."

Cash piped up from the back, his arms crossed firmly against his chest. "So what you going to do about it?"

"I got an idea." Anson glanced at Sadie as he rubbed his beard. "I'll lay it out for you and you guys try and punch holes in it. Sound good?"

The rest of the group nodded in agreement.

"Let's bring in the rest of our food and hash it out." Anson motioned at Wynter and Ransom. "There's a burger and fries for each of you… dreamwakers eat, right?"

Ransom gave him a toothy smile. "Yup."

"Let's get going," Anson said. "Time's a-wasting."

Everyone collected their remaining meals and settled in around the conference table. Over the next hour, the group formulated a plan that hopefully would get Jezebel put away for good.

"I got to make a call." Anson pushed his chair away from the table and headed out to his office. On his way, he stopped by Jake's chair. "And we're going to find Quinn. You have my word."

"Thanks." Jake followed Anson out with his eyes, then cast a dubious look at Cash. "You think this is going to work?"

Cash glanced at Wynter and Ransom sitting on the opposite side of the table talking between themselves. He spoke quietly so only Jake could hear. "Jezebel's a wild card, but so is *he*." Cash motioned at Ransom. "Honestly, I don't know."

HEROES

Jake watched Anson back out of his parking stall from the front entrance of the station. Sadie rode shotgun and Wynter and Ransom sat in the back, holding hands, with Jake's camcorder sitting on the seat between them.

"You sure you don't want to tag along?" Anson called out to him from his open window. "You could hang out in the back seat." He cast a casual glance at Sadie. "Probably not 'by the book' but fuck it. I'm the sheriff of this town."

"Nah. This cast just gets in the way," Jake said. "But come and get me after. We still got to find Quinn."

"I haven't forgotten," Anson said.

Jake's eyes shifted to Wynter's, and he offered a small smile and wave. "You guys be careful, okay?"

Wynter and Ransom nodded.

"And take care of my camera. You remember what to do?"

"We got it, Jake," Anson said. "See you soon." He pulled away from the station and followed Main Street through town and across the interstate. Wynter watched Jake shrink in Sadie's side mirror.

Stedford Plaza passed by on the right and Wynter followed the parking lot and the familiar entrance with her eyes. She wondered if Hunter and Daytona were working today. Had Vinny fired her yet? So much had changed in a month and she looked forward to it all going back to normal.

But what is normal now?

Anson caught her worried glance through the rear view mirror. "You okay back there? Need more time?"

Wynter managed a smile. It felt fake but she hoped it appeared genuine. "No, I'm good."

Anson passed Jones Avenue and the entrance to Sven Dwarfs, heading deeper into southie territory and closer to Jezebel for what Wynter hoped would be the last time.

The Suburban rolled to a stop at the side of the road. Anson shifted into park and killed the engine. "Time to rock and roll."

Sadie was out of the vehicle in a shot and opened Wynter's door. "Let's double-check your wire and vest."

Wynter scooted to the edge of the seat and stood.

"I think we have the mic well attached," Sadie said. "I'm going to lift the back of your shirt up a little bit and take a listen." She tugged up at the T-shirt's hem. Behind Wynter's white Kevlar vest sat a miniature tape recorder attached to the small of her back with wide strips of white tape.

Sadie plugged in a pair of Walkman headphones into the headphone jack of the tape recorder. The orange puffy ear pads looked like a pair of mini donuts held firmly to her head.

"I had headphones like that before..." Wynter stopped herself.

Sadie pressed record. "Say something again for me, will you, hon?"

"Today, Thursday August 7, 1986, Jezebel Caine's luck runs out."

"Amen to that." Sadie rewound the tape and played it back. She listened, nodded, and disconnected her headphones, then pressed record. She let the T-shirt's hem fall naturally. The vest was a little bulky but Wynter's loosely hanging T-shirt covered it up well.

Anson and Ransom joined Sadie at the side of the Suburban. "All set?"

Sadie gave a thumbs up. "You're good to go."

Wynter couldn't hide her worry. "You sure we need to do this?"

Anson softened his gaze. "The more hard evidence we have, the better."

Wynter chewed at her lower lip. "Maybe Cash didn't—"

"Wynter, listen to me." Anson placed his hand gently on her shoulder. "Cash knows what's at stake. And he knows *you*." He smiled warmly, then looked at Ransom and the camcorder strapped to his hand. "You know how to operate that thing?"

"Sure do." Ransom peered at the side of the camcorder. "Autofocus is on. Power is on. Press record and point and shoot."

"Alright," Anson said. "If we're lucky, we'll have Jezebel behind bars by the end of the night."

Wynter glanced at Ransom, then down Woodpark Avenue toward Jezebel's run-down house. Even through she had lived in the same southie neighborhood all her life, Wynter had never set foot in Jezebel's yard or knocked on her door. She rubbed her damp palms on her jean shorts. "I don't believe in luck anymore."

Sadie caught Wynter's lingering worry. "Just take your time and remember to breathe. We're literally right around the corner. Let us do the hard part."

Wynter nodded and tried to swallow the lump in her throat without success. She searched for Ransom's free hand. He took it willingly as they both headed down the cracked and crumbling sidewalk.

Wynter paused and looked back at Anson and Sadie standing beside the Suburban. "The hard part... is being the bait." She resumed her approach without waiting for a response. She didn't need one.

The distance from the junction with Main Street to Jezebel's house couldn't have been more than three blocks, but the walk seemed to take forever, as if Wynter was walking on a treadmill.

The early August evening was comfortably warm. Combined with Wynter's nerves and the tight-fitting bulletproof vest, she could feel beads of sweat build up on her back and channel down along her spine.

Wynter and Ransom approached a small hedge next to Jezebel's yard. Beyond it sat the infamous Barracuda. Frankie's shit-box Pinto was gone, probably parked outside the Itty Bitty Bar.

Good. It'll be just you and me. And backup.

"You hide in here and get it all on video."

"I will," Ransom said. "Point and fucking shoot."

Wynter peered around the hedge and up at the porch landing. "Time to enter the lion's den."

Ransom kissed her, then squirmed into the hedge. He pressed record with his thumb. "Rolling."

Wynter stepped onto the weed-infested front lawn.

"Hey girl..." Ransom's whispery voice floated out of the hedge behind her. Wynter paused mid-stride, afraid to look back in case she blew Ransom's cover. He continued, "You're bad to the bone."

Wynter stifled her smile and continued across the grass. The Barracuda's engine clicked intermittently as she passed, a clue that the engine was still warm. She wanted to touch the hood to confirm, but instead focused on her mission.

The wooden steps to the porch groaned and creaked with each footfall. She expected one of the steps to break under her feet like it had in her dream, but the wooden planks held.

Wynter stretched forward to knock on the door when she felt the tape recorder affixed to her back slip down. Her sweat had compromised the tape's adhesive strength.

There's no going back now.

Wynter knocked on the door. The vibration traveled down her arm to her shoulders and the tape recorder slipped a bit more. She hoped the vest and the waist band of her jeans would stop the device from falling further.

She heard thumping footsteps from inside the house, then silence. Wynter casually glanced at the front window and noticed the rotting curtains moving ever so slightly. She was about to knock again when the footsteps resumed.

The deadbolt slid back into the door with a *clunk* and Jezebel pulled the front door wide open. Wynter caught a whiff of rancid grease and stale beer, and her stomach did a backflip. She took a step back.

The two teenagers glared at each other, each wanting the other to make the first move. Wynter surprised herself by beating Jezebel to the punch.

"Where is she?"

A scowl curled at the edges of Jezebel's lips. "Get the fuck off my porch, *Whinerrr.*"

Both rage and panic welled up within Wynter. It didn't take much from Jezebel to press her buttons, but she found she no longer cared. Wynter made an abrupt step forward that took Jezebel by surprise. The tape recorder slipped a little more. "Where's Quinn?"

Jezebel looked past Wynter and shrugged. "How the fuck do I know? You dykes are usually joined at the hip. Now get lost."

"I'm not leaving until you tell me where she is."

Jezebel crossed her arms against her chest. "Don't know what you're talking about. Get the hell out of here or I'll call the cops."

Wynter laughed. "You? Go for it." She waited for Jezebel to make a move. "No? Always figured you for a chickenshit. The cops saw right through your Trojan horse dreamwaker bullshit, too."

Jezebel's jaw tensed in angry angles.

"You don't have your *boy-toy* anymore, so you got to make dreamwakers of *yourself.*" Wynter scowled and gave Jezebel a once-over. "Pathetic."

"Get the FUCK out of here!" Jezebel stepped out onto the porch, practically nose to nose with Wynter. "NOW."

"Thank God Ransom chose *me* instead of *you.*" Wynter locked gazes with her nemesis and stood her ground. She pictured Jezebel in a *Looney Tunes* cartoon, steam blasting from her nostrils. The image made her smile.

Jezebel retreated into the house and slammed the door, her footsteps thumping somewhere inside.

Wynter had no idea if her dustup with Jezebel would help Anson or not. She didn't care. This time she had won. It was the small victories, right?

As she stepped off the porch, the tape recorder slid out from under the vest and swung at her left leg, tethered by the microphone cord. Stopping on the grass, Wynter shot a panicked look at the hedge where Ransom had hid. She grabbed the device and tried to stick it back in place, but it was an impossible task to do behind her back.

Would it fit in her pocket?

Wynter's thought came a second too late. She heard the front door to the house click open again. Looking back, she saw Jezebel standing in the doorway, a LadySmith .38 Special in her right hand, and her eyes locked on the tape recorder in Wynter's hand.

"You fucking bitch."

Wynter dropped the tape recorder and raised her hands. "No! Wait—"

But Jezebel didn't wait. She aimed the gun and pulled the trigger. The shot rang out into the neighborhood and Wynter flinched at its deafening sound, despite being outside. Her quick reflex reaction probably saved her life as she heard the bullet whistle through her hair, just barely missing her head.

Jezebel bounded down the steps in hot pursuit. Wynter ran for the hedge, then spotted Ransom and the camcorder in the shadows. She reversed toward the Barracuda, knowing she had lost her lead. The abrupt change in direction caused the tape recorder to disconnect from the mic cord and break apart as it hit the sidewalk.

Jezebel stopped, aimed at Wynter, fired, then continued her pursuit.

Wynter ducked and leaped behind the Barracuda as the bullet hit the grass behind her. In a low crouch, she kept herself moving, staying on the opposite side of the car from Jezebel.

"You can't avoid me forever, *Whinerrr.*"

Wynter remained silent. Any response would give away her position. The plan would have worked if Jezebel hadn't reversed direction.

"Hello, fuck face."

Wynter rolled back and reversed around the Barracuda's back bumper as she heard Jezebel fire the gun again. A searing pain burned through her left shoulder and rivulets of blood traced their way down her arm. She had been shot but had no idea how bad it was and had no time to check. The adrenaline had kicked in and as long as Jezebel had bullets, running was Wynter's only option.

She bolted down the right side of the house with Jezebel twenty feet behind and gaining. Wynter led the chase through the cluttered and overgrown back yard and back along the left side of the house toward the street. She punched the latch on the rickety gate, but it stuck.

Jezebel used the moment of weakness, aimed, and fired. The bullet struck Wynter's right calf, shattering her fibula. She screamed and pushed with all her strength.

The gate budged open just enough for Wynter to escape. But Jezebel had used Wynter's struggle to gain lost time and distance. Almost upon her, Jezebel took a moment to steady the .38 Special aimed at Wynter's back and squeezed the trigger. The bullet's impact knocked the wind out of her, sending Wynter sprawling forward onto the front lawn.

"You're dead, bitch." Jezebel stomped through the weeds, her gun poised. "Finally."

Wynter flipped onto her back, scrambling backward through the pain of her injuries, and raised a pleading hand.

"Go to hell, *Whinerrr.*" Jezebel pulled the trigger.

Click.

Wynter began to laugh as the irony overwhelmed her. "Stupid... bitch..."

Jezebel raged and curled her finger against the gun's trigger several times, cycling the cylinder through empty clicks.

The Suburban screeched to a stop in front of the house. Anson and Sadie leaped out and drew their weapons.

"Drop it, Jezebel. Now." Anson had his gun locked on Jezebel's head.

Ransom stepped out from the hedge, his camera trained on Jezebel and Wynter. He picked up the shattered tape recorder and handed it to Sadie. "The tape might still be okay." She took the shambles of electronics and tossed it into the front of the Suburban.

Jezebel's short-lived surprise shifted back to anger. She alternated her seething gaze between Wynter and Ransom. "You think you're so *fucking* smart," she hissed.

Sprinting footsteps echoed down the avenue backed by the crescendo of a siren in the distance. Cash burst past the hedge, his eyes bugging out at Wynter's bloodied arm.

THE AMBULANCE ROLLED to a stop behind the Suburban. Anson stepped up to the passenger side window. "Hey guys, thanks for doing this. We owe you one."

The male and female paramedic in the cab nodded. "We're between gigs, so...," the driver said.

Anson peered down Woodpark Avenue. He could still see Wynter and Ransom making their approach to Jezebel's house. "Things are going to happen fast. We'll we roll out, secure the scene, then Sadie will signal you over the radio."

"Copy that," the driver said.

"Now, about that stowaway..." Anson offered a small grin.

The paramedic riding shotgun hopped out and unlocked the ambulance's side door. Cash jumped out and met with Anson and Sadie.

"I sure hope this works." Cash spotted Wynter and Ransom in the distance and began to pace.

"Everything will work out fine," Anson said. "Jezebel's number is up."

Ransom crawled into the hedge and Wynter disappeared around it.

"Ransom's in place and Wynter's on the move," Sadie said.

Seeing Wynter had helped ground Cash. Now that the sidewalk was empty and she was out of view, his internal alarm bells went off. "What if she catches on? Jezebel's fucking smart."

Anson placed his steady hands on Cash's shoulders. "She is, but we're smarter. She won't realize what hit her until it's too late."

Cash took in several deep breaths in an attempt to calm himself. It didn't work. "Is this even legal? What if she gets off on some technicality?"

"Cash, it's going to be okay," Anson said. "It's—"

A gunshot echoed out across the neighborhood.

"Wynter!" Cash bolted, sprinting toward Jezebel's house with nothing in his head except Wynter's well-being.

"Cash! Wait! Shit." Anson turned to the paramedics. "Wait for our signal." The paramedics gave him a thumbs up as he scrambled into the Suburban. Sadie slammed her door closed and Anson keyed the ignition.

The Suburban's engine failed to start.

"Jesus Christ not now." Anson tried the ignition and pumped the gas. Another shot rang out. "Come on, dammit!"

"Anson," Sadie said. "I know you're the sheriff and all, but you need to calm the fuck down."

"All hell's breaking loose and you're telling me to calm down?"

"Listen. The engine's flooded." Sadie locked her gaze with his. "Don't pump the gas. Floor it for a couple seconds, then turn the ignition."

Anson did as instructed and the engine caught, first try. "You got hidden talents, Buckley." He gunned the gas and the engine responded greedily, the tires peeling out in the same direction Cash had gone. A third shot, more of a *pop,* reverberated past the Suburban's open windows. Anson flipped on the light bar without siren.

Cash had moved fast. He was halfway to Jezebel's house when Anson zoomed past. The sound of another two gunshots floated past the window, just loud enough to overpower the rev of the Suburban's engine.

Anson shared a concerned look with Sadie before slamming on the brakes and skidding to a stop in front of Jezebel's house. "Don't shoot her," he said.

"Speak for yourself."

Anson and Sadie burst from the Suburban, guns drawn. Anson aimed his pistol at Jezebel and flicked off the safety for the first time in years. "Drop it, Jezebel. Now."

In his peripheral vision, Anson saw Ransom hand something to Sadie. He ignored them and advanced on Jezebel. He had a clean shot. He could end it right here and now and no one would give a damn, with the exception of Frankie. Maybe.

Cash's frenzied sprint carried him past Ransom, his eyes now locked on the expanding red patch on Wynter's shoulder.

Anson held up a hand to Cash to stop and kept his gun trained on Jezebel. "Drop the gun." He advanced onto the sidewalk, then the lawn, Sadie securing his flank.

Cash skidded onto the lawn, then backed up a few steps to avoid blocking the view of Ransom's camcorder. It was obvious he wanted to go to Wynter's side, but he acknowledged the gravity of the situation and gave Anson the space he needed.

"The chamber's empty, Deputy D—"

Anson slapped the gun out of Jezebel's hand, twisted her arm behind her back, and pushed her prone onto the grass. "When I say drop it, you *drop it.*"

Sadie collected Jezebel's .38 and placed it in an evidence bag, then unhooked her radio handset. "Go for medics." Right on cue, an ambulance siren faded up from the end of Woodpark Avenue.

Anson pulled out his handcuffs and secured Jezebel's hands behind her back, right, then left.

"Oh, *daddy!*" Jezebel grinned through a clump of weeds. "You know I like it rough."

"Shut up!" Anson pulled Jezebel back up to her feet just as the ambulance arrived, stopping just beyond the Suburban.

Seeing that Anson had Jezebel restrained, Cash dropped to his knees at Wynter's side, his eyes heavy with tears, wanting to comfort her but not knowing where to start. "Are you okay? Where does it hurt?"

Wynter managed a smile. "It's okay, Cash."

"I'm so sorry." He grabbed Wynter's right hand and held it to his chest.

As Anson led Jezebel back to the Suburban, she sneered at Ransom. "You can have her, asshole." She raised her voice to a scream. "But I'm not done with you yet. *All of you.* You're *all* going to *pay!*"

"Save it for the judge." Anson directed Jezebel towards the Suburban with brusque movements. "You're going to need all the help you can get."

Paramedics unloaded a stretcher, extended the wheels, and rolled it toward where Wynter lay. One paramedic caught Jezebel's eye as she passed. Her brown skin and braided red hair under a medic's baseball cap gave her an intense feeling of déjà vu.

But it wasn't déjà vu at all. It was Wynter, dressed as a paramedic. "Gotcha, *bitch,*" the paramedic whispered before breaking into a wide smile.

"What?" Jezebel thrashed against Anson's hold. Sadie hooked

her arm under one of Jezebel's arms and helped drag her to the Suburban. "They fucking set me up! This is bullshit! Let me GO!"

Sadie pulled open the door to the Suburban's back seat and Anson deposited Jezebel inside the vehicle. As soon as the door closed, Jezebel flipped on her back and began pounding at the door with her feet. Anson and Sadie took their seats in front.

"She's a *dreamwaker!* The bitch double crossed me!" Jezebel screamed.

"She sure did." Anson gave Cash and the two Wynters a thumbs up, then twisted in his seat to look back at Jezebel. "And if you want destruction of police property added to your shopping list of charges, keep it up."

Jezebel sat up and looked out the Suburban's window. The two paramedics had secured the injured dreamwaker, Wynter Too, to the stretcher and guided her toward the ambulance, with help from Cash and Wynter.

As the group rolled by the Suburban, Wynter Too waved at Jezebel, a sly satisfied smile on her face. The wave morphed into a raised middle finger. "Suck on that, *motherfucker.*"

"Later, folks." Anson started the SUV's engine and tapped the outside door panel. "Will keep you posted, Wynter."

The paramedics waved as the Suburban drove away and loaded Wynter Too into the back of the ambulance. Wynter followed one paramedic inside, then turned to Cash, who was standing at the back bumper.

Wynter smiled at him, then her eyes flicked to Ransom, still standing by the hedge holding the camcorder.

"Cash." Ransom nodded him over.

Cash gave Wynter a wary look, then strolled over to him.

Ransom handed him the camcorder. "Get this back to Jake for me, okay?"

Cash took the camcorder and slung the strap over his shoulder. "Thanks. Jake would've flipped if it had gotten busted."

"No problem." Ransom's eyes floated past Cash to Wynter standing at the back of the ambulance.

Cash noticed. "Hey. I'm not going to, like, get in the way of... you know."

Ransom smiled broadly at Wynter, his eyes glistening. Then his lips morphed into a grin as he gave Cash a sideways glance. "You don't get it, do you?"

"Get what?"

Ransom took a step off the curb toward Cash. "It's you, Cash. It was always you." Ransom's face drew serious. "She loves *you*."

"She loves you, too."

"But not in the same way." Ransom let his eyes find Wynter again in the distance. "Not in a way that lasts." He extended his open hand toward him.

Cash hesitated for a second, then took Ransom's hand. The two teens shared a firm handshake.

Ransom turned and walked back toward Main Street. "See you in your dreams."

"No offense, but I hope not," Cash said.

Ransom gave him a thumbs up without looking back, like a lazy hitchhiker, and continued walking. "Touché."

Cash watched Ransom walk half a block before he heard Wynter behind him.

"Coming?"

Cash turned to see Wynter holding out her hand. He took it at once and they both climbed into the back of the ambulance. The second paramedic closed the back doors.

Cash settled himself on one of the bench seats along the wall and buckled himself in. "I hope I don't see the inside of an ambulance again for a long time."

The first paramedic had already placed a tourniquet on Wynter Too's leg and a pulse oximeter on her index finger. She grabbed a blood pressure cuff from a pocket on the side of the portable cardiac monitor.

Wynter stopped the paramedic with a gentle hand. "Long story, but we're not going to need this. Trust me."

"Sorry, it's standard procedure," the paramedic said, and she continued wrapping Wynter Too's arm with the blood pressure cuff.

"Just drive us to Sven Dwarfs. The sheriff will back me up." Wynter gazed down at herself on the stretcher, then glanced back at Cash. "Your dreamwaker version of me is pretty awesome. Fooled Jezebel."

"Thanks," Cash said. "I've been studying you for years."

Wynter let out a small laugh. "You really came through."

"We all did." Cash saw pain flash across Wynter Too's face and reached for her hand. He looked at the paramedic. "Can you give her something to take the edge off?"

"I'll see what I can do."

"Wait." Wynter dug into her pocket and pulled out a baggie with the last three zees in it. She and her clone shared a knowing look. She removed them and placed the little cubes in Wynter Too's hand.

The paramedic gave Wynter a look of concern. "What *is* that?"

"Don't worry," Wynter said. "It's an all natural sleep aid."

Wynter Too ate the zees before the paramedic could stop her.

"You better not get me into trouble," the paramedic said.

"More like we're keeping you *out* of trouble." Cash laughed at the paramedic's puzzled look. "You'll see why soon enough."

The ambulance followed 19th Street across the interstate, through Newhaven, and back to Sven Dwarfs Trail'r Park along Main Street. It was like a mini-tour through recent-memory lane, much of it unpleasant. These paramedics could have been the same ones that had cared for Wynter after her fall, but Cash couldn't be sure.

The ambulance rolled to a stop in the vacant parking spot outside Cash's trailer normally reserved for Ernie's Civic. Like clockwork, Wynter Too had just fallen asleep, the zees having done their magic.

The paramedic watched in awe as Wynter Too drifted in a sweeping arc of blue charged light. The blood pressure cuff, pulse oximeter, and tourniquet all fell limp onto the stretcher, on top of the Kevlar vest and the microphone Wynter Too had been wearing. All evidence of blood was gone. The smell of ozone hung heavy in the small, enclosed treatment space of the ambulance.

The paramedic alternated her gaze between Cash, Wynter, and the empty stretcher. "Holy fucking shit."

"It's better if you don't ask questions." Cash slid his arm around Wynter's waist. "But you got one hell of a story now."

The paramedic opened the side door and let the teenagers out first, then followed. She climbed into the passenger seat.

The driver glanced at her, puzzled. "What about the patient?"

The first paramedic shook her head, but kept her eyes on Cash and Wynter, now standing on the front landing to the trailer. "Just drive."

"What?" The driver looked back through the portal window in the back of the cab. "Where is she?"

"Just fucking drive."

The paramedic behind the wheel looked at his partner, not sure if he saw terror or amazement on her face, and backed the ambulance up.

Wynter and Cash waved as the ambulance followed the ring road out of the trailer park.

"You think we just blew her mind?"

Wynter nodded. "Most definitely. They're going to have lots to talk about on the trip back to Halston."

Cash unlocked the front door. They both stepped inside and he locked it behind him. He crossed the room to the phone and dialed. There was barely enough time for the line to trill before the call connected. "Hey, Jake. The plan worked. We got her."

"Fucking awesome!" Jake's excited voice buzzed from the handset's speaker. "Wynter okay?"

"Yup. I'm looking at her right now." Cash sent Wynter a weary smile.

"What about Quinn?"

"Nothing yet, but I'm sure Anson's on it."

Jake's mood deflated a little. "Okay. Thanks for the update." He lowered his voice to a whisper. "Now make your move, dude."

Cash laughed. "Right. Talk to you later." He hung up the phone, took a deep breath, and let himself fall back against the wall. "I can't believe we got her. What do you want to do now?"

Wynter gazed at him in the August twilight that filtered through the trailer's windows. She took his face in her hands, inched up on her toes, and kissed him deeply.

It was a kiss that Cash had dreamed about more times than he could count. And when Wynter finished, she took his hand and led him to his bedroom.

"I don't think I've seen your hair braided like that before."

Wynter flipped her single braided ponytail back and forth. "What do you think?"

"It's nice..." Cash locked his gaze with hers.

"But?"

"I like it down, too. Can I?"

Wynter smiled at him, nodded, and turned her back to him. She reached out and flipped on the clock radio. KROK was in the middle of their "Ballad Box Hour" and Lionel Richie was crooning "Stuck On You."

Cash slid off the small hair elastic securing the end of Wynter's ponytail, then starting mid-back, he pulled gently, extracting intertwined loops of red hair. The strands felt like silk against his fingertips.

With her hair loose in his hands, Cash held it to one side and kissed her neck. He sensed a shiver run up her back and smiled.

Wynter turned and kissed him on the lips again. She grabbed

hold of the hem of his T-shirt and raised it over his head. She ran her hand down his strong, lean body, instantly reminded of Ransom. But that made perfect sense. She had used Cash as inspiration.

Cash placed his hands on Wynter's hips and moved them up over her shirt, inching toward her breasts, touching but not quite. He discovered that his hands were trembling.

"I'm a little nervous," he said. "I've never done this before."

Wynter placed her hands on his and guided them to where they both wanted them to be. "Don't worry. I've never done this before either."

"But... you and Ransom?"

Wynter shook her head slowly and smiled. "Just kissing." She pulled her T-shirt over her head, exposing her bra, and wrapped her arms around his body. She peppered his chest with kisses.

Cash hooked his thumbs into the waistband of her jeans, ran them around to the small of her back and traveled up to the strap of her bra. His fingers searched clumsily for a clasp but found none.

"It clips in the front," Wynter whispered as she unhooked both sides of the bra and allowed the cups to fall open and slide off her shoulders.

The radio faded into "I Want to Know What Love Is" by Foreigner. Goosebumps rose all over Wynter's body as she and gazed up at him. "I love this song. I want you to be my first."

Cash swallowed with surprise, then smiled. "That makes two of us." He ran his fingertips across the smooth skin of her back.

Wynter placed one hand behind his neck, pulled him in for a kiss, and let the other wander across his taut jeans. She could feel his excitement under the zippered denim. "Do you have..."

"Protection?"

Wynter nodded.

Cash went to the bottom drawer of his dresser and pulled out an unopened box of condoms.

Wynter gave him a curious glance. "Are you *sure* you're a virgin?"

"Yeah, a hundred percent." Cash tore into the box and extracted a foil pouch. "I've had these, like, forever."

"They're not expired, are they?"

"Uh..." Cash examined the box. "They're not *that* old."

Wynter pulled him onto his bed. "I'm kidding."

"I was saving them for the right moment."

"Like now?" Wynter popped the button on his jeans and unzipped his fly, revealing the waistband of his boxers.

"Like now." Cash mirrored the move and unfastened Wynter's jeans, sliding them off her long, slender legs. He wriggled out of his own jeans and threw them on the floor. With a flick of his wrist, he billowed the top sheet over top of them like a tent and lay next to her.

Time seemed to stand still as they explored each other's bodies, playfully, reverently, the heat between them rising. Finally, both naked under the sheets, their dreams and longing for each other became real. Their first time together didn't last long, but they didn't rush it either. Both Cash and Wynter's hearts were full of the intense first love that never happens again in quite the same way.

Afterward, Wynter had snuggled up against Cash's chest, his heart beating strong in her ear. He had laid his arm across her back as they both enjoyed the deep peace of their intimate time together. They felt like adults, and in this important way, they were.

She lazily ran her fingertips across his chest, doing her best not to tickle him. "Do you think your dad would, like, freak out if he knew what we just did?"

Cash didn't take long to think about the question. "No." He cast his eyes back at the open box of condoms on his dresser. "We were responsible."

Wynter propped herself up on one elbow. A suggestive smile

crossed her lips as her eyes set upon the condoms. "How many of those are in a box?"

Cash studied her face and returned her smile. "I don't know. I wasn't paying attention. My mind was on *other* things."

Earlier, they both had felt modest about exposing their bodies and had used the top sheet to cover themselves up. Everything had changed. Wynter pushed herself up and stretched her body past Cash, reaching out for the condom box. The top sheet fell away, leaving her smooth curves in full view. Cash wanted to touch her skin but chose to memorize the view instead.

Wynter rested her body on Cash's chest as she flipped the box around in her hand. She reached inside and pulled out a flat, silver snake of condom packages. "It says there's a dozen in here." She moved her body back and set her chin on her arm, her nose almost touching Cash's. "Since we're being responsible..." Her eyes positively sparkled. "Want to be responsible again?"

Cash sank his fingers into her hair, kissed her, then rolled on top of her. He could feel his body awakening again. "You sure?"

"Most definitely," Wynter said between kisses.

"I think I'm going to like being responsible."

"Me too."

Cash applied a fresh condom for the second time in his life. The wait had been worth it. Their bodies moved slowly together as the top sheet slid to one side. They no longer cared about their nakedness with each other, secure in each other's arms with the night to themselves.

RANSOM FOUND HIMSELF back where it all began, at the railing of the Main Street Bridge looking out over a never-ending stream of interstate traffic.

He knew his time was coming to an end, at least in the form of a dreamwaker. He had seen it in Cash's eyes. And in Wynter's.

Ransom cast his gaze to the sky, the August reds and oranges dissolving at the horizon into the blues of a summer night. Even through the exhaust of the vehicles below, the warm breeze carried the sweetness of summer past his face. If he had to go, this was as good a time as any.

He climbed up onto the railing, curving his feet over the top edge, and raised his arms up from his sides like he was praising God. A few vehicles heading east honked their horns at him, either in concern or acknowledgment. He didn't care which.

A familiar song rose up to his ears from the highway below. Ransom traced the source to the cars and trucks racing east and west, their radios all tuned to the same wavelength. Then he heard the lyrics and everything made sense.

"I want to know what love is," the chorus rang out.

Ransom smiled to himself. Now that Wynter had shown him what love was, his job as a dreamwaker was done. He drifted a second later in a burst of vibrant sapphire blue energy, leaving Newhaven for Wynter and Cash to navigate together, hopefully without Jezebel.

ANSON REACHED THE END of Woodpark Avenue, gave Sadie a knowing glance, then turned left down 19th Street.

Jezebel twisted in the back seat to try and look out the back window of the Suburban. She couldn't see much but knew that they were driving away from the station. Ahead was the parking lot to Ollie's MovieTyme, the giant ghostly white movie screen looming in the distance.

"Where are you going? This isn't the way." Jezebel's attempt to hide her panic failed.

"Oh, I think you know where we're going." Anson raised an eyebrow at her through the rear view mirror.

Jezebel's mind raced. She had to calm herself down. Freaking out now would do her no good.

Anson drove past Ollie's, following 19th Street to the last road on the left: Sheffield Avenue.

Oh shit.

Jezebel watched derelict houses lit by sodium vapor streetlights pass by on the left and right side of the Suburban until one particular house stood out ahead. She had been there only once before but once was enough.

Anson slowed and parked at the curb. "You know whose house this is, right?"

The orange glow from the streetlights made the silver Fiat X1/9 in the driveway look bronze. It didn't make the car look any better and it was still ugly as hell.

Already Jezebel had begun to regret ratting out Monty. This could get bad fast. But she had to roll with the fallout and decided keeping her mouth shut would be the best plan.

"Jezebel Caine at a loss for words? Note this day in the history books." Anson glanced at Sadie. "Let's go arrest a drug dealer." He popped open his door.

"You got the warrant?"

Anson nodded and tapped the inner pocket of his jacket. He leaned into the Suburban far enough to get a clear view of Jezebel again. "Be good. If there's any damage to my ride, I'll make sure the judge takes it out of your ass."

Jezebel continued her silent vigil as the two police officers closed their doors and approached the house.

MUFFLED SOUNDS OF CAR CHASES and gun fire punctuated the blue light that flickered through the threadbare curtains covering Monty's large front window. Anson hoped that the violent ambiance wouldn't become prophetic. If given the choice, he would rather have a peaceful arrest without struggle.

"You cover the back," Anson whispered to Sadie. "I'll take the front."

Sadie nodded, drew her pistol, and disappeared along the darkened side of the house. Anson stepped up the bulky concrete front stoop. Unlike at Jezebel's, Monty's house had no porch. Reduced working room meant that he'd have to keep his wits sharp.

Anson placed his hand on the grip of his pistol but left it in its holster. Its cool weight grounded him. He cast a glance back at the Suburban and saw Jezebel had remained exactly where he had left her, her eyes glowering at him in the dim orange street light.

He took a breath and knocked on the door. Somewhere inside the house a bottle fell to the floor and rolled.

Floorboards creaked just beyond the door's threshold.

Then nothing.

Anson knocked again. "Myles Mancini. This is Sheriff Jacobs from the Newhaven Police Department. I have a warrant for your arrest. Open the door, please." He paused briefly to give Monty a chance to respond, then continued. "Monty. Open the door. Running's only going to make things worse."

Sounds of a struggle echoed back from deep within the house. If Monty had tried to exit through the back, Sadie would have stopped him. Anson had full confidence in her abilities under pressure.

"Drop it!" The thickness of the front door had done little to block the volume of Sadie's command from within the house.

Anson drew his pistol, flicked off the safety for the second time, and kicked open the front door. The front hallway ran the length of the house, dividing it in half, much like Jezebel's house and many others in southie territory. Low income, cookie-cutter housing had its advantages.

Backlit by the kitchen lights, Anson identified Monty standing in the kitchen at the end of the hallway, a .38 snubnose gripped in his right hand. Sadie stood near the back door, her gun trained on his chest.

"Drop the gun, Monty." Anson aimed his pistol at Monty's back, taking care to avoid Sadie's line of fire. "This isn't worth dying over."

"You got a fuckin' warrant?" Monty yelled back, careful not to make any sudden moves.

"I said I did." Anson spoke calmly as he slid the warrant from the inside pocket of his jacket and shook it open. "Got it right here. Drop the gun and you can read it."

Monty hesitated. "What's the charge?"

"Possession of a controlled substance with intent to distribute." Anson took a silent step forward, then another. "Those are serious charges. Cooperation will go a long way."

"Fuck you. That don't mean SHIT."

"Better than leaving in a body bag." Anson's eyes flicked to Sadie's as he took another step forward. She held her aim steady on Monty. "You ready to die today?"

As Monty choked on a response, Anson advanced another foot forward and the floorboards let out a strained creak.

Monty turned his head to confirm Anson's position, momentarily taking his eyes off Sadie's gun.

It was time to act. This degenerate had too much control. Sadie used the moment to make her move. She lunged at him, leading with her gun.

Monty registered her movement and raised his snubnose, swinging his arm wide. He pulled the trigger. The gunshot echoed within the small kitchen and exploded the overhead light.

Sadie managed to grab his right hand just as the light bulb fizzled out in a shower of sparks.

Anson pulled his flashlight from his belt, turned it on, and crouch-ran toward the two of them. It was impossible to avoid the snubnose's wild aim as Sadie and Monty struggled on the floor.

Slamming Monty's right hand against the wall was all it took. The snubnose slipped out of his grasp, bounced off the baseboard, and slid toward Anson.

Sadie rolled Monty onto his chest, placed her knee on his back, and holstered her pistol. With cuffs in hand, she reached for his left wrist, but Monty had no intention of cooperating and repeatedly evaded her grasp.

Anson kicked the snubnose farther down the hallway, dropped his flashlight on the floor aimed at Monty's face, and forced Monty's left wrist to the small of his back.

As Sadie locked one cuff, Monty jammed his free hand under his body, but the two officers' speed and strength were no match for his weakened physical condition. Selling drugs and couch surfing didn't offer much in the way of exercise.

Anson pulled Monty away from the wall and dug out his arm far enough for Sadie to take over. She locked the other cuff around his right wrist with a quick flip of her hand.

The three of them sat on the floor, spent and catching their breath.

"I'm goin' to sue your fuckin' asses for police brutality," Monty said through a pool of drool that had collected on the floor near his cheek.

Anson propped his elbows on his bent knees and rolled his eyes. "Can't wait." He shared a tired but satisfied glance with Sadie. "You feel up to getting what we came for?"

Sadie returned a smile a mile wide. "Fuck, yeah." She stood, brushed herself off, and walked back toward the front door, then detoured into a side room and flicked on the light.

"Where she goin'?" Monty called out. "There's nothin' in there."

"You sure about that?" Anson grabbed his flashlight as he stood, then hooked his hand around Monty's left bicep and pulled him to his feet. He led him down the hallway to the doorway to the room Sadie had entered and pressed Monty chest first against the wall.

Anson stowed his flashlight and held up the official arrest warrant. "Want to read what you're going down for? Just so everything's by the book?"

Monty spat on the creased piece of paper and scowled.

"I figured as much." Anson wiped off the spit using the back of Monty's T-shirt and tucked the warrant back into his jacket.

Sadie's voice floated back out of the side room. "Anson, you're going to want to see this."

"Bring it out here." Anson braced his right forearm against Monty's shoulders. "Monty's telling me there's nothing in there."

Sadie appeared at the doorframe and held up a large Ziploc bag, filled to capacity with assorted pills in all shapes, sizes, and colors, all separated into separate smaller baggies.

"Fuck," Monty cursed to himself.

Anson leaned in to Monty's left ear. "What was that?"

Monty fell silent and his resistance melted away, his mind somewhere else.

"I'd guess that's going to get you ten years, minimum." Anson flashed Sadie a thumbs up. "Nice job, Deputy."

"I can't fuckin' do ten years," Monty said. "What if I gave you somethin'?"

Anson exchanged a dubious look with Sadie. "Nothing's going to reduce your sentence."

"You solve that murder yet?" When Anson and Sadie didn't respond immediately, Monty continued. "You know, that cabbie from Halston?"

"You know something about that?" Anson tightened his grip on Monty's arm. "Who'd believe you?"

"Hey, my fuckin' arm doesn't bend that way, asshole." Monty pushed back and Anson eased his grip. "You don't need to believe *me*. Just use your fuckin' *eyes*."

"Going to have to give me more than that," Anson said.

"I got photos." With his face pressed against the wall, Monty strained to look at Anson. "What's that worth to you?"

"I'd have to see the photos." Anson looked at Sadie and she nodded back, her curiosity piqued. "Where are they?"

"Left back wheel," Monty said. "Where my stash was."

Sadie disappeared into the room. Sounds of plastic breaking and clattering to the floor echoed back through the doorway. "Well I'll be dipped in shit." She returned to the hallway, a roll of Kodak T-MAX 100 tweezed between her thumb and index finger.

"Don't stand there gawkin'." Monty rolled his shoulders. "That goin' to be enough?"

"If it leads to an arrest... maybe," Anson said. "Ultimately, it's up to the judge." He heaved Monty backward and pushed him out the front door.

Sadie placed the .38 snubnose into an evidence bag, picked up the bag of narcotics, and followed Anson out.

"You goin' to fix my fuckin' door?"

"Eventually." Anson led him toward the Suburban.

Monty spotted Jezebel in the back seat. "What the *fuck* is she doing here?" He tried to twist around to look back at Anson. "Did she rat me out? If I find out—"

"Monty, you have the right to remain silent," Anson said. "Anything you say can and will be used against you in a court of law. You—"

"Blah fuckin' blah. Whatever."

"Suit yourself." Anson opened the passenger door opposite to Jezebel, guided him onto the bench seat. He closed the door and met Sadie at the back bumper.

"Un-fucking-believable." Anson scanned the street for any spectator activity. "They ratted each other out."

"Two perps, one stone," Sadie said, grinning.

"Got that film handy?"

Sadie passed the film canister to him, and Anson slipped it into a pocket. "Let's get these pillars of society back where they belong."

"Copy that."

Both officers returned to the cab of the Suburban. Anson threw the vehicle into drive and began the short trip to the station, glad that the night was over.

But good things usually happen in threes and tonight was no exception.

JEZEBEL AND MONTY had surprised Anson. He had expected his two criminals to tear into each other on the way back to the station. Instead, they both sat quietly on their sides of the back bench seat.

Perhaps his earlier attempt to read Monty his Miranda rights had invoked his self-preservation. The evidence against him was damning and whatever was on the film would not change his fate much.

Monty held his tongue, but his face told a different story. His rage was palpable. If looks could kill, Jezebel would have died multiple times. Anson wondered if the feeling would have been mutual had Jezebel known about Monty's photographs.

Sadie and Anson unloaded their captives from the Suburban and led them toward the station. Sadie pushed Monty brusquely up the front steps, still riding on adrenaline from their scuffle at the house. Anson led Jezebel into the station content to know that she wasn't a dreamwaker. Once back at MacLeod County

Juvenile Detention Facility in the morning, she wouldn't be getting out any time soon.

Anson locked Jezebel and Monty individually into the two adjoining holding cells and removed their handcuffs through the bars.

Monty walked to the bench, laid himself out on his back, and tucked his hands behind his head. "Rockwell will have me out by tomorrow morning."

Sadie had just returned from the Suburban, Monty's drug stash held firmly in her hand. "I wouldn't count on it. There's enough felony convictions in this to last a lifetime." She scanned the contents through the clear plastic. "You've really screwed yourself this time."

"No! Someone *else* screwed me." Monty aimed his index finger like a gun through the bars at Jezebel and cocked his thumb. "Your ass is grass," he said through clenched teeth.

"Fuck off, asshole. I didn't do nothing to you that you didn't already have coming." Jezebel leaned against the back wall and closed her eyes.

"Just you wait, bitch," Monty said under his breath. "You'll get yours soon enough."

Jezebel wiggled her fingers. "Ooh, I'm so scared."

"Truth is, you *should* be scared, both of you." Anson appeared at the door to his office. Sadie handed him the bag of drugs. "These charges are serious and they're not going away."

Jezebel jumped to her feet and ran to the bars. "But I was set up! That's fucking *entrapment*."

"Big words... but using a gun on Wynter was *your* choice, Jezebel," Sadie said. "We just lucked out. Right place, right time."

Anson took the overstuffed bag of drugs from Sadie and placed them into the box with all of Jezebel's evidence. The canister of film in his jacket was burning a hole in his pocket. How important would the photos be? Would they help nail Jezebel's case closed like Monty had alluded to?

He pulled the canister out and rolled the cool metal cylinder between his fingers. Tomorrow he'd visit Minit Prints and find out.

Anson carried Jezebel's fate to the evidence lock up room in the back of the station. He started a second box for Monty and transferred the bag of drugs into it. As he secured the mesh door closed, he heard angry voices rising up from the main office. "What the hell are those assholes going on about now," he muttered to himself.

As he strode by the bathrooms at the end of the hallway, he heard Jezebel's voice plain as day.

"You better not cross me, you bitch."

Anson passed the conference room and into the main office area. Monty hadn't moved from his reclined position in his cell, taking in the show with a smirk on his face.

Jezebel stood at the bars of her cell, shrieking at Sadie. At least that's what it looked like at first. As Anson approached the front of the office, he discovered that Sadie's body had blocked his view of Roxy sitting opposite her.

"The plot thickens," Anson whispered to himself. He walked around to the side of Sadie's desk. Roxy gave him a wary glance. "What the hell is going on here?"

Sadie shook her head. "Sorry, Anson. She won't shut her mouth."

"Don't listen to her!" Jezebel jammed her arm through the bars and pointed at Roxy with an angry finger. "She doesn't know what the fuck she's talking about."

Anson side-eyed Jezebel, beyond fed up. "I don't know what *you're* talking about. So how about you stow it for a second." He turned his attention to Roxy. "Can I help you with something?"

Roxy scanned the office and intentionally avoided eye contact with Jezebel. It was clear that she hadn't expected to run into her partner-in-crime and her expletive-laced outbursts.

"Want to talk in my office?"

Roxy nodded.

Anson motioned to his open door. "Come on."

"Fucking bitch. She's a *liar!*" Jezebel screamed, both her hands gripping the bars as if ready to rip the door of its hinges.

Anson stood just outside his office as Roxy stepped inside. He followed her in and closed the door. The door offered some respite from Jezebel's tirade but not nearly enough.

"That child sure has a set of lungs on her."

Roxy met Anson's eyes for a second, then shrugged and looked away.

"Have a seat." Instead of sitting on the opposite side of his desk, he took the chair next to Roxy and moved it around to face her. "What brings you here on this unusually busy Thursday night?"

Roxy was conflicted. She looked back at the closed office door. Jezebel's voice still assaulted their ears through the wood and glass. "I'm sorry. I shouldn't have come."

She stood and beat a path toward the door, but Anson placed a gentle hand on her arm and stopped her.

"Easy, now. Sit." Anson went to the door and opened it wide enough to poke his head out. "Sadie, you recording everything Jezebel's saying out there?"

"Every word." Sadie winked at him. "Ever since she got here."

"What?" Jezebel said, momentarily distracted. "So?"

"You're a smart girl, Miss Caine," Anson said. "Anything you say can be used against you in court. So, you might want to *shut up*." He closed the door without waiting for an answer and returned to the chair beside Roxy.

Refreshing silence descended over the station. Anson waited a moment. "Think it's going to work?"

Roxy shook her head. "Probably not."

Jezebel began wailing in protest again.

Anson and Roxy exchanged a smile. At least they were on the same page now.

"What did you want to talk to me about?"

Roxy bit her lip.

"If you're afraid, let me reassure you. Jezebel's going away for a long time."

"But she holds a grudge."

Anson sat forward, rested his elbows on his knees, and clasped his hands. "Roxy, let me be straight with you. You're linked with that psycho out there for some of her charges, specifically the LaCroix arson. You will face some kind of punishment. That's for certain. But you coming in here today with whatever information you have is a show of good faith. It may affect the judge's decision regarding your actions." He detected worry on her face. "Did you expect no consequences?"

Roxy's eyes fell to the floor, and she shook her head. "No. I was there. I knew what could happen. And I knew it was wrong."

"Okay. So what's on your mind?"

Roxy sat back in her chair and sighed. Jezebel's ranting had decreased but her protests still floated through the door. She wrung her hands nervously and cast her eyes around the office. "Fuck it." She glanced at the closed office door. "No. Fuck *her*." She found Anson's gaze and matched it. "I know where Quinn is."

Anson pulled out his notepad and pen, careful not to look too eager. This was good information that could save a life. "Whenever you're ready."

"You know Ollie's?"

"Ollie's MovieTyme?" Anson looked to Roxy for confirmation. "The old drive-in on 19th?"

Roxy nodded. "There's this shed, in the back, like, behind the screen. Jezebel locked... I mean *we* locked her in there."

"When did this happen?"

"This morning." Roxy found a clock on Anson's desk. "Maybe around nine?" She shook her head. "Jezebel had already hit her in the head with a bat and knocked her out. I just helped getting her into the shed."

"And you kept that information to yourself until now?" Anson's anger battled against his gratitude for Roxy's willingness to confess. "Did you leave her with any food or water?"

Roxy shook her head.

"Was she conscious when you put her in the shed?"

"I don't think so."

"You don't *think* so? People die from head injuries, Roxy."

"I'm sorry." Roxy covered her face and sobbed. "Jezebel didn't care if Quinn died. She said she'd kill me, too."

Anson tucked his notepad and pen away and stood, sending the chair sliding backward. "Look. Coming to me was the right thing to do, but you should have done it sooner."

"Am I going to jail?"

"Stand up."

Roxy wiped her tears and stood.

"As for jail, I don't know," Anson said. "That's up to a judge to decide. A lot rests on whether Quinn is okay or not. Understand?"

Roxy sniffled and nodded.

Anson placed his hands firmly on her shoulders. "Are you a flight risk?"

Roxy blinked back at him.

"If I let you go home for now, can I trust you not to run?"

"Yeah," Roxy said. "I'm done running."

"Good, because this isn't over." Anson locked his gaze with hers to emphasize the gravity of Quinn's situation. "Go straight home. I'm going to get Quinn to the hospital. You better pray she's okay."

"I'm sorry, Sheriff."

"Yeah. So am I." Anson grabbed the doorknob. "Don't say anything to Jezebel." He opened the door and escorted Roxy out of his office.

Jezebel launched herself off the cell bench and jammed her arms through the bars to try and grab Roxy as she passed by. "What did you say to him, you *bitch*? Tell me!"

Roxy kept her eyes forward.

"You're fucking *dead!*" Jezebel screamed. "You're going to *pay* when I get out of here!"

"Sadie." Anson jerked his head to the front entrance. "A word." He led Roxy out of the station, stopping just outside the doors. "Normally I'd drive you home but Quinn's my priority. Remember, straight home and stay there. That's best for your case going forward."

Roxy nodded and ran into the night along Main Street.

Sadie stood part way out of the door. "What's up?"

"Roxy fessed up," Anson said. "Quinn's locked in a shed behind Ollie's. Jezebel assaulted her earlier so I'm going to run her to the hospital and get her checked out. You okay to stay here?"

Sadie rocked back, cocked her ear at Jezebel's ruckus, and laughed. "She's losing steam. Probably be asleep by the time you get back."

"Right." Anson ran down the steps toward the Suburban. "Keep you posted."

"Copy that." Sadie moved back into the station.

Anson jumped behind the wheel of the Suburban, rocketed backward from his parking space, and tore down Main Street headed south, following the same route he had taken to Monty's house earlier. The thought occurred to him that he could have rescued Quinn earlier if he had only known, no thanks to Roxy. Fucking Roxy. If Quinn was severely injured or worse, a delayed confession was as good as no confession at all. He hoped it wasn't too late.

Luckily, traffic in Newhaven was light on a Thursday night. After crossing the interstate, Anson skidded right onto Jones Avenue, past Sven Dwarfs and the Starlite, then left on 19th Street. He turned on his light bar, floored the gas, and shot past the weather-beaten "Ollie's MovieTyme" sign. Had he not been watching for the shed behind the screen, he would have missed it.

The Suburban slid to a stop on the loose gravel at back of the shed, the headlights aimed at the door and back wall, the rest of the surrounding area awash in undulating red and blue light.

Anson leaped out of the vehicle and grabbed a tire iron from the back. The tool wasn't ideal but would have to do. He ran to the door and pounded on it. "Quinn? You in there?" He listened only for a second before ramming the flat end of the tire iron between the door and the frame.

Anson pulled with all his weight. The leverage made easy work and the lock loop snapped off the door in one piece. With a rusty creak, the door swung inward and revealed Quinn lying in a fetal position on a dirty mattress. Dried blood smeared the fabric near the back of her head and vomit spilled off the opposite edge of the mattress.

Anson's stomach dropped. "Dear God, Quinn." He kneeled beside the teen and touched her neck, preparing himself to feel nothing but her cold skin. But she surprised him. There, strong and steady under his fingertips, was her unmistakable pulse.

Quinn groaned and rolled over, taking the brightness of the Suburban's headlights full on. She raised her hand to block the light.

"Easy, now." Anson slid one arm behind her back and the other under her knees and heaved her up. Quinn slumped into his chest and shielded her face in his jacket. He ran on bent knees to the SUV, pulled open the back passenger door, and eased Quinn onto the back seat, belting her in.

Anson returned to the cab and picked up the radio handset. He considered calling for an ambulance from Halston, but it would take almost an hour to get here, then an hour back. He could transport Quinn directly to the hospital in less than half that time. "Sadie, package intact and en-route to Halston. Anson out." He threw the Suburban into reverse and followed the same route back toward I94.

He glanced into the rear view mirror. "Quinn? How you doing back there? You okay?"

"Jake?" Quinn's eyes fluttered open. "Jake."

"What about Jake?"

"I need him," Quinn said.

"Quinn, you need a hospital."

"I need Jake."

Anson found Quinn's eyes in the mirror, and he couldn't deny their urgency. A detour to Jake's house might delay them several minutes but could make a world of difference to Quinn's recovery and well-being. Besides, with his light bar on, he'd have the interstate to himself.

"Okay," he said. "Next stop, Jake's. Then the hospital."

Two minutes later he found himself bounding up the walk to Jake's front door. Mirielle answered but Jake was dressed and ready to go, a can of Coke jammed in his front pocket. Anson led him back to the Suburban.

Jake opened the door to the back seat and peeked inside. "Mustang, this is Maverick, requesting fly-by."

Quinn's eyes flicked open. "Jake!" She unbelted herself, slid across the bench seat, and threw her arms around him.

He smiled at her. "How you feeling?"

Quinn groaned. She had moved too fast. "Hurts."

"Watch her head," Anson said. "She's got one hell of a goose egg."

Jake climbed inside, positioning his cast in a comfortable angle, and buckled Quinn and himself in. "Here." He popped the tab on the Coke and offered it to her.

Quinn raised the can to her lips and took a healthy drink. She let loose a small burp, sighed, and leaned into him. By the time Jake had taken the can and placed it between his legs to prevent spilling, Quinn had fallen asleep.

"Keep her awake, Jake. Until doctors can assess her. Concussions are serious."

"I'll do my best, Anson." Jake kissed Quinn's forehead and roused her from sleep. He offered her another sip of Coke, which she drank willingly.

Anson saw the two teenagers embraced in his back seat and knew that he had made the right decision. "Next stop, Halston Medical Center."

Jake thumbed the brim of his baseball cap at him and gave him a head nod.

Anson threw the Suburban into gear and navigated back to the interstate. With light bar blazing, he made it to the hospital in just under forty minutes.

An ER doctor and a nurse examined Quinn, gave her fluids, and began to stitch up the gash on the back of her head. Jake and Anson stood close by and waited until the doctor had completed his examination.

"You were a real johnny-on-the-spot earlier," Anson said.

Jake smiled, his gaze still settled on Quinn in the hospital bed. She had perked up considerably since getting proper medical attention. "Yeah, well Cash called earlier and told me that you got Jezebel. So I called the station."

"You were checking up on me."

Jake shrugged. "What can I say? Quinn's my girl."

"I don't blame you," Anson said. "I would've done the same thing for Mercy." He paused, shifting his eyes between the two teens. "You two make a nice couple."

"Thanks," Jake said, beaming.

"One more charge to add to Jezebel's shopping list."

The doctor approached Anson. "All done. She's lucky. Just a mild concussion. She's good to go any time."

As Anson and the doctor continued to talk, Jake walked over to Quinn's bed and examined the bandage on the back of her head with a gentle hand. "Did they take out the Indigenous eel larva?" he asked with a smirk.

Quinn gave him a sideways glance and scrunched her nose at him. "Khan Noonien Singh would not be pleased."

"I'm so glad you're okay." Jake reached for her hand.

"Me, too." Quinn took Jake's hand in hers and let their fingers interlock.

The doctor scanned the ER. "You taking her or are her parents here?"

"Speak of the devil." Anson jerked his head toward the entrance to the ER. Lotus Benoit, wearing black pants and a blouse under a bright yellow jacket with exaggerated shoulders, approached the doctor with quick strides. Her straight, black hair framed perfect makeup, and her purse matched her shoes with each intentional step.

"Am I seeing this right?" The doctor looked at his watch. "At this hour?"

"Quinn's mom is quite the fashion plate," Anson said. "But don't let her looks fool you. She's a riot."

The doctor nodded.

Lotus took Anson aside and hugged him. "Thank you. For everything."

"My pleasure, Mrs. Benoit," Anson said. "Glad Quinn's okay. I've got to head out, but Doc here will fill you in."

The doctor walked Lotus back to Quinn's bed, sharing the results of his examination. At the entrance to the ER, Anson turned to take one last look back on the scene. Quinn's ER microcosm exuded happiness but he reminded himself that in Jezebel's hands it could have gone the opposite direction just as easily.

Anson headed out to the Suburban and began his journey back to Newhaven. He tapped the film canister in his pocket and wondered what secrets it would hold, if any. Minit Prints would deliver the answers to those questions, but not until morning.

THE STEDFORD PLAZA parking lot outside Minit Prints was mostly vacant when Anson arrived the next morning. He drained the last of his travel mug full of Lucy's coffee and headed for the locked exterior door. With a rap of his knuckle, he caught the attention of a clerk inside.

"Open up," he said.

The clerk twisted the deadbolt and pushed the door open. "What's going on, Sheriff?"

Anson held up the film canister. "Going to have to commandeer your store until this is developed. Is that going to be a problem?"

"Uh... no sir." The clerk stepped aside to let Anson pass.

"Lock the door and keep it locked."

The clerk secured the door. "There *is* a job running already." He gave Anson a concerned look. "You'll have to wait for that to finish."

"Sure." Anson handed the canister to the clerk. "How long will it take?"

The clerk examined the canister. "T-MAX huh? High end stuff." He scanned the side of the blue minilab machine. "I can start the film developing now, and the current print job is almost done, so... For one set of prints, maybe twenty minutes? Half an hour tops."

Anson nodded and walked around to the end of the machine. A continuous strip of untrimmed photos exited on rollers behind a clear plastic window before disappearing back into the machine to be cut into individual prints.

"What's this about?" the clerk asked.

"Sorry. I can't discuss an ongoing criminal investigation."

The clerk's brows shot up in surprise.

Anson waved his hand at the clear window at the back of the

minilab. "Going to ask that you stay away from this side of the machine too," he said. "The film may contain sensitive material."

The clerk nodded. "I understand." He loaded the T-MAX canister into the developer and set the machine running.

"And I'll need to collect the prints myself if you don't mind," Anson said.

"Because of the sensitive material... right. No problem."

After the developer had processed the T-MAX film, the clerk transferred the negatives to the printing machine. "Do you need more than one set of prints? If you do, it'll take longer than my original estimate."

People had begun pacing at both the exterior door and the security gate that opened the store to the plaza. Anson answered without hesitation. "One set is good. Don't want to hold you up any longer than I have to."

True to the clerk's estimate, the T-MAX photographs completed their journey through the printer in twenty-five minutes. He handed Anson a paper envelope and showed him where to collect them.

"How much do I owe you?"

The clerk shrugged and shook his head. "Nothing? This is official police business, right?"

Anson dug out his wallet and pulled out a twenty. "Will that cover it?"

"Yeah," the clerk said. "Let me get your change."

"Keep it." Anson tipped his hat at him. "For your trouble."

"Thanks."

Anson twisted the deadbolt on the exterior door and let himself out into the parking lot, which had filled considerably in the past thirty minutes. "Sorry for the delay, folks. Minit Prints is back in business."

He strolled to the Suburban and hopped in. Anson stared at the Minit Prints envelope in his hand and wanted nothing more than to tear into it. But Sadie had played a big part in this case.

He could hold out a few minutes more. He threw the vehicle into gear and drove the half-mile to the station.

ANSON ENTERED THE STATION to relative silence compared to the obscenity-laced state he had left Sadie with the previous night.

An unpleasant scenario flashed through his mind. "We haven't had a jail break, have we?"

Sadie's voice floated back, "No. Just a little breakfast from Lucy's." She poked her head around the corner holding a plate of pancakes. "Want some?"

"What the hell?"

Sadie shrugged and speared a bite of pancake with her fork. "Prisoners still need to be fed."

"Last meal, more like." Anson approached her, slipped the Minit Prints envelope part way out of his jacket, and lowered his voice. "Interested?"

"Fuck, yeah."

"Meet me in my office," Anson said. "And bring some of those flapjacks with you. Please." He stood at the doorway to his office and watched Monty and Jezebel in their cells. Each of them had a disposable cup of coffee and their own stacks of pancakes balanced on paper plates. They ate without utensils. Anson shook his head in partial incredulity. Both had been elusive for so long, yet here they were, in his custody, both with mountains of evidence against them. He worked to suppress a smile.

"Where's Roxy?" Jezebel spoke around a slurry of chewed food.

"Finish your breakfast, Miss Caine," Anson said. "You may not be eating at Lucy's for a long time."

"She ratted me out, didn't she?" Jezebel threw her plate onto the cell bench. "Fucking bitch is dead."

"At least she's consistent," Sadie said as she entered Anson's office with an extra plate of pancakes, a fork, napkins, and a single-serving container of syrup.

Anson closed the door behind her, then pulled out the Minit Prints package from his jacket and threw it on his desk. "Thought you'd want to do the honors."

Sadie handed him his plate. "You haven't seen them yet?"

"No." He took joy in her excitement. "God help me, I wanted to, though."

Sadie smiled at him as she wiped her hands. "Thanks, Anson." She opened the envelope and slid out almost three dozen black and white 4"x6" prints.

"We'll get enlargements made of the important ones."

Sadie flipped through them one by one. "Monty's been busy. Looks like some of these were taken somewhere else, maybe on a different day." Three-quarters through the stack she paused, and her eyes widened. "Holy shit."

She swallowed hard and handed a print to Anson. The shot showed Jezebel holding a knife to the cabbie's neck. The next several prints she handed him showed the knife buried in the cabbie's chest as Jezebel fled the scene. The last photo was closer and the dark, bloody patch surrounding the knife in the cabbie's chest had expanded, taking the man's life with it.

Anson flicked his eyes up from the print to Sadie. "We got them."

Sadie nodded, satisfaction creeping across her face. "We got them *both*."

"With help from some *meddling* kids," Anson added with a wink.

"Some *awesome* meddling kids," Sadie said. "Couldn't have done it without them."

"Damn straight." Anson set the prints down on his desk in exchange for his plate of Lucy's finest breakfast fare. He doused the pancakes with syrup and tore into them. He tapped his loaded fork with Sadie's. "Good work, Deputy. Cheers."

Cold pancakes had never tasted so good.

September

THE NEXT SIX WEEKS moved quickly for Wynter, Cash, Quinn, and Jake. With Ransom gone for good, the four friends spent most of their non-working waking hours either together or as separate couples.

Wynter stepped back into the shoes of her old job at Shooters. Wisely, Vinny offered no opposition and no reprisals in the wake of her return. Perhaps the guy had a human heart after all.

Jake suggested she use her photography skills to help promote the store. "Make sure the asshole pays you extra for it. Your stuff is really good. Don't forget that."

She continued to stay with Cash. It was a convenient arrangement and Ernie enjoyed the extra help as much as the added female energy Wynter brought with her.

After the hospital had discharged Nolan, he joined Madeline's mission to find a new place to live. Their pad rental at Sven Dwarfs had already been paid for the year and replacement trailers of comparable size were easy to find. Getting insurance to follow through and pay out remained the biggest hurdle.

Cash returned to Finn's Gas N Go part-time. When he wasn't hanging out with Wynter, he spent his remaining time working with Jake on their video game venture.

"I'll make the games. You sell them. Together we get rich." That had been Jake's mantra for the rest of August. Now that dream was actually happening, and it offered a change of scene from school and working at Finn's that Cash hadn't realized he had needed.

Quinn quit her job at FreshWhip.

"You're too good for that place," Jake had told her. "You need a job where you can kick major ass, and do what you're good at."

Using Jake's encouragement as a confidence booster, Quinn remembered Wynter's suggestion and talked her way into a small job reviewing movies for the *Newhaven Register*. Working within the time constraints of school, she reviewed up to three movies a week, one theatrical release on the weekend and two VHS video releases during the week. Quinn loved it. The free movie admissions and video rentals were a bonus.

Jake became the hidden glue of the four friends. After he had his cast removed, it was like someone had lit a fire under his ass. He immersed himself in all things related to video game programming. When his grades began to slip, his priority shifted to convincing his parents to try and imagine the lucrative future of video games. It was a monumental task made somewhat easier when Wynter, Quinn, and Cash backed him up. But he recognized that school had to come first. He just needed a little more balance.

Their senior year at Newhaven High School began with an unexpected perk, not only for Wynter and her friends, but for the whole student body. The wheels of justice sometimes move quickly and the Friday after Labor Day saw Jezebel and Roxy convicted of arson and attempted murder. Both received ten years behind bars, beginning at MacLeod County Juvenile Detention Facility, then transferred to Sheyenne Women's Correctional Center on their eighteenth birthdays to serve the remainder of their sentences.

Teachers and students hadn't realized how much of an oppressive influence Jezebel and Roxy had had on the school until they were gone. Other bullies remained to take their place but none with nearly as much clout. Evil took a blow at Newhaven

High, and as a result friendships across the school strengthened, including Wynter's.

THE INDIGENOUS PEOPLE of the Sheyenne grasslands had recorded seasonal changes for hundreds of years, well before European explorers "discovered" North America. The people of Newhaven had celebrated the equinox since 1976, a day when the hours of daylight equaled the hours of darkness. The autumnal equinox also signaled the beginning of Fall.

Every year Nolan celebrated his Indigenous heritage as well as the equinox with a simple family barbecue, but this year he had much more to be thankful for. He had survived a gunshot, had lived through a heart attack, his legs had mostly healed, and most important of all, Wynter had made a full recovery from her coma.

To repay his good fortune, he expanded his celebration to include Wynter's friends and family, as well as Finn O'Connor, and the police and fire department. While he couldn't afford to open things up to the entire town, neighbors who showed up from the trailer park were not turned away. He set up tables, chairs, a collapsible tent awning, and a large barbecue in the common field at Sven Dwarfs.

A loudspeaker placed on Ernie's front stoop blasted John Lennon out into the field, entertaining anyone who would listen with lyrics about "instant karma."

Madeline used her employee discount with FoodXpress to supply the celebration with hot dogs, hamburgers, condiments, cupcakes, and assorted beverages.

Nolan stood near Ernie's trailer, surveyed the field, and beamed. The only detail left was to man the barbecue.

"It's going to be one hell of a shindig, ain't it?"

Nolan looked to find Ernie, dressed in a worn T-shirt and sweatpants, leaning on the railing in front of the door to his trailer. Nolan raised his voice over the music. "Sure will. I've got much to give thanks for. Starting with you."

Ernie scrunched up his face. "Me? What're you going on about?"

"For accommodating the noise." Nolan tapped the loud speaker. "But especially for allowing Wynter to stay with you and Cash. It's been a Godsend while Maddie and I track down a new trailer."

"Happy to do it," Ernie said. "She's a real gem."

"That she is." Nolan glanced at his watch and his face clouded with worry. All at once Ernie's clothing made sense. "Shit. This is your wake up time, isn't it?"

Ernie shrugged and waved him off. "Relax. It's Saturday. Perfect timing, I think." He looked out to the food that had been set up next to the barbecue. "I know what I'm having for breakfast today."

Nolan nodded and smiled. "Whatever you want. As much as you want." He spotted a familiar vehicle approaching along the trailer park's ring road. "But you better get to the food before the teenagers do."

Ernie snapped his fingers. "Good point," he said and disappeared into the trailer.

Madeline parked the Plymouth Reliant on the grass next to Ernie's Honda Civic. Cash and Wynter hopped out of the back seat, unloaded assorted groceries, and transported them to the tables.

Madeline strolled to where Nolan stood, kissed him on the cheek, and snaked her arm around his waist. "You did good, Hon."

"We did good." Nolan pulled her into a hug and whispered into her ear. "I got some good news. Our settlement came through."

Madeline stepped back, surprise etched on her face. "We got it?"

Nolan nodded. "All of it. The insurance company called the motel just after you left this morning. We may have a new trailer by this time next week."

"I have to admit, I'm a little surprised."

"It might have something to do with Jezebel being in the news again," Nolan said. "Denying payout to the victims of a convicted arsonist would look incredibly bad."

"Don't you mean a convicted murderer?"

"Don't count your chickens, Maddie." Nolan gazed at her, rediscovering all the little details he had fallen in love with seventeen years ago. "The jury's still out."

Wynter and Cash, hand in hand, crossed the field toward them. Madeline smiled wistfully at their approach. "Our baby is growing up."

Nolan took Madeline's hand and kissed the top of it. "She sure is."

"Mr. LaCroix?" Cash eyed him earnestly.

"Cash, it's *Nolan*." Now that Wynter and Cash were a couple, "Mr. LaCroix" held a formality that Nolan didn't care for. But Ernie had raised Cash to respect his elders and it was hard to fault him for that.

"I know," Cash said. "I'm working on it. I'm just used to it the other way."

"Sure. What can I do for you?"

"Well, actually..." Cash glanced at Wynter. She nodded in encouragement. "I know this is your party and all, but since there's more people this year, I was thinking... I could help you at the grill. If you want."

"You were thinking, huh?" Nolan tilted his head toward Wynter. "You put him up to this?"

"No, Dad. I swear," Wynter said. "This is, like, all Cash's idea."

Nolan gave Cash a once-over and took pleasure in letting the young man squirm a bit. But there wasn't any point to drawing it out.

"Well, Cash. Since you're *family* now, I think that's a damn fine idea." He hooked his arm playfully around Cash's neck and lead him toward the barbecue.

"I think you got yourself a keeper, there, Wynnie."

"I hope so, Mom." Wynter watched Nolan give Cash a tour of the grill. "He's pretty cool."

"Handsome, too." Madeline leaned in and kissed Wynter's head. "Help me get set up? People will be here soon, and I got onions, tomatoes, and pickles to chop."

"Let's do it."

Just as they both began walking toward the awning next to the barbecue, Wynter froze.

"Wynnie? What is it?" Madeline would have gone into full blown panic mode if she hadn't detected a small grin emerge from one side of Wynter's mouth. "Honey?"

Wynter looked back over her shoulder and spotted a dust cloud billowing close on the bumper of Blue Belle as the little car roared around the ring road toward Ernie's trailer. "Quinn and Jake are here. I'm going to wait for them, then we'll all come and help."

Madeline chuckled to herself as she carried on toward the awning. "Don't take too long."

Quinn parked beside the Reliant and hopped out. Jake bounded out of the passenger seat, no longer encumbered by his leg cast. He squared up his Nintendo baseball hat and ran to catch up with Quinn.

"Bug! Oh my God! Bug!"

Wynter stared are the two of them as they ran toward her. "What? What's going on?"

"You're not going to believe this," Quinn said between raspy breaths.

"Go on. Tell her." Jake flicked his eyes between the two girls.

"Tell me what?"

Quinn spotted Cash and Nolan setting up the barbecue and raced toward them. "Everyone needs to know," she called back.

"What the hell, guys," Wynter said as she and Jake followed.

Quinn stopped at the barbecue, gasping and practically vibrating with excitement. "Everyone. Listen. I have news."

Ernie crossed the field and joined the small gathering. "Rub-a-dub-dub. I'm here for the grub." Everyone looked at him like he had just spoken a different language. "I'm *not* here for the grub?"

Cash stood by Ernie's side. "Shh, Dad. Quinn's got something to tell us."

All eyes settled on Quinn. She looked to Jake, then back at the crowd. "The jury found Jezebel guilty of first degree murder. It was unanimous."

"Well, goddamn," Ernie said. "Lots of folk are going to be happy about that."

Madeline took Nolan in her arms and held him tight, then extended an arm to Wynter and pulled her into a close family hug. "It's over."

"Only after she's behind bars," Nolan whispered in Madeline's and Wynter's ears.

"It'll be in tomorrow's paper." Quinn beamed with satisfaction. "And on the news tonight. Most definitely."

"Justice finally caught up with her," Cash said.

"Fucking awesome." Jake slapped his hand to his mouth self-consciously but too late to self-censor.

The parents of the group looked at him in surprise until Nolan stepped up and pat him on the back. "Couldn't have said it better myself." He glanced back let Cash. "You coming, grill-master? The barbecue calls."

Jake intercepted Cash as he walked past. "Hey. Dude." He hooked a thumb at the speakers back at Cash's trailer. KROK cranked out Styx's "Renegade" as if Quinn's news had determined the song. "Nice, eh?"

"Yeah. Totally righteous, man." The two teens bumped shoulders as they passed.

Jake propped his chin on Quinn's shoulder. "So, hot stuff. Any movie recommendations?"

"Nothing you don't know about already," Quinn said. "But I get to see a sneak preview of *Crocodile Dundee* next week. Supposed to be mega good. Want to come?"

"Big time." Jake planed a quick kiss on her cheek. "I'll pay for gas and snacks. Your parents coming today?"

"I think so."

"Mine too. Let's help get things set up before they arrive."

Everyone pitched in with setup, except for Ernie. He tried but Madeline simply refused. For his generosity with Wynter, plus being the only night-shift worker in the group, she gave him special treatment. He was first in line for a "breakfast" of hamburgers and hot dogs with the works.

The Petersons, Benoits, Finn, and Anson and Mercy arrived a short while later, along with Sadie, Chief Embers, and several firefighters. The gathering of friends and family ate well and the gossip flowed. Nolan couldn't have been more pleased. Their world had begun to find balance again.

WORKING THE NIGHT SHIFT five days a week meant that weekends followed the same schedule. While Cash and Wynter slept, Ernie roamed the trailer and flipped back and forth between crappy late-night television and his latest paperback. He liked to think his wanderings helped dissuade weekend make-out sessions behind closed doors, but he also knew teenagers could be quietly mischievous if so inclined. He was young once too.

Ernie heard the paper hit the front stoop just before six o'clock.

He opened the front door, picked up the *Newhaven Register's Sunday Edition,* and unfolded it on the kitchen table.

"Dreamwaker Killer Sentenced 25 Years," read the bold, black headline.

"Jesus Christ," Ernie whispered to the empty living room. The local TV news had covered Jezebel's conviction the previous night, just as Quinn had said it might. Even a few local affiliates had carried the story. But it was different to see the story in black and white in his small town newspaper. Somehow it made it more real.

He made an instant decaf coffee and settled in. *The Register* had managed to find an unsympathetic photo of Jezebel in a full, hateful scowl. It didn't do her any favors.

The story ran over the first two pages and documented the murder of Travis Higgins, a cab driver from Halston. The newspaper had included a couple of Monty's non-graphic photographs, as well as a reprinting of Jezebel's arson conviction, adding to her psychopath portrait.

On the bottom of the second page, the fate of Myles "Monty" Mancini took up less than a quarter of a column. He received a nine year sentence without parole at MacLeod County Correctional Center for drug possession and distribution. One year had been shaved from his original sentence for providing "pivotal" evidence against Jezebel.

Ernie heard movement from Cash's bedroom and for a moment he thought he might overhear something that should remain private. Then Cash's bedroom door squeaked open, setting his mind at ease.

The sleep-addled footsteps of a teenager shuffled toward the kitchen table. "Hey, Dad."

"Sorry if I woke you." Ernie slid his kitchen chair to the side. "You're going to want to read this."

Cash rubbed the sleep out of his eyes as he focused on the

headline. "*Dreamwaker* killer? Ugh. Jezebel ruins everything." He sat and began reading.

"What is it, Cash?" Wynter moved from the bedroom to the bathroom, pushing the door closed to a sliver.

"They're calling her the 'dreamwaker killer,'" Cash called back.

After the flush and sounds of hand washing, Wynter strolled to where Cash sat reading the front page. "They came up with that nickname when her lawyers tried that insanity defense, remember? 'My dreamwaker clone did it, blah blah blah.'" She sat next to him.

"Yeah," Cash said. "Doesn't make it right."

MacLeod County District Court had tried Jezebel as an adult for Higgins' murder and she had received twenty-five years in prison without possibility of parole.

Ernie placed his empty coffee mug in the sink. "I'm going to bed, kids. Try and keep it down to a dull roar, okay?"

"Sure thing, Dad."

Ernie kissed Cash's head lightly and gave Wynter's shoulder a tap as he passed behind the two teens on his way to his bedroom.

"Says she's going to be transferred to Sheyenne Women's Correctional Center this week. And she also gets to serve her arson conviction at the same time." Cash flipped the front page, then slumped back in his chair, and sighed. His brain was tired of Jezebel.

"Who cares? She's right where she belongs," Wynter said just before kissing him on the cheek.

"But 'dreamwaker' was your thing."

"Actually, it was Jake's idea." Wynter rested her head on Cash's shoulder and closed her eyes. She didn't need to read the story. "Dreamwakers are a thing of the past now."

"Jake's going to be pissed."

"I'm sure Quinn can keep him *distracted,*" Wynter said with a grin.

Cash caught Wynter's vibe and smiled too. He placed his arm around her shoulder. "Can you still summon?"

"I don't know and I don't care," Wynter said. "That's, like, ancient history."

Cash folded up the newspaper and tossed it aside. "I feel like pancakes. How about you?"

"Most definitely."

Cash and Wynter stepped to the kitchen counter and busied themselves with pancake preparation. Making new memories to push out the ones of Jezebel came easy for them both.

JUST AS QUINN AND JAKE found their seats for the sneak preview of *Crocodile Dundee* at the Essex Theater in Halston, Jezebel grabbed her state-issued towel and bar of soap and made her first trip to the showers.

Her transfer from MacLeod County Juvenile Detention Facility to Sheyenne Women's Correctional Center just outside Sanwood had taken place two days earlier.

News of Jezebel's transfer had circulated through the prison within hours of the news breaking the previous Saturday night. With such a high-profile case, the warden had expected inmate interest in Jezebel to be high. Not many seventeen-year-old murderers had graced the prison's steps and having one on your crew would be seen as a definite advantage. Curiously, the inmates gave her a wide berth.

Jezebel's cell was located in D Block, which she later learned stood for "Degenerates." It was a far cry from the "Divas" pod back at MacJuvie, but that was fine by her. She'd been called far worse, most recently during her trial.

She kept to herself the first two days, skipping the daily hour of recreation and exercise, and only venturing out for meals.

Jezebel ate alone in the cafeteria but not unobserved. Crews sat and watched, biding their time until the right moment. The guards could sense building undercurrents of tension.

Jezebel interpreted her newfound autonomy as a sign of respect. Why not? She had subjected Newhaven and the surrounding area to a reign of criminal behavior unmatched in recent years. Certainly no one close to her age had been so bold.

Everyone should *respect me.*

Jezebel passed through the corridor on her way to the communal showers.

I should be picking my *crew, not the other way around.*

I *should be the queen around here.*

Inmates gossiped in whispers as they watched her stroll by. Jezebel dismissed them all. Clearly, they were all beneath her.

She pushed open the swinging door to the showers. Four dingy stalls with translucent curtains lined one common off-white tiled wall. Benches for changing and one toilet sat opposite. Green-tinged overhead fluorescents cast dim light over the entire perpetually moist environment.

At the line of four sinks on the back wall, two inmates combing their wet hair spotted Jezebel in the stainless steel mirror. They collected their supplies, threw them into their towels, and made their way to the exit.

"That's right." Jezebel dead-eyed the two inmates as they disappeared out the swinging door. "Keep walking."

She slipped out of her red jumpsuit, socks, shoes, and underwear, and hung them with her towel just inside the stall. Jezebel turned both faucet controls on. A jet of cold water hit her body and took her breath away momentarily before the temperature warmed to a comfortable level.

The prison had supplied her with one bar of soap. "State soap" one guard had called it. All purpose, to be used for everything. Hair, body, and clothes.

Jezebel wet her hair, rolled the bar of soap in her hand, and worked the frothy lather into her hair. It was nothing like the Pert she had at home. Her hair hung in wet, greasy strands, the lather disappearing inexplicably. She made a mental note to visit the commissary for better shampoo.

A soapy drip found its way into her eye and caused a burning sensation so intense that it forced her eyes shut in response. Jezebel hissed in pain, shoved her face in the shower stream, and twisted her wrists against her closed lids.

The sound of the shower and her discomfort hid the small squeak of the swinging entry door. Three inmates stepped inside, one acting as lookout as the other two, one shorter and stockier than the other, advanced on Jezebel's stall.

The two inmates rammed Jezebel from behind, pinning her to the wall and knocking the wind out of her. The heavier woman pressed all her weight into Jezebel, while the other produced a shiv made from two toothbrush handles taped together, one end sharpened to a point.

Jezebel regained her wits enough to begin a struggle, but the two inmates wasted no time. In a span of less than ten seconds, the taller inmate perforated Jezebel's right abdomen more than two dozen times, shredding her liver, kidney, and intestines. Pain bloomed white in front of Jezebel's eyes.

The taller inmate leaned into Jezebel's ear. "Monty don't like snitches." She flipped Jezebel around and pressed her against the wall. "Neither do we." She jammed the shiv into the center of Jezebel's chest as far as it would go and snapped off the handle.

Jezebel slid down the shower wall and landed hard on her bare ass. Bright red blood flowed in torrents from her multiple wounds, cascading off her body and swirling frothy pink down the drain between her legs.

Both inmates spat on her. "Fuckin' rat *bitch*." The heavier inmate gave her a kick for good measure. Their mission complete, they rejoined their lookout and left the showers.

Jezebel sat on the grimy tile floor and slumped to one side, her arms slack and her eyes focused on nothing as the shower went cold.

It won't hurt for long.

The corners of her mouth curled towards a smirk, then in the grim light, it was almost as though her eyes had flickered a bluish glow... just for a second.

March 18, 2022
Victoria, BC, Canada